MARKSWOMAN

MARKSWOMAN

BOOK 1 OF ASIANA

RATI MEHROTRA

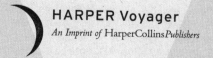

HARPER Voyager
An Imprint of HarperCollins Publishers

MARKSWOMAN. Copyright © 2018 by Rati Mehrotra. All rights reserved. Printed in the United States of America. No part of this book may be used or reproduced in any manner whatsoever without written permission except in the case of brief quotations embodied in critical articles and reviews. For information, address HarperCollins Publishers, 195 Broadway, New York, NY 10007.

HarperCollins books may be purchased for educational, business, or sales promotional use. For information, please email the Special Markets Department at SPsales@harpercollins.com.

Harper Voyager and design are trademarks of HarperCollins Publishers LLC.

FIRST EDITION

Designed by Michelle Crowe
Lotus ornament by teamplay/Shutterstock, Inc.
Map illustration by Amy Goh

Library of Congress Cataloging-in-Publication Data

Names: Mehrotra, Rati, author.
Title: Markswoman / Rati Mehrotra.
Description: First edition. | New York : Harper Voyager, 2018. | Series: Asiana ; Book 1
Identifiers: LCCN 2017036176 | ISBN 9780062564542 (softcover)
Subjects: LCSH: Secret societies—Fiction. | Assassins—Fiction. | BISAC: FICTION / Fantasy / Epic. | FICTION / Action & Adventure. | GSAFD: Fantasy fiction. | Science fiction. | Dystopias.
Classification: LCC PR9199.4.M45954 M37 2018 | DDC 813/.6—dc23 LC record available at https://lccn.loc.gov/2017036176

ISBN 978-0-06-256454-2

18 19 20 21 22   LSC   10 9 8 7 6 5 4 3 2 1

CONTENTS

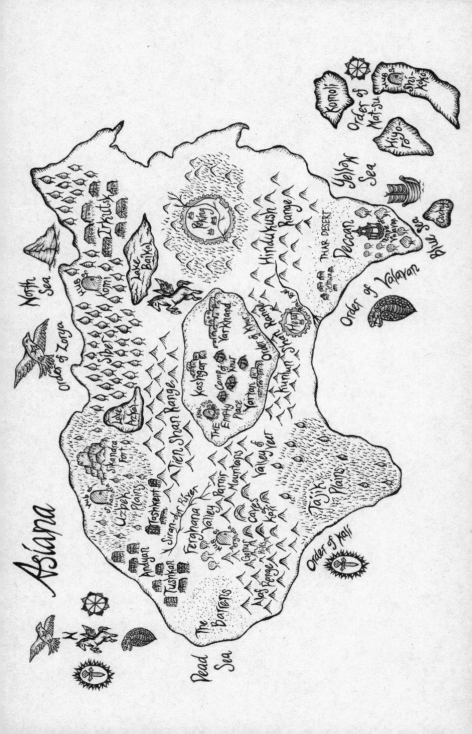

MARKSWOMAN

PART I

From *The Orders of Peace—Our Place in Asiana*, by Navroz Lan of the Order of Kali

> None may take a life but those who carry a kalishium blade and are sworn to the Orders of Peace. This is the law—the Kanun of Ture-asa—which binds all the clans in the valley, the mountains, and the desert beyond.
>
> There are five Orders in Asiana, and the Order of Kali is the oldest, commanding tithe from all the clans in the Ferghana Valley. Our symbol is an inverted katari encircled by a ring of fire.
>
> The Order of Valavan rules the Deccan: tall, dusky women who excel in dueling and the Mental Arts. The mere sight of the banner of Valavan with its striking cobra has been known to end battles and strike terror into the hearts of the most hardened outlaws.
>
> In the farthest north, at the edge of the habitable zone in Siber, lives the Order of Zorya. Fierce fighters they are, and the most

skilled in the art of survival. They strap varnished animal bones to their feet, and skim across the ice faster than the wind. The Hub of Komi connects them with the rest of Asiana, but the soaring white falcon with the star on its breast—the symbol of Zorya—is seldom seen south of the town of Irkutsk on Lake Baikal.

The Order of Mat-su dwells far to the east on the islands beyond the Yellow Sea, and rules the eastern borders of Asiana with severity and grace. The Mat-su symbol is the eight-spoked wheel of life, and the Order aspires to enlightenment through the eightfold path of right thought and right action.

Last and youngest of all is the Order of Khur, but we do not talk or think overmuch of it.

It is whispered that the power of the Orders is beginning to fade. This heresy, first uttered in one of the clan councils of Tushkan, is no truer now than it was then. While we hold a katari in our hands and the Kanun in our hearts, a word from us can still raise armies and crumble mountains.

CHAPTER I

FIRST MARK

Kyra stood in the shadows and watched the guard as he paced the camp, shifting the weight of the kalashik on his shoulder. Her nerves thrummed in anticipation. It was Maidul; she was sure of it. She was lucky he was on guard duty tonight, his thoughts louder than the whistling wind. If he had been asleep in his tent, she might not have been able to identify him.

She gripped her katari—the dagger she was bonded to—and swallowed hard. This was it: the ultimate test. Did she have what it took to be a Markswoman? Could she kill a man? She crept forward, footfalls soft on the sand, taking care to stay in the pools of darkness cast by the flapping tents.

But Maidul must have sensed something. He spun around, his eyes darting from the tents to the thorny ditch that surrounded the camp. Kyra froze, katari in hand. Surely he could not see her? There was no moon tonight, though the stars cast their silvery light on the dunes.

Oh no. She remembered, too late, the telltale glow of the

blade of her katari. How could she have been such a fool as to forget it? Maidul stared right at her and whipped the gun down from his shoulder. Heart racing, Kyra summoned the Inner Speech, binding him before he could fire.

"DROP YOUR WEAPON."

He let go the kalashik; it landed with a soft thud that made her wince. But nothing stirred in the camp except the wind.

"YOU WILL NOT MOVE OR MAKE A SOUND," said Kyra in her most compelling voice. She approached him, trying to slow her pulse. *Control yourself before trying to control others*, the Mahimata always said.

Maidul's face contorted. His forehead beaded with sweat, his jaw clenched in a snarl. She could tell that he was struggling to move, to shout. But he wouldn't be able to, not as long as she held the mental bonds of the Inner Speech over him.

Kyra took a deep breath and said in a normal voice, "By the power vested in me by the Mahimata of Kali and the Kanun of Ture-asa, I, Kyra Veer of the Order of Kali, have come to grant you, Maidul Tau, the mercy of my blade. May you find forgiveness for your crimes."

She raised her blade for an overhead strike. But as she saw the plea in Maidul's eyes, she paused, the blade hovering.

Kill him, you idiot. What are you waiting for?

But she couldn't bring herself to do it. He looked helpless, terrified, his eyes darting from her blade to her face, his breath coming in short gasps. And he was young—no older than her. It didn't feel right or just. How did the other Markswomen do it so easily? Why hadn't Shirin Mam warned her she might react to his unspoken entreaty for life?

Maidul broke loose from her bonds. It was her fault; she hadn't been paying attention, had underestimated his strength.

He threw himself on her, knocking her to the ground and pinning her beneath his weight. He gripped her blade hand, twisting it back until something tore inside her wrist. She gasped with pain and let go her weapon. As the katari slipped from her trembling fingers, a bubble of panic rose inside her.

Maidul clamped her mouth shut with his other hand. Did the moron think she needed to speak aloud to use the Inner Speech? She fought down her panic; his face was so close to hers, she could see his pores, smell his rancid breath. He didn't look frightened now. He was grinning.

"Not so sure of yourself now, are you?" he snarled. "Wait till my father sees what I've caught. He hates Markswomen. You know what we're going to do to you?" He pushed her body harder into the ground. "We like to start by cutting bits off. Fingers, toes, ears. But don't worry, we won't let you bleed to death. You'll be alive and awake the whole time to enjoy it."

Kyra relaxed in his hold, shutting out his voice. "THANK YOU," she subvocalized.

Maidul stopped talking and looked at her, confused. "What?"

"YOU HAVE SHOWN ME WHAT I MUST DO." Kyra smiled into the hand pressed against her mouth.

His eyes widened as realization dawned on his face. He let go her hand and half-rose, wrapping his fingers around her throat. His knees gripped her hips, holding her down. Struggling to breathe, Kyra extended her arm and bent her mind to the katari. *Come to me.* The blade glided into her outstretched palm like a homing pigeon.

Maidul did not notice. He was too busy squeezing the life out of her body. *For you, Mother,* thought Kyra, gasping for breath, and she thrust the blade up between his ribs.

Maidul's grip loosened; he stared in shock at the katari

protruding from his chest before slowly toppling over backward with a gurgling sound.

Kyra dragged herself out from under him and got to her feet, cradling her aching wrist. Her throat was on fire. Maidul twitched and bled into the ground, and her stomach twisted. The bile rose in her throat and she thought she would vomit.

Breathe, she told herself. *Focus*. She closed her eyes and summoned her inner calm, shutting out the man dying before her.

Then Kyra bent down to retrieve her katari, taking care to avoid looking into Maidul's sightless eyes. She trembled as she grasped the smooth leather grip and withdrew the blade from his ruined chest. It came out with a squishy, sucking sound that almost undid her a second time. She closed her eyes again and gulped. She would *not* be sick. This was the moment she had trained for and dreamed of for many years. The moment she had almost ruined with her foolish hesitation. What would Shirin Mam say if she knew?

She focused on the katari's silvery green blade. It was, as expected, sparkling clean. Nothing could tarnish kalishium, the telepathic metal with which the blades of all kataris were forged. It was her bond with a kalishium blade that allowed a Markswoman to use the Inner Speech. The deeper the bond, the greater the ability, Shirin Mam was fond of saying. Kyra had bonded with her blade five years ago, at the completion of her coming-of-age trial.

She kissed the tip of her katari. "Thank you," she whispered. "You saved my life." The slender, tapering blade glowed in response.

Now for the next part. Kyra took a deep breath and slashed a notch into her own left arm, below the elbow, just as Shirin

Mam had told her to do. *We must remember who we kill and why. Our blood for theirs.* Still adrenalized from the fight, she barely felt the cut.

She slid the katari back into the carved wooden scabbard that was corded to her waist. Time to be gone. She threw a last glance around the camp, memorizing details to share with Shirin Mam: the number of tents, the size of the corral, the absence of water. At least fifty people, and they would be moving soon.

The tents flapped in the wind, concealing those who had butchered her clan, as if the night itself could not bear to look upon them. Kyra could kill many of them now if she chose. They would be unprepared and half-asleep, no match for her blade and the Inner Speech.

But Shirin Mam's instructions had been explicit; her first mark had to be *one* person, and who better than Kai Tau's eldest son, Maidul? It would be both a warning and a punishment for the outlaw chief.

Take me, mistress. Then you can kill them all.

The cold voice cut through the darkness. Startled, Kyra stared at the kalashik lying at her feet.

It would be easy, the voice went on. *Slaughter them as they lie sleeping, as they slaughtered your family. Fulfill the vow you made to yourself. Take me.*

Kyra bent down, her hands reaching for the elongated barrel. Her fingertips brushed the surface of the hard metal, and a shiver ran through her.

Shots ring out, deafening in the hollow bowl of the valley. Screams rise, only to be abruptly cut off. The child trembles in fear, tastes blood in her mouth.

Kyra jerked back to the present, breathing hard. She

straightened up and kicked the gun away. It gleamed in the starlight like a living thing, but it did not call out to her again. What had Shirin Mam said? These guns were made before the Great War. Men wanted to use kalishium to make them, but were forbidden from doing so by the Ones. So they tried to duplicate kalishium, and instead created a metal unlike anything seen in Asiana. It was telepathic, like kalishium, but in a deformed way. It was *evil*.

She walked away, heart thudding at the narrowness of her escape. Suppose she *had* picked the kalashik up. Would she have gone on a murderous rampage like the Taus? Shot and killed everyone in the camp?

Better not to know. Better not to test herself. Kyra scrambled up the thorny ditch around the Tau camp, back to her mare, Rinna. Unbidden, the voice of Shirin Mam touched her mind yet again. *Let the past be what it is. Let the future bring what it will. Stay in the present. Be aware of yourself and who you are. It is all that matters.*

A simple philosophy, but it formed the heart of the Mahimata's teachings. The first thing novices learned was detachment. Shirin Mam called it the art of forgetting. Parents, siblings, teachers, friends—none of them mattered once you joined the Order. Well, that was what you were supposed to learn, anyway.

Kyra mounted her mare with one hand, wincing as the pain in her right wrist flared anew. It was easy for the others. They had only normal lives to forget. None of *them* had been forced to scare away vultures from the bodies of their parents. She hadn't been able to keep the scavengers away from the others, of course. At one point she had given up and crawled inside the hut to join her sisters. Her three little sisters . . .

As Kyra rode between the dunes, the wind rose and fell from a high-pitched keen to a deepening roar—an eerie sound that made her skin crawl. The sand stung her eyes, her throat was parched, and she ached all over. She urged Rinna on; she longed to be out of the Thar Desert, back home in the Ferghana.

She almost missed seeing the door by the side of the fossilized dune. It was half-hidden by a mound of fresh sand. Perhaps there had been a micro sandstorm in the last hour.

Or perhaps the door had *shifted*.

Kyra dismounted, brushed clear the door, and inserted the tip of her kalishium blade into a barely visible slot. The slot glowed blue and the door swung open, and she had a moment of dislocation.

Being in a Transport Hub always did that to her. Hubs didn't belong in this desert landscape, or anywhere else in Asiana for that matter. The elders said that the Ones had come down from the stars to help humans build the Transport system. Hubs were artifacts left over from a world that no longer existed, the remnant of an ancient civilization that had destroyed itself many hundreds of years ago.

What a strange world it must have been when wonders like these were commonplace. Kyra could not even imagine what it would have looked like. Perhaps people had homes in the sky and all the homes had Hubs, and every time you wanted to see anyone or go anywhere, you merely stepped through a door.

It wasn't quite that simple now, of course. If you were an ordinary person who needed to travel, you had to take the long, slow route by horse or bullock cart or camelback. Only kalishium could open a door, and only the Orders had access to kalishium. It was just as well. No one truly understood how Transport worked, and some of the doors had begun to fail.

There were stories of Markswomen who had never returned, or who returned raving mad and had to be locked up for their own safety.

Kyra gave herself a shake. She was going to Transport, and everything was going to be fine. She peered inside the Hub. The corridor stretched into darkness, lined only by the glowing slots on each of the doors within. It looked the same as it had a few hours ago, but that didn't mean it was still the same Transport Hub.

She tightened her grip on the reins and led Rinna forward before she could change her mind. The door swung closed behind them and the mare whinnied and jerked her head.

"Hush, Rinna," said Kyra, stroking her neck. "You don't like it, do you? Don't worry, you're safe."

Safe. If only she could believe that herself.

Kyra coaxed her mare along the corridor until they came to the fourth door on the right, where she once again inserted the tip of her katari into a slot. This time a numbered screen slid out and she tapped in the Transport code Felda Seshur, the Order's mathematician, had given her: 116010611.

The door slid open and the tight knot in her stomach dissolved. The code still worked; this should still be the right door.

She led Rinna across the threshold and pale blue lights came on, revealing a circular room with seats melded to the floor. Kyra sat down on one to wait, and it moved fractionally beneath her, adjusting to her shape. This part always made her skin crawl. Chairs weren't supposed to move, not the ones made of wood or stone or metal, at any rate. Who knew what material had been used to forge these? Kyra sat erect on her seat, trying not to think about what she was doing. She had

Transported a few times before, but always in the company of the elders of Kali. Her journey here had been the first time she'd done it alone.

The room began to spin. Rinna whinnied again and backed to the wall, where the spin was greater. She almost lost her balance, crashing against the curved surface of the chamber. Kyra frowned. She should have tethered her mare. Something to remember for the next time.

"We'll soon be home, Rinna," she said in a soothing voice.

But the room kept on spinning. What if it never stopped? If they were stuck there forever, a rotating nightmare between one world and the next?

No, that was irrational. She was giving in to fear, a monster without a face that was born from her own dreams. Kyra closed her eyes and practiced Sheetali, the Cooling Breath, until she sensed the spinning slow down and stop.

CHAPTER 2

THE CHOSEN ONES

They emerged from the Hub on a hill overlooking the windswept plain that was the realm of the Order of Kali. Kyra inhaled the cool, mulberry-scented night air: the smell of home. They had reached Ferghana safely. Surrounded by mountains and watered by the great Siran-dyr River, the fertile valley was a mix of cropland, pastures, orchards, and forests—a living, breathing land, unlike the desert she had just left behind.

The door swung closed behind her and the Hub slept, quiescent—a metallic hump that shone with an eerie light. Kyra shivered and moved away from it. By the Goddess, she was glad to be out of there.

Rinna pranced, also relieved to be outside again. Kyra patted her flank, feeling empty somehow. All those months of anxiety and anticipation, going over various scenarios with Shirin Mam, and it was over now.

A familiar figure scrambled up the hill toward her. Nineth? Trust her to know the minute Kyra was back. But of everyone in the Order, it was her face that was most welcome now. Elena would have wanted to come too, but would have allowed Nineth to overrule her, as she usually did.

"Come on, Rinna." Kyra caught hold of the reins and made her way through the tamarisk bushes that lined the path down-hill.

"Kyra!" Nineth met them halfway and flung herself into Kyra's arms, almost knocking her over. Behind them, Rinna whinnied a greeting. "You've been gone so long. I was imagining all sorts of horrible things. What happened? No, don't tell me. It is Shirin Mam you must talk to first. She said to tell you that she's waiting."

"I would've been back sooner, but it took a while to find that nest of vipers," said Kyra. "And on my way back I was stuck in the Transport Chamber. I have no idea how long I was in that spinning room, but it felt like hours."

Nineth hesitated. "Did you . . . is he . . . ?"

"Yes. Maidul is dead," said Kyra flatly. She should have had a sense of accomplishment as she said it, but she felt nothing—just a deep, aching tiredness.

Nineth's eyes widened with awe. With a pang, Kyra realized that a gulf now separated her from her friends. She had killed with the katari and was no longer an apprentice. Would Elena and Nineth distance themselves from her? She hoped not; she had been lonely in the Order until they arrived. At five, she had been the youngest novice the Order had ever seen. And also, despite Shirin Mam's efforts, the most damaged. It had taken years to come out of the darkness that had threatened to consume her. Even now, the ghosts were never too far away.

"Where is Shirin Mam?" asked Kyra.

"In the cavern," replied Nineth, "pretending to read some

old book, and waiting for you with all the patience of a fox outside a rabbit hole."

Kyra grinned at the image. "I'd better hurry."

"She had me scrubbing the cavern until I thought my skin would come off," said Nineth, taking the reins from her. "The initiation will be tonight. There hasn't been one for three years, not since Tonar Kalam. All the elders are excited. Aren't you?"

Nervous, more like. "You'll be next," said Kyra with a smile she didn't quite feel as they walked downhill. "You'll find out how exciting it is."

Nineth gave an exaggerated shudder. "Oh no, not yet. Shirin Mam says I am not even ready to kill a wyr-wolf, let alone a man. I'm quite happy being an apprentice."

Kyra looked at her with affection. Plump, cheerful Nineth with the brown hair hanging over her eyes and the perpetually crumpled robe—there were many in the Order who wondered why Shirin Mam had chosen her as a novice, from all the girls of the Dan tribe that dwelled in the eastern end of the valley. Kyra could have told them the reason, but what would be the use? Most Markswomen measured prowess by one's ability with the Mental Arts or in Hatha-kala. Something as nebulous as "spirit" wouldn't make sense to them—but Nineth had it in spades.

"You can't be an apprentice forever," said Kyra. "You'll be seventeen next month."

Nineth snorted. "So what? You're two years older than me. And don't forget dear Akassa. She's champing at the bit. Probably claw me apart if I get my first mark before her."

Kyra laughed. Akassa Chan was another apprentice, and a favorite of Tamsyn's, the Mistress of Mental Arts. Come to think of it, now that she herself was going to be initiated as a Markswoman, Nineth, Elena, and Akassa were the only apprentices left. True, there were four novices who had yet to pass the coming-of-age trial and earn their kataris, but it troubled Shirin Mam that she hadn't found more girls with the ability to bond with a kalishium blade in recent years.

They parted at the foot of the hill, Nineth leading Rinna to the horse enclosure and Kyra heading for the cave system where the Order of Kali dwelled. The entrance to the caves was a crawlway on the base of a hill opposite the Hub. After the first few meters, the narrow passage of the crawlway widened into a broad corridor. Keep walking, and you arrived at the immense cavern where all the sacred rites were held.

"You are back."

Kyra jumped. But it was only Ria Farad, a tawny-haired, slender Markswoman who was often on guard duty outside the caves.

"You startled me," said Kyra. "I should have known you would be here, imitating the night."

Ria laughed. "You don't imitate the night, young one. You *become* the night."

She melted once more into the darkness. Kyra scanned the surroundings to catch another glimpse of the Markswoman. She could be anywhere: among the rushes that bent and swayed in the wind, behind the trunk of the ancient mulberry tree, or even right in front of her. But it was no use trying to see her, and Kyra gave up.

She crawled through the narrow passage to the caves, shaking with fatigue. Her wrist throbbed and her throat was still raw and painful from being squeezed by Maidul's fingers. She would have to be careful what she said to Shirin Mam.

The main cavern was empty save for the Mahimata. The

light from a hundred sconces flickered on the walls, bringing the ocher and charcoal paintings on them to life. Kali the demon-slayer danced across the walls, holding aloft the sword of knowledge to cut the bonds of ignorance and destroy her enemy, falsehood.

Kali, whose name literally meant "the dark one," had been worshipped by millions before the Great War, Shirin Mam had told them. She was the oldest in the pantheon of deities that once flourished in Asiana. She was there at the beginning of things, and would be there when everything ended. Protector of devotees and bestower of boons, she was nonetheless a fearsome warrior, called by the gods to the battlefield when all else failed.

Black-skinned and four-armed, adorned with a garland of human skulls and a girdle of human arms, in the paintings the Goddess carved her way through a multiplicity of mythic monsters: a demon with the body of a water buffalo, another that could kill with his roar, and yet another that could duplicate himself with every drop of his blood that fell to the ground. One of the paintings showed Kali catching the demon's blood with her tongue before it could fall. From the detailed depictions of her battling demons with sword, spear, and dagger had grown Hatha-kala, the style of fighting unique to the Order of Kali.

But some of the paintings showed a slightly different version of Kali: a blue-skinned woman wearing a wolf-hide skirt and holding one of her four hands out in benediction. This was Tara, the maternal aspect of the Goddess. The mother loved her children as much as the warrior hated demons.

But who still worshipped the Goddess beyond the caves? Did anyone else remember what she stood for?

Perhaps only the Markswomen of the Order of Kali did, they who took her name when they went into battle.

Shirin Mam—slim, gray-haired, and black-robed—sat on one of the dozen wooden benches that surrounded the raised central slab. Behind her was the silver gong, suspended from a metal frame, its rune-covered disc gleaming in the torchlight. The Mahimata's head was bent over a book; she appeared completely absorbed by it. Kyra felt a rush of relief at the familiar sight. Her first impulse was to run and hug her teacher, but she controlled it and waited for Shirin Mam to notice her.

Shirin Mam raised her head and fixed a stern gaze on her. "What kept you?" she demanded.

Kyra bowed. "I apologize, Mother. The camp was not easy to find."

"No, I meant what kept you *after* you returned here. No doubt you were chattering with Nineth and Ria."

That wasn't fair. Kyra wanted to protest, but then Shirin Mam smiled—a smile that transformed her face so that she looked, for a moment, quite young. Kyra found herself smiling back, warmed from within. The moment passed and Shirin Mam said, "Is it done?"

"It is done, Mother," replied Kyra.

"We will have your ceremony at dawn. Tell me everything."

Kyra gave the Mahimata a brief account of the events of the night, leaving out the bit about how she had hesitated and almost been strangled as a result. When she came to the part where the kalashik had spoken to her, Shirin Mam frowned.

"Those guns know they do not belong in our world. You were wise to leave it there, although I think the clan of Arikken would have been grateful if we had returned it to them for safe-keeping. The weapons were stolen from them, as you know."

As I know. Those guns slaughtered my entire family.

"Cannot something be done about them, Mother?" asked Kyra. "Can they not be destroyed?"

"Fire does not burn them," said Shirin Mam. "Water does not rust them. Even the blade of a katari cannot cut them. Throw them into the sea and they will find their way into a fisherman's net. Bury them in the deepest pit, and they will be dug up again. Kalashiks were made before the war and if there is a way to destroy them, it is lost to us now. The best we can do is keep what caches remain safe from the hands of the ignorant and the evil. Unfortunately, it is always the ignorant and the evil that the dark weapons seek to align themselves with."

Kyra shuddered as she remembered how the kalashik had exhorted her to slaughter the Taus. "It was all I could do to ignore its voice," she confessed.

"It is a voice few could resist," said Shirin Mam gravely. "Thank your kalishium blade for protecting you from it. Tell me, how did it feel when you killed Maidul?"

Kyra was taken aback. "It felt . . ." She hesitated. Should she tell the truth? Would Shirin Mam think less of her if she did?

But she needn't have worried. The Mahimata said, "You found it repugnant, did you not? It will never be otherwise for you." She nodded, almost to herself. "Still, you will do what needs to be done."

"How do *you* feel when you have to kill someone?" Kyra blurted out.

Shirin Mam's expression gave nothing away. "To be evil is to suffer, and there is joy in releasing others from suffering. Now you must change your robes and prepare for the ceremony. But first, a special assignment. A reward for your success." She withdrew a folded piece of parchment from her book and held it up to Kyra.

Kyra took it, puzzled. Her mystification increased when she unfolded it and saw that it contained nothing but a meaningless string of numbers. "What is this, Mother?"

"A secret," said Shirin Mam, her eyes dancing. "Felda Seshur derived it from a formula in one of her oldest tomes. Decode it, and come to me when you are done." She reopened her book, adding, "Speak of it to no one. Now go."

Kyra stuffed the parchment in a pocket and left, glad to get away from Shirin Mam's piercing eyes. She was too exhausted to try to hide her thoughts from her teacher, and she didn't want Shirin Mam to guess that she had almost failed to kill her first mark.

All around the cavern were openings into passageways. Kyra took the narrow passage that led to her own cell, trying to ignore the empty chambers yawning on both sides. Each Markswoman and apprentice had a cell to herself for sleep and meditation. But most of the chambers of the cave system were empty. The Order numbered just thirty-three these days, not counting the four novices, instead of the hundreds that used to inhabit the caves of Kali.

Before she had gone more than a few steps down the passage, a figure stepped around the corner holding up a lamp.

"Kyra," came a mellifluous voice.

She blinked in the sudden light, and her heart sank as she saw the beautiful face behind it. *Tamsyn.*

"Elder." Kyra bowed and made as if to move past her.

But the elegant, ebony-haired woman fell in step beside her. "Is it done?" she asked in a husky whisper, raising the lamp and peering at Kyra's face.

No one but Shirin Mam had the right to ask her that. But Tamsyn Turani was the Hand of Kali, Shirin Mam's executioner of choice. Her left arm was crisscrossed with scars, and the pelts of a dozen wyr-wolves carpeted the floor of her cell.

"It is done," said Kyra. She hoped the disinterest in her voice would put Tamsyn off, but the elder laughed in delight.

"You hated it, did you not? But now you are a real Markswoman and not a mere apprentice. Oh, anyone can take down a wyr-wolf or two. But it takes a Markswoman to kill a man."

Kyra didn't want to think about Maidul as a man, to recall the look of surprise on his face when her katari passed through his chest. It was easier to think of him as a mark for her blade. She averted her face and brushed past Tamsyn. But the elder caught up with her again and grabbed her arm.

"Wait," she said. "I want to see you." She put the lamp down and pulled Kyra around to face her.

"You see me every day, Elder," Kyra protested.

"Not like this," said Tamsyn. She whipped away Kyra's cloak and took a deep intake of breath. Her gaze traveled from Kyra's blood-spattered robe to her tangled hair. Kyra tried not to squirm, but it felt as if she was being dissected, every moment of the last few hours analyzed and judged.

"As transparent as ever." Tamsyn shook her head with a pitying look. "You can hide from *her*, but you cannot hide from me. What went wrong?"

Kyra suppressed her discomfiture as best she could. "Nothing, Elder. I achieved my first mark, and my initiation will be at dawn."

"Indeed." A smile slid across Tamsyn's face. "After the ceremony, I shall give you a special private lesson. After your success, you deserve it."

A private lesson with the Hand of Kali? As if it wasn't enough, being punished by her every day in the Mental Arts class. "I have my regular classes to attend after the ceremony, Elder," said Kyra. "I do not deserve, or indeed desire, special private lessons with you." She bowed, catching the fleeting look of rage on Tamsyn's face before it rearranged itself into its customary smoothness.

She ducked into her cell, but not before hearing Tamsyn's parting shot. "We are more alike than you think, little deer. And Shirin Mam will not always be around."

Kyra shuddered with indignation and something else—a chilling sort of anxiety—as she lit a candle and removed her soiled robe. She was *nothing* like the scheming elder. And why did she say that Shirin Mam would not always be around? Shirin Mam was barely sixty. She would lead the Order of Kali for a good many decades yet, the Goddess willing. It had been an odd threat, even for Tamsyn. Kyra didn't like it.

She wiped herself with a damp cloth. A proper cleansing would have to wait till morning, when she could go to the stream-fed pool nearby.

After she had dried herself, Kyra slipped on a clean robe, reveling in the softness of the finely woven garment. Then she lay on the woolen rug, letting the fatigue seep from her body into the stone floor. How still it was, how silent. This quality of silence was what she loved best about the caves. No screech of wind or howl of wolf could penetrate their endless depths. Here there were only your own thoughts, your own memories.

Kyra breathed deep and slow, trying to relax into the first-level meditative trance. But Maidul's face floated in front of her, dead yet somehow still alive—half-mocking, half-reproachful.

No. Maidul deserved what he got. She would not see him the way she saw the others. Her mother, sitting at the ancient wooden loom in their hut and weaving a blue rug. Her father, turning the spit to roast mutton at a clan wedding, giving that deep belly laugh she loved. Her younger sisters, trotting after her on chubby little legs, mimicking everything that she did.

Kyra had been in the privy behind their hut when the guns started firing and people started screaming. Instead of running back to her family, instinct made her seek the refuge of an oak tree, climbing to the highest branch she could reach. There she waited, cold and terrified. An hour passed, or perhaps two, before the sounds of the machines stopped.

She slithered down the tree, scratched and bleeding, her throat dry. She went past her own dwelling, averting her face from the two bodies that lay awkwardly at its entrance, refusing to see them. Because if she saw, that would make it real.

She wandered blindly through the village littered with corpses, coldness blooming in the pit of her stomach. She went from house to house, hoping that someone was still alive—a cousin, an aunt, a grandfather. But no one answered her calls; no one stirred at her footsteps. Finally she returned to her own hut. Perhaps she had imagined it; perhaps her family had fled into the forest when the bad men came.

But the scene outside her hut was unchanged: two blood-drenched bodies at the entrance, the open door leading only into darkness. *Come in*, the darkness beckoned. *I have a gift for you.*

She stood there a long while, biting her fingers until they bled. The sun rose in the sky, and still the darkness waited behind the door, and at last she could put it off no longer.

There was a chance, a small chance, that her sisters might still be alive.

She stepped over the bodies of her parents and crept inside, praying *please oh please Mother Goddess let them be all right, I'll never be bad again*. Her eyes burned with unshed tears of hope and fear.

But inside the hut was nothing but the stench of blood and death. Her sisters lay in a tangle of broken limbs and torn clothes. The side of Ishira's head had caved in. Ishira the baby girl, who loved to comb her older sister's long dark hair. Kyra went out and sat at the entrance next to her parents, hugging her knees, rocking herself.

How long before Shirin Mam came? Hours? Days? Kyra could remember being lifted by strong arms and tied to a horse, but she had no memory of the actual journey to Ferghana.

In the caves of Kali she was put under the care of Navroz Lan, the healer. Navroz forced her to drink the bitterest of brews every night to help her sleep, but Kyra wondered later whether the potion had made the nightmares worse. That was the darkest of times, when madness held her in its relentless grip. Often, she could not tell what was real and what was not. Her days were filled with raw grief. She cried constantly, but tears brought no relief—no mother to hold her, no father to lift her on his shoulder. She dreamed of nothing but an endless series of doors and a terrible blank void that lay beyond them. She opened one after another, chasing the ghosts of those she'd loved, and finding only emptiness. It wasn't until she was older that she learned to separate dream and reality, though the doors haunted her still.

The gong sounded, reverberating through the caves.

Goddess, was it already time for the ceremony? Kyra leaped

up and grabbed a comb to run through her long hair. She tried to get the tangles out, but it was impossible, and at last she gave up and tied it in a loose bun, hoping she looked neat enough. She took down a tiny mirror from a shelf above and brought the candle close to her face to check for smudges. Her features—the snub nose, dark brown eyes, and generous mouth—reflected back at her as always. But today, it wasn't just the face of Kyra. It was the face of a soon-to-be Markswoman.

She tossed the mirror back on the shelf and withdrew her katari from its scabbard.

The Markswomen filled the cavern, all dressed in the brown, loose-sleeved robes with divided skirts that were the uniform of the Order, embroidered with their symbol: an inverted katari encircled by a ring of fire. White novice robes and green apprentice robes were conspicuous by their absence; only a full Markswoman could attend the initiation rites. Kyra knew this, but the fact that she was the only one wearing green made her heart beat faster. The katari almost slipped from her sweaty palm. She discreetly wiped her hands against her sides and clutched it. She would *not* drop the blade and make a fool of herself.

The women streamed out of their cells in silence, looking not at each other but at their blades. Kyra joined them at the wooden benches surrounding the central slab, but she found it hard not to fidget. Her last hour as an apprentice.

When everyone was seated, Shirin Mam stepped into the cavern and took her place by the platform in the middle. She looked different, somehow, from the small, slight woman who had spoken with Kyra a short while ago. Her back was straight, her robe a shimmering black, the katari shining before her in translucent diamond-like splendor. Her face in the torchlight was neither young nor old, neither good nor evil. She simply *was*, Shirin Mam the Mahimata of Kali, leader of the most ancient Order of Peace in Asiana.

". . . and Ture-asa, the last king of Asiana, decreed that to live we must die, and to rule we must serve, and to uphold the peace we must kill. Thus was the Order of Kali born and to this day we, the chosen ones from all the clans, the shining outcasts, do follow the path laid down for us. In our sacrifice lies the salvation of Asiana. And so it will ever be."

"And so it will ever be," they all intoned, their voices echoing through the cavern.

Shirin Mam's voice grew deeper. "This day a new Markswoman is born among us. Rise, daughter of Kali, and come to me."

Kyra rose and advanced to the central slab.

"Kneel," commanded the Mahimata.

Kyra knelt and Shirin Mam touched her forehead with the tip of her lucent blade. Kyra closed her eyes and held herself rigid as the Mahimata's katari seared her flesh for a long, excruciating minute. This was the mark that would brand her as a Markswoman of Kali forever. Through a haze of pain she heard Shirin Mam's voice ring out like a bell on a clear autumn day:

"May you walk on water and pass through fire. May the blood that you shed nourish the soil and the bodies you strike feed the crows. May the katari protect your flesh and Kali protect your soul. And when your work is done, may the Ones take you with them to the stars for the last journey of your life." Shirin Mam grasped Kyra's shoulders, helping her up. "Drink," she said.

Kyra stared at the swirling red liquid in the wooden bowl that had materialized in her hands. It looked like wine or . . . *blood*. Wyr-wolf blood? The rumors were true. *Yuck*. Kyra shuddered but there was no help for it. She took the bowl and raised it to her lips. A collective sigh rose from the Markswomen.

Kyra drank without stopping, without thinking, without tasting. When she had drained the last drop from the bowl, a mighty cheer rang through the cavern. Her head swam and faces danced before her eyes.

Shirin Mam slashed open Kyra's apprentice robe with her katari and led her to the slab.

Kyra lay on the raised platform, clad in just her shift, trying to ignore the goose bumps on her skin. The five black-robed elders—Navroz Lan, Chintil Maya, Felda Seshur, Mumuksu Chan, and Tamsyn Turani—surrounded her. The first four touched her forehead with their kataris, their lips moving in silent benediction. But Tamsyn, her face distorted in the torchlight, laid the bloodred tip of her weapon in the middle of Kyra's chest, just above the heart. Pain rose like a scream within her, then subsided to become a distant, bearable thing.

Kyra struggled to stay conscious but the effort was too great. The last thing she heard was the singing of many voices, sweet and low. The song lifted her from pain and took her by the hand into the corridor of sleep. As Kyra walked down that corridor she saw, as plain as if it were her own reflection in a mirror, the serene face of her mother, beckoning at the far end. Joy filled Kyra and she ran toward her. *Mother, I've missed you.* She ran and ran, but her mother was no nearer than before. The corridor stretched away into the distance and her mother's form dimmed. *No*, Kyra tried to shout, *don't leave me again.*

But no words escaped her lips and her mother faded away, still smiling, still beckoning. Kyra collapsed, sobbing in frustration and despair. Then she smelled ash, and felt the metallic taste of blood in her mouth.

A blue-skinned, four-armed woman with a vermilion-streaked forehead and bloodshot eyes stood over her. Twice as tall as Kyra, her black hair rippled in turbulent waves over her wolfskin skirt to her bare feet. A garland of skulls rattled around her neck as she presented Kyra with a lotus in one hand, a pair of scissors in another, and a sword in the third.

Kyra gaped at the fearsome form in disbelief. *It cannot be.* She wanted to grovel at her feet. She wanted to run away. In the end, she did neither. And as the Goddess flicked out her long red tongue and held out the final hand in benediction, her eyes bore into the depths of Kyra's soul, and Kyra's world went dark.

CHAPTER 3

THE JUDGMENT OF KHUR

There was no glory in being a Marksman.

Rustan had learned that quickly living with the Order of Khur, in the cold desert that festered in the heart of Asiana.

And yet, did it have to be quite so *inglorious*?

"Please," said the kneeling man—the *mark*—again, tears running down his cheeks and dripping to the dusty street. "I am innocent. Please don't kill me." He continued to blubber, a bald, middle-aged man with the paunch that came from too much kumiss and too little labor.

They all said that, when confronted with the katari. They all became innocent and fearful and pitiable, no matter how heinous their crime. And this man's crime was of the most despicable kind. He had been found guilty of the murder of his own estranged father by the elders of the Kushan council—a matter of greed and inheritance, the council had concluded. And yet, it took all of Rustan's willpower to ignore the man's entreaties. It had been too long since he'd done this.

It was the first such case in Tezbasti in several years. This close to the camp of Khur, violent crime was rare; premeditated murder even more so. People kept to the law and paid their tithe to the Order of Khur, and the Marksmen kept them safe from marauding bands of outlaws. This was the compact, had been since the Order of Khur was founded hundreds of years ago.

Go with my blessing, the Maji-khan had said. *Deliver the judgment of Khur.*

I will be honored, Rustan had replied, not knowing how little honor he would find in the task.

He suppressed his disquietude and slid off his camel's back. Time to put a merciful end to the man's whimpering. "It will not hurt," he said, withdrawing his katari. "That I promise. Do you wish to confess?"

"I have nothing to confess," the man cried, stumbling to his feet. "My trial was a sham. The council wants my land. I've been framed."

Rustan delved into him—lightly, so his presence would not be felt—and found nothing but anger, fear, and, overriding them both, a deep sense of guilt. *If only I had reconciled with my father and asked his forgiveness while he was still alive.*

It was enough for Rustan. "Your father forgives you," he said, and let fly his katari, straight and true, right into the mark's throat.

The man toppled over, still maintaining that expression of outraged innocence, while a fountain of blood gushed out of his severed artery. Rustan waited before bending down to recover his blade. He wiped the blade against his sleeve—a gesture born of habit, nothing more, for it was clean as always—and exhaled the breath trapped in his chest. It was not his first mark, or even his second, and it would not be his last. So why this knot of tension in his stomach? Why this feeling of things unfinished or badly done?

No matter. Tezbasti would be safer, cleaner, without this patricide breathing its air.

The sand-blown streets were empty, eerily so for midday. The inhabitants of Tezbasti would not emerge until Rustan had gone. But a sound came from one of the mud-walled huts, a high, keening noise that echoed in the flat horizon, setting his teeth on edge. The man's wife, perhaps. Or a sister. Or a child. Rustan did not know if the man had had a family. It was better not to know such things, for then you would find yourself mourning with them, for them.

Rustan sheathed his katari and leaped on his camel's back. "Let's go home, Basil," he muttered. "Our work here is done."

The camel snorted and heaved itself up. Twenty miles across the sandy wastes to Khur—they could make it before midnight, even with a short break in the afternoon. Rustan had hoped to rest his camel in Tezbasti itself, but all he wanted now was to put as much distance as possible between the wailing noise from the hut and himself. As if distance could make him forget it, grief made audible, and the guilt of his own hand, his own heart. As if distance could answer the questions, rearing serpent-like inside him: *What if he was truly innocent? Who am I to take a life, even a wicked one?* And—*what is wrong with me, that I feel this way?*

This was foolish. He had simply obeyed orders. He was a Marksman and this was what he was trained for. In the two years since his last mark, he had become soft, forgotten the dark edge of a Marksman's reality. No wonder the Maji-khan had selected him for this assignment. The Order was testing him.

But the mark two years ago had been different; he had ridden with Shurik and the others between the dunes, chasing a band of outlaws, dust tearing his eyes, his throat hoarse with shouting. There had been excitement and danger, even a kind of heroism to it. The outlaws were armed with bows and arrows, and two of the Marksmen had suffered flesh wounds.

In truth, all his marks thus far had been, if not exciting, then at least gratifying. Rustan earned his first mark while protecting a caravan bound for Kashgar from bandits, and his second while breaking up a fierce fight between warriors of the Kushan and Turguz clans. He'd killed the leaders from each side, ensuring that the rest laid down their arms and turned to Barkav to mediate peace. It was an achievement to be proud of.

Whereas this . . . this was an execution.

Rustan urged Basil on, but the sounds of lamentation followed him still, until he wanted to close his ears and shout: *I did my duty. That is all.*

⚜

A pale and bloodless moon had risen in the sky by the time Rustan returned to the Khur camp. A vast dune shimmered in the moonlight ahead of him like an immense silver shield. Rustan made out the cluster of tents at its base, and his heart lifted. He was home. He would make his report to the Maji-khan, and everything would be all right. He would sleep, and wake rested to a normal day. He would tell Shurik everything; Shurik would listen to him and grin and punch his arm, say he was too sensitive, that he was *lucky* to be selected by the Maji-khan.

An apprentice was waiting at the camel enclosure, rubbing his hands and shivering in the cold wind. Rustan handed over

Basil to him, inhaling the familiar, pungent aroma of the enclosure with pleasure.

He stopped short outside his tent. A tiny, hooded figure was standing at the entrance: Astinsai, the seer and katari mistress of Khur. What was the Old One doing here at this hour? She barely deigned to speak even to the elders; her presence here could mean nothing good.

Rustan bowed. "Mistress," he said warily, "you could have summoned me to your tent. I would have come anyway, after making my report to the Maji-khan."

"Barkav can wait," said Astinsai, her voice hoarse with age and smoke-weed. "This cannot. Follow me."

Why? he wanted to ask. But he kept quiet and followed her as she slowly made her way toward her tent, despite his growing bewilderment. Astinsai was one of the few people alive who could make kataris from the kalishium that the Ones had left behind when they went back to the stars. It was a long and arduous process, and it was now many years since she had accepted a new assignment. But she had made many of the kataris that the Marksmen of Khur now carried, including Rustan's. He could not have disobeyed her, even had he wanted to.

They reached Astinsai's tent at the southern edge of the Khur camp, Rustan bending almost double to squeeze inside. He could not remember the last time he had been in the Old One's smoky little home. She did not often invite anyone inside, preferring to keep to herself or, if needed, summon people to the council tent.

Astinsai lowered herself to sit cross-legged on the felt carpet, and the hood fell away from her seamed face and sparse white hair.

"So, you become stronger and braver, Marksman?" she said, dark eyes flashing in the lamplight with an emotion he could not identify. "Let me see your katari."

Feeling light-headed from exhaustion and from the close air of the tent, Rustan withdrew his katari and proffered it. The kalishium blade pulsed with a soft blue light and, as always, he was struck by its beauty. It seemed more alive than either him or the bent old woman who had forged it.

Astinsai's expression clouded. "Put it away," she said. "I have something for you. Something that will set you on a path you cannot yet imagine." She rose and hobbled to the back of her tent, where she removed the stopper from a decanter and poured a clear liquid into an earthen cup. She held the cup up to him.

"Drink," she commanded.

"Is that Rasaynam?" said Rustan, dumbfounded. "There are easier ways to kill me."

Rasaynam was a spirit Astinsai brewed for herself that was rumored to drive men mad. Even she partook of it but sparingly.

Astinsai's face softened. "There are, but this is the one we must choose. Rasaynam will show you the truth of what happened today."

The terrible doubt that had seized Rustan in Tezbasti rushed back. He swallowed. "The truth is that I took down a mark. I obeyed orders. I should go to the Maji-khan now and report. He will be waiting for me."

Astinsai put down the cup. "I cannot force you," she said. "You must *want* to know, for it to work for you. You must need it. But ask yourself this: How will you atone?"

Again Rustan heard the wailing sounds that had followed

him out of the village and into the open desert. Again he heard the man's pleas of innocence.

Rustan reached for the cup with a hand that was not quite steady. The liquid was bitter tasting, as if flavored by grief itself. Although he wanted to stop and spit it out, he swallowed each drop. And he knew, in the depths of his soul, this was the start of his punishment. For when he had drunk to the bottom of the cup, he saw, instead of Astinsai, the face of his mark, clutching his ruined throat as if trying to prevent blood from spilling out of it. But it spilled out anyway, running between his fingers, leaving red tracks on his arms. And the specter said, full of reproach, "I *told* you I was innocent."

Rustan rose, the cup tumbling out of his hand. He tried to speak, but the scene shifted. Two elders of the Kushan council sat down to a meal with the murdered man, the father of his luckless mark. There was much talking and laughter. And then the flick of a wrist over a cup of tea—the slow-acting poison that would claim the victim's life later that night. One of the elders stabbed a finger at Rustan. "Do you see?" he said, jovial. "See how we fooled the council and the Maji-khan. See how we fooled *you*."

The victim's face had become swollen, purple. He opened his frothing mouth and echoed Astinsai's words, "How will you atone?"

"I will kill them!" shouted Rustan, and he reached for his katari. But the scene shifted, back to Astinsai's tent. The old woman had not moved; she sat in the same position, watching him like a hawk.

"Is that what you will do, Marksman?" said Astinsai, a note of pity in her voice.

Rustan wiped the sweat from his forehead with a sleeve. His head was pounding as if someone had hammered nails into it. How could the Maji-khan have sent him to Tezbasti to kill an innocent man? Rustan had always trusted his elders, had never questioned them. That trust had been betrayed, his world turned upside down. And no matter the reason, it was Rustan himself whose katari had done the deed. How could he ever rely on his blade again?

"Why tell me now," said Rustan, trembling with anger, "when there is nothing I can do about it? Why not tell me earlier?"

"I am sorry," said Astinsai, not sounding sorry at all, "but I did not know. Not until your blade took his life."

"I must tell the Maji-khan," he said, wondering at his ability to speak so calmly, so normally, after what he had witnessed. "The Kushan elders will be punished."

"But that will not bring back the dead man," said Astinsai. "It will not undo what you have done."

No, it won't. He wanted to smash something, wipe that knowing look off the Old One's face. It was as if she saw the torment he suffered, had, in fact, planned it.

Instead, he left Astinsai's tent without another word, almost at a run, to find the Maji-khan.

CHAPTER 4

MENTAL ARTS

Kyra raced up the flower-strewn slopes behind the caves of Kali, where Tamsyn liked to hold Mental Arts. Once again, she'd slept through the gong for morning assembly. She couldn't afford to be late for class, especially not Tamsyn's, but it was happening with depressing regularity since her initiation. She now had to take advanced classes with older, more experienced Markswomen, in addition to the classes she usually took, and it was hard to keep up. Most days, she was covered with bruises by the time she lay down to sleep.

But her sleep was filled with disturbing dreams, and brought little rest, especially since she had decoded the message Shirin Mam had given her. Kyra had hoped the parchment would be a secret of some kind, some special counsel that Shirin Mam divulged only to those who had been initiated as Markswomen. Instead, the number string had resolved into a perfect pyramid of palindromic primes. She had stared at the solution, coldness creeping up her limbs.

"Mathematics is the language of the universe," Felda had once told her, "and primes are the building blocks of that language. The Ones probably used primes to generate codes for all their doors, even in their home world—and palindromes are beautiful in their symmetry and easy to remember. Lucky for us they used base ten in Asiana."

Transport codes were always palindromic primes.

And Shirin Mam never did anything without a reason.

A reward for your success, the Mahimata had said, without a hint of irony. And now every night Kyra was haunted by the dream of a door that waited for her to open it, waited to engulf her in darkness.

Kyra reached a terrace midway up the hill and stopped, panting. Tamsyn was already in full flow. Students surrounded her, sitting on the rocks that dotted the terrace, listening with every appearance of raptness to the elder's deep voice.

She tried to sneak in behind the others while Tamsyn's back was turned, but someone said loudly, "Oh, it's you, Kyra. You startled me."

It was Akassa, of course. Arrogant and beautiful with sleek black hair and olive skin, the eighteen-year-old thought that she was ready for her first mark. She had been furious when Kyra was chosen ahead of her.

Tamsyn broke off her lecture mid-stride and cast her gaze upon Kyra. A little smile of anticipation played on her lips. Kyra stood rooted to the spot, wishing that one, Tamsyn would look away from her, and two, Akassa would drop dead.

"Look who has decided to grace my class with her presence," said Tamsyn lightly. "The newest Markswoman, no less."

There were a few sycophantic titters. Kyra, who had been

wondering whether to apologize, realized it would make no difference what she said. Tamsyn had already decided what she would do.

"I was explaining to the class the difference between Inner Speech and Compulsion," said Tamsyn. "Perhaps you would like to offer your expert opinion on this matter?"

There was a snort of laughter from Akassa. Elena and Nineth gave Kyra sympathetic glances. It was a simple question Tamsyn had asked, but Tamsyn's simple questions never had easy answers.

"Inner Speech is the gift of kalishium," said Kyra. "Properly trained, a Markswoman can read and control other people's minds and actions. Compulsion is a misuse of this gift and punishable under the Kanun."

"So, the difference between the two is that one is allowed and one is not?" said Tamsyn, her lips curling. "You give a whole new dimension to the field of Mental Arts. Thank you for this great insight."

There were more titters. Akassa gave a derisive bow to Kyra, her eyes glinting with amusement.

Kyra kept quiet, but inwardly she fumed. She had answered correctly, even though she hadn't elaborated. But of course, that was not good enough for Tamsyn, who delighted in mocking her students as a means of "teaching" them.

"My, my, what turbulent thoughts you have, little deer," said Tamsyn. "You really need to work on controlling those wayward emotions of yours."

It was as if Kyra had been turned inside out, with every thought she had ever had on display for all to see; such was the force of Tamsyn's gaze.

The dark, hypnotic eyes turned away from her and Kyra sagged with relief. Sweat beaded her forehead and her heart thumped.

"Make no mistake—Inner Speech is not a 'gift,'" Tamsyn told the class. "It is an art to be learned and practiced every day of your life, if you aspire to any degree of skill. The bond you have with your kalishium blade allows you to hear the thoughts of those around you, but to delve into individual minds and exert control requires years of dedication. There are four rules. First, that we use Inner Speech sparingly and in great need. Second, that we never use it against another Markswoman—"

"Or Marksman," murmured Nineth unthinkingly. She clamped her hand on her mouth with a stricken look on her face, but it was too late.

Tamsyn's face went red, her lips pressed in a thin line. She glared at Nineth. "Is not one prize for stupidity every year enough for you? Must I inform the Mahimata how utterly un-deserving you are to be an apprentice of the Order of Kali? The very word 'Marksman' is a blasphemy. The Kanun of Ture-asa says nothing about men being able to bond with kalishium. There are *four* Orders in Asiana: Kali, Zorya, Valavan, and Mat-su. The fifth is nothing more than a bunch of outlaws. Understand?"

"Yes, Elder," said Nineth meekly.

"Obviously, it is something you find hard to remember. You will carve it for me on a stone tablet as a penance."

On *stone*? Kyra winced. That would take ages. Poor Nineth.

"Where was I before being rudely interrupted?" said Tamsyn. "Yes, the rules of Inner Speech. The third rule is that we must not use it for personal gain. Fourth, that we do not use it to take a life. That is what the kataris are for. When we break the rules, it is called 'Compulsion' and—as our *cleverest* young Markswoman pointed out—punishable by law. One more thing: Inner Speech does not usually work on animals, but it does have some effect on wyr-wolves. This is to our advantage when we hunt the beasts. Questions?"

Predictably, there were none. To ask a question in Tamsyn's class was an act of optimism bordering on lunacy.

The class came to an end. But before Kyra could escape with Nineth and Elena, Tamsyn called her back and told her to do a hundred sun salutations as "a small penance for being late."

Kyra glared at the elder's graceful, retreating figure, not bothering to try to hide how she felt. It was noon; the penance would cause her to miss the start of the midday meal, which was no doubt as Tamsyn had intended. Kyra considered simply ignoring the elder's command, but the penalty for that was a meeting with the Mahimata and her entire council of elders.

No, it wasn't worth defying Tamsyn. Kyra fell into the sequence of twelve poses that comprised the sun salutation. If she hurried, she could still reach the kitchen in time to eat something.

Somewhere between her sixtieth and sixty-third asana, a prickly sensation crept up her spine. As if someone was watching her, contemplating stabbing her between the shoulder blades.

She froze, fighting the urge to spin around. She was being foolish—hungry, exhausted, and now imagining things.

After the hundredth asana she stopped, swayed, and toppled to the ground. The grass was spiky and unpleasant to lie upon, but she was beyond caring. It was good to rest. She drew in deep breaths, trying to muster the energy to move. And then it came again, the lingering sensation of being watched, strong enough that she dragged herself to her feet. She brushed the hair from her face and started walking downhill, glancing cautiously around her.

A bone-chilling howl split the air, nearly stopping her heart. Kyra leaped and stared at the dense cover of spruce trees on either side of the hill, blade in hand. Nothing moved. Still she waited, every sense alert. The wind blew soft through the trees and insects chittered in the grass, but beyond that the world was silent. At last she slid her blade back into its scabbard, calming herself.

It could have been an ordinary wolf. Wyr-wolves rarely came down to the valley in the warmer season. But sometimes a goat or a calf or—rarely—a human would go missing, and the telltale tracks of the beasts would be seen, elongated and clawed. Nothing was ever recovered of the victims—not a scrap of clothing or a shard of bone. The Markswomen followed the trail when they could and relied on their instincts when they could not. It was dangerous work; wyr-wolves were twice as big and fast as ordinary wolves and far more deadly, at least during the full moon. No one had ever seen them during the new moon, not even Tamsyn herself. The kiss of a wyr-wolf meant certain death, for in their saliva was enough venom to paralyze a horse.

Kyra had ridden in three hunts last year, a necessary prerequisite to becoming a full Markswoman. The first and second times, the wyr-wolves outran their horses and the Markswomen returned with nothing to show for the night's work. But the third time, the pack of seven wyr-wolves they were tracking wheeled around to attack their pursuers. Kyra had been shocked at the size, speed, and slathering fury of the fearsome beasts. Ria Farad's blade had flashed through the darkness, lopping off the head of the snarling pack leader.

Kyra herself had killed one. She had waited, terrified, until the beast was almost upon her and she could smell its fetid breath before thrusting her katari up into its massive chest. The encounter lasted less than three minutes. At the end of it, five wyr-wolves lay dead on the forest floor. Two escaped, much to Ria's chagrin.

Later, Kyra had wondered what she would do if she had to face a pack, or even just one wyr-wolf, on her own.

Keeping a wary eye about her, Kyra continued down the hill. It must have been an ordinary wolf. Wyr-wolves knew better than to come anywhere near the caves of Kali. But she didn't care to hang around, waiting to find out. Such bravado could be left to the likes of Tamsyn and Ria.

The Order's kitchen was a roomy space hollowed out of the hillside, part of the same cave system that contained the main cavern and the individual cells of the Markswomen. But it had a separate entrance, a wide wooden door that was open during the day and padlocked at night to keep the food safe from animals.

Kyra entered through the door, inhaling the aromas of Tarshana's cooking and feeling herself relax. The Order of Kali might rule the Ferghana, but Tarshana ruled the Order's kitchen. A big-boned, red-cheeked woman with a thick plait of gleaming black hair, she had worked for the Order of Kali for over a decade, and her mother and grandmother had had the job before her. She stood now, perspiring over an enormous pot that hung above the fireplace.

"What's for lunch, Tarshana?" called Kyra, making her way

to Nineth and Elena, who had saved a place for her between them.

"Everything you like," said the cook, grinning. "Pilaf, fried eggplant, and potato samsas."

Delicious. Kyra eagerly settled down on the kilim-covered stone floor with a plate in front of her, ready to dig in. Just as she had taken her first bite, Helen Pichto, a plain-faced little novice with serious eyes, scurried over to whisper in her ear. Shirin Mam wanted to see her.

"Right away," murmured Helen before bending to collect the empty dishes in front of the other Markswomen.

With a sigh of longing, Kyra pushed her plate away and stood up, hunger and dismay warring within her.

"You're not eating that?" said Nineth, reaching for Kyra's plate.

"Are you all right?" said Elena.

"Sure," lied Kyra, and gave them a big smile before heading out of the kitchen. She had been expecting this summons for a while—ever since the night she returned from her first mark and Shirin Mam gave her that "special assignment," in fact. But did it have to be right *now*? This was the third meal she'd be missing in four days.

She walked down the corridor to the Mahimata's cell, thinking of what she could say, what excuse she could make for not having visited as soon as she had solved the puzzle. But there wasn't any. She'd been delaying the inevitable.

Shirin Mam sat at her desk: a huge carved affair of solid oak that had been gifted to her predecessor by a grateful petitioner. A bronze candlestick with three candles threw a small pool of yellow light on the books and scrolls scattered on the desk. In one corner of the Mahimata's cell was a pallet, and in another, a grass mat for meditation.

As always, Kyra was struck by how little of the Mahimata's personality this room reflected, how insignificant it seemed. There was nothing to indicate that it was the seat of power for the most formidable woman in Asiana.

Shirin Mam put down her quill. "When were you going to tell me you had decoded Felda's string of numbers?" she asked without preamble.

"I'm sorry, Mother," said Kyra. "It must be all the meals I'm missing." It was out of her mouth before she realized how insolent it sounded. But what she wanted most right then was to go back to the kitchen and wolf down some eggplant and pilaf before the next class. Her stomach rumbled in agreement.

Shirin Mam rose from her desk. "You are not a fool, and neither am I. It has been two weeks now and you did not come to me with the answer. Why?"

Kyra felt the first stirring of anger. Shirin Mam had all but ignored her for the past few weeks. She hadn't even mentioned the assignment again after giving Kyra the parchment. "I've been busy and I forgot," she said curtly.

"Is that all?" said Shirin Mam, her expression unreadable as always. "Or is there something else you wish to tell me?"

Of course there was something else. There was the dream she'd had over and over again. There was her fear the dream was connected to this "special assignment." But it was nothing she wanted to tell Shirin Mam about. When she was a child, she could run sobbing to the Mahimata, telling her of doors that ate her, that made the world disappear. Shirin Mam would hold her close and soothe the fears away—sometimes even sing her to sleep. For the rest of the world, she may have been the leader of the most ancient Order of Peace in Asiana, but for Kyra, Shirin Mam had taken the place of the mother she had lost.

But that was years ago. Kyra was a Markswoman now and if such dreams still came to her, she was not a child to be comforted.

The tension stretched between them like a tightrope. Kyra's eyes watered but she did not speak, willing her limbs not to tremble from fatigue.

Finally, it was Shirin Mam who broke the silence. "The solution, Kyra. I know that you carry it with you."

Kyra fished out a crumpled piece of parchment from an inner pocket of her robe. "It was simple," she said. "I rearranged the numbers and got this pyramid."

2

30203

133020331

1713302033171

12171330203317121

15121713302033171712151

1815121713302033171215181

161815121713302033171215181

33161815121713302033171215181613333

933316181512171330203317121518161613339

Shirin Mam barely glanced at the parchment before returning it to Kyra. "And what do you think it is?"

"There are ten primes," said Kyra. "They must be the codes to a set of doors." She hesitated before asking the question that had been haunting her. "Why me, Mother?"

"Felda thinks that special sets of primes might hold the key to every door in any Hub," said Shirin Mam, ignoring her question. "There is more than one Hub in the Ferghana, you know. Keep these safe."

Kyra felt a chill creep up her spine. "You mean me to use these codes, don't you?" she persisted.

The Mahimata cocked her head. "Not I, Kyra," she said gently. "You mean to use them yourself. Why else would you carry them around with you?"

What was Shirin Mam talking about? Kyra had the codes because she had forgotten the parchment was in her pocket—that was all.

"Let us try again," said Shirin Mam. "Why did you not come to me with the solution?"

"Because of the dream." The words spilled out before she could stop them.

A door—there was always a door. It stood in the middle of a featureless landscape, and Kyra would walk up to it and extend her katari to open it.

No! The real Kyra would shout to the dream Kyra. *Don't. Can't you sense the emptiness beyond?*

But dream Kyra couldn't, or wouldn't listen. She would slide the tip of her katari into the slot, the slot would glow blue, and the door would slide open. Beyond was utter blackness, and the black would open its maw to suck her in, drowning her in nothingness.

Shirin Mam was watching her.

"What will come, will come," said the Mahimata. "A dream is only a dream, but you make it more so with your fear."

"Is it only my fear, Mother, that there is a door I will open that would eat me alive? That would eat this entire *world* alive?" Kyra's voice shook slightly at the end.

Shirin Mam's tone became cooler. "Regardless of your fear, you will do what you have to do. And I don't know what lies in your destiny."

You lie, thought Kyra.

"Not to my knowledge," said Shirin Mam drily. Kyra flushed. "Is there something else you wish to talk to me—or *not* talk to me—about? You are going to be late for Mathematics. Felda will have something to say about that."

Kyra knew when she was being dismissed. But she drew a deep breath and plunged ahead. "Yes, Mother, there is something else. It has been a few weeks since my first mark. Is it not time for my second?"

"Good," said the Mahimata. "I like a sense of duty. The elders of Kalam have sent an urgent missive. They need a Markswoman to deliver justice. It is but a few hours' ride from here. I had meant to send Tonar Kalam; it is her clan, after all, and they have asked for her. But you will do just as well. Go the day after tomorrow, with my blessing."

Kyra's mouth dropped open in dismay. She had asked, so she had no one to blame but herself. But she didn't want to go around executing random strangers, and she definitely didn't want Tonar's mark.

Shirin Mam frowned at her expression. "What is the matter, child?"

As if you do not know. "Mother, I have vowed to wipe out the outlaw clan of Tau."

"You plan to kill them all?" asked Shirin Mam. "There must be over thirty of them now, not counting the women and children."

"I will kill all who deserve it," said Kyra. "And Kai Tau will be the last. Let him watch his people die one by one." Her heart contracted. *Let him suffer as I have suffered.*

Shirin Mam gave her a penetrating look. "You are not ready for your second mark, Kyra. I will have to send Tonar Kalam after all. You will accompany her, as a penance." The Mahimata held up her hand. "No, not another word. You remember all your pain, you carry it on your back, and you are so bowed down by its weight that you cannot see the truth. I have told you before that being a Markswoman is not about taking revenge. If you kill in anger, you are no better than the ones you execute. The katari is not meant to be used in this way."

"You let me execute Maidul Tau," said Kyra.

"I set Maidul as your first mark because by executing Kai Tau's eldest son, you strike at the heart of the Taus. You deprive them of their future," said Shirin Mam. She paused and added, "I had hoped that your first mark would teach you something. I was wrong."

Kyra's face burned, but she said, "Mother, at least let me take down the original twelve who murdered my family."

"No. I'll not have any Markswoman of mine throw her life away."

"But, Mother," protested Kyra.

"One day," said Shirin Mam, "the time will come and you will confront Kai Tau. For now, I expect you to concentrate on your classes, obey your elders, and practice the art of forgetting. The one thing you have not learned."

"Yes, Mother." Kyra bowed and backed away, unsettled and dissatisfied. Before she had taken more than a few steps, Shirin Mam said, almost as an afterthought, "Be here at the hour of dinner tomorrow night. You need an extra lesson."

Kyra's heart sank. The Mahimata must have heard about her abysmal performance in the advanced classes. And now she was going to miss the evening meal tomorrow. A coincidence? Or punishment for her earlier insolence?

As she walked out of the cell, she replayed the unsatisfactory conversation. She'd gotten no clear answers about the set of primes and why she might need it. And she was no closer to a second mark than before—though she was grateful she would not be taking Tonar Kalam's mark.

It wasn't as if she thought there was any honor in killing. Maidul's look of shock as he stared at the katari protruding from his chest still haunted her.

But she would not be weak. When the chance came to take down another Tau, she would grab it with both hands. If only she could find their camp again. Why did Shirin Mam not let her try? It was both her right and her duty. She had never questioned the Mahimata's judgment, and she didn't want to start now, but why couldn't Shirin Mam have given her some sort of explanation, or perhaps a timeline? One Tau murderer a year, leaving Kai Tau for the last. Twelve years to take her revenge, twelve years to "learn" whatever it was that the Mahimata seemed to think she lacked. Wasn't that reasonable?

"I could have told you that you'd get nothing out of her."

Kyra spun around, hand going to her katari.

Tamsyn laughed and stepped out of the passage where she had been standing.

"I have named you well. You startle as easily as a deer."

"Forgive me, Elder. I must be going." Kyra made as if to pass her, but Tamsyn blocked her way with a slim, outstretched arm.

"Felda can wait a little longer, don't you think?" The elder's mesmeric eyes held her. Kyra tried to still her thoughts, knowing that it was hopeless.

At last Tamsyn withdrew her gaze. "You are so *simple*, Kyra. Almost the worst at Mental Arts among the younger girls. You should have accepted my offer of extra lessons. It would have done you some good. At least your thoughts would be a little quieter than they are right now."

Kyra controlled herself with an effort. The worst of it was that there was truth in what the elder was saying. She resolved to focus better during Tamsyn's lessons, no matter how the Mistress of Mental Arts goaded her.

Tamsyn's eyes narrowed. "Shirin Mam will never let you go back to the Thar, little deer. You can wait forever, but she'll not give you the command to kill another Tau. You have killed the eldest son of the outlaw, and that is punishment enough."

The words—hard-edged and true—stabbed Kyra. "What of the twelve who slaughtered my clan?" she said.

"Shirin Mam has told you that being a Markswoman is not about taking revenge."

"I have made a vow and she knows it," retorted Kyra, realizing that she should stop talking, disengage from Tamsyn and step away, but unable to help herself.

"What is your vow to her?" said Tamsyn contemptuously. "You'll dance on her strings like everyone else does." She gave a flick of her fingers and went on, her voice somehow deeper and more compelling: "Years will go by and your vow will fade in everyone's memory, even your own. The Taus will breed and multiply like the vermin that they are, while the name of Veer will be forgotten. And you—what will you be but a mediocre old Markswoman whom no one respects? Perhaps you will inherit Felda's miserable little hoard of number-books."

Kyra closed her eyes. Tears pricked her eyelids and she suppressed them with difficulty. *Never weep in front of your enemy*, Shirin Mam had said once. *Your inner strength flows out from your tears and into your enemy's grasp.*

When she opened her eyes, she found Tamsyn watching her. "What would you have me do, Elder? I must obey the Mahimata."

"Yes. But perhaps a way can be found. Perhaps I can help you."

"Help me?" echoed Kyra. How could Tamsyn do that? And more importantly—why?

Tamsyn leaned forward until her lips were close to Kyra's ear. "If it were up to me," she whispered, "I would *command* you to kill the Taus. I would not rest until I had seen you avenge your family. I would walk with you into their camp, blade to blade, and butcher them in their sleep. The desert would drink their blood and I would garland you with their skulls, like the Goddess Kali. I would teach you all the words of power I know—words in the ancient tongue that can bend anyone to your will. And then *you* would be the most feared Markswoman in Asiana, the bane of outlaws and the scourge of wyr-wolves."

"But," stuttered Kyra, and stopped. The vision was too bright, too strong. She saw herself walking proud and fierce through the remains of the Tau camp, bodies falling before her katari like puppets. She saw Kai Tau kneel before her and beg for mercy. She saw herself swing her blade down onto his lowered head, and slice it off from his undeserving body.

The vision wavered and she rubbed her eyes. A small, sane voice within reminded her that it was *not* up to Tamsyn, and she should thank the Goddess that it wasn't.

Tamsyn leaned back and smiled, as if satisfied with what she saw. "My time will come," she said, soft. "And yours will too. Are you with me?"

"Yes, Elder," said Kyra, making her voice humble. She waited, but Tamsyn was silent. ". . . I should go for class now."

Tamsyn waved her away and Kyra made her escape, trying not to run.

For the rest of the day, Tamsyn's words and the vision she had spun kept dancing through Kyra's head. She thought she should go to Shirin Mam and tell her about the encounter, but something held her back. Perhaps it was the vision itself, and seeing her dream of revenge come to fruition. Or perhaps it was that uneasy feeling that she should have stopped Tamsyn from speaking, and defended Shirin Mam in some way.

But that was ridiculous. As if Shirin Mam needed anyone to defend her. The Mahimata knew her Markswomen inside out, and was stronger than any of them. Even if Tamsyn did make a bid for leadership, Shirin Mam would soon squash her. And Tamsyn knew it.

Still, if it was Tamsyn in charge, she would send Kyra back to the Tau camp. She would order Kyra to execute the killers who still walked free, fourteen years after her own loved ones were dead and gone.

The knowledge haunted Kyra. She felt she was betraying Shirin Mam and, miserable, began to dread her upcoming lesson with the Mahimata.

CHAPTER 5

THE SHINING CITY

The next evening, Kyra and Nineth joined Elena in her cluttered, candlelit cell. The deft, petite sixteen-year-old was Navroz Lan's favorite student—a "natural healer," the elder called her. Jars of pastes and bottles full of swirling liquids jostled for space on the floor. Bunches of dried herbs and roots hung from the ceiling. On the walls, she had stuck parchments scribbled with her favorite remedies. Shadows danced over them, blurring the words and dimming the drawings. A faint smell of honey lingered in the air.

"What does the Mahimata want with you?" asked Elena, massaging Kyra's left shin. Kyra had hurt it in a mock duel during Hatha-kala practice that afternoon. "You're not in trouble, are you?"

"Of course not," said Kyra, trying not to wince. "She's giving me an extra lesson."

"Better you than me." Nineth shuddered. "As if it's not enough, having classes all day."

Silently Kyra agreed with her. It had been a long day and

she was bone-tired. Felda had been deeply annoyed that Kyra missed most of Mathematics yesterday, never mind that it was the Mahimata herself who had summoned her. She had been even more displeased today when Kyra was unable to solve the "simple" derivations she set for the class. Nor was Kyra able to concentrate in Healing afterward; she couldn't get Tamsyn's words out of her head, and she couldn't figure out what she would say to Shirin Mam.

The worst class was Hatha-kala; fatigue and hunger had conspired to dull her fighting skills, and she had been beaten by each one of her opponents. Every part of her body throbbed.

Kyra sighed as Elena's fingers worked their magic on her shin. "It doesn't hurt at all now," she said. "What did you use?"

"Figwort, arnica, and calendula extract," said Elena, closing the lid on a jar of green-brown paste. "Oh, and a bit of horse dung."

"What?" Kyra sat bolt upright and glared at her friend. Elena's shoulders shook with suppressed mirth, and Nineth grinned.

"Very funny," said Kyra, annoyed. "I won't need any more of this ointment, will I?"

"You might," said Elena. "You're really not in any trouble? Or is there something you're not telling us?"

The sound of the gong summoning them for dinner saved Kyra from having to reply.

❦

Shirin Mam was working at her desk. *Does she never eat?* Kyra paused outside the Mahimata's cell. Markswomen were supposed to need less sleep and food as they grew older and more adept in the Mental Arts. Not that Kyra felt in the least hungry herself right now. There was a tight knot of tension in her stomach that threatened to push itself out of her throat. She didn't want to see Shirin Mam. What she really wanted to do was go back to her cell, pull the rug up over her face, and sleep for the next twelve hours.

"Come in before you collapse at my door," came Shirin Mam's voice. "If you would but pay attention instead of day-dreaming through my lessons, you would not need more than four hours of sleep a day. Even those hours you would grudge, knowing that sleep is a kind of death, just as death is a kind of sleep, however temporary."

Kyra swallowed. She entered and bowed, trying to summon the courage to say the words she had mentally practiced a hundred times now. *I'm sorry I listened to Tamsyn. There's something wrong with her. Maybe there's something wrong with me too. Maybe I don't deserve to be a Markswoman.*

Shirin Mam steepled her fingers. "The past couple of weeks have been hard, yes? It is always so. Everyone else is more skilled and experienced than you. You think you don't belong, like you can never match up to the more advanced Markswomen. It was the same for me also."

Kyra gazed at the Mahimata, astonished. Somehow she had never thought of her teacher as being a young novice, or an apprentice who had yet to prove herself.

"Everyone goes through this phase," said Shirin Mam. "In this you are not unique. Even Lin Maya, the founder of the Order of Kali, was filled with misgivings."

"Surely not," Kyra blurted out, her worries about Tamsyn temporarily forgotten. Lin Maya and her cohort were the stuff of legends. They were the first Markswomen of Asiana, and they had brought peace to the Ferghana Valley, brokering accords between warring clans, forcing them to accept the authority of the Order.

"I have been reading a copy of her memoirs." Shirin Mam indicated a tattered old book on her desk. "They are quite enlightening. Apparently, she questioned whether we should use kalishium to kill anyone. She was, you should be aware, the first to fashion a blade for herself using the metal."

"But the Kanun of Ture-asa says that only Markswomen can take a life, and they should use kataris to do so."

"We forget that Ture-asa was just a man," said Shirin Mam. "He was a wise man and a king, but he was not God. Nor was he a mouthpiece of the Ones. He wrote the Kanun just over eight hundred fifty years ago, long after the Ones had returned to the sky. He foresaw the emergence of the Orders from the chaos that reigned after the Great War, but he did not foresee how kalishium would dwindle, and how the ability to use it would vanish over time. Who still lives now who can forge a true katari?"

Shirin Mam fell silent, her face shadowed. Then she raised her head and fixed her gaze on Kyra. "Doubt is not your enemy. Face your doubts and fears so you can understand yourself better. Work hard—harder than you ever have before—and you will begin to chip away at the distance between you and the more advanced Markswomen." Her tone became brisk. "This brings me to the reason I have called you here tonight. I want to take you to *Anant-kal*, the world beyond time."

"What is this place, Mother?" asked Kyra, with a sinking feeling. "How come I've never heard of it?"

"It is the world as perceived by our kalishium blades," said Shirin Mam. "The ability to enter it unaided is quite rare. I myself have done it several times, but I am the exception. As you will be."

Kyra swallowed. "And how exactly do you get there?"

"When we bond with our blades at the end of the coming-of-age trial, it opens up a bridge that most Markswomen will never see. Cross that bridge and you enter *Anant-kal*."

"So it's an actual place?"

"It's real enough, but not in the physical sense," said Shirin Mam. "You'll understand what I mean once you've walked there. You must enter the second-level meditative trance to find the bridge to *Anant-kal*. We can try this right now. I will help you."

A bubble of apprehension rose in Kyra's chest. She didn't want to go to this *Anant* place, whatever it was. It sounded eerie—a place that was real, but not in the physical sense. Wasn't that the same thing as a dream? She had enough to deal with at night without seeking more strangeness in her waking hours. "But I have not yet achieved second-level meditation," she protested.

Shirin Mam waved a dismissive hand. "You will achieve it today," she said. "Too much food and sleep binds us to our bodies. Missing a meal or two can help, especially if you've never done it before."

Kyra blinked at the Mahimata. So she had made her miss dinner on purpose.

"Close your eyes and empty your mind." A thin, cool hand closed on Kyra's. "The only barrier is the one that you create yourself. Why so attached to this limited body? Why so fond of this restless mind? Let it go; let it all go, until only the real you remains."

"The real me?" echoed Kyra, bewildered.

"That which is timeless and beyond the constraints of the physical world," said Shirin Mam. "It is the real you that I call for. Come, walk with me."

Kyra closed her eyes and was surprised at how easily she slipped into the first-level meditative trance. Shirin Mam had helped her in some way, but it felt natural. She relaxed and breathed. What had she been afraid of? She couldn't remember. The light-headedness she'd been feeling from lack of sleep and food morphed into a warm, hazy sensation.

Shirin Mam's voice, gentle yet commanding: "Remember what it was like when you held your katari for the first time. Remember *katari-mu-dai*, the moment you laid your lips on the blade and welcomed it into your soul. Focus on the bond you have with your blade."

Kyra slipped deeper into the trance, and the world dimmed. Her blade shone in front of her, a silvery green beacon glowing with intention. How beautiful it was. The light bobbed ahead of her, beckoning. Kyra followed. As she moved, the light moved too. It darted ahead and she had to run to keep up with it. Beside her, and a little behind, she sensed Shirin Mam keeping pace with her.

The fog cleared. The light of her katari grew bigger and brighter until it was a blaze. The blaze elongated into the shape of a door—a rectangular opening of light in a dark world—and Kyra ran toward it without thinking, knowing only that she must go through the door of light before it closed.

She emerged on a grassy cliff perched under a deep blue sky. Blinded by the sudden sun, she gasped and reeled, reaching out for something to hold on to, but falling to her knees instead.

A long, narrow bridge curved impossibly over a dark canyon.

At the other end of the bridge, a vast city sparkled in the sunlight. It was unlike anything she had ever seen or dreamed.

Kyra crawled to the edge of the canyon and peered down. Her heart lurched at the sight of the yawning abyss below. Shading her eyes against the sun, she looked up.

Gleaming metal towers that appeared to be holding up the heavens.

Gigantic white domes resting on fluted columns.

A disc-shaped structure hanging unsupported in the sky, like a strange moon.

She closed her eyes but there was no escape from what she had seen. It followed her still, deeply familiar, yet utterly alien.

"What is it?" she managed to croak. "What is it, Mother?"

And Shirin Mam's voice, tinged with sadness: "I wish I knew."

Kyra began to sob. She couldn't help herself. Sunlight shimmered on the gossamer bridge, the tall towers, and the white domes. But the glittering city was empty of life. There was nothing but cold, dead beauty.

Shirin Mam held out her hand. "Will you cross the bridge with me?"

Kyra stopped sobbing. Cross that cobweb bridge? There were no railings, nothing to hold it up that she could see—no beams, ropes, or abutments. What if it broke and she fell into the abyss below?

"No," she said, her voice shaking. "Please, no."

"As you wish."

The light faded, leaving them in the dimness of the second-level trance. They were back where they had started. It was unbearably dull after the brief, bright glimpse into that other world, and Kyra had no wish to linger there. She surfaced from the trance and the physical senses rushed back. She raised a hand and touched her cheeks. They were wet with tears.

Shirin Mam gazed at her with compassion.

Kyra tried to speak calmly. "What was that place, Mother?"

"An aspect of *Anant-kal*. What the kataris chose to show us today."

"The world as perceived by our blades?" Kyra tried to understand.

"The world changes with time," said Shirin Mam. "But kalishium carries the memory of all that has been."

"That was our past? The world before the Great War?"

"It was *a* past," said Shirin Mam. "Does it matter?"

"Have you . . . have you seen . . . ?" Kyra choked, unable to complete the question.

But the Mahimata understood what she meant. "The Ones from the stars? No. The past is empty of life, unless you walk within living memory."

Kyra yearned to see that city again, even as she struggled to comprehend what the Mahimata was trying to explain. She wanted to walk down its streets, climb those glittering towers, and get a closer look at the odd, disc-shaped thing hanging in the sky. Even more, she longed to see the people who had built it.

But the past was gone, destroyed by war and its toxic aftermath. The fantastic city had vanished and the people who had once lived in it were long dead, their bones crumbled to dust.

"What use is it?" said Kyra softly. "Why show this place to me?"

"There is no one else I could have shared it with," said Shirin Mam. She looked diminished somehow, older.

Kyra sensed the deep loneliness of the most powerful woman in Ferghana. To go through life knowing something like this, and not be able to tell anyone. How had she borne it?

"You understand," said Shirin Mam.

"Yes, I do," whispered Kyra. On an impulse, she reached forward and did something she hadn't done in years: she embraced Shirin Mam.

"Hush, child." Shirin Mam's hands stroked Kyra's head. "It will be all right."

And Kyra, sobbing into the Mahimata's shoulder, had a sudden, unreasonable flaring of hope that it would.

CHAPTER 6

THE MARK IN KALAM

The Kalams were horse breeders and dwelled in the tree-less, grassy highlands to the west of the Ferghana Valley, between the mountains of the Alaf Range and the wasteland known as the Barrens. Kyra and Tonar left before dawn and rode without a break, yet the sun was high in the sky before they arrived at the cluster of circular white yurts that were the homes of the people of Kalam—their temporary homes, of course, for the Kalams could dismantle them and move at an hour's notice.

Kyra was glad to arrive, although she wasn't looking forward to the display of Tonar's markswomanship skills. The sooner this was over with, the better. Shirin Mam hadn't been joking when she called it a penance. Kyra had slept little the previous night. The vision the Mahimata had shown her refused to leave her thoughts, and before she knew it, Tonar Kalam was poking her awake, telling her to be ready to leave in five minutes.

Normally, Kyra liked the short, muscular Markswoman with her square jaw and deceptively mild eyes, her blunt black fringe perpetually falling across her forehead. Tonar was gruff and straightforward, rather like Felda. She was also the Markswoman closest to Kyra in age, being but three years older.

However, she had been simply insufferable throughout the ride to Kalam. She had taken Shirin Mam's instruction to "teach by example" to heart, and kept up her badgering until Kyra wanted to scream. It was too bad, because with different company, Kyra would have loved the ride. The Alaf Mountains were topped with snow, the foothills covered with lush pine forest. The sky was a cerulean blue, dotted with fluffy clouds, and the grass beneath their horses' hooves was fresh and green. The scent of pine and grass filled Kyra with peace. Or it would have, if Tonar wasn't shouting at her from horseback, explaining the difference between doing one's duty and mere self-gratification.

"Whoever my mark today is, I will know them," said Tonar. "It is my clan, my family. I grew up with these people. It could be a cousin, an aunt, an uncle. By the Goddess, it could be my own brother! But did I flinch when Shirin Mam gave me this mark? Did I plead with her to send someone else? No. I was proud of her trust in me. Just as *you* should have been proud when she offered it to you."

Kyra rolled her eyes, but she knew in her heart that Tonar was right. She hoped, for Tonar's sake, that the mark today—Tonar's fourth—was not a close relative of hers. For all Tonar's lecturing, Kyra could detect an undercurrent of nervousness in the Markswoman's voice.

Nervousness was evident also in the people of Kalam as they stood outside their yurts, watching the Markswomen approach.

The Kalams usually kept to themselves and had their own laws, rigidly enforced by their council of elders. Only in the case of murder, or a dispute with another clan, was the Order of Kali invoked. It had been several years, apparently, since they had appealed to Shirin Mam for help.

"They're afraid," murmured Kyra, noting the rigidity of their stance, the way some of the men and women had covered their mouths with their hands, and the absence of any children.

Tonar frowned. "Well, of course," she said. "We're Markswomen." She dismounted from her horse and Kyra followed suit.

A middle-aged woman in a green embroidered dress and black waistcoat stepped forward and bowed, placing her right hand over her heart. "I, Aruna Kalam, headwoman of the clan of Kalam, am honored to welcome you," she said, her voice trembling. "We had expected only one Markswoman—we are indeed *fortunate* to receive two."

The emphasis on *fortunate* was not lost on Kyra, although Tonar did not appear to notice it.

"Greetings, Aruna," she said. "I bring you Shirin Mam's blessings, and thanks for the beautiful fillies you sent us last year."

Aruna gave a strained smile. "No more than our duty," she said. And still that break in her voice, as if she was deathly afraid.

"Talking of duty, I am here to do mine," said Tonar. "Who has committed a crime so grave that it calls for a Markswoman? You did not give the Mahimata any details, beyond requesting my presence. While I am glad that you asked for me, you must remember that I will show no favor. Bring forth the accused, present the evidence, and read out the sentence."

Aruna swallowed hard and unfurled a parchment. Behind her a knot of six elderly women, whom Kyra took to be the council of Kalam, twitched and trembled. A wave of tension swept over the entire crowd, as if they were holding their breaths, waiting for something terrible to happen.

Please, Kyra prayed, *let it not be Tonar's mother or father or brother* . . .

"For the crime of killing my son, Asindu Matya," read out Aruna in a shaking voice, "I, Darbin Matya, do sentence you, Tonar Kalam, to death."

Tonar stared at Aruna slack-jawed, but Kyra had already begun to move with the headwoman's first few words. With an almost audible click she sensed the trap close, and lunged at Tonar, throwing the Markswoman hard on the ground. A hail of arrows ripped through the space that Tonar had occupied, and vanished harmlessly across the grassland. A couple buried themselves in a yurt opposite. Kyra rolled off Tonar, heart pounding, her blade flashing green fire in her hand.

People screamed and dropped to the ground, trying to crawl to safety away from the Kalam camp as more arrows flew through the air. From somewhere came a wordless, frustrated shout and the sound of running footsteps.

Tonar rolled fluidly up from the ground, spitting grass and mud. "Behind the horses," she barked, and Kyra obeyed, although her heart clenched at using the horses as shields. They scooted across the ground on their elbows and crouched behind the horses. Rinna and Dvoos, Tonar's black gelding, stood calm and motionless amid the chaos. From underneath Rinna, Kyra spied a large, powerfully built man throw a lighted torch at one of the yurts. *Oh no*. There could be people inside.

Kyra focused her anger to a pinpoint of pure rage and unleashed it at the assailant in a burst of Inner Speech.

"PUT OUT THE FIRE," she commanded. "RESCUE ANYONE WHO IS INSIDE."

The man hesitated, his mind blocking her, and Kyra realized he was out of her range. She streaked from her hiding place, pulse racing. An arrow grazed her shoulder and she stumbled, caught herself, and pushed forward again, this time staying low to the ground.

The blood thundered in her ears. She summoned the Inner Speech once more, putting all her force into it, her muscles straining and aching with the effort.

The man tried to resist, but this time, she broke through his defenses. He lurched forward and beat the flames out with his coat, thrusting aside the burning wood of the doorway to crawl inside. A Kalam man and woman followed, ripping aside the smoking canvas of the yurt to reveal the precious ones trapped inside: over a dozen little children, huddled together, their faces terrified. A man stood over them, holding aloft a wickedly curving sword, looking angry and bewildered as his compatriot—acting under the bonds of Inner Speech—tried to wrest it away from him. The hostage keeper.

Kyra's breath caught. She didn't stop to think. Her blade flew from her hand and buried itself in the sword-wielder's throat. Blood gushed from the wound and spurted over the children in a hot river as they screamed in panic. Kyra ran toward the body to retrieve her blade, hoping the children were uninjured.

She and Tonar had to put an end to this now. Kyra kept the bonds of Inner Speech tight over the man who had tried to burn the yurt, although her head felt like it was splitting in two.

Tonar, meanwhile, had not been idle. She had thrown her blade at the lead archer, stopping him dead in his tracks. The blade embedded itself in the middle of his forehead, and his bow fell uselessly to the ground. She darted forward to retrieve it while simultaneously using the Inner Speech to fell another attacker.

Kyra reached the remains of the smoking yurt as the Kalam adults began carrying the weeping children away. She bent and closed her fingers over the hilt of her blade, yanking it out from the mess that was the corpse's throat.

Later, she would wonder who he was, and why he had chosen an outlaw's path.

But not now. Now there was only the fight.

She ducked behind another yurt, ignoring the cries of pain and fear around her. *Four down*, she thought. *How many left?*

She sensed, too late, a malevolent presence behind her. A noose slipped around her neck—which was still sore from having been squeezed by Maidul Tau. Kyra's katari dropped to the ground. She gasped and brought her hands up to her throat, trying to tug the thin, silken rope off. But all she did was tighten it even more. Panic fogged her thoughts as the noose cut off the supply of blood to her brain.

"Die, scum of Kali," hissed a woman's voice behind her.

It was the name of the Goddess that galvanized Kyra's fading strength. She drove her elbow hard, behind and up, and connected with the woman's groin. There was a gasp of pain, and the hands that held the noose momentarily lost a bit of their desperate power.

That moment was enough. Kyra gripped the hands and twisted up the fingers, breaking several with an audible crack.

The groan turned to a scream and her assailant stumbled

back. Kyra sprang up and delivered a hard back kick to her chest, then spun around and followed it up with a front kick to the throat. The woman tumbled to the ground, blood frothing from her mouth.

Tonar appeared behind the yurt in a half-crouch, her face nearly unrecognizable in a twisted snarl.

"Any more?" she hissed.

Kyra grabbed her katari and massaged her neck, trying to breathe normally and still the fierce roaring in her head. "Not that I know of. Let's check the camp."

They circled the camp twice, throwing aside the canvas of the yurts, kicking open the wooden-frame doors. All were empty; the Kalams had fled to safety farther up the grassland where their horses were grazing.

Four dead bodies were sprawled on the ground; the man whom Kyra had bound with the Inner Speech sat in front of a yurt, a vacant look in his eyes. It would be a long time before he remembered who he was.

Three Kalam men and one woman had been injured by arrows; Kyra stopped where they lay whimpering and tried to soothe them with the Inner Speech as best she could, although she hadn't much of herself left to spare. Fatigue stole up her limbs and spine, and she longed to lie down on the grass and close her eyes.

A hand grasped her shoulder. "Enough," said Tonar, her voice hoarse. "Don't empty yourself, or you'll be the one in need of healing."

Kyra got to her feet, but it was hard; her legs felt like rubber. She took in the scene of destruction around her—the bodies, the burned and broken yurts—and shuddered. It was beginning to sink in, what had happened. She had taken down her second and third marks, and not one of them had been a Tau. "Goddess," she muttered.

"It could have been worse," said Tonar. "The Goddess watched over us all right." She wiped her damp brow with a sleeve. "Let's get those fools back here so they can clear up the mess and explain themselves."

Kyra glanced at Tonar's exhausted face. "Who was Asindu Matya?" she asked quietly.

"My first mark," said Tonar. She pointed with a boot to the body of a man who lay crumpled on the grass a few feet away, his head caved in. "His father was my fourth."

Kyra swallowed as she gazed at the corpse. She couldn't help feeling sorry for him, whoever he was. Then she remembered the children kept hostage in the yurt—the children these people had been ready to kill—and her pity vanished.

"Don't be sorry for them," said Tonar, as if she had read Kyra's mind. "His son killed a woman after abducting and violating her. A violent criminal, who deserved to be put down."

Kyra nodded, not trusting herself to speak.

Tonar walked to the edge of the camp and summoned the Kalams, using the Inner Speech.

One by one, they straggled back. Some were wounded and limping, leaning on their kinsmen for support. Some wept openly. A few hurried to help the injured, headed by the black-robed medicine woman of Kalam. Parents had their arms protectively around their children. The sight smote Kyra. She hoped Tonar wasn't going to punish them.

Aruna Kalam was one of the first to return. She knelt in front of Tonar, her face gray. The elders of Kalam clustered behind her, looking equally abject. "I have betrayed you, Markswomen of Kali," Aruna quavered. "I beg the mercy of your blade."

"Oh, do get up, Auntie," said Tonar irritably. "Tell me what happened, although I think I can guess."

The headwoman stood and wiped her eyes. "They arrived a week ago," she said. "Four men and two women, four armed with swords, two with bows . . ."

"That means one escaped," interjected Kyra in dismay.

Tonar's face hardened. "She won't get far. The Order of Kali will find her, sooner or later. Go on, Auntie."

"They had two of our children at sword-point," said Aruna, wringing her hands. "They must have found the children on the steppe, grazing the horses. They threatened to kill them unless we did as they asked. They rounded up all the other children, and made us write a letter to the Mahimata, asking for your presence."

Tonar pursed her lips. "Fools," she said loftily, "thinking they could fight a Markswoman of Kali."

Kyra didn't say anything, but she knew Tonar would have been dead in the first hail of arrows if she hadn't pushed her aside.

"We apologize deeply," said one of the Kalam elders. "We will accept whatever punishment the Mahimata deems fit."

"One of our elders will be here tomorrow," said Tonar. "I am quite sure the Mahimata will send Eldest, our healer. As for punishment, I cannot speak for Shirin Mam, but I doubt she will be angry. You have been foolish, but not malicious. You were trying to protect your children, after all." She glanced at the scene of carnage around them. "Bury the dead. Bind the one who still lives; his mind is gone, but it may decide to return. Eldest will deal with him."

Aruna Kalam bowed. "Thank you, Markswomen, for your mercy. May we . . . may we offer you our hospitality?"

Tonar gave a short laugh. "No, thank you. We'll be on our way. You have much to do before nightfall. Take care of your injured and your young. Till we meet again, the Goddess be with you."

"The Goddess be with you," they echoed.

Tonar and Kyra mounted their horses and cantered away, leaving the damaged camp behind. It was late afternoon now, and the golden, slanting rays of the sun made it seem as if the foothills were on fire. The wind had picked up—a sign that the night would be cool. Kyra inhaled deeply, grateful to be on her way back home. Grateful to be alive.

"Lucky I was with you today," she said, glancing at Tonar sideways. "Shirin Mam's penance turned out to be good for something."

Tonar snorted. "Shirin Mam sent you with me today for a reason—a reason that had nothing to do with penance or luck."

"Surely you don't think she knew what would happen?" said Kyra, skeptical. If Shirin Mam could have predicted this, she would have sent the Hand of Kali. Tamsyn could have taken on all six outlaws single-handed without so much as flinching.

Tonar shrugged. "The Mahimata must have sensed something amiss. Perhaps in the way the letter was phrased." She paused and said in a different tone, "I'm glad you were with me." She smiled at Kyra—an event so rare that it struck Kyra speechless. They were quiet for the rest of the ride home, and did not arrive at the caves of Kali until dusk had deepened the sky to violet.

CHAPTER 7

THE MAJI-KHAN
OF KHUR

No," said Barkav, his voice implacable. He knelt opposite Rustan, a huge, gray-bearded man with power radiating from every sinew of his massive frame. Clad in white robes with the symbol of Khur—the winged horse—embroidered on his chest, he could not have been anyone other than the Maji-khan, the head of the only Order of Peace in Asiana composed of men.

"But the Kushan elders . . ." began Rustan.

"Ghasil will take care of them," said Barkav. "Do you not agree that the Master of Mental Arts is the most capable among us to delve into their minds? They will fall over themselves in their hurry to tell him everything. Ghasil will make an example of them." His gray eyes darkened. "No one will dare lie to us again. No one will dare try to frame an innocent man."

But what about me, Rustan wanted to shout. *What role will I play?*

They were in the Maji-khan's tent, which was the biggest in Khur, save for the communal and council tents. It was also better appointed, with thick carpets, woven hangings, and brass lamps. Wooden trunks stuffed with books and scrolls lined the walls; on top of the trunks were figurines of every shape and size, made from bone, wood, metal, and clay. Gifts from petitioners and souvenirs from the Marksmen's travels, Barkav had told him once. Rustan caught sight of an exquisite clay camel, a gift from the Kushan council, and suppressed the desire to smash it.

"Please, Father," he said. "Grant me this, that I may be the one to liberate the souls from their bodies. It will lessen the evil I have done."

Barkav frowned. "What evil? I am the one who passed judgment. You simply followed my orders. If there is guilt here, it is mine. I should have examined the evidence and questioned the elders more closely. Instead, I trusted these men. I have been punished for my complacence, and it will never happen again."

Was that all the Maji-khan would say about his own culpability? How could he bear the burden of this mark so lightly? An innocent life should matter more.

"Yes, I obeyed you," said Rustan, "and all I ask is for the opportunity to obey you again. Let me take down the two marks."

"For the third and last time," said Barkav, his voice like flint, "no. It is not your place to seek vengeance. If you would obey me, then do not ask for this again."

Rustan gritted his teeth. His katari burned through its sheath, reflecting the turmoil within him. "So I just continue as usual?" he said, forcing calmness into his voice. "Pretend to the others that everything is fine?"

"You can tell the others what you wish," said Barkav. "The elders know, and sympathize."

Rustan swallowed the retort on the tip of his tongue, the one about where the elders could put their sympathy, but he couldn't quite hide it from Barkav, who always knew how he felt and could often read his thoughts.

The Maji-khan's grim face relaxed into a small smile. "I'm sure you won't mean that, not when you've had a chance to cool down. Rustan, there is a lesson in this, and the learning of it will be the making of you as a Marksman. You are accomplished in both katari-play and the Mental Arts. But sometimes, the real talent lies in knowing when to do nothing. Knowing how to step back, forgive, and let go."

"The day I forgive those two men is the day they stop breathing," said Rustan.

"I was talking about forgiving yourself," said Barkav calmly. "A much more difficult task, is it not?"

Rustan had nothing to say to that. After the Maji-khan had dismissed him, he stepped into the blinding white light of the afternoon sun. Almost everyone else would be resting in their tents. It was why he had chosen this time to confront Barkav. A part of him had known it would be an exercise in futility—but he had to make one final attempt.

He had killed an innocent man. What would the others say if they knew? And truly, did it matter what they thought? The fact of the man's death was what was important.

Rustan remembered again the sounds of lament that had followed him out of Tezbasti, and his stomach clenched. It was a sound that poisoned his waking hours, that haunted his dreams.

If only there was someone he could turn to now, someone not of the Order, who could listen to him, perhaps even guide him.

But there was no one. Rustan had never known his father, and had known his mother too briefly to be able to call on her, or even remember her very well. There were the elders of the Pusht clan, who had adopted him and raised him for the first eight years of his life, but would they tell him anything different from what Barkav had said?

He doubted it.

He walked beyond the tents to the grove, wanting to meditate. The novices had planted shrubs of jessora, spicebush, spineberry, and ephedra there. Given enough moisture, the shrubs would bear fruit in the spring—provided a sandstorm did not destroy them first.

Rustan knelt on the sandy earth and closed his eyes. He waited for his whirling thoughts to still, but they did not. He waited for his burning katari to cool, but it did not. He had been uprooted, and there was nothing for him to hold on to, not even the katari he was bonded to, for the katari had failed him. Or he had failed the katari. Was there a difference?

Astinsai's words echoed and clanged in his mind: How would he atone?

PART II

From *History of the Order of Kali*, by Navroz Lan of the Order of Kali

> *It is said that of all the Mahimatas of Kali, none were as wise as Shirin Mam, and of all her pupils, none were dearer to her than the orphan Kyra Veer. That is why she set her a test of the utmost difficulty at the coming-of-age trial.*
>
> *The coming-of-age trial in the Order of Kali has four phases. The first is Veeran—isolation of the spirit and starvation of the body, so that one becomes an empty vessel, translucent and receptive to the visions of Kali. The second is Seeran, when the Goddess gives her disciples the dreams that will tell them who they are and what they might become. The third is Jeeyan, the unique task set by the Mahimata that the novice must complete in order to win her place among the Markswomen of the Order. In the fourth and final phase, Katari-dan, the Mahimata awards the successful novice the katari that will henceforth be her constant companion.*

Kyra was fourteen when Shirin Mam judged her ready for the coming-of-age trial. This is not early; most Markswomen undergo the trial between the ages of twelve and fourteen. If they are not ready for it by then, the saying goes, they never will be.

The trial commenced at dawn. The Mahimata gave Kyra a flask of water fresh from a mountain stream, and bade her seek a place of solitude and quiet. There she must stay for three days without food or water or companionship. She was to drain herself of feeling and memory, words and desire. On the third day, she was to take just one sip of water from the flask. Then she must gaze into the water and pray to Kali. The rest was between her and the Goddess.

Kyra was gone for seven days, the longest that any novice had taken with the first and second phases of the trial. Some of the Markswomen of the Order were troubled, but the Mahimata was not.

When Kyra returned with the flask she was a wraith, weak and emaciated. Her eyes shone fever-bright and her step was lighter than a deer's. The elders plied her with questions, but all she would say was that she had been in a cave up on the mountain, and that she had dreamed of doors.

Kyra had gone close to the spirit world, and the morning light seemed to pass through her. Her ties to earth and flesh had never been weaker. It was time for the third phase, Jeeyan.

The Markswomen gathered around to watch, thinking that the Mahimata would take pity on the novice and set her a simple task. Was not Kyra a favorite?

But Shirin Mam withdrew her blade and spoke a syllable in the old tongue, and the Markswomen gasped and stepped back.

The ring of fire: an ancient test that had not been used in the memory of any save myself, eldest of the elders.

The flames leaped high and the heat seared Kyra's face. She looked at her teacher, and Shirin Mam nodded once. Kyra closed her eyes and stepped into the ring. The smell of singed hair and flesh wafted over to the Markswomen. Inside the circle, Kyra cried out in fear and surprise. When she entered the ring, she was captured within the walls of the enchantment that had created it. She could no longer see or hear the world outside. Only the fire that was now closing in on her.

The Markswomen waited, hardly daring to breathe, watching Kyra turn this way and that, searching for an escape. They understood that what Kyra was seeing was not merely an illusion that Shirin Mam's katari had conjured. It was as real as anything else, and Kyra could burn to death if she did not know how to counter the flames.

But of course, the test was not as simple as that. Once more Kyra cried out, for she beheld a form lying on the ground before her. It was a girl child, barely three years old, sleeping with her thumb in her mouth and one hand tucked beneath her head. Kyra grabbed the sleeping child. But the child would not move. Kyra tugged and tugged, but she could not so much as shake that child, let alone lift her up. Finally, with the fire just a few meters away, Kyra doused herself with water from the flask and hunched over the child, covering the little form with her own body.

The tongues of flames reached out, caressed Kyra's damp body, and vanished. The Markswomen let out a collective breath of relief and gave a ragged cheer. Kyra stood, looking around as if she could hardly believe that she was still alive. The child was gone, back to where it belonged: in Kyra's deepest childhood dreams.

Shirin Mam smiled and bowed low to Kyra, welcoming her as an equal into the Order of Kali. She presented her with a new blade, bidding her use it well, for it was made by Urhul Mirranthir, one of the last great katari masters of Asiana. Kyra knelt before the Mahimata and accepted the katari with both hands. She laid her forehead on the kalishium blade for katari-mu-dai, the moment of bonding, and shuddered as awareness exploded within her soul.

I applied healing salves to the burns on Kyra's face and arms, and there followed the usual feasting and singing in the central cavern. But Kyra did not rejoice overmuch. She understood the symbolism behind the trial of the ring of fire. The child was gone, safe from the flames, but consigned forever to the deeps of memory. The journey to adulthood had begun, and Kyra had only her wits and the blessings of the Goddess to carry her safely through.

CHAPTER 8

THE FESTIVAL
OF CHORZU

Summer had arrived in the Ferghana Valley, bringing long days of sunshine and pleasant nights. Everyone in the Order of Kali was looking forward to the festival of Chorzu. It meant two days away from the daily drudgery, days to mix with the ordinary folk of the valley and enjoy the show put on by traveling musicians, jugglers, and storytellers.

The elders were more relaxed than usual and there were fewer classes. Felda decided not to give them any derivations at all, and Mumuksu regaled them with stories of her girlhood spent in a caravan of performers. Even Tamsyn was subdued, as if she was directing her energies to something other than torturing students for a change.

Shirin Mam did not single Kyra out again, apart from praising her and Tonar's quick action at Kalam in front of the entire Order. "Exemplary discharge of duties and display of courage," she pronounced with a warm smile, making both

Kyra and Tonar blush. "But don't get bigheaded about it," she added, which brought them back down to earth.

Nor did the Mahimata summon Kyra for any more lessons, but still Kyra sometimes dreamed of *Anant-kal*. It was almost as bad as the dreams of doors; the idea that she could enter the realms of the past—or at least, the past as perceived by her blade—was both fascinating and repellent. Besides, she was embarrassed whenever she remembered how she had embraced Shirin Mam and wept like a child. One simply did not show such familiarity with the Mahimata.

Shirin Mam did send her one enigmatic note, a couple of days before the festival started:

"When in doubt, ask my katari where to go."

Kyra puzzled over this for several minutes. Surely Shirin Mam meant that she should ask her *own* katari where to go? Maybe she made a mistake while writing the note. But even if she did, whatever did she mean? Kyra went to her cell to ask her for an explanation, but the Mahimata was too busy to see her and waved her away. Perhaps it was a test of some kind? Kyra put the note in her pocket and resolved to figure it out after the festival.

The novices had to be accompanied to Chorzu by an elder, but the apprentices could be accompanied by any one of the Markswomen. This meant that Kyra and her friends could, for the first time ever, be completely on their own. Last year Tonar Kalam had accompanied them with rather bad grace, scolded them when they tried to sneak off to see a puppet show, and made them return early before the fun started.

Nineth was the most excited of the three. She kept counting the few bronze coins she had, and speculating what she could buy with them.

"We could pool our money and buy a palm-reading for you," suggested Kyra. "You never know, there might be a fortune hidden away in your future."

None of them had much money, and for most of the year this did not matter. Only during the festival did their penury pinch. There was a lot to buy, and little to buy it with. The elders sometimes paid them in coin for special tasks, or they would have had nothing at all. Elena was by far the richest of the trio, with several silver coins she had earned for her healing work.

"I'd like to buy a snakeskin if I can," she told the other two. "They are said to have a lot of healing power, especially for broken bones and torn muscles. I hope I find a good one."

Nineth and Kyra exchanged a quick, worried glance. Kyra hoped fervently that Elena would find no such thing; they were counting on her silver coins to purchase several little treats.

It was difficult to concentrate during the last class on the day of the festival—a combined Meditation class for the apprentices and younger Markswomen. They sat cross-legged on the grass, enjoying the scented evening air and half-listening to Mumuksu talk about the opening of the third eye.

Mumuksu ended the class by reminding them of the rules for attending the Chorzu festival. "No spirits, no fortune-telling, and no fighting. Wear your traveling cloaks over your robes, and keep your kataris and identities hidden. Of course, many of the Chorzu folk will still recognize us, but the outsiders won't, and the villagers know to keep their silence. You must be in groups of at least three, and apprentices must be accompanied by a Markswoman. You need to return by midnight. Remember, the penalty for being late is that you spend the whole of tomorrow sweeping the caverns instead of enjoying yourself back at the fair."

Kyra grinned at her friends and they grinned back at her. But the happy smiles were wiped off their faces at Mumuksu's next words: "Kyra, I know you are planning to escort Elena and Nineth to Chorzu. You will include Akassa in your group. The three apprentices should stay together."

She lectured them some more on the good behavior that was expected of them, but it was all empty wind as far as Kyra was concerned. She stared at Elena and Nineth in dismay and horror. The only silver lining was that Akassa looked equally horrified.

Sure enough, she blurted out, "Please, Elder, do I have to go with Kyra? I overheard the Mistress of Mental Arts saying that she needed to buy some things in the village. Perhaps I could help her carry them."

Mumuksu frowned at the apprentice. Although they were of the same clan, the elder showed Akassa not the slightest favor. "The Mistress of Mental Arts has more important things to do tonight than go to a village festival," she said. "You will go with Kyra and the other apprentices. Remember, stable your horses at the Kokand Inn."

She swept away, and the students scrambled up off the grass, laughing and talking.

Kyra went to her cell to retrieve her cloak. How like Mumuksu to saddle her with the loathsome Akassa. Perhaps they could slip away without her?

But when Kyra emerged from the caves, all three apprentices were waiting outside, cloaked and ready to leave. Akassa tapped her foot and looked at the sky, as if she had been waiting a long time.

"Finally!" she said, rolling her eyes when she saw Kyra. "Let's go get the horses."

"We're walking," Kyra retorted. She had meant them to ride

to the festival, but something stubborn and unreasonable inside made her want to punish Akassa, just for being there. She felt a small stab of satisfaction at Akassa's look of dismay.

"You're joking, right?" said Akassa. "Everyone else is riding. It's miles to the village. It's going to be dark before we get there, and it's a full moon tonight. Do you *want* us to be attacked by wyr-wolves?"

Kyra ignored her and started walking. Nineth and Elena exchanged worried glances before falling in step beside her. Kyra snapped, "The festival doesn't begin until sunset, and it's a lovely evening for a walk."

"We didn't say a word," muttered Nineth. Elena stayed silent.

But if they held their peace, Akassa did not. She kept up a loud and constant stream of complaints throughout the two-mile walk to Chorzu. The grass was damp, her feet were sore, they would miss the drumming at the start of the festival, they would be late coming back, they would be ripped apart by wyr-wolves, and so on and on until it was all Kyra could do to stop herself from slapping the girl. It quite spoiled the walk, which was a pity, because the valley was beautiful at this time of the year. The pink sky was a perfect backdrop for the distant snow-covered peaks, and the air was full of the scent of the red and white wildflowers that stretched as far as the eye could see.

Akassa need not have fretted about the time; they arrived in Chorzu at sunset, just as the first drumroll echoed across the evening sky. Forgetting their bickering, they picked up their robes and ran toward the field behind the village where the festival was being held. An offshoot of the Siran-dyr River rippled by the edge of the field. Later that night, young girls of the village would float flower offerings to the Moon Goddess on the water.

But for now, all attention was focused on the drummers: a group of bare-chested young men standing on a mound in the center of the vast field, drums slung around their necks and red scarves tied to their wrists.

"There must be thousands of people here," said Nineth in awe.

Men and women dressed in the loose white shirts, sleeveless black coats, and wide trousers typical of the valley thronged the field. But there were also clowns on stilts, black-robed medicine women, and veiled merchants from Tushkan. Children ran underfoot, laughing and shouting.

Nineth's words were drowned by the next drumroll. The drummers began to beat out an age-old invocation to the stars for friendship, light, healing, and unity. Elena slipped her hand into Kyra's and Kyra held it hard, her heart accelerating to the beating of the drums. How far back did this ritual go? Did anyone even remember what it meant? She thought back to the vision of the past she had glimpsed in *Anant-kal*, and her throat tightened. Perhaps the Ones were still out there somewhere, watching and listening.

When the last drumroll died away there was a roar of approval from the crowd. The drummers bowed, their faces shiny with sweat.

"Wasn't that beautiful?" said Elena.

"Not bad," said Akassa disdainfully. "But it was better last year."

Kyra shot Akassa a disgusted glance. "Where shall we go first?" she asked Nineth and Elena.

It was a good question. The field was dotted with dozens of little tents that were already doing a brisk business, to judge by the lines snaking out of them. Off to one corner, a tent larger than the others proclaimed "Marvels and Magick: Come and Be Amazed!" in golden lettering. The fragrance of freshly baked potato pies drifted up from a row of open carts tended by a group of Chorzu women.

"I'm hungry," said Nineth, sniffing the air.

"After that enormous lunch you ate?" sneered Akassa. "Be careful or you'll get too fat for Hatha-kala. As it is, you can barely spar as well as a novice."

Nineth's face went bright red and her eyes widened in hurt.

"Shut up, Akassa." Kyra glared at the apprentice. "Or I'll send you back to the caves right now."

"Let's go buy some pies," said Elena hurriedly, before Akassa could snap back at Kyra.

Akassa didn't want any, as expected. So the three of them joined the queue in front of one of the carts. The woman who was tending it gave them one quick glance and averted her eyes, obviously recognizing them. She handed them three potato pies and waited with discomfort as Elena counted out six bronze coins.

Kyra wished she could pat the woman on the arm and tell her there was nothing to be afraid of. They were just a group of friends out to have fun at the festival.

But that would not have gone over well. The Order of Kali had ruled the Ferghana for centuries, acting as peace brokers, protectors, and executioners. The Mahimata ensured that her Markswomen followed the law scrupulously, but as far as the villagers were concerned, they held the power of life and death over everyone else in the valley.

Kyra and her friends took their pies and stood beside the Marvels and Magick tent to eat. Akassa wandered away scowling, pausing to inspect a peddler cart stacked with colorful wares with such scorn that she scared away several potential customers.

"Mmmm, this is good," said Kyra, biting through the crispy shell of the pie to the buttery center.

"I could say that myself," said a deep male voice from somewhere over her left shoulder.

Kyra jumped and veered to face the speaker, a stocky young man who was leaning against a tent pole. He had full lips, blue eyes, and reddish hair, and was passably handsome, apart from his too-prominent teeth. He bowed and doffed an imaginary hat. "Hattur Nisalki at your service. What are three such lovely ladies doing outside my tent?"

"This is *your* tent?" Nineth gazed at the garish lettering on the white canvas flap. "What are the marvels and magic inside it?"

Hattur flashed a toothy grin. "In answer to the first question, dear lady, the tent and its wonders belong to my father, but I take care of day-to-day business. As for your second question, why not come in and see for yourself? One silver coin each and I'll toss in a personal tour for free."

Nineth's face fell. "We don't have that much money to spare."

Kyra had already turned her attention back to the potato pie when Hattur drawled, "Oh well, seeing as I'm in such a good mood, how about a kiss instead?"

Kyra almost choked. *How dare he.* No one talked to the Markswomen of Kali like that. She glared at Hattur's grinning face, wishing she could break a few of his gleaming teeth. But their instructions were quite clear: they must not draw attention to themselves during the festival.

"Let's go," she muttered, tugging her companions along

with her. Hattur shouted a cheerful apology after them, but she ignored him.

They wandered around the field, jostling shoulders with ordinary folk, light-headed with freedom. There were all sorts of goods on display, from wooden toys to love potions, perfumed soaps, and mulled wine. There was even a tent that offered massages to cure every possible ailment, from infertility to rheumatism.

They caught glimpses of other groups of Markswomen, and once they saw the four novices, hurrying after a scowling Felda, who was striding along as if the entire field belonged to her. Akassa kept her distance from them, which was a blessing.

As evening deepened into night, a full moon sailed into the sky. Lamps winked into existence at every tent and cart, their oily smoke mingling with the aroma of roasted kebabs and pilaf. The crowd became even more densely packed, especially around an impromptu stage where a riddling contest was being held.

The girls bought sweet buns stuffed with walnuts, and Elena delighted them with a silk scarf each—green for Kyra and blue for Nineth, to match the color of their kalishium blades— having failed to find a snakeskin that was to her satisfaction. Akassa sniffed in disdain at the scarves, but Kyra could tell she was irritated that Elena did not buy her one too.

For herself, Elena replenished her stock of black silk ribbons to tie her plaits. She always wore her long black hair parted in the middle and neatly plaited—unlike Nineth, whose brown hair was always falling in front of her eyes. *Makes me think you're trying to sleep during class*, Felda had told her once in a waspish tone. Nineth had mumbled an apology, pushed the hair away from her face, and widened her blue eyes at Felda in an attempt to look interested in the laws of motion. It hadn't worked; Felda had seen through her and set her extra problems.

They made their way to the rivulet, munching the buns, Akassa following slowly with a sour look on her face. Soon it would be time for the unmarried girls of the village to float their flower offerings, and they would have a perfect view of the ritual right on the banks. For now, though, the area was deserted, and the peace and quiet were a relief after the noise and smoke of the crowds at the other end of the field.

They had settled down on a dry patch of grass when a familiar voice spoke up behind them: "I see you lovely ladies did not forgive me after all."

It was Hattur Nisalki. Kyra suppressed her irritation. A lone lamp hung from the branch of an old chenar tree above Hattur, highlighting his half-earnest, half-jesting expression.

He bowed deeply. "Dear ladies, please accept my humble apologies for my forwardness earlier this evening."

"What forwardness?" whispered Akassa.

"As recompense," Hattur continued, "I would like to offer you all *free* entry to the tent of Marvels and Magick."

"No thank you," began Kyra in an indignant voice, but Nineth scrambled up, looking excited.

"Nineth!" said Akassa. "Have you gone mad? Come back here right now."

Although this was exactly what Kyra herself had been about to say, she said instead, "Go on, Nineth. Just be back in time for the rite of flowers. You wouldn't want to miss that."

Nineth threw her a grateful look and beamed at the young man. He offered her his arm and they disappeared into the darkness of the trees.

For a moment the remaining three were speechless, struck by the magnitude of what had happened.

Akassa said, her voice tight with ill-concealed triumph, "You wait until I report you to the elders. You're supposed to be a *Markswoman*? You don't have the sense of an apprentice. They should demote you back to being a novice."

"Yes, you'd love that, wouldn't you?" said Kyra, although she was already regretting her rashness in letting Nineth go off with a strange man. "But it won't happen. You just can't accept that you don't have what it takes, not now, perhaps not ever." The words were harsher than she had intended, but a sudden anxiety, a feeling of not-rightness, made her speak without thinking.

Akassa leaped up, her face distorted. "You're so proud of yourself," she hissed. "But it's only because you're the Mahimata's favorite that she even let you go for your first mark. I bet she doesn't let you go after the Taus ever again."

The words hit home and Kyra also sprang up, snarling. Elena tried to hold her back, but she shook off her friend's hand and advanced on Akassa.

Akassa laughed, a high, brittle sound. A blue glow in the darkness betrayed the presence of the katari in her hand. "Let's see whose blade is sharper, *Markswoman*." She invested the last word with such venom that it sounded like a curse.

"Kyra, don't." Elena's voice was small and frightened. Kyra ignored it. She focused on Akassa, the blade in her hand, and the stance of her crouching body, outlined against the trees on the other side of the rivulet. Akassa's back was to the dark, rippling water; this was to Kyra's advantage.

Never draw your kataris on each other. It was the first thing apprentices were taught. The penalty, for a full Markswoman, was permanent exile from the Order. An apprentice, of course, could still be forgiven.

"I give you one chance to sheathe your blade, apprentice," said Kyra, "and express your remorse."

"Why, little deer, are you afraid?" taunted Akassa.

It was the use of the derisory *little deer*, which no one but Tamsyn ever called her, that goaded Kyra to action. She did not draw her blade; to do so would have been to fall into the trap that Akassa had sprung, and she wasn't that foolish.

Your blade is but an extension of yourself, Chintil had told them. *Your hands are but an extension of your blade. Armed or unarmed, it is all the same.*

Kyra crossed her palms in front of her face and slipped into the dance of Empty Hands—the art of bare-handed defense—without pausing to think.

Akassa blinked in surprise and stepped back, whether from the silence and swiftness of the attack or because her opponent had not drawn her katari, Kyra did not know and did not care. The moment's advantage was enough; she swung around with a side kick that caught Akassa on the chest, and the girl gasped and stumbled back farther. *A little more*, thought Kyra.

Akassa's blade flashed in the darkness, a streak of deadly blue light that took every ounce of Kyra's skill to deflect. Akassa did not mean to kill her, or she would already be dead. But the blade grazed the side of her face, and she cried out with pain and anger.

Akassa laughed. In the blue light of her blade she looked quite demented. "How did you like *that*, little deer?" she sneered.

Without bothering to reply, Kyra closed the gap between them and Divided the Wind, a risky maneuver that opened you up to attack, but could break the arms or hands of a foe. She swept up her forearms to knock Akassa's hands aside, and then brought the sides of her palms down hard on both of the other girl's wrists. Akassa cried out with pain and dropped her blade. Kyra seized hold of Akassa's neck, spun her around, and hurled her into the cold black waters of the rivulet. Elena gave a small shriek, then covered her mouth with her hands.

Akassa emerged a few moments later, gasping and sputtering, hair clinging to her face. In the moonlight, it looked as if a rather bedraggled river nymph was rising from the swirling water.

"I hope you haven't mislaid your katari," said Kyra, hardening her heart against the girl. "I can't even imagine the penalty for losing it."

A look of fear crossed Akassa's face and she dove back under the black surface. She was gone for two whole minutes. When she came up for air, her hands were still empty, and her expression had gone from merely fearful to wild with panic.

Elena came to stand beside Kyra at the bank. "When are you going to tell her that you have her katari in your hand?" she whispered.

"Oh, maybe an hour or four from now?" Kyra laughed at her expression. "Don't worry, I'll tell her when she next comes up for air. I don't want the entire village watching an apprentice of Kali make a fool of herself." She examined the slender blue blade in her hand. She was uncomfortable holding it. She did not like Akassa and the weapon was hers; an alien hostility emanated from it.

"Kyra, your face—you're bleeding!" Elena cried.

Kyra reached up to touch the side of her face; it was slick with blood and throbbing with pain. The katari pulsed in her hand, and she fought down fear.

No. I will not be afraid. I bested your mistress fair and square. She glared at the weapon as Elena swabbed away the blood from her face and tied the green scarf around her neck to hide the wound.

Akassa emerged from the water again, panting and shuddering. "Help me," she called out in a thin voice. "I can't find my katari."

"I have your katari," said Kyra. "You can come out now."

Akassa dragged herself out of the water, ignoring Elena's outstretched hand. She stumbled toward Kyra, snatched the katari from her hand, and kissed the blade, weeping soundlessly.

"Let's get you dry," said Elena. But Akassa brushed past them and ran toward the sheltering darkness of the trees.

"Let her go." Kyra caught hold of Elena's arm as she made to follow the weeping girl. "She'll be all right."

In truth, Kyra was ashamed of herself. Yes, Akassa had attacked her, but hadn't she goaded her into it? She should have ignored the girl's insults and walked away. Shirin Mam would be most disappointed in her.

At the thought of Shirin Mam, the feeling of not-rightness returned with such force that Kyra had difficulty controlling her breath.

"What's the matter?" Elena's eyes were large with concern as she took in the expression on Kyra's face.

"I don't know," Kyra whispered. "Don't you feel it?"

Before Elena could answer, sounds of laughter and excited voices broke the silence. Little flames of light came bobbing through the wood. Behind them glowed the faces of young girls holding their offerings—lotus-shaped containers filled with flowers, incense sticks, a candle, perhaps a bronze coin or two.

In a minute the place would be packed with people and Kyra and Elena would not be able to move, even if they wanted to.

"Should we go look for Nineth?" said Elena, anxious now.

"Yes. Something is wrong, but I can't put my finger on it," said Kyra. She had lost all interest in watching the rite of flowers.

They slipped out between the trees, past the line of girls and the groups of young men who were cheering them on.

Elena grabbed her sleeve. "Look, there she is!"

They hurried out of the wood into the open field. The crowd had thinned and some of the peddlers were already packing up for the night, although there were still enough lamps to see by.

Nineth sauntered toward them, her brown hair even more ruffled than usual, a little frown marring her normally cheerful face. Kyra felt a rush of relief. It was not Nineth who was in trouble after all. And it couldn't be Akassa, because the feeling of something not-right had come upon her before the apprentice ran away.

"What took you so long?" Elena demanded as soon as they were in earshot.

"We had visions of Hattur Nisalki carrying you off," added Kyra teasingly, although her heart was not in it.

"Oh, that almost did happen," said Nineth. "But I gave him a black eye and he changed his mind."

"Nineth," exclaimed Elena. "You *hit* him?"

"Once," said Nineth. "I didn't show him my katari or anything stupid like that, but he grabbed me and I didn't know what else to do. Besides, he'd already shown me the tent and it wasn't much—a bearded lady, a dwarf, a poor little wildcat in a cage, and a magic show with funny instruments called scopes. I'm glad we didn't waste any money to see it."

Despite her mounting worry, Kyra snorted with laughter. She couldn't help it. "Poor Hattur didn't get his kiss after all?"

Nineth flushed. "I'd rather kiss a horse." She looked around. "Where's dear Akassa? Don't tell me you've managed to lose her."

"She and Kyra had a fight," said Elena. "Kyra threw her into the river."

"What?" Nineth looked dumbfounded. "Kyra, how could you?"

"I know, I shouldn't have." Kyra hung her head, chastened.

"I mean, how could you have not waited for me?" said Nineth. "I always miss the fun! Wait, she's not still in the river, is she? We might have some explaining to do to Shirin Mam if she is."

As soon as Nineth said Shirin Mam's name, the feeling of not-rightness grew until it enveloped the entire world. "We should go back to the caves," said Kyra.

"But it's still two hours to midnight," Nineth protested.

"I'm sorry," said Kyra. "But something's wrong; I can feel it. I think we should get back." Her urgency bled into her voice, and she knew Nineth and Elena could hear it, because they joined her without further protest.

She walked away fast, but it wasn't enough. She could not outrun the knowledge that something was horribly wrong back at the caves. If she didn't hurry, it would be too late to stop something terrible from happening. The katari at Kyra's side burned with urgency. She began to run, run as she never had before, away from the dying festivities of Chorzu and into the moonlit night.

Behind her Nineth and Elena followed, stumbling in their haste over the familiar, grassy paths, calling to her to wait for them.

But Kyra did not wait. Her heart thudded with every step and twice she tripped over an unseen rock and bruised herself. Somewhere, not far distant, a wyr-wolf howled: a lonely, drawn-out wail that sent shivers up Kyra's spine.

She did not stop running until she had crested the hill that overlooked the caves of Kali.

CHAPTER 9

BUT ANOTHER DOOR

A cool wind chased ragged clouds across the dark sky. Kyra stood on the hill overlooking the shadowy hollow in front of the caves and tried to overcome her dread. Whatever had happened here, it was over now; the sense of wrongness had abruptly withdrawn as she reached the top of the hill. She drew her katari as she advanced down the slope. Behind her, she sensed Nineth and Elena follow suit. They ducked into the crawlway of the caves and made their way through the widening passage into the torchlit cavern.

It was empty; the others hadn't returned yet. They would be on their way, though. They would have sensed, as she did, that some balance had been disturbed.

Kyra walked into the middle of the silent cavern and slowly circled it. The Goddess Kali danced on the walls, flickering in the firelight as she vanquished one demonic force after another. It all appeared as it should. Then why this cold prickling certainty of the world turned inside out? Just because Shirin Mam wasn't sitting at a bench, reading one of her old books?

The Mahimata must be meditating in her cell. Kyra would go and check, and Shirin Mam would rebuke her for disturbing her, and all would be well.

Wouldn't it?

Kyra's blade began to burn. She gripped it, letting its warmth flow into her arm, its strength into her heart.

"Stay here," she told Nineth and Elena, before making her way to Shirin Mam's cell.

The walk down the Mahimata's corridor was the longest Kyra had ever taken. The lamplight flickered, and the faces of previous Mahimatas gazed sternly down at her from the portraits that hung on the walls. Each step she took increased her sense of unreality.

And then she arrived at the entrance to the Mahimata's cell, and could put off the moment no longer. Kyra grasped the white horsehair curtain, lips moving in wordless prayer, before pushing it aside.

The cell was dark. Kyra blinked and called out, "Mother?"

No one answered.

She sheathed her blade and went back into the corridor. She took down one of the torches from the wall, trying not to shake. The Mahimata must have been called away by a petitioner. An emergency of some sort, a life in need of saving.

But in her heart, she knew that was not true. She reentered the cell, holding aloft the torch, afraid to breathe.

A body lay in a small, twisted heap on the floor next to the pallet. A thin arm was outstretched, the fingers curling over a lifeless blade.

The blood rushed away from her brain and Kyra thought she would faint. She leaned against the wall and tried to inhale.

But it felt like all the air had left the world and she would never be able to take another breath.

Get ahold of yourself. Shirin Mam needs you. She might be ill.

Kyra hooked the torch to a sconce on the wall and ran to where the Mahimata lay on the floor, her legs trembling. She knelt and placed two fingertips gently on the inside of Shirin Mam's wrist. *Please, please be alive.*

There was no pulse.

Kyra's self-control broke. "Mother!" she cried, grasping her teacher's face with both hands. "Wake up. It's me, Kyra. Look at me!"

Shirin Mam's eyes stared sightlessly back at her. That emptiness told Kyra what she had known ever since she entered the caves of Kali.

Shirin Mam was dead. *Dead.*

Kyra rocked back on her heels, gasping. The sob started in her chest and burst out of her mouth like an animal's cry of pain. She put a hand across her mouth to stifle the sound.

"Kyra! What is it? What has happened?"

Navroz Lan stood framed by the entrance to the Mahimata's cell. Her white hair was disheveled, her mouth open in distress.

Wordlessly, Kyra pointed to the body on the floor.

Navroz rushed to her side and bent over Shirin Mam. She felt for a pulse, as Kyra had done. She shook her head, muttering under her breath, and went to work. She laid Shirin Mam straight on her back, and placed the heels of her hands on her chest, one on top of the other. She began chest compressions, hard and fast, counting aloud.

Kyra watched, hope blooming like a treacherous flower inside her.

After a minute, Navroz stopped. She lifted Shirin Mam's chin and tilted her head up. She bent to listen, then breathed into Shirin Mam's mouth, pinching her nose shut.

Navroz repeated the whole process again, then again. Each time, Kyra scanned her face for some sign that it was working, that Shirin Mam's heart had started beating of its own accord.

But at last the elder sat back, her face tight with grief. "I'm sorry, Kyra," she said, her voice breaking. "She's gone."

No, Mother. Kyra doubled over, hugging herself.

Navroz slipped an arm around her shoulders and held her as she cried.

"How?" sobbed Kyra. "Why?"

But Navroz didn't have the answers. It was Kyra who knew what must have happened.

Shirin Mam will not always be around, she had said. *Are you with me?* she had asked, and: *Yes, Elder,* Kyra had meekly replied.

Tamsyn had all but told her she would do this, and what had Kyra done to stop her? Nothing.

Navroz continued to hold her for a while. Then she grasped her by the arms, looking straight into Kyra's eyes. "I know you loved Shirin Mam," she said softly. "So did I. We both will grieve. But right now, I need your help."

Help? What could she possibly do that would mean anything? Kyra shook her head and shied away from Navroz's gaze. All she wanted was to crawl into a dark corner and never emerge again.

"Please, Kyra. You'll have to be strong for Shirin Mam's sake. You meant a lot to her. Don't let her down now."

But I already did. Kyra's chest hurt. She couldn't speak, couldn't breathe.

Navroz pulled her up to her feet. "Listen. The others will be here soon and I would like her to be ready for them. You don't want them to see her like this, do you?"

"No," whispered Kyra. Not like this. Helpless, undignified, soiled.

"Then let us clean her and change the robes before we take her to the main cavern."

Bile rose in Kyra's throat but she pushed it down. *Help me, Goddess. Make me strong.*

They worked in silence, straightening the body and removing the robes. Kyra tried not to look at Shirin Mam's face, her empty blue eyes. As long as she didn't look, she could believe that her teacher was still alive, and that this thin, shrunken body belonged to someone else. She wiped the skin with a damp cloth that Navroz handed her, checking for any marks or clues as to what had happened. But there were none.

Kyra swallowed and made herself speak. "She looks untouched."

"That doesn't mean anything," said Navroz.

Eldest was right. A katari in the hands of a trained Markswoman like Tamsyn could kill without seeming to—not a drop of blood, no cut to the skin, just a stopping of the breath and a stilling of the heart. But Shirin Mam was skilled in the art of katari defense. Surely no one could have taken the Mahimata by surprise, she who had taught them all how to see with the third eye?

But how else could Shirin Mam have died? She had been healthy and strong, at the peak of her powers.

They dressed the body in a fresh robe that Navroz dug out from a chest in the corner. The elder combed Shirin Mam's hair and closed her eyes.

"Quick now," she commanded. "The others are almost here."

Kyra grasped the corpse by the shoulders while Navroz took hold of the feet. Kyra was shocked at how light the body was. It was like carrying a child.

Back in the cavern, Nineth and Elena still waited, pale and anxious. They both burst into tears at the sight of the body.

"Hush," said Navroz. "I won't have you wailing like farm-wives. Shirin Mam would not like it. Remember who you are."

Elena stopped at once but Nineth continued to sob, stuffing her fists in her mouth to stop the cries escaping her throat.

They laid the body on the slab. Navroz told Elena to fetch the Mahimata's katari, which was still lying on the floor of her cell. When Elena returned, Navroz laid the katari on Shirin Mam's chest, folded her hands over it, and stepped back.

"It looks as if Shirin is only sleeping," said Navroz, her voice tight with suppressed emotion.

But Kyra could not look at the still, black-robed figure on the platform. She watched Navroz instead. The elder seemed to have aged ten years in one night. Her face was drawn, her eyes bright with unshed tears.

"Elder," said Kyra, "I must speak with you."

Navroz shot her a warning glance, and she heard what the elder must have already sensed: low, worried voices and the rustling of robes.

Chintil and Tamsyn were the first to arrive. Chintil's hands flew to her mouth and she fell to the floor in shock. Tamsyn gave a cry of grief and circled the body on the platform, wringing her delicate hands. *Like a vulture*, thought Kyra numbly. *Closing in to finish its meal.*

The others began to arrive one after another, including a red-eyed and subdued-looking Akassa. Kyra stared hard at her but Akassa refused to meet her eyes. Everything they had been fighting about now seemed stupid and trivial, and Kyra was filled with self-loathing. To think that she had been baiting an apprentice while Shirin Mam lay dying in her cell. If only she hadn't gone to the festival, or fought with Akassa. Perhaps she would have sensed something was wrong much sooner than she had, and returned in time to help her teacher.

The last to arrive was Felda. She led the four novices to a corner, hugging them one by one when they began to cry.

When everyone was assembled, Navroz clapped for silence and said, "Shirin Mam, our beloved Mahimata, is no more." Her voice was hoarse but it did not waver.

She waited until the cries had subsided. "I have examined her body, and found no marks. I do not know the cause of death. Perhaps she simply chose to leave us? I cannot say. I know this is a shock to all of you. Do not hesitate to come and talk to one of us if you need to." She paused to swallow. "Shirin Mam was our teacher, friend, and mother. Many years ago, she was also my most challenging pupil. She questioned me in everything, and in turn forced me to question myself. She taught me to take nothing for granted. But in this I am guilty: I took *her* for granted. I did not expect to outlive her." She bowed her head and was silent for a moment. When she raised it again, her face was calm and resolute. "We must prepare Shirin Mam for the last rites. You may come to your Mahimata one by one and say your farewells."

The Markswomen streamed past the raised platform, folding their hands and murmuring their goodbyes. One or two paused to kiss the hem of her robe, and Noor Sialbi laid a white wildflower at Shirin Mam's feet.

When it was Kyra's turn, she forced herself to look at the

slab where Shirin Mam lay, the slender katari on her breast, eyes closed as if in sleep. Small and still, diminished in death. There should have been an aura of power around her still, something to tell the world what a remarkable person she had been. Kyra's soul cried out at the unfairness of it all. Did death make everyone ordinary? Did it make no difference who you were, what you had accomplished?

No, of course not, came Shirin Mam's gentle, chiding voice. *Death is but another door I have walked through. You see my husk, the part I have left behind, and mistake it for the whole. I am elsewhere, a place you cannot reach—not yet.*

Kyra sighed. Her teacher's voice was still with her. If nothing else, she still had that. She bowed her head and moved away.

The elders bent to whisper together. Kyra could see Tamsyn gesticulating with her hands, and Felda shaking her head and scowling. What was going on?

She found out soon enough.

"Tradition holds that the Hand of Kali succeeds the Mahimata in the event of a sudden death," said Navroz. "While we wait for the formal ceremony, I see no reason to delay in informing you that the Mistress of Mental Arts has agreed to take over the Mahimata's duties."

Kyra gasped. This could not be happening. Tamsyn the new Mahimata of Kali? What was *wrong* with the elders? How could they be so blind? The Hand of Kali was the only Markswoman who was even remotely capable of killing Shirin Mam.

Tamsyn went to stand near Shirin Mam, gazing at everyone in turn, as if she was carrying on a special conversation with each. *You fraud,* thought Kyra, her anger growing until she felt she would burst. *Your grief is all pretense. Why can no one else see through you?*

Tamsyn pinned her with a piercing stare, and Kyra lowered her eyes and emptied her mind. Tamsyn gestured to Baliya, the Markswoman standing nearest the gong. Baliya bowed and struck the raised central boss of the gong with the mallet. The clear tones echoed through the cavern. It was time for the song of farewell.

Tamsyn began to chant, her voice high and clear:

"Even the katari will wear out one day,
what is this skin that I leave behind.
Even the sun will dim one day,
what is the fading of this one life.
Even the Ones will leave one day,
the sky empty like my eyes.

Time will eat all
Only Time will remain
And Kali formless in the dark
Will return to the night from which She came."

Kyra observed the faces around her, the women she had grown up with, the elders with their depthless eyes and composed faces, the novices quite still, not daring to move, though their eyelashes fluttered as they glanced at each other. And all the others, young and old, her companions during sunlit hours of working in the orchards, rubbing down the horses, meditating on the hilltops. They were all she knew, and yet how well did she truly know them? Would they accept Tamsyn's leadership simply out of fear? She searched the faces—Ria Farad, Tonar Kalam, Ninsing Kishtol, Sandi Meersil, Noor Sialbi, and all the others—but she found no answer.

No one noticed Kyra staring. They were transfixed by Tamsyn's melodious voice and the words they had known by heart for most of their lives. Tamsyn continued to chant and the other elders joined in one by one:

"O Divine Mother
Demon Destroyer
Mistress of three worlds
Enchantress of Shiva
Giver of life, Bringer of death
Most noble assassin
Bless your daughters
In whom you dwell."

The chanting died away and the cavern fell silent once more. Heartsick, Kyra stole a last look at the tiny woman lying on the platform. She looked peaceful. And old. Shirin Mam had never looked old, not while she was alive.

Why did you die? Kyra wanted to shout. *Why did you leave me?*

"Stay well, Shirin Mam," she whispered. "The blessings of Kali go with you."

She backed away from the cavern, eyes lowered so that no one would see the glimmer of tears in them.

The novices were sobbing. Nineth still wept, red-eyed and blotchy. Mumuksu laid a comforting hand on her shoulder.

Kyra escaped into the cool night air, still fighting her tears. She should go back inside. Her absence would be marked and remembered. Navroz would be anointing Shirin Mam with sacred oil to prepare her for meeting Agni, the Fire God. It was he who claimed the flesh of all Markswomen when they died, destroying the earthly doors that bound them to life.

But the caves of Kali were no longer the safe home Kyra had known for fourteen years, and she was loath to go back in. Shirin Mam was dead and Tamsyn was the new Mahimata. Either the elders *wanted* Tamsyn to lead the Order and were utterly oblivious to her true nature, or they were in her power somehow and did not dare to oppose her. Kyra didn't know which was worse.

She leaned against the gnarled trunk of the mulberry tree and looked up at the branches framing the dark sky. The wind whispered through the leaves, as if telling secrets.

If only she was more adept in the Mental Arts. Or as skilled in combat as Chintil Maya. If only she had some talent—any talent—that could help her now. She couldn't even enter *Anantkal* unaided, and now that Shirin Mam was dead, perhaps she never would again.

Or could she?

Kyra glanced around to make sure she was alone. She drew in a deep breath, focusing on the present moment. The sounds of the night—the soft breeze, the chittering of insects, the distant hoot of an owl—calmed her. She closed her eyes and folded her hands. There was no time for the complete ritual, the slowing down of the breath and the gradual strengthening of the meditative trance. But Shirin Mam used to say that need was the greatest motivator; when the time came, the lowliest novice could embrace the oneness of space-time and see where her true path lay.

Kyra let the wind blow her thoughts away. Her mind emptied as she sank into the first level of the trance. And in place of the grassy patch before the entrance to the caves of Kali, there was now a pool of water glittering under the light of a full moon, tall banks of reeds around it. The pendulous boughs of a stately old elm reached down to caress the water. The fragrance of damask roses filled the night air with sweet longing. The sights and scents of this place were familiar; Kyra knew she had been here—but when?

"For shame, little deer; have you no respect for the soul of our departed teacher? You have missed the lighting of incense and the last prayers."

Kyra jumped and broke out of her trance. The pool of water vanished. Tamsyn stood before her with folded arms, a frown on her oval face.

"You can never know the love and respect I had for Shirin Mam," said Kyra, biting the words off.

Tamsyn drew her lips in a thin line. "Oh, but I do know. I know it well. But you are a Markswoman now, not a foolish little novice. I told you my time would come, and it has come, a little sooner than everyone expected, that is all. I am going to make some changes around here; are you not looking forward to it? To going back to the Thar and fulfilling your vow?"

Not at this price.

"Poor Kyra," said Tamsyn. "It must be difficult to lose a mother for the second time in your life. I forgive you your weakness. Tomorrow I will not be so kind."

"Shirin Mam was kind to you, was she not?" said Kyra, guilt and rage driving away the last of her caution. "Did she regret it in the end?"

Tamsyn took one step forward and grabbed Kyra's hair, forcing her head back. "Be careful, little deer," she whispered, her voice laced with the Inner Speech. "Apologize, before I make you *regret* your rudeness."

Kyra's throat tightened with fear. She tried to stop the words, but they tumbled out anyway. "I'm sorry, Elder."

Tamsyn's teeth flashed. She let go Kyra's hair and Kyra stumbled back, her scalp stinging.

The gong boomed: once, twice, thrice.

"Time to build the pyre," said Tamsyn calmly, as if nothing had happened. "The burning of the old, the anointing of the new." She inhaled deeply. "I can smell it already."

She turned and left, her black robe swirling behind her. Kyra followed, her feet like lead. *Keep walking*, she told herself. *Do what you must.*

CHAPTER 10

THE BLADE OF
SHIRIN MAM

They worked by firelight, building the pyre on a metal grate that faced the wind. The sacred wood of the chenar tree mixed with the sweet wood of cinnamon; strong and bittersweet would be the burn.

Kyra bent low as she dragged another heavy stake of wood from the pile to the pyre. Her back throbbed and her eyes burned. Drag, heave, shove the stake into place. Do it again. And again. She welcomed the ache in her body, the rawness of her palms, the sweat trickling down her forehead. It helped keep her mind empty, helped deflect the probing tendrils of Tamsyn's gaze.

She looked up once and caught Elena's eye, and wished she hadn't. Elena's face was strange in the flickering firelight; they all were. A sense of unreality took hold of her. Who were these hollow-eyed women and what was she doing with them?

A touch of red lit the eastern sky. "Fifteen minutes," Navroz announced, her voice cutting through the clearing. "We must light the pyre at dawn to release Shirin Mam to the stars."

Kyra stopped in her tracks; she had been on her way to the store for more wood, but the stacks were four feet high now. Shirin Mam was tiny. She would not need so much wood to burn. Then again, a long and dignified ceremony was vital; the last rites were the last chance to say goodbye.

The Markswomen went back into the cavern, their footsteps slow and heavy. Kyra lingered behind until she was sure Nineth and Elena had gone in; she didn't want to talk to them yet.

When she went inside at last, the elders were standing next to the slab, speaking of Shirin Mam. The others clustered in a half-circle, their hands folded, their eyes lowered.

"Shirin and I were novices together," said Mumuksu, so soft that Kyra had to strain to hear her words. "We shared a cell and we shared every secret. I helped her reach the third level of the meditative trance, and she helped me learn how to fight. She was my dearest friend. The day she became the Mahimata and we swore our oaths to her, the gong sounded of itself, so loud that it drove us out of the cavern. That had never happened before, and it will never happen again." She stopped, and looked at Felda.

Felda cleared her throat. "What can I say? Words cannot describe how I feel," she said, her gruff voice uncharacteristically hesitant. "Shirin Mam is—was—the most accomplished leader our Order has seen in centuries. With everything else she did, she did not forget the importance of mathematics, and helped me acquire several tomes that were critical in the understanding of doors. She brought the light of knowledge and wisdom wherever she went. I will miss her, as I know you will too."

Felda stopped speaking, and everyone turned to Chintil.

But Chintil shook her head, unable to speak, and at last it was Tamsyn who spoke, her voice like honey. "I have Shirin Mam to thank for everything that I am today," she said. "I was just a poor orphan begging on the streets of Tashkent when she took me into her protection. She was on a mission, but she made time to test me, and decided I was worth bringing back to the caves of Kali. If I am alive today, it is because of her."

And yet, thought Kyra, *this is how you chose to repay her*. She had to use every ounce of self-control not to scream at the devious woman standing there with big, sad eyes, as if she was going to burst into tears at any moment.

"It is time," said Navroz. "We must now carry Shirin Mam to the pyre."

Felda, Mumuksu, and Chintil turned toward the slab. But before the elders could do more than lay their hands on the body, Tamsyn's voice rang out, sharp and clear: "Wait. I claim Shirin Mam's katari."

A collective gasp rose from the Markswomen. Some murmured to each other.

The fog of unreality surrounding Kyra lifted. It was like waking from a nightmare only to discover that the nightmare was real. She stared at Tamsyn, shocked. How dare she claim the ancient weapon that she knew should go into the fire with Shirin Mam? Not that kataris could be destroyed by fire, of course, but it was an essential last step in the relationship between a Markswoman and her blade. Just as *katari-mu-dai* was the moment of bonding, placing the katari in the pyre was the moment of release; it unraveled the bond and freed the soul. Afterward, the katari was placed with the ashes in an urn and taken to the funerary chamber, a vast cavern two levels below the main living area.

Kyra took an involuntary step toward the body, as if she could somehow stop Tamsyn. Suddenly, she remembered Shirin Mam's note. *When in doubt, ask my katari where to go.*

Tamsyn smiled, her dark eyes challenging them all. "Yes, the katari is usually consigned to the flames with a Markswoman's body and placed with the ashes in the sacred urn. But consider this. Unlike the rest of us, Shirin Mam inherited her katari from the previous Mahimata's grandaunt. Before that, we do not know what its history might be. It could be as old as the Order itself. It is a powerful weapon and it would be wrong to relinquish it, especially now that Shirin Mam is gone. We need all her guidance and strength."

Her words were so reasonable, her voice strong and sincere. Kyra could see the other Markswomen nodding, their faces clear of the frowns that had been there a minute earlier. Would no one see through Tamsyn and challenge her?

Navroz spoke, her voice dry and cool: "Shirin Mam's guidance and strength come to us from her teachings, not from her katari."

Tamsyn's eyes flickered. "Eldest, you speak well. I too have the teachings of Shirin Mam to thank for my own learning. Nevertheless, I claim the katari. As the soon-to-be-appointed Mahimata, I have the best interests of the Order at heart."

"Perhaps we should discuss this in closed council," said Navroz.

Tamsyn smiled. "There is no time. The fire and the closing of the doors wait for no one." She glided forward and reached down to pluck the katari from Shirin Mam's breast.

Kyra clenched her fists, wondering how to stop her. But before she could move, Tamsyn sprang back with a shriek of pain. She cradled her right hand in her left, her face a mask of rage. The katari had bitten her. Kyra could have sung for joy. But the reprieve did not last long. Tamsyn swung around and blasted the Markswomen with the Inner Speech:

"WHO LAID THE WORD OF POWER ON THE KATARI? WHO THWARTS ME IN THIS WICKED MANNER? CONFESS OR YOU SHALL PAY THE PRICE."

The command rolled into Kyra's head. She had an absurd desire to shout, *It wasn't me, Tamsyn.* The novices fell to their knees; Elena and Nineth clung to each other. Even the older Markswomen looked shaken. Anger did not seem to dull Tamsyn's skills, as Shirin Mam had warned, but to sharpen them.

Navroz answered, her voice as calm as ever, "It is no word of power and there is no call for you to resort to the Inner Speech, Tamsyn. A part of us dwells in our blades, as you are well aware. Perhaps the part of Shirin Mam that still remains in her katari wishes not to be touched."

"Is that so," said Tamsyn, her words falling like bits of ice on a cold winter night. "In that case Shirin Mam is not ready to meet the Fire God, for how can we carry her to the pyre without touching her? She must lie here until the katari yields itself to me."

"But Shirin Mam must meet Agni at dawn," said Chintil, alarmed. "Else the door to the stars remains forever closed to her."

"It is as you say," said Tamsyn, "but we must obey Shirin Mam's wishes. She does not wish to be disturbed."

Kyra blurted out, "That is not true."

"What?" Tamsyn snared Kyra with her gaze. "Who speaks so boldly among the elders? Is it the little deer?"

Kyra's throat was so dry she could barely continue. But there was no help for it. She couldn't let Tamsyn take Shirin Mam's blade, not when the Mahimata herself had told her that she would need it. She swallowed and continued, "It is not true that Shirin Mam does not wish to be touched. I will prove it to you. I will take her katari myself."

She walked up to the slab before she could lose her momentary courage, before Tamsyn could recover from her surprise, and before any of the elders could command her to stop. She reached over Shirin Mam, heart thudding. *Oh, Kali, help me now, or all is lost for your disciple.*

Then the katari was in her hands, so quick and smooth that it seemed to come there of its own accord. Kyra's palm tingled and confidence rushed through her blood. She held Shirin Mam's katari aloft so that everyone could see it, the beauty of the transparent blade that reflected the purity and power of Shirin Mam's soul.

She did not know how long she stood there gazing at the blade, surrounded by the awestruck silence of her companions. Perhaps she would not have seen Tamsyn gliding toward her if someone—Nineth, perhaps—had not coughed in warning.

Kyra swung around to face Tamsyn. The elder stopped a few feet away, her eyes slits of hatred, her lips curved in that smile that seemed to say, *How delicious, I will eat you now.*

But Kyra was not afraid of her, not while she held Shirin Mam's katari in her hands. And Tamsyn knew it.

"See, Elder?" said Kyra. "Shirin Mam *does* want to go into the fire. But she didn't want you to have two weapons. Two weapons would divide your power and put your soul in danger. Even in death, Shirin Mam teaches us something."

The four other elders murmured their approval.

"How right you are, little deer," said Tamsyn sweetly.

"Certainly, the wisdom of our respected teacher cannot be doubted. You have taught me a good lesson. Now put the katari back where it belongs and let us proceed immediately with the last rite."

Kyra hesitated, caught in the trap of her own cleverness. If she put the katari back, she would be plain Kyra again, with none of the protection and strength that Shirin Mam's weapon offered. In Shirin Mam's katari lay centuries of power—she had sensed it at once.

Perhaps Tamsyn had killed Shirin Mam not only to take her place, but also to take her katari. If Tamsyn could not obtain this ancient weapon herself, she would want it out of Kyra's reach. And once that happened, she would certainly punish Kyra for daring to challenge her—and Kyra stood no chance against the deadly Hand of Kali.

"Well, Kyra?" Tamsyn tapped her foot as if she wished to delay the last rite no longer. "What are you waiting for?"

For inspiration, thought Kyra. She gazed at the blade in her hand. "I think," she said slowly, hoping that it would not appear as if she was making things up on the spur of the moment, "Shirin Mam must want me to be the guardian of her katari. Why else would she let me pick it up?" Her voice grew stronger. "Perhaps the katari is intended for someone who is not yet known to us? Yes, that must be it. The katari comes to me from Shirin Mam to protect as the inheritance of someone who is yet to be revealed."

"Kyra," said Navroz, her voice sharp. "Enough. Please return the katari so we can proceed."

Felda, Chintil, and Mumuksu were staring at Kyra, their faces taut with worry.

Tamsyn was clapping her hands, laughing. It was not a pleasant sound. "That is a good story, little deer. Except that it is quite untrue. If Shirin Mam wanted to pass on her katari to someone else, she would have told us years ago." A note of command entered her voice. "Put the katari back, Kyra. It is I, the new Mahimata, who tells you this."

Kyra bowed. "I am sorry, Elder, but the old Mahimata tells me something else. It would be disastrous for the Order to ignore the voice that comes from her katari. In fact, the katari tells me that I must leave at once to search for its true successor."

Tamsyn tried to stop her, as Kyra had known she would, summoning all her mental forces against her. Without the protection of Shirin Mam's katari, Kyra would have crumpled senseless to the floor. But the katari acted like a shield, bathing her in its silver light, and Tamsyn could not come near her, mentally or physically. The other Markswomen stood back as Kyra strode from the cavern. She could sense the elation of some of her companions, the dismay of the others. Most of all, she could sense Tamsyn's fury. It was a monster, straining against the fraying leash of the rules of the Order, hungry for revenge. What would it feed on in her absence?

CHAPTER 11

A NEW ASSIGNMENT

In the middle of the Khur camp was an open, circular space surrounded by tents, and it was here that Ishtul, the blade-master of Khur, liked to hold his class. The sand was hard-packed by decades of use, and ideal for fighting.

It was midmorning and the sun beat down on the heads of the Marksmen who clustered around the elder, awaiting instructions. Rustan stood to one side, barefooted and loose-robed, as they all were for the combat class. In the last year, Ishtul had begun to treat him more as an assistant than as a pupil, and usually Rustan loved this class more than any other.

But not today. Maybe not ever again. His katari was tainted, and so was he.

"Pair up for katari duel," barked Ishtul. "Shurik, you will duel Rustan. Try to stay upright for more than a minute."

Inwardly, Rustan groaned. Shurik was his closest friend in the Order, despite the three-year age gap. He had shared a tent with Shurik when the boy first arrived in the Order, and mentored him as a novice. Now, he was the person Rustan wanted to avoid the most. Shurik could sense, even if the other Marksmen couldn't, that something was wrong with Rustan.

Shurik sauntered over as the others fell into pairs and Ishtul circled them, shouting instructions and curses.

"Why the long face?" He grinned. "Afraid I'll finally beat you and take your place as Ishtul's favorite?"

Despite himself, Rustan laughed. The dour, hook-nosed blademaster of Khur never minced words about Shurik's abilities—or rather, his lack of them. "Jests will not win you a duel," he said.

Shurik flexed his muscles. "Worth trying. Anyway, I think you're slipping. Standing there so slack and glum, I could have stabbed you three times by now."

"Three times?" Rustan shook his head. Shurik was gifted in the Mental Arts—more so than perhaps anyone in the Order. But combat was not his strongest suit. Rustan withdrew his katari and held it in both hands, one on the grip and the other on the glowing blade. "Talk less and concentrate. If you can but touch me with your blade, I will concede."

Shurik did not have to be told twice. He gripped his katari in his right hand and lunged, aiming for a downward diagonal stab at Rustan's shoulder.

Rustan danced away and blocked Shurik's blade with his own, striking upward so that sparks flew from both kataris. The force of the clashing blades vibrated through his wrist and down his forearm. Shurik must have felt it too; his face spasmed with pain and he staggered back. Usually, Rustan would have waited for him to recover, but he wanted to end this particular bout. He dove forward and twisted Shurik's blade arm back until he had forced him to his knees.

"Yield," he said, holding Shurik down with his own right knee pressed into his back, and his blade on Shurik's neck.

"Never," gasped Shurik. "That was less than half a minute. Kill me now, before Ishtul does."

Sure enough, the elder stalked up to them, his face like thunder. "Abysmal," he growled. "Must I send you to train with the apprentices?"

Rustan released Shurik and stepped back. Shurik rose and hung his head, trying to look ashamed. But since it was something Ishtul threatened him with in every other class, Rustan knew it was all pretense on his friend's part.

"Perhaps, Elder, it is not a bad suggestion," said Rustan. "If Shurik were to actually *teach* the apprentices, he would learn more."

Don't don't don't . . . Shurik thought at him frantically. Rustan suppressed a grin.

"I will consider it," said Ishtul. "But I don't want the apprentices to suffer either. Rustan, I'm afraid you must miss the rest of this class. Astinsai wants to speak with you."

Again? Since the day she made him drink Rasaynam, Rustan had warred with two impulses: First, to burst into Astinsai's tent and demand another taste of it. And second, to steal away from Khur in the dead of night and never show his face again to the Order.

Both options were untenable. But so was Rustan's current situation. His face must have betrayed something of what he was feeling, for the elder frowned. "Remember who you are," he said softly. "And remember who she is."

Shurik raised his head and scrutinized Rustan, gauging his depths, seeing the darkness even the elder could not.

Rustan bowed and turned away from both of them, trying to control his emotions. What new horror did the katari mistress have in store for him? He walked toward her tent, filled with misgiving.

But, in the end, what she had to say was not horrific at all. It was simply incomprehensible. She had a new assignment for him, one that made no sense.

"You want me to do *what*?" he asked, when he was seated opposite her.

"I want you to watch the Akal-shin door from sunup to sundown every day," repeated Astinsai, with more patience than she normally displayed.

"Why in the sands would I do that?" said Rustan. "No one has come through that door in centuries. What am I supposed to do there?" The Akal-shin door was only a mile away, embedded in the base of a massive cliff, but the codes were long since lost.

"Watch and wait," said Astinsai, clarifying nothing. She added, with a return to her usual asperity, "Or is that too difficult a task for you, Marksman?"

Not difficult. Futile. But Rustan held his tongue. At least it was something to do, even if it felt more like a penance than an actual task. And it would keep him away from Shurik's inquisitive eyes.

CHAPTER 12

AGAINST THE DARKNESS

The sky had lightened to lavender by the time Kyra cantered out of the horse enclosure on Akhtar, Shirin Mam's bay stallion. Rinna whinnied in indignation at being left behind by her mistress, but Akhtar was the fastest horse in the stable, and Kyra needed to move quickly. Besides, he had belonged to Shirin Mam. It seemed right to choose him.

She cast a last look back at the caves of Kali, and urged Akhtar to a gallop across the twilit valley. Her heart felt as though it was tearing in two. She was leaving the only home she had known for the last fourteen years. She was leaving her friends. But it was too late for regrets.

Poor Nineth. How would she fare with the poisonous Tamsyn as the new head of the Order? *Take me with you*, she had thought to Kyra as she left the cavern. And gentle Elena, who tried and failed to hide her shock and betrayal at Kyra's abrupt departure—how would she cope?

At least they had each other. And Kyra hadn't planned on

running away. That was just the way it happened. Once she picked up Shirin Mam's katari, she didn't have much choice.

Again and again the scene played out. Throwing aside the curtain to the Mahimata's cell. The sight of the body, lying twisted on the floor. The blood and the stench of death. The vultures circling overhead.

Vultures? No, her memories were playing tricks on her. Kyra wrenched her mind away and focused on the task at hand. *Do what you have to do. Grieve later.*

She didn't know where to go, except away from the caves. Something impelled her to ride toward Yashmin-Gah, the sacred grove in the hills of Gonur where Shirin Mam had led a meditation one full-moon night a few years ago. Was this the right way? Was the Mahimata's spirit guiding her?

Kyra slowed Akhtar to a walk, closed her eyes, and relaxed into a meditative trance. At once she sensed the powerful presence of the alien blade, pulsating against her skin. Her own blade seemed subdued in comparison—not any less than what it had been, but overshadowed by a more ancient weapon.

She fought against her instinct to repel Shirin Mam's katari; instead, she opened herself up to it. She sought again the vision of the pool of water, and asked for the knowledge that lay outside her reach: Where was this place? What should she do there?

The answers danced in her mind like bits of flame. Hidden in Yashmin-Gah was a disused Hub, a surefire escape from Tamsyn. If Kyra could pass through a Transport Hub, the elder would no longer be able to sense her whereabouts.

Shirin Mam's blade was full of secrets. Perhaps she had suspected Tamsyn's treachery and wanted to make sure Kyra could flee the Order with the Mahimata's ancient weapon. In that case, might not the blade be able to tell Kyra how its owner had died? Or what Kyra was supposed to do after putting as much distance as she could between herself and the Hand of Kali?

Emptying her mind, Kyra sank into the trance once more. But this time she was disappointed, for she got no further answers.

Kyra put the blade out of her thoughts and concentrated on her destination. Yashmin-Gah *was* the right way to go. She remembered walking through the ancient trees of the sacred grove after Shirin Mam's meditation exercises, and almost stumbling into a little pool of water. The smell of roses and the sighing of rushes in the wind swept over her. Her heart quickened as she thought of the door, hidden where no one could see it. Shirin Mam had left this knowledge in her blade for Kyra to find.

At last, Kyra understood why the Mahimata had given her that "special assignment" with the codes that could unlock any door in any Hub. Her teacher had been prepared for the betrayal. Why, then, had she done nothing to stop Tamsyn? It was a painful riddle; one day, she would have the truth of it.

The sun slipped into the sky; she didn't have much time. The last rite would be complete when the first rays of the sun touched Shirin Mam, no matter how long the body took to burn. Tamsyn would waste no time in coming after her.

A wyr-wolf howled, long and low-pitched. Another joined in, and another. Kyra risked a quick glance back across the valley. Were those wolf shapes in the distance?

Wolves often hunted at dawn. If she was being followed

by a pack, Kyra would stand no chance. Akhtar was swift and strong, a true descendant of the golden stallion Shamsher himself, but this pace would soon exhaust him. The wolves would bring him down with ease. How many of them would she be able to kill with her katari? Two, maybe three. But the fourth would get her, and crush her neck between its massive jaws.

Another howl, louder than before. Answering howls to its left and right. They were closing in. Kyra fought down a wave of nausea. Had she escaped Tamsyn only to be devoured by wyr-wolves? She urged Akhtar on, but the horse needed no urging from her. He galloped as hard as he could, trembling with exertion and snorting in fear.

As abruptly as they'd sounded, the howls stopped. For several long minutes, there was silence. When the howls started again, they were much farther behind, to the southwest.

Kyra let out a long, deep breath. What had driven them off? The presence of the kataris? Perhaps they had sensed weaker prey elsewhere. Whatever the reason, she offered up a fervent prayer of thanks to the Goddess Kali.

"It's all right, Akhtar, you can take it easy now," she said, stroking the horse's neck. "We'll soon be there."

But Akhtar did not slow down, and Kyra sensed his terror sharpen. *Oh no.* They were still being followed. Kyra almost fell from her saddle when she saw huge shapes unfold from the darkness behind the stunted trees on her left and right. Two blurry shapes with long snouts and powerful haunches, loping to keep pace with her.

Horror turned Kyra's veins ice-cold. The wyr-wolves were here, right beside her.

The hills of Gonur loomed ahead, the uneven ridges like broken teeth against the blue sky. *So close, and yet so far.*

With all her strength, Kyra pushed aside her fear. She had two kataris. By the Goddess, she would go down fighting. She would not let these dogs smell her fear.

When they were almost at the feet of Gonur, Kyra commanded Akhtar to stop, pulling one rein to turn him around and face the beasts. Akhtar stamped and trembled, but he obeyed her. She withdrew both blades, heart hammering inside her chest.

The two wyr-wolves were huge, half the size of Akhtar himself. One had a thick gray mane and a white streak on its ridged forehead. The other was pure black, except for its yellow eyes.

The beasts stopped some distance away from her. The smaller one made a whuffing sound. The larger one yawned, displaying a cageful of deadly fangs. The kataris almost slipped from her sweaty palms at the sight.

And then, as if at some unspoken signal, the two wyr-wolves turned and trotted away. Kyra watched them go, her mouth dry. Before long, they had vanished beyond the undulating landscape.

She couldn't understand it. Maybe they had decided that just two of them would not be a match against an armed Markswoman? Perhaps they had gone to fetch the rest of the pack.

But they hadn't appeared that interested in her—more as if they simply wanted to see her, and be seen by her.

There was no time to puzzle it out, for every minute that passed brought Tamsyn closer to her heels. Kyra turned Akhtar around to try to find a way up to Yashmin-Gah.

It wasn't long before she spied the rock-strewn path to the forest in the upper reaches of the hills. They climbed, Akhtar picking his way among the rocks, Kyra scanning the horizon. No sign of pursuit yet. No sign of the wyr-wolves either, and it was getting to be daylight. Good; Akhtar should be safe then, if she sent him back to the caves.

They entered the old spruce forest, dense with undergrowth and sweet with the scent of rhododendron. Kyra dismounted and patted the stallion's head. "Go home, Akhtar. Nineth will take care of you." The horse whinnied and nipped her shoulder.

"Go back, Akhtar." Kyra put as much command as she could muster into her voice.

Akhtar snorted and trotted away, down the path they had come. Kyra felt bereft. The last link to the Order, and she was sending him away.

Now was not the time for sentimentality. Anyone seeing Akhtar returning riderless might assume she was dead or injured. It could throw Tamsyn off her trail, at least for a little while.

She went deeper into the forest. It was cool and dark. Birds chittered at her and she saw a monkkat, its whiskered black face splitting in a snarl before it leaped away. She moved through the undergrowth, pushing aside branches and vines from her face, letting instinct guide her.

She came upon it suddenly, as she had all those years ago, a little pool of water surrounded by rushes, the boughs of an old elm touching its surface. The water was dark and still, like an unseeing eye.

She parted the rushes and stood by the edge of the pool, scrutinizing the area. The door was close now, hidden somewhere a few feet from her. Her skin prickled with the certainty of it. She walked around the pool, summoning the vision that had brought her there.

The third time she circled the pool, she caught a glimpse

of the door from the corner of her eye. It was beside the elm, beneath a mound of earth covered by a prickly bush. She stooped in front of the mound and pushed aside the spiky green plant, ignoring the scratches to her hands and arms. She scrabbled away at the earth with her fingers, feeling the hardness beneath her palms. And there it was—no more than two feet high—a dark rectangle embedded in the ground, unused for decades, perhaps centuries.

Kyra carefully held her katari to the slot on the diminutive door. As with every other Hub, the slot glowed blue and the door swung open, as she had hoped it would, revealing a low, dark tunnel inside. She smiled. Easy, it had been easy. With a sigh of relief, she bent her head and squeezed in, crawling into the tunnel.

Behind her the little door swung shut, engulfing her in darkness.

Kyra stopped smiling and her sense of triumph vanished, replaced by dread.

It wasn't merely the darkness. It was the dreams, except that the dreams were real now; she was in them and there was no escape. The door had closed behind her and she was five years old, weeping because she was trapped and they were all dead. No, she was dead and they were trapped and what difference did it make whose face she saw; the door would be how everything ended.

Stop it. Stop it now. You're okay. This is an old Hub no one's used in a while, that's all.

Kyra counted her breaths, trying to slow them down.

She went farther in. The tunnel became larger and she was able to stand up in the corridor without hunching. The glowing blue slots of Transport doors stretched away into the darkness. All was as it should be, so why was she having trouble breathing? Why was her heart thudding away fit to burst her rib cage?

She placed her katari on her palm and spoke a word of power to summon light—a simple word, and the only one that apprentices were taught. *"Rishari,"* she whispered, and the katari glowed, a beacon in the dark.

Still her dread did not go away. She had dreamed of this many times. A foretelling? No, it could not be. She couldn't possibly be meant to die, not yet.

She took a step toward the first door and placed her palm upon it. Perhaps she would be able to sense what lay beyond.

The world *twisted*. Kyra blinked, blinded by the bright light of a midday sun.

The Transport corridor had disappeared. She stood at the edge of a narrow, crowded street. It was cold; people wore thick furs and woolens, and the sloping roofs dripped icicles. Tiny shops jostled for space with inns, shrines, and food counters. Open vats of soup steamed next to loaves of freshly baked bread. Men carrying palanquins shouted at passersby to make way for them. At one end of the street, an arched blue and white stone gateway glinted in the sunlight. The air was thick with smells: smoke, spices, open drains.

"Please can you help me?"

Kyra jerked around, almost falling over her robe. So intent had she been on the street before her that she had not noticed the child, a small figure huddled to her left, dressed in an oversized patchy gray coat that blended with the gray stone of the walls behind him.

"What—who are you?" she stammered.

The boy sidled up to her. His dark, intense eyes held her

gaze. "I am Arvil. Do you have any food? We haven't eaten in three days."

"Three days!" Kyra was horrified. Now that he was standing next to her, she noticed how thin and hollow-cheeked he was. "Don't you have parents?"

"No," said the boy, keeping his eyes fixed on hers.

He was an orphan, just like her. Kyra wished she could do something for him. But how? "I—I don't belong here," she said. "I don't have any food. Perhaps those shopkeepers over there . . . ?" The words trailed away. The boy's face filled with disappointment and she grew hot with shame.

"Arvil, what are you doing? Come here."

A thin, sharp-faced little girl stood in an alley glowering at them, arms akimbo and feet planted apart, as if ready for a fight. She was dressed like the boy, in a long woolen coat with folded sleeves and pinned-up hem.

The boy trotted over to the girl. She cuffed him on the ears. "How many times have I told you not to talk to anyone? I'll find us some food. Don't I always find us food?"

The pair walked away. Kyra started to go after them, but . . .

The world spun. The sun blinked out. She was once more in the dark corridor, leaning against the first door. Her forehead was beaded with sweat and she was trembling. What had happened? Had she actually used that door, or had she imagined it? That look of crushed disappointment on the little boy's face—she wouldn't forget it, as long as she lived. Impulsively, she inserted the tip of her katari into the glowing slot on the door. She had to get back to those children; they needed her help.

She waited for the door to open, for the world to shift, but nothing happened.

She ground her teeth in frustration and tried again.

The world remained unchanged.

Defeated, Kyra slumped against the door. Why would it not open for her katari?

And still this fear, as if something in the corridor watched and waited for her to lower her guard. She straightened, but of course there was nothing to see. She steeled herself and walked to the second door. She hesitated only a moment before placing her palm upon it.

The world *twisted*.

Shirin Mam sat on a rug in what looked like her cell, reading a book. She glanced up and an expression of annoyance flashed across her face.

"Wasting time as always, child. Go now. This door is not the right one."

"But—but you're dead," Kyra whispered, her breath catching at the sight of her beloved teacher, seemingly alive and well.

Shirin Mam threw her an exasperated look and waved her hand in dismissal.

"No!" Kyra shouted, but the world spun again.

She leaned against the smooth hardness of the second door, sobbing.

"Shirin Mam!" she cried. "Please don't go." She picked up her katari from where it had fallen on the floor, and with a shaking hand inserted it into the slot.

But once again, nothing happened. Kyra could not move. She clung to the door, her cheek against its cool metal surface, hoping that it might transport her back to her teacher.

At last Shirin Mam's words echoed through her mind: *Wasting time as always.*

She wiped her eyes with a sleeve. She should check the other doors. But it was hard to let go of this one. It had shown her what she wanted most. With an effort, she pushed herself away and stumbled to the third door. She paused, for here she sensed the vast sweep of nothingness beyond. What was behind this one? She reached a hand out to it, and hesitated.

It was not the fear that stopped her. Fear had been her constant companion since she'd crawled into the Transport corridor. It was the growing conviction that out of all the doors in the Hub, *this* was the devastating one.

Kyra wavered. Time to choose. She could step away from this door and move on to the next one.

But in truth, she didn't have a choice, only the illusion of one. She couldn't walk away from this.

Taking a deep breath, she laid a palm upon the door and the world *ended.*

There was nothing. No light, no sound, no sensation. Kyra—an idea of Kyra—floated, a disembodied spirit in the manifold of space-time.

There was no fear, no pain, and no fatigue. There were no emotions at all, for emotions require a physical body and Kyra had left her body behind—wherever *behind* was. Was this what it felt like to die?

Time had no meaning in the vast emptiness of deep space. The dust mote that was Kyra floated, peaceful in the void.

But wait, what was that distant banging sound? Whose inhuman cries were those? Kyra hung for a moment between the two realities of being and not-being.

The world came rushing back in a nauseous flood of sensation—pain, terror, the taste of blood in her mouth. She was back in the corridor. Her fingertips were raw; she must have been scrabbling at the door. Her katari had fallen to the floor, and this time its light had gone out.

Kyra hugged her knees and closed her eyes against the darkness. This was the door that had haunted her sleep since childhood. This was where she would one day go to die.

After a while—it could have been hours or minutes—she uncurled herself and reached for her blade. For it wasn't over, was it? There was still something that needed to be done: a door to be chosen, a way to be found. It wasn't the time for *this* door yet. She dragged herself up. What would the next one do to her?

But the fourth door was only a door. When Kyra laid her palm upon it, nothing happened. She could not sense what lay beyond. Trembling, she inserted the tip of her blade into the slot. A screen slid out, numbers glowing. She swallowed, and tried to respool her thoughts. This was the fourth door in the Hub, so she should use the fourth palindromic prime from the pyramid she had drawn on Shirin Mam's parchment: 1713302033171. She tapped it in, wondering if it would work, almost hoping that it would not.

But it did work. The screen withdrew and the door swung open. As she walked into the chamber, lights came on. A voice like rustling silk whispered through the room:

"Code override. Code override."

She tried to back out, but the door had closed. The chamber began to spin.

From somewhere, there came a faint metallic laugh.

CHAPTER 13

THE MARK OF KALI

Dawnlight transformed the Empty Place; the sands rippled red and gold, as if they were alive. Even the drab tents of Khur were regal in that transitory light, as if kings or queens might live there.

Rustan inhaled deeply, trying not to shiver as he practiced breath control outside his tent. The temperature would not go up to zero until the sun rose. Most of the Marksmen were still asleep, wrapped in their felt rugs. But he had an assignment that week, set by Astinsai herself. Or perhaps it was a punishment. It was hard to know, with Astinsai, what she truly intended.

Shurik, unfortunately, had also woken up. The youth was lying inside Rustan's tent, his tousle-headed face poking out. "What happened in Tezbasti?" he asked, his voice heavy with sleep. "Did you have trouble with the mark?"

Rustan breathed in and out, ignoring his friend.

"Come on, you can tell me," he wheedled. "You've been back for over two weeks now and you still haven't talked. You've become more closemouthed than a Peral River oyster."

Rustan gritted his teeth. "You talk enough for the two of us, so I guess it evens out. There was no trouble in Tezbasti, okay?"

It was the first time he'd ever lied to Shurik, but he couldn't bring himself to tell his friend what had really happened. He could picture it all too well. *I killed an innocent man*, he would say, and Shurik's face would collapse in shock and pity. Then the questions would start: *How could the Maji-khan not know? Why did your blade not tell you something was amiss? What will you do now?* Questions that tormented Rustan in every waking hour; questions to which he had no answers.

He caught Shurik's skeptical expression and added, "If you don't believe me, ask Barkav," knowing full well that the Maji-khan would reveal nothing of what had transpired.

"And have my head bitten off?" said Shurik with a shudder. "No thanks. But if there was no trouble, why did Barkav send Ghasil to talk with the Kushan clan elders?"

Rustan got to his feet, trying to control his irritation. What had happened in Tezbasti wasn't Shurik's fault, but why couldn't he leave it alone? His friend was too curious for his own good.

Shurik blinked, then scrambled out of the tent and stood beside him. He put his hand on Rustan's shoulder. "You're thinking of going away, aren't you?"

As always, Shurik's perceptiveness surprised Rustan. It shouldn't anymore. He'd have to be careful what he said and thought in front of his friend, or Shurik would make his own deductions about the events in Tezbasti. "Honing your talent in the Mental Arts, are you?" he said lightly. "Ghasil must be happy."

Shurik snorted. "The day that Ghasil is happy with me is the day this desert turns into a wetland." He paused and added,

"The Master of Mental Arts returned from Tezbasti last night. I suppose you know that?"

"I know." Rustan walked away. "Time for me to go." *Time to end this conversation.*

Shurik followed him. "Breakfast?" he said. "Or am I getting your share of Luthan's poisonous mash this morning?"

Rustan forced a laugh. "Better you than me," he said. "And I have to be at the Akal-shin door by sunup, or the Old One won't let me hear the end of it."

"Why did she give you such a useless task? Is it a penance?" Shurik yawned.

"I don't know," said Rustan. "Perhaps, if she confides in you, you will enlighten me?"

"Haha, very funny," said Shurik. "Honestly, can we trade places? I'd like a day off from Ishtul."

"And I'd like a day off from you," said Rustan. He veiled the lower part of his face, and before Shurik could ask him any more questions, he strode away.

Shurik called out, his voice fading into the cold, gritty wind, "You won't escape that easily."

The novices were already up, all seven of them hard at work. One of them waved to Rustan as he passed by the camel enclosure. Rustan waved back, envious. What he wouldn't give to be a novice again. To fill the water troughs for the camels, tend the grove that would bear fruit in spring, plant the windbreaks around the camp. What he wouldn't give to have *not killed*. Odd, how he had longed for exactly the opposite as a novice.

The sun rose over the dunes, a great orange orb that promised warmth later in the day. Rustan neared Akal-shin, the long, steep ridge of red rock that had once sheltered the

Marksmen from a terrible sandstorm. His fifth day guarding this place and still he could not get used to it, from the lonely grandeur of the jagged peaks to the absurdity of the narrow door at its base. What purpose had it served before the Great War? He could not imagine who would have wanted to dwell in this barren waste of shifting sands and freezing nights.

He took a long swallow from his waterskin and settled down to his usual station beneath the shade of a rocky overhang opposite the door. *Watch and wait*, Astinsai had said, nothing more. Well, it suited him fine. At least here he was spared his fellow Marksmen's questions and puzzled looks. Maybe that was why she had sent him here—a kind of enforced isolation that would bring some self-knowledge, some way for him to heal.

Rustan's head ached. He leaned his head against the cool rock and closed his eyes. In his mind, he saw once again the face of his mark, tears running down his cheeks. He heard once again the man's pleas for a retrial, his protests of innocence.

He pressed his katari to his forehead and groaned. Shurik was right; he wanted to leave Khur, at least for a while. Would Barkav agree to it?

Movement caught his eye and he scrambled up in time to see the Akal-shin door swing open. A girl staggered out, her dusky face half-hidden by the wild disarray of her dark hair. In her right hand, she clutched a silvery green kalishium blade. Rustan sprang forward, heart pumping adrenaline, his own katari flashing blue fire. As the door swung closed, he caught a glimpse of a corridor curving ghostlike into the darkness.

The surprise visitor knelt on the hard ground and sobbed, her shoulders shaking.

The girl—the *Markswoman*, Rustan corrected himself—

smelled of terror. She had not noticed him yet. Rustan found his voice. "Who are you?" he demanded.

The reaction was remarkable. She stopped sobbing and leaped up with a snarl, all trace of helplessness gone. Before Rustan had time to blink, she had pinned him to the rock wall, her blade at his throat, his knife hand paralyzed by an advanced zenshao-lock behind his back. His katari clattered to the ground, and he felt a sharp pang of separation.

The Markswoman spoke, her voice ragged. "When is this?"

When. Not where. Was she mad? At least she hadn't tried to actually stab him. Yet.

"You could have asked nicely," said Rustan. He brought up his left arm fast, knocking away her weapon and gripping her wrist, twisting back the elbow. It must have hurt but she did not utter a sound, and she did not lose the zenshao grip on his other arm. At least, not until he flipped his wrist and she tumbled to the ground.

Rustan bent to retrieve his katari, but quick as a snake she lashed out with her right leg. The kick would have broken his neck if he hadn't ducked in time. He grabbed her leg, hooking and twisting it until she was on her stomach, face on the ground. With his other hand, he reached for his katari and pressed it against her neck.

"Why don't we start at the beginning?" said Rustan, breathing hard. "Who are you? No, don't move. My blade sits right above your throat."

"My name is Kyra." The Markswoman's voice was muffled. "Let me up."

"Your clan and Order, and the reason for your presence here." Rustan pressed the hilt of his blade a little harder against her neck.

"Let me go! Is this how you treat visitors?"

Rustan snorted. "Visitors don't attack their hosts."

There was a pause. She spoke as if the words were being dragged out from her. "I . . . I'm sorry. I was surprised."

Rustan bent over her, considering. "Fine. But you will not touch your weapon without my permission." He released her and stood, backing away.

The Markswoman sat up, massaging her leg. Her face was expressionless but her dark eyes blazed with fury. He offered her his hand but she ignored it, rising to her feet with dignity, for all her dirty robes and smudged cheeks. She looked young, and she came barely to his shoulder, but she had a fighter's stance and a determined chin.

She pushed the hair out of her face, revealing a diamond-shaped scar on her forehead. *The mark of Kali.* Rustan felt the winds of fate blow around him, and he understood why Astinsai had chosen him to watch the Akal-shin door.

He tapped the rock wall with the hilt of his blade. "Your clan and Order, and the reason for your presence here," he repeated.

"I am Kyra," said the Markswoman, "of the clan of Veer, may its name endure, and the Order of Kali, the Goddess be praised. As to why I am here, I don't know, save that this was the only door that behaved like a door. It seemed like the right thing to do."

She wasn't making any sense. Rustan could see that she was itching to pick up her katari. He hesitated, but it was unlikely she was going to attack him again. "Go ahead, take it," he said at last.

The Markswoman snatched her katari and sheathed it, her

relief palpable. Her gaze went to the jagged peaks of Akal-shin. "What is this place?" she asked. "When is this?"

There was that *when* again. "This is the third day of the dark half of the seventh lunar month in the year 853 of the Kanun, and you are in the Empty Place," said Rustan.

Her eyes widened. "Two months," she muttered to herself. "I lost two months."

Rustan glanced at the door. "What do you mean, you lost two months?"

Her face took on a haunted look. "It was the fifth lunar month when I left the Ferghana Valley. And yet, I wasn't in the Hub for more than an hour."

What? How was it possible to lose time in a Hub? Rustan had never heard of such a thing happening before. Doors were meant to be shortcuts through space. He suppressed his unease. "You had better come with me," he said. "Perhaps our Maji-khan and his council of elders will know what to do with you."

"All right," she said. "I'll come with you."

As they started to walk away from Akal-shin, she muttered, almost to herself, "I don't know if I can use this Hub again. And what is there for me to go back to but death by Tamsyn's blade?"

"Tamsyn?" said Rustan, curious. "The Hand of Kali? I don't know much about your Order, but surely you have no reason to fear one of your own elders? And surely Shirin Mam, your Mahimata, can protect you from anyone?"

Kyra laughed—a small, unhappy sound. "Are you so cut off from the rest of Asiana that you do not know? Shirin Mam is dead. I think Tamsyn had something to do with it. I have been entrusted with Shirin Mam's katari. While I have it, Tamsyn cannot touch me."

She withdrew a second katari from a back scabbard hidden behind her hair, and held it aloft.

The transparent blade caught the white light of the sun and broke it into a many-colored rainbow.

So beautiful, thought Rustan, and he closed his eyes. *Just like I remember it.*

CHAPTER 14

THE WINGED HORSE

The landscape was vast and empty; it hurt the eyes to look at it too long. Kyra observed her companion instead, a lean, brown young man with coal-black hair and slate-blue eyes. He was handsome, in a hard, serious sort of way, with features that looked as if they had been chiseled from granite. She tried asking him questions about the Order of Khur but he ignored her. Perhaps he was not supposed to give her any information. They walked in silence between the enormous dunes, their feet sinking into the sand.

She should not have attacked the Marksman without provocation, but his unlooked-for presence outside the door, after everything that had happened inside the Hub, had robbed her of the last vestige of self-control.

That he had defeated her was deeply irritating. Of course, she had not been at her best. She was mentally and physically drained after what she had been through. Not that this was any excuse. What would Chintil have said? *Don't get into a fight, but if you do, make sure that you win or you're no pupil of mine.* Inwardly, Kyra chastised herself for failing her teacher.

The camp of Khur was a cluster of tents on the lee side of a vast dune that curved to the north and east. Kyra felt a mixture of apprehension and excitement as they neared it. She knew little about Khur, apart from the fact that it was the only Order composed of men. Founded by Zibalik a mere four hundred years ago, it was also the youngest Order in Asiana. Not a single Markswoman in the Ferghana could claim to have visited it.

Kyra recalled the stories she had heard about the men of Khur, the depth of their bonds, their matchless fighting skills. Fewer men than women had the ability to bond with kalishium, but those men who *did* have the ability were rumored to be as powerful as a highly skilled Markswoman. *No wonder Tamsyn hates them.*

At the edge of the camp, a giant of a man with flowing gray hair and beard waited for them. He had such a commanding presence that Kyra guessed at once he must be the Maji-khan of Khur. Behind him stood seven grim-faced men clad in gray robes—the elders of Khur. They must have sensed the arrival of alien blades into the heart of their territory. To the Maji-khan's right was a tiny, bent old woman with wispy white hair.

The Marksman halted in front of the gathering and bowed. Kyra followed suit, heart skipping a beat. She had not expected such a formidable reception committee. Not that she had really expected anything after emerging from that door. The fact that she was alive and unhurt was miracle enough. That she had arrived in this time and place, and was now in the presence of the elders of Khur, was beyond belief. She felt awkward and tongue-tied, unprepared for what was surely a historic moment.

The Marksman said, "Father, I bring before you Kyra of the

Order of Kali and the clan of Veer. She came through the Akal-
shin door."

The elders of Khur stared at Kyra with varying degrees of
amazement and disapproval on their faces. Perhaps they were
irked that a stranger had used their door. Or maybe they disliked Markswomen on principle. She hoped the Marksman
would not tell them how she had attacked him.

But the young man had already retreated. Perhaps he would
give the elders a more detailed account later on.

"Welcome to Khur," said the Maji-khan. "I am Barkav, the
head of the Order. This is Astinsai, our seer and katari mistress."

A katari mistress? Kyra could scarcely believe her ears. Men
and women who could forge kataris from kalishium had become increasingly rare over the years. She had never met such
a one before, but they were said to have strange powers. She
swallowed nervously and bowed again. The old woman's eyes
stabbed her with a piercing gaze, and Kyra felt exposed, as if
the seer had seen through her to all the events that had led to
this present moment.

The Maji-khan continued, "These are the elders of the
Khur council: Ghasil, Saninda, Afraim, Ishtul, Falad, Samant,
and Talbish."

There was a pause while they inspected her. Seven elders,
like seven hawks. Kyra tried to keep her face neutral and relaxed under their scrutiny, but it was hard. At least they weren't
trying to delve into her thoughts. Hopefully, they followed the
same rules of Inner Speech that the Markswomen did.

The elder called Ishtul—a tall, thin man with a hook nose—
leaned forward. "It is the first time in over three hundred years
that the Akal-shin door has opened. What brings you here,
Markswoman?"

Kyra hesitated. How much should she tell them? How much would it be *safe* to tell them? "It's a long story, Elder," she said at last. "And I have not eaten for a while."

Ishtul scowled, but the Maji-khan looked at her thoughtfully and then beckoned to a youth hovering behind the group.

"Shurik will get you food and water, and show you to a tent where you can rest. While you are at Khur, you are our guest. Ask Shurik for anything you need. We can speak later tonight in the council tent."

With that the Maji-khan walked away, followed by the elders. Kyra was relieved she had been dismissed; she had gained a little time. The youth Barkav had assigned to be her guide trotted up to her. A stocky young man with a cheerful face and curly brown hair, he was grinning from ear to ear.

"I can't believe it," he said. "A real, live Markswoman. Here in Khur! You're going to give Ishtul and Ghasil nightmares."

"I'm not that scary," said Kyra. She looked down at her crumpled robe and ran a hand over it in a futile attempt to smooth out the creases. "At least, I won't be after I've had a wash and something to eat."

Shurik bowed with a flourish. "Happy to be of assistance. Let's go see what food there is. Luthan's cooking today, so don't get your hopes up."

He led her through the camp to a large rectangular tent made, Shurik said, from camel hair. "Cool in the daytime and warm at night," he explained.

As they approached the tent, fragrant smells of cooking wafted into the air. An elderly Marksman with crinkly eyes in a weather-beaten face sat at the entrance, stirring an enormous vat. She bowed in gratitude when he poured a generous portion in a large clay bowl for her. As they went inside the tent where she could sit down and eat, Shurik told her it was millet porridge with camel's milk.

Camel's milk? Kyra inspected the steaming bowl doubtfully. Well, whatever it was, she would have to eat it. She took a tentative spoonful, and another. Why, it wasn't bad at all. It was actually quite good. It tasted a bit like Tarshana's wheat porridge, except thicker and chewier. She ate ravenously after that, stopping only to ask for another bowl, much to Shurik's amusement.

When she had eaten her fill, he took her around the Khur camp. He began with the camel enclosure, a large roped-in area where around two dozen camels sat, chewing the cud and gazing at their visitors with supreme indifference. A couple of young boys were at work in the enclosure, filling the water trough and cutting squares of feed from compressed bales of grass.

Kyra wrinkled her nose as the pungent odor of the camels hit her. Shurik chuckled at her expression. "The smell of Khur," he said. "You'll soon get used to it. Hey, Jeev, Darius, come and greet our visitor."

The two boys scampered up to the fence and bowed low, their dark eyes alight with curiosity. Kyra bowed back, amused and a little uncomfortable. She was clearly a figure of interest here.

"Jeev and Darius are novices who have yet to earn their kataris," Shurik told her. "Barkav has great hopes of them. Personally, I think they are destined to be camel-boys forever."

By the tone of his voice and the grins on the boys' faces, Kyra realized this was an oft-repeated joke, and if she were not around, they would have made a suitable retort. As it was, the novices did not say anything, but stared at her until Shurik shooed them away.

Next, he took her beyond the camp to a grove of tall shrubs. The small patch of greenery looked absurd and out of place in the vast, yellow-brown landscape. "This is where we sometimes meditate," he said as they walked down a path between thick clusters of stunted trees and dense shrubs. "Or at least, the others meditate and I try my best not to fall asleep."

Kyra laughed. "But how does anything grow here?"

"Sheer willpower," said Shurik. "We do have a well, of course. Zibalik, the founder of Khur, would not have chosen this spot without knowing there was water underground. The dune gives some shelter against the wind, and we've planted windbreaks everywhere. Do you see those plants on the slopes of the dune?"

They had reached the edge of the grove. Kyra shaded her eyes and looked in the direction he was pointing, at the dune that towered over the camp of Khur. The slopes were crisscrossed with improbable rows of spiky plants and grasses.

"They may not be much to look at," said Shurik, "but they don't need irrigation, and they help stabilize the sand. That dune has not moved more than a few centimeters in the last several years. You can see a crust of soil has already formed on the dune's surface."

"Fascinating," said Kyra, and she meant it. This place was desolate, but it had a beauty all its own.

"Must be different from what you're used to," said Shurik, a wistful note in his voice.

"Very," said Kyra, and left it at that. She allowed him to show her the highlights of the rest of the camp, even though she was dying for a drink and a wash: the stone well, the Maji-khan's tent, and the open, circular space in the middle where Ishtul was leading a combat class.

Marksmen stopped fighting to stare at her, the younger ones gaping quite openly, the others more discreet in their curiosity, until a snapped command from Ishtul brought them back to attention.

Shurik sniggered and steered Kyra away from the class. "They can't help looking at you," he said in a loud whisper. "Sorry."

"I suppose it's because I came through the Akal-shin door? That elder said it hasn't been used in centuries," Kyra mused.

"Er, no," said Shurik, looking a little abashed. "It's because you're a girl. I mean, a Markswoman. Most of us haven't seen one before." He stopped walking to gaze at her himself, as if he wanted to memorize every detail of her appearance before she vanished as mysteriously as she had arrived.

But Kyra had had enough of being scrutinized. "I'd like to wash, please," she said firmly. "Is there a place I can change and rest?"

"Of course, of course, please follow me. We have a tent reserved for special guests." Shurik led her to a small tent that stood by itself, not far from the Maji-khan's tent. Kyra untied the flap and peered inside while he went off to fetch water for her from the well. The tent was quite cozy, with brown camel hair rugs patterned with colorful cotton threads covering most of the floor and walls. At the top was a smoke hole for the stove. She had to stoop to enter, and could barely stand upright inside, but it would do her just fine.

Shurik returned, bearing a pail of water and clean clothes: a thick brown robe, a hooded camel-wool cloak, and a pair of soft leather boots.

"Gifts from Khur," he said, beaming, and with that he left her alone.

It was a relief to wash away the grime and sand from her skin and put on clean, warm robes, even though they were far too large for her. She transferred the crumpled parchment with the secret codes into a pocket of her new robe, and belted the scabbard to her waist. When she was done, she lay down on the thick rug on the floor of her tent. Perhaps she could sleep for an hour or two before the council meeting. She needed her wits about her to deal with the elders of Khur.

But as soon as she closed her eyes, the vast emptiness of the third door in the hidden Hub came rushing back, threatening to swallow her. She jerked upright, fighting nausea and fear.

No. She would *not* think of that.

You simply postpone the inevitable.

Shirin Mam's voice, distant and amused.

Kyra groaned. Was it any easier thinking of what the second door had shown her? Or even the first? A little boy had asked for her help and she had refused. And what about that voice she had heard in the Transport Chamber, that high, crazy laugh?

Perhaps she had imagined it all and the dreams had finally driven her mad. There was always that possibility. But how had she lost *two months*? She could have sworn she hadn't been in the Hub more than an hour or so.

There was no point in trying to sleep. Kyra splashed her face with some of the cold water left in the pail, and settled back to practice the 108 moves Chintil had taught her to focus the mind and build internal strength, until it was time to meet the Khur council.

∞

The Khur council tent was rectangular, enclosing a long, low space that was warmed by the stove in the middle. The walls were covered with woven hangings that depicted lush flowers, grassy fields, and blue lakes. Kyra, sitting cross-legged on a thick rug near the entrance of the tent, guessed they were the handiwork of homesick young Marksmen who yearned for the milder climes of their birth. She had been startled by the steep drop in temperature after sundown and the sharpness of the wind outside. The walls of the tent thrummed, the wind sang its eerie song, and Kyra gathered her cloak more closely around herself. The elders talked on, heedless of the bitter night.

The cold can freeze the marrow in your bones, Shurik had told her when he came to fetch her for the meeting, and the wind can cut your throat. He had attached himself to her, would have even followed her into the council tent had the elder called Ghasil not grabbed his ear and told him to go round up the camels for the night.

The Maji-khan sat on a cushion in the middle of the tent—the senior-most position, as befit his status. He was speaking, but not everyone appeared to be listening to him. Rustan—this was the name of the Marksman who had bested her—sat outside the circle of seven elders around Barkav, staring into space. Astinsai, whom everyone referred to as the Old One, watched Kyra out of dark, glittering eyes.

"We all know that this is the first time in over three hundred years, perhaps more, that the Akal-shin door has opened," said Barkav. "But what—"

"Will it open again, do you think?" interrupted one of the elders, a bald, heavyset man.

"Not for us, Talbish," said Barkav. "I went to Akal-shin an hour ago. The door still does not respond to my blade. Perhaps it opens only from inside." He looked at Kyra. "Or perhaps it will open for you?"

Kyra shuddered at the thought of entering that Hub again. "I don't know, Maji-khan. Perhaps it will. But I lost time while traveling and I suspect the doors have shifted."

"How convenient," said Ishtul coldly.

Barkav frowned. "How so?"

Ishtul spread his bony hands. "Can you not see this for what it is? A trap. We are a month and a half from the annual clan meeting in Sikandra. Now here is this—this *girl*—sent to sow disharmony in our Order."

Kyra flushed, a flash of anger running through her. "I'm sorry, but you are mistaken. I certainly never planned on coming here."

Ishtul leaned toward her. "Then *why* are you here?" he demanded.

The question hung in the air, sticky and unanswerable. All eyes were on her. The Maji-khan motioned for her to speak.

Kyra took a deep breath. There was no point in lying to the elders of Khur, even if she wanted to. They would see through it at once. It was time to tell them what had happened. "You all know that I belong to the Order of Kali," she said. "What you may not know is that Shirin Mam, our Mahimata, died . . ."

There were gasps from those gathered around.

"Died?" echoed the Maji-khan, his composure slipping for the first time.

"Over eight weeks ago, if I have lost so much time between doors." She stopped, unable to go on, nausea rising again at the thought of losing time. Where had she been, all this while? And what had happened back home in her absence?

"This is bad news you bring, Markswoman," said Barkav gravely, glancing at Rustan.

"There is more," said Kyra. "Tamsyn, the Hand of Kali, has been declared the new head of our Order. And I suspect she had something to do with Shirin Mam's death."

The elders recoiled, shock and disbelief on their faces. Barkav's frown deepened.

"That is quite an accusation, young one. What makes you think so?" said Ishtul. "Do you have any proof?"

Kyra knew she couldn't repeat the things Tamsyn had said to her; the Marksmen would not understand the seriousness of them, because they did not know the Hand of Kali the way she did. Too, there was the matter of her own culpability. Why had she not gone to Shirin Mam and reported her conversation with Tamsyn?

"I have no proof," she said quietly, "but there is no one else in our Order who is as powerful—or as power-hungry—as Tamsyn. The other Markswomen are either in her thrall or too afraid to speak against her. But Shirin Mam's katari has chosen me as its temporary guardian. I listened to the voice of my teacher and it has brought me to you. I could not tell you why."

"You have run away," said Ishtul. There was a contemptuous note in his voice. "Do you expect to find a safe haven with us?"

"I expect nothing," said Kyra. "If it is the will of the council, I will leave Khur."

"Where will you go, if not through the door?" said another elder, a white-haired old man with ebony skin and a reed-thin frame. "You wouldn't last two nights in the desert. Of course, we could provide you with an escort to Kashgar or Yartan, and you could make your way from there."

"Saninda, the Akal-shin door has opened, and you would simply send away the one who has walked through it?" argued Barkav.

"What else are we to do?" demanded Ishtul. "She is a defector and if we give her refuge we are subject to retaliation by her Order. That is the law; has everyone forgotten it? I say return this renegade to her Order and let the new Mahimata deal with her."

"I am *not* a renegade." Kyra couldn't stop the anger spilling into her voice. "I am a Markswoman. My first duty is to my blade and my blade tells me that Tamsyn is not the true Mahimata of Kali."

The elders ignored her outburst. "I think it's a trap," said one of the younger ones seated near Barkav, twirling a bushy mustache. "Tamsyn is trying to set us up with this Kyra. She will use this as an excuse to make open war on us."

There was a murmur of worried assent from the elders.

"You are all fools." Astinsai finally spoke, and everyone went quiet. "It is obvious that the girl is telling the truth. Besides, consider who she is and what is owed to her."

Kyra frowned. What was *owed* to her? The Marksmen owed her nothing; they didn't even know her. What did the old woman mean?

Ishtul cleared his throat. "That's not the point. Even if she is telling the truth, it would be dangerous for us to harbor her."

"And it would be churlish to turn her away," said Barkav. "I think she should come with us to the annual clan meeting at Sikandra Fort. Envoys from all the Orders and clans will be there. She can explain herself to them."

"A woman?" said the mustache-twirler who had spoken before, amazement creeping into his voice. "You will take a *woman* to represent us at the annual clan meeting?"

"No, Ghasil, not to represent us," said Barkav. "Only to accompany us."

"Tamsyn will be there," Ishtul pointed out. "Don't you think our position will be a bit, shall we say, *difficult*?"

"Not at all," said Kyra, speaking without thinking. "That will be perfect. For I am going to challenge her to a katari duel. If all the clans are present, she will have no choice but to accept." Kyra was not certain at what point this had become her plan, but she knew in that moment it was the best path—the only path, if she wished to return to her Order.

"You? Katari duel with Tamsyn?" exclaimed Saninda. The elders regarded her with incredulous faces. "How long have you harbored a death wish, young one?"

Ishtul laughed, his thin shoulders shaking with mirth. "Tamsyn's blade is famed throughout Asiana. And you—are you not still an apprentice? Do you think she will let you die an easy death?"

Kyra spoke calmly, although her heart was racing. "I am a Markswoman. The manner of my death is written already, and so it does not concern me. If I defeat Tamsyn, the Order of Kali will be free forever from her power. If I die, as you think I will, it will be an honorable death. Either way, the Order of Khur will suffer no retribution."

Astinsai cackled. "Brave words, from one so young."

"Are you certain this is the correct choice to make?" said Barkav. "A month is little time to prepare yourself for a duel."

"I know," said Kyra. "But I think I must. There is no other way that I can see." *No other way for me to go back home.* The enormity of it began to sink into her and she strove to look composed, as if challenging the Hand of Kali to single combat was something she'd thought long and hard about.

"You could make a public apology," said Barkav. "As you point out, if you do it in front of the entire clan assembly, she will have no choice but to accept. At the very least, it will ensure your safety. After all, you have no evidence of wrong-doing. Perhaps you are mistaken about her."

"I am not mistaken, Maji-khan," said Kyra, putting as much conviction as she could muster into her voice. "Tamsyn had something to do with Shirin Mam's death, and I *will* challenge her to a duel. As long as she's the Mahimata of Kali, no one's safety is ensured."

Barkav stroked his beard. "So be it. Rustan will help you train for the duel. He's one of our best in combat."

Rustan started at the mention of his name. "What's that? What do you want me to do?"

"You will give her lessons," said Barkav. "Start tomorrow morning with the Shokuhara and Alemik schools of bare-handed defense, and work your way toward the thirty-six known styles of katari duel. After that, we shall see." He got to his feet, looming over the rest of them, signifying that the council meeting was at an end. The elders rose, talking in low voices among themselves as they filed out of the tent.

But Rustan continued to sit, his mouth twisted as if he had eaten a bitter lemon.

"You want *me* to teach her how to katari duel?" he said to Barkav. "Why? What have I done to deserve this, Father?"

Kyra shot Rustan a furious glance. "I don't need anyone to teach me how to katari duel, Maji-khan, especially not *him*."

Barkav gazed at both of them out of calm eyes that were the color of a leaden sky. He didn't say a word, but after a moment, Rustan lowered his head. Kyra's cheeks burned. She wished with all her heart that she had not spoken. To her relief, Barkav gave a curt gesture of dismissal. Kyra almost tripped and fell in her hurry to leave.

CHAPTER 15

A PRICE TO PAY

The wind had fallen silent. Kyra stood outside her tent, drinking in the stark splendor of the scene. A silver moon rode high in the sky, dimming the stars and bathing the sands with its phosphorescent light.

"Beautiful, is it not?" a voice rasped behind Kyra. It was Astinsai. In the moonlight her tiny, wizened form and hooded face took on an almost inhuman cast.

Kyra shivered. "Beautiful but cold."

"There is always a price to pay for beauty," said Astinsai with a gap-toothed grin. "Or for love. Oh, never mind me," she added. "I am old and sentimental and cannot say anything original anymore. But come to my tent, if you will. I want to see your face by the light of my own fire."

Kyra was bone-tired, and she would have to get up before dawn for the so-called lessons with Rustan. But an invitation to spend time with the last living katari mistress did not come every day. So she bowed and said, "I would be honored."

She was curious to see how the katari mistress lived. Would

there be shelves of glass pitchers filled with colorful potions? Bunches of roots and herbs hanging from the ceiling to ward off evil spirits? Luxurious silk cushions and rugs lining the floors? Glass mirrors and bronze urns? Kyra's imagination soared as she followed the old woman to the edge of the Khur camp.

In this, however, she was sorely disappointed. The Old One lived in a small, nondescript dwelling. Kyra had to duck her head to enter it, and by the wavering light of the stove, she could see that the carpet on the floor was ragged and the felts lining the walls were stained with age and smoke. Incense burned at a tiny altar behind a wooden pallet; its heavy, sweet scent permeated the air. Books and scrolls made an untidy heap on one side of the pallet. It hardly seemed a suitable abode for a renowned katari mistress and seer.

Astinsai lowered herself on a cushion and studied Kyra out of bright little eyes. *Like a wrinkled old spider, waiting in its lair for some tasty treat*, Kyra couldn't help but think, though she quickly brushed the thought away as she knelt opposite the seer. "Is it my face that you want to see or my honesty that you wish to test, mistress?" She had not meant to speak, but the words spilled out anyway.

Astinsai cackled. "Oh, I have no doubt of your honesty. But I do wish to see your face. After all, this is the first time a pretty young woman has come into our midst. I am sure the younger ones are already half in love."

"We are bound by the Kanun of Ture-asa," said Kyra, striving to maintain her deferential tone. "None of us can forget the vows we have made in the names of our ancestors."

"Oh, nonsense," said Astinsai. "Ture-asa may have been the last king and prophet of Asiana, but he was sick with metal poison when he wrote the Kanun. Sick, blind, and dying. The Great War was almost over and poison had spread into every field and lake."

Kyra listened, fascinated. She had never heard Ture-asa referred to except in the most reverent of tones. She knew that the Orders had come into being because of Ture-asa's writings, not long after his death. He had predicted as much, and laid down the laws that would bring Asiana out of the dark aftermath of the Great War. Copies of the original text were much prized, and preserved by the clans with great care. They were heirlooms, passed from one generation to the next. The Order of Kali had a copy of a copy; it was kept locked in the Mahimata's trunk, only removed on the most special of occasions.

"Ture-asa's son was killed and the line of kings was broken forever," Astinsai continued. "Ture-asa knew that he had little time left, and he wrote his Kanun in a hurry. All the rules about chastity are there to lend weight to the text, and I wouldn't be surprised if they were added later by one of his overzealous ministers. In any case, they are wrong. Why do you think the ability to bond with kalishium is becoming rarer? If Markswomen do not breed, how will they pass on their talents to future generations?"

"You think the ability to bond with kalishium is *inherited*?" said Kyra, flabbergasted.

"Of course," said Astinsai. "What did you think, it is some sort of mystical power you are graced with? No. The Ones must have altered certain humans when they first came here, perhaps to communicate with them. Those who were altered passed the trait down their bloodline."

This was too much to take in. Kyra was sure there was nothing in Ture-asa's texts about any of this. She wondered how the elders of Kali would feel about such an interpretation of their abilities. They'd probably call it heresy and forbid her to talk nonsense. But Astinsai seemed sure of herself, and it wasn't the most far-fetched theory. The Ones had brought kalishium from the stars; perhaps people had to be changed before they could use it.

"How do you know all this?" said Kyra. "Are you descended from Ture-asa himself? They say that only those who can call a king ancestor are blessed with the far-sight."

Astinsai snorted. "I don't even know my own parents," she said. "I make no claims to royal ancestry. And my visions are not always to be trusted. There was a time when I could work kalishium to make kataris. No more. I grow older than I dreamed possible." She shook her head, as if to rid it of unpleasant thoughts. "Enough. Tell me about yourself, child. Do you truly think your life is best spent seeking vengeance for those who will never return?"

The change of subject caught Kyra off guard. "How do you know about that?" she asked.

"Every elder knows the fate of Veer. The eldest grandchild of the headwoman was the sole survivor of the massacre, and you bear her name. There is no one else to speak for the dead. Besides, we heard rumors about the execution of Kai Tau's eldest son." She paused. "You did not answer my question."

Kyra hesitated, unwilling to admit her need for revenge to the katari mistress. But Astinsai seemed to know everything already. "I'm not going to spend my whole life on this task. At least, I hope not," she said. "But until I punish the men who killed my family, I will have no peace. I was five years old when my world came to an end. Yet I have lived on for fourteen years; to what end?"

"To what end indeed," said Astinsai. "Did you never wonder why the Taus destroyed your clan? And why they spared you?"

Kyra frowned. "The Taus are outlaws. I survived because I hid in a tree."

Astinsai sighed. "I see Shirin Mam told you nothing. Well, perhaps it is better so. Not all things are meant to be known. Not all things are meant to be taken into account. If they were, how would we ever act? How would we take sides?"

"What do you mean?" said Kyra, her pulse quickening.

Astinsai leaned forward and whispered, "Are you sure that you want to know?"

From her breath came the smell of smoke-weed, and something else: the thin, sharp odor of malice.

"Yes," said Kyra. If the katari mistress had knowledge that would help her make sense of the brutal killing of her family, then she needed to hear it.

"Why?" asked Astinsai. It was not a mere question; it was a command to speak. If Kyra did not give the correct answer, she knew she would not get another word from the old woman. She thought hard before replying.

"Because it is better to confront the truth, no matter how terrible it is," she said finally. "I am the last of my clan and if I don't know its history, no one ever will."

"Well said." Astinsai leaned back and smiled with hooded eyes. "Remember these pretty words of yours when I have finished telling you what I know. It is not the whole story, and it is not the whole truth. That last is something you will have to find for yourself." She reached for a pipe attached to a clay bowl and inhaled deeply before blowing a ring of sickly sweet smoke into the air. Kyra held her breath until it dissipated.

"One winter twenty years ago, it was so cold that snow

covered the desert and the well water froze," she said. "In Tezbasti, the village nearest to us, people were reduced to eating snow and straw. Maheshva, the old Maji-khan of Khur, sent a team of men with the strongest camels across the desert to Yartan to barter for food and other supplies. The Akal-shin door was of no use to us; even then, it would not open." The Old One paused, her eyes glinting like rocks in a pool. "But you have come through the door. What was it like, child?"

Kyra flinched. "It was—not something I care to speak of. Please go on with your story. Did the men reach Yartan safely?"

"They reached safely and returned with enough provisions to last us through the bitter months that followed. All but one. The best of them all was lost to us in Yartan to a blade sharper than any katari. It was a wound he never recovered from. A wound of the heart."

"He fell in love?"

"Love, lust, *deewangee*. There are many names we give to this thing, and they are all inadequate." Astinsai stared at the fire, her eyes turned inward. Was the old woman remembering her own youth?

Kyra had a sudden vision of a slender woman in a marketplace giving sideways glances to a young man seated on a white horse. The young man gazed down at her as she pretended to select the herbs that her aunt, a medicine woman, had sent her to buy. She picked bunches of mint and lemon balm, complaining to the seller about their quality and freshness, but all the while she was thinking of how fine-looking the young man was, how well he sat on his horse, and how smart his clothes were.

Astinsai moved and the image flickered out. Kyra realized with a start that she had looked unbidden into the other's past.

She cleared her throat. "What happened to them?"

The Old One's mouth twisted, as if knowing the vision Kyra had accidentally seen. "What can such madness lead to but tragedy? He was brave and handsome, but he was now a renegade who had forsaken his Order. She was good and beautiful, but she was also the eldest daughter of a headwoman, and the heir of her clan.

"They left Yartan, thinking perhaps to make for the small mountain villages farther northwest. For two weeks, they must have known love, sweet and delirious. Despite the hunger, fatigue, and fear, they must have known happiness. For a while, they were free from the anger and envy of those they had left behind.

"But eventually, they were found. They were caught in a pass in the Spirit Mountains, trying to cross into the Skyol Highlands. It was the girl's clan that found them. It might have gone better if the Order of Khur had reached them first."

"The headwoman was angry with her daughter?" guessed Kyra.

"There is justifiable anger, and there is blind rage—two entirely different things," said Astinsai. "The headwoman was fierce and proud. She had sent her sixteen-year-old daughter with a few trusted companions to Yartan to select a mate from the clan of Kushan. She was not merely angry; she was ready to kill the daughter who had caused her to lose face among the clans of Asiana. Faced with this rage, the girl betrayed her lover to save herself. An old story, but we never tire of it, do we? Life is a series of patterns, ugly and scarred. What would you have done in her place, child?"

Kyra flushed. "I would never have run away from my duty in the first place."

"Is that what you think?" said Astinsai. "Or is it what you have been taught to think by your Order? No, you don't have to answer me. But ask yourself this: Where do your loyalties lie? I will not make a prophecy for you, but I can see that your way is unclear. Doubt and misgiving will follow you no matter which path you take."

Kyra felt a chill creep up her spine. "If that is so, all I can do is try my best and pray to Kali to protect my soul."

"I too pray for you," said Astinsai. "I pray that you find what you are looking for, and that you do not meet an untimely end, like your—like the young girl of my story did."

Kyra sensed the barb in her too-sincere words. The story was about to end with a painful twist that her inner eye could almost see.

The Old One gave a deep, theatrical sigh. "There is not much more to add. The girl told her mother that she had been kidnapped by the young Marksman and forced to lie with him. It was easy to believe—especially because her mother wanted to believe it. The headwoman had the Marksman flogged in the main square of Yartan, as was her right by law. The young man protested his innocence with every lash and called in anguish to his paramour to declare the truth of their love." Her face darkened. "I watched, helpless to intervene. I hoped that pity and shame would move the girl to beg for clemency on his behalf.

"But the girl was silent, her face hidden by a veil. Perhaps she regretted her lie? I do not know. I only know what happened next. The headwoman and her daughter returned to the Valley of Veer, where they dwelled, and the whole sordid tale was never referred to again."

Shock coursed through Kyra's veins, ice-cold, numbing. The Valley of *Veer*? "No," she stuttered. "That can't be true."

"Save your distress," said Astinsai. "I am not finished yet. The girl—your mother—was married off a few months later to a suitable young man from the clan of Tenaga. Meanwhile, her lover escaped from the Order of Khur the night before he was to be executed. He went on to form a clan of his own, an outlaw clan, vicious and violent, that has grown in strength and cunning until it is now the most powerful one in southern Asiana. You know which one I mean."

A roaring filled Kyra's ears. Astinsai was talking of the Tau clan. Kai Tau and her mother. Her mother and Kai Tau . . . no, it was impossible.

"The past is past," said Astinsai softly. "We cannot change it. We can only change our own perception of it. For years, I blamed myself for what happened. Then I realized it would have happened anyway. Kai would have found his path to evil with or without me."

Kyra's mouth was dry, her throat tight. "You helped him to escape, didn't you?" she said in a ragged whisper.

Tears glimmered in Astinsai's eyes. "Kai was always my favorite. I believed in him. I knew he was telling the truth and that he had been terribly wronged. Yet, had I guessed the carnage he would wreak in the name of vengeance, I would have cut my own throat before I freed the bonds that had been laid on him."

The firelight flickered, casting shadows on the tent wall. Kyra's hands were like stones on her lap, her katari cold within its sheath. "You have not told me why I was spared." Her voice sounded flat, distant to her own ears.

"I made a prophecy to Kai before he left that he would die by the hand of a daughter of Veer, and no other. This is his penance and his destiny. He waits for you, all these long years, to free him from the evil he has done. Not until you kill him will he know any rest." The Old One closed her eyes. "That is all I have to say. Go now, for I am tired and can speak no more."

Kyra stumbled out of the tent and into the cold, quiet night, her mind full of tortured images. Her sweet-faced mother, in the willing embrace of the brute who would destroy the Veer clan. The blood-soaked bodies littering the streets of her village. The broken limbs and the stench of death. The circling vultures and the darkness behind the door. Except that the darkness was inside her now and there was no escaping the horror of it.

Was Kai Tau her father? Had she killed her own half brother in the name of vengeance? And if so, what kind of monster did that make her?

It was a long time before she could calm herself. She walked away from the camp until she could no longer see the flickering lights of the lamps and stoves. The moon had slipped below the horizon and the stars and planets shone with undimmed splendor. Kyra sat on the sand, gazing at the vast, silent space that surrounded her, listening to the slowing beat of her own heart.

CHAPTER 16

FORMS OF THE DANCE

Dawn found Rustan in the grove beyond the camp, practicing breath control as he waited for his pupil to arrive. He had told her to meet him in the grove at first light; the tall shrubs would shelter them from the midday sun as well as from the sharp wind.

He breathed in the frigid air, trying to relax his mind and his body. Little as he liked the task that had been given to him, he would fulfill it to the best of his abilities. He had risen two hours earlier to prepare the forms of bare-handed defense that he planned to teach Kyra today.

Except that she wasn't here yet.

Rustan pushed aside his irritation and focused on his breath. This time alone in the grove was a *gift*, and he would use it well. He settled down to meditate.

The sun had slipped into the sky when racing footsteps alerted him to Kyra's arrival.

He opened his eyes and regarded her as she stood before him, panting. She looked even younger than she had yesterday, with her hair tied back and her slight frame lost in the over-sized robe that Shurik had given her. The dark circles under her eyes betrayed that she had slept little.

"You're late," he said evenly.

"Sorry," she muttered.

"No matter," he said. "It is only our first lesson. But it should not happen again. To be late is to be disrespectful. And where there is no respect, there can be no learning."

The Markswoman did not respond; she merely gazed through him, as if her mind was elsewhere, on more important things.

Rustan rose and said, more harshly than he had intended, "I have no more desire to do this than you. But the Maji-khan has assigned me to teach you, and I intend to do the best I can. What about you—what do you intend?"

Once again, she did not respond, only looked at him bewildered, as if he spoke in a strange language. He noticed that her eyes were red-rimmed. Had she been crying?

Rustan relaxed his tone somewhat. "You don't have to do this, you know," he said. "If you're afraid . . ."

Kyra thrust her chin out and glared at him. "I am not afraid," she said through gritted teeth. "I will do what I must."

"It's your funeral," said Rustan, relieved that she had started talking to him, even if it was through gritted teeth. "Personally, I think Tamsyn will take less than a minute to disarm you, which is why it is important to learn bare-handed defense."

"I am not that easily disarmed," snapped Kyra.

"No?" said Rustan. "Let us see."

He raised his palm and uttered a word of power that Barkav had taught him a few months earlier.

Kyra gasped as her katari flew from its scabbard, straight into Rustan's waiting hand.

She reached for it, pausing just short of snatching it back. "How did you do that?" she asked, scowling. When she saw Rustan was smiling, her scowl deepened. "Do you laugh at my incompetence?"

Rustan stopped smiling at once, sensing her humiliation. "No. I was only able to call your katari to me because it knew I meant no harm, that I was demonstrating a lesson that may prove valuable to its mistress."

"And the lesson is what?" said Kyra as he handed the katari back to her. "How easily you can kill me?"

"The lesson is, expect the unexpected," said Rustan. "The Hand of Kali is skilled in all the arts of katari-play. Your only hope is to stay calm no matter what move she makes. Anticipate her when you can—after all, you have known her for years—and when you cannot, be ready with counterattacks of your own. Inner Speech is not allowed in the course of the formal katari duel. This is to your advantage; use it. Focus on the bond you both have with your blades, for that bond will be crucial in the outcome of the duel."

He stopped. Kyra was no longer listening to him; she was studying her katari, turning it this way and that.

"What are you doing?" he demanded.

"I can still feel your hand on my blade," she replied. "You shouldn't have taken it from me like that."

A wave of frustration broke against Rustan's core of inner calm.

"Take your stance," he said.

Kyra looked up, startled. He felt almost sorry for her. He made his move without waiting, using a small outside kick of the Kawamuri style to sweep her off her feet. She lay on the ground, stunned.

"You should have been able to counter that easily," he said, shaking his head. "But you weren't paying attention."

Kyra snarled and leaped to her feet. He certainly had her attention now.

She came at him, as expected, with a classic hip technique of the same Kawamuri style.

So predictable, he thought, and countered her with a reverse hip throw.

This time she was slower to leap at him. At least she switched forms, but he was still able to foresee the Kawashi axe kick before it came close to connecting.

He knocked her down six times before saying in exasperation, "No, no! You are going about it all wrong. You are trying to watch me with your eyes when you should be watching me with your mind. Where is the wisdom of your third eye? *Anticipate* me, or all the moves of all the schools in Asiana will not keep you on your feet."

Kyra got up, spitting dirt, her eyes black slits of fury. He wouldn't have been surprised if she'd started hissing at him like a banded snake. He didn't care, as long as she listened to him.

"Anger will cloud your judgment and blunt your weapon," he said. "You must be quiet in body and mind to be able to listen to your opponent. Where is her balance? What does she intend? If you know this, the fight is won before it starts." He paused. "What are you smiling at?"

Kyra's smile vanished. "You sounded like Shirin Mam just then," she said quietly.

That stopped him cold—as if she *had* anticipated what could hurt him most. "Back to work," he snapped. "This time, use your elbows, feet, hands—whatever it takes to counter my moves."

They continued sparring until the sun was overhead in the sky. Rivulets of sweat trickled down Rustan's face and back as he danced and spun with the Markswoman. He was in a place outside time where he didn't have to think or feel. There were only the forms of the dance, and the opponent he must cut down time and time again. How to explain this to her? The fight was unimportant, the enemy even less so. There was only the self and the need to prevail.

At last, when Kyra looked ready to drop from exhaustion, he said, "We'll break for the midday meal. Eat sparingly and be back here within the hour."

He strode away before she could speak, breathing hard. Feeling and memory returned. There was a dull ache in his head and chest. He sounded like Shirin Mam, did he? It was going to be even more torturous teaching this Markswoman than he had thought. One more punishment added to everything else—when would the scales balance out?

The month until the next clan meeting stretched before him, each grueling day worse than the previous one. And for what? So that her blood could stain the floors of Sikandra Hall.

Get ahold of yourself, he thought as he walked to his tent, ignoring the curious glances of his fellow Marksmen. *It's not as if she doesn't know what she's doing.*

But that was the problem. He doubted very much that she did.

⚜

Kyra gazed at Rustan's retreating back with a mixture of frustration and anger. What was the matter with him? If she bothered him so much, he should tell Barkav that he didn't want to teach her. Then maybe Barkav would pick someone like Shurik, who would have been happy to spend all day with her.

But reviewing the lesson·in her mind, she had to admit that Rustan knew his stuff. For all his chatter and friendliness, she doubted Shurik was as skilled as his brooding fellow Marksman.

Rustan was also right about the fact that she was afraid, though she'd die before admitting it to him. Even without the use of Mental Arts, Tamsyn was the deadliest bladeswoman in the entire Order. Better than even Chintil, it was rumored. How was Kyra going to defeat her?

Yet defeat her she must if she wanted to live.

Irritated, she ran her fingers through her hair, dislodging clumps of dirt. She cursed, knowing it would take ages to comb it all out. She shook the strands as best she could, and tied them into a semblance of neatness. As she walked in the direction of the camp, she caught sight of the small tent that the Old One occupied.

Though she had tossed and turned all night, she had not spared a thought for Astinsai's incredible story during the last few hours. *Too busy being beaten up.* If nothing else, training for the duel with Tamsyn would help keep her mind focused on the present. But she could only train for so many hours a day . . .

"Hey, Kyra." A cheerful voice broke into her thoughts. It was Shurik, standing outside the communal tent. "Come quick or the food will be all gone."

Glad for another distraction, she hurried to join him. Inside the tent, Marksmen were already seated in two rows opposite each other, being served by the novices. Some inclined their heads in greeting and some stared at her. Most simply went on eating.

Kyra let Shurik take her arm, covertly scanning the tent for Rustan. But she couldn't spy his lean, grim face among the others. Perhaps he was eating by himself. Well, *she* certainly didn't care where he was. She let Shurik guide her to a place at the end of one row and thanked the novice serving her with a smile of such toothy brilliance that the boy almost fell over in his attempt to get away. She noticed the elder called Ghasil glowering at her, and made a mental note to be more careful.

The millet and onion stew was simple but tasty and she ate it with relish, dipping in pieces of flatbread to soak up the spiciness.

"Who does the cooking around here?" she asked Shurik between mouthfuls.

"It changes every day," said Shurik. "Today it is Gajin and he's a fair cook, which is why the stew is tasty. Tomorrow it is David and we will be lucky if he serves us something edible."

"Everyone cooks by turn?" asked Kyra, trying and failing to imagine Barkav sweating over a cooking pot.

"Everyone except the elders," said Shurik, grinning. "I expect you'll get a turn too and we'll see how well the Order of Kali eats." He noticed her aghast expression and added, "What's the matter, haven't you cooked before?"

"Not for so many people," mumbled Kyra. It wasn't a lie, not exactly.

"Oh, don't worry," said Shurik. "If you can cook for one, you can cook for forty, Gajin always says." He continued to shovel food into his mouth.

Kyra stared at her plate, appetite gone. Was it not enough that her combat skills had been found lacking? Would she be judged on her nonexistent cooking skills as well? No one in the Order of Kali knew how to cook. That was what Tarshana was for. A wave of homesickness swamped Kyra; she desperately longed for the world she had left behind.

The world that no longer exists, she reminded herself.

CHAPTER 17

VISITOR FROM VALAVAN

Watch out, here she comes," whispered Nineth. Elena leaped up from where she had been slumped on the floor, and both girls began to sweep the cavern as if their lives depended on it.

"Not slacking, are you?" said Akassa, amused. The glossy-haired girl paused at the passageway that led from her cell to the central cavern. "What shall I tell the Mahimata? Should the apprentices be spared further punishment, or should they be separated from their blades?"

The girls longed to retort but continued sweeping, heads down and eyes fixed on the floor. Akassa might only be trying to frighten them, but it was better not to anger her in any way. She was, after all, Tamsyn's pet. And they were in trouble, having performed dismally in the Mental Arts class that morning. In truth, they had been in trouble ever since Kyra left.

"The Mahimata says I am ready for my first mark," said Akassa, leaning against the cavern wall. "I've been ready for a long time. Shirin Mam couldn't see it, but she can."

"Wishful seeing," muttered Nineth.

"What? Did you say something, apprentice?"

"Oh, just that I wish I was ready," said Nineth sweetly. "But I'm not."

Akassa laughed. "No one in their right mind would think you were. Maybe you're a forever-apprentice. Or maybe you'll run away, like your precious Kyra did." Her tone turned venomous when she said Kyra's name. Anger coursed through Nineth, but she controlled it and said nothing. Every word she spoke would be reported to Tamsyn.

At last Akassa got bored watching them sweep, and drifted out of the cavern.

"Probably gone to filch potato pies from Tarshana," muttered Nineth, leaning on her broom and gazing at the single shard of afternoon light that stabbed the cavern through the crawlway.

"Hungry?" said Elena. "Me too." They seemed to miss most of the midday meals these days, what with random penances handed out by Tamsyn's favorite few Markswomen.

"I miss her so much," said Nineth. "I wish she had taken us with her."

"Hush." Elena glanced toward the dark holes that marked the passageways out of the cavern. Talk of Kyra was forbidden. Since the day she vanished from the Ferghana Valley, Tamsyn had developed the worrying habit of pouncing on anyone she believed was even thinking of her. As Kyra's best friends, Nineth and Elena had been summoned to the Mahimata's cell and subjected to an hour-long interrogation by the Mistress of Mental Arts—a title she retained, even as the Mahimata. It had not been a pleasant experience and neither of them wished to repeat it.

"No one's listening," said Nineth. "I would know it if they were. Where do you suppose she went? She didn't have more than a fifteen-minute head start, yet Tamsyn and the others couldn't find her."

Elena sighed. They had been over this many times, and it just didn't make sense. Tamsyn should have been able to find Kyra no matter how fast she'd ridden Akhtar. A Markswoman's bond with her blade was a beacon in the dark for those who were adept in the Mental Arts. If she was anywhere in the Ferghana Valley, Tamsyn should have been able to track her down. Unless—and Elena tried to push the thought away but she couldn't quite succeed—unless she was dead.

Nineth's voice became lower still as she bent toward Elena. "I think she found a *door*."

Elena looked at her friend in exasperation. "Don't be silly," she said. "If there was another door or Hub in the Ferghana, the elders would know about it."

Nineth's face fell. "Yes, I suppose they would, wouldn't they?"

Elena's voice softened. "Give it up, Nineth. We don't know where she went. We can only hope that she's fine, wherever she is. Let's hurry up and finish this floor, okay? We might be able to grab some potato pies ourselves before the next class."

Nineth brightened and fell to sweeping with renewed vigor.

❦

"Looking for something, Eldest?" Tamsyn's voice at the entrance to the Mahimata's chamber was coldly inquiring.

Only the decades of training prevented Navroz Lan from squeaking with surprise. As it was, she took her time straightening up from Shirin Mam's old desk, smoothing her robe, and turning around. Damn the woman, how had she been able to sneak up on her unawares?

Navroz squelched her betraying thoughts. "My apologies for disturbing you, Tamsyn, but there is a matter of some import. We have a visitor from the Order of Valavan. The Order has received disturbing reports of violence in the Thar Desert, and wishes to discuss them with us. I thought you might like to meet her at once."

Tamsyn's smile was glacial. "Indeed," she murmured, gliding into the cell and sitting at the desk. "Is she an elder? No? You and Felda should be enough for her. It is not fitting that the Mahimata of Kali receive every Markswoman who takes it into her head to come to our caves."

"As you wish." Navroz backed away, eyes lowered. Near the entrance she straightened, permitting a tiny bubble of relief to escape her lips.

"A moment, Eldest."

Navroz stopped, pulse quickening as she raised her eyes to gaze at the new Mahimata.

"Is this what you were searching for?" Tamsyn tossed a linen-wrapped package on the desk and leaned back, watching her with a hooded gaze.

Despite herself, Navroz's eyes darted toward the package. She had hoped that Shirin Mam had left a message or a clue for her to find, but it seemed Tamsyn had found it first. Well, she wasn't about to reveal her dismay to the Mahimata. "I don't know what you mean, Tamsyn," she said. "I was here to inform you of the visitor from Valavan. What is in this package? Is it something important?"

"I found it in a hidden drawer in this desk," said Tamsyn.

"Perhaps it is something from Shirin Mam. Would you like to open it? I can see that you would. Here, take it."

Navroz stared at her, concealing her surprise. This woman was more devious than a demon. The package must be sealed with a word of power, or Tamsyn would have opened it herself. Obviously, Tamsyn was testing her. Aloud she said, "I thank you for the honor, but it is not my place to open it. If it is from Shirin Mam, it is intended for you, the new Mahimata. You will inform us of the contents if you deem it appropriate. Now if you will excuse me, I must see if the elders can join me in meeting our visitor."

She bowed and left before Tamsyn could say anything further. As she walked down the torchlit passage that led to the central cavern, her eyes strayed to the last portrait hanging on the wall. Shirin Mam's face smiled back at her and she wanted to curse. What had Shirin Mam been up to, those last few days?

It was a cool, crisp afternoon, at least ten degrees lower than the Deccan village from which the petite and dusky Derla Siyal had come, but if she was cold, she did not show it. Navroz studied her composed face with grudging admiration. Derla had never Transported before, but she had used two sets of doors to arrive at the Ferghana Hub. To look at her, sitting serene and regal under the mulberry tree, one would have thought she'd arrived by palanquin. Navroz was not surprised that Faran Lashail, the head of the Order of Valavan, had chosen her as the Order's new ambassador. She had "elder-in-the-making" written all over her smooth brow.

Felda's arrival interrupted her train of thoughts. The squat, scowling elder looked even grimmer than usual, although she made an attempt at a smile for the visitor.

"Chintil Maya is taking an advanced combat class and Mumuksu Chan is in meditation, but we will have them join us if you stay long enough," said Felda, dropping down on the grass next to them.

"I'm sorry that the Mahimata is otherwise engaged," added Navroz. "She means no disrespect."

Derla raised her delicate eyebrows. "Perhaps you did not convey the seriousness of the situation? Faran will be *most* disappointed. First I will have to tell her that her dear old friend Shirin is no more. Then I will have to tell her that the new Mahimata does not deem a visitor from Valavan significant enough to grant her an audience."

Navroz almost snorted. *Dear old friend* indeed. Shirin Mam and Faran Lashail went back a long way, but they had been as "friendly" as two cats fighting for the same bit of fish. She said, "As the new Mahimata, Tamsyn has her hands full right now. But you have the ears of the elders of Kali. Now, please tell us what brings you here. It is not often that the caves of Kali have such a distinguished visitor."

Derla smiled, but the smile did not touch her eyes. "It is not often that we hear of entire villages in the Thar being laid waste by the dark weapons."

Her words hung in the air like bits of ice. Navroz swallowed. "Entire villages? Are you certain?"

"Certain?" said Derla. "No. Although our authority extends into the Thar, we do not often venture there. The only door to the middle of the desert that we know of is here in the

Ferghana Hub. We have a door to Jhelmil, northeast of the desert, too far to be of much use. But we've questioned a couple of survivors who made it to Jhelmil. It appears that an army is in slow march to the north, mowing down any that stand in its way."

"Kai Tau," said Felda.

"Kai Tau," agreed Derla. "The Taus are the only outlaws equipped with death-sticks. You know that they stole twelve kalashiks from the clan of Arikken several years ago. The remaining weapons in Asiana have been under constant guard since then, in the Temple of Valavan."

She paused. Navroz and Felda exchanged a meaningful glance. There had been much secrecy surrounding the location of the remaining weapons cache, with Faran Lashail refusing to admit that such a cache even existed.

Derla continued, "The point is, why now? We left the Taus alone and they were careful not to draw attention to themselves. We probed a bit further, and heard disturbing rumors of a mark. Apparently, Kai Tau's son was executed by a Markswoman of Kali some months ago. Now I am sure that you will tell me I am wrong, because the Thar is *our* territory, and Shirin Mam would not have done such a thing without Faran Lashail's permission and approval." She sat back, fixing her calm gaze on them.

Felda began to speak but Navroz forestalled her, knowing that Derla was baiting them, trying to draw them into a defensive position.

"You may have nominal territorial jurisdiction over the Thar," she said. "But as you have confessed, your Markswomen hardly ever go there. The Order of Valavan may number eighty-five compared to our thirty-three, but you are still too thinly spread over the subcontinent to enforce the Kanun in every field and dune. Perhaps Faran needs to step up her recruiting?"

Derla's face flushed with anger and she opened her mouth to speak, but Navroz raised a hand, cutting her off. "Wait. I am not finished. You may have territorial jurisdiction over the Thar, but the Order of Kali has moral jurisdiction over the fate of the Taus. It was Kyra Veer who executed Maidul Tau."

"The Taus are murderers and must be brought to justice sooner or later," added Felda. "Just because they are better equipped than the average outlaw doesn't mean that they are beyond the Kanun."

Derla exhaled slowly. "It is as Faran suspected. The Markswoman Kyra is allowed to take revenge for a past tragedy, and the Order of Valavan is left to handle the bloody aftermath. This is not what we expected of Shirin Mam."

"Shirin Mam rarely did what was expected," said Navroz. "Rest assured that you understand her even less than we did." She frowned. "That said, we will certainly not leave you to 'handle the bloody aftermath' alone. When I said that we have moral jurisdiction, I meant it."

"And what will you do?" said Derla. "Engage them in open battle? That is the surest way to die. Kalashiks can kill over a distance of several hundred meters. For us to use our weapons, we must be able to get close to the outlaws."

"Is that why the Taus still live?" said Felda. "Because the Markswomen of Valavan are afraid?"

"Felda!" Navroz's voice was cold, carrying every bit of authority she possessed as the eldest of the elders.

Felda colored, mumbled something that could have been

mistaken as an apology by someone a little hard of hearing, and glared into the distance with folded arms.

Navroz said quietly, "I think we all know why the Taus still live."

The three were silent. They did know, and it was nothing to be proud of. It was the massacre of Veer, after all, that had silenced the voices that complained of the tithe they gave to the Orders, the voices that had insinuated that Markswomen belonged to an era that was dead and gone.

Yes, they had played an important role once. For many years after the Great War, people struggled to survive, to find clean water and grow food to feed themselves and their diminished families. But everything was tainted by the toxic remains of the decades-long conflict. People sickened and died in large numbers—more even than had been killed during the war itself.

But among them were always one or two who led the rest, who never sickened, who defended the weak and fought off marauders, human and animal alike. They were the descendents of the followers of Ture-asa, the last king of Asiana. Under their protection, small groups managed to survive here and there. And in time, as the poison leeched out of the fields and villages grew into more than just a few wretched huts, from among their number was born the first child who would fashion a blade from kalishium and call herself Markswoman: Lin Maya, the founder of the Order of Kali.

But as the Orders grew in power and strength, so too did the clans of Asiana, until now hundreds of thousands of people lived and farmed on communal land, secure in the belief that they were safe. The dark years were over, the light of the Kanun shone in almost every corner of Asiana, and the towns and villages were well able to deal with the infractions of their local populace. It had been decades since outlaws had dared to attack a major settlement. Clan leaders began to chaff at the authority of the Orders. Why didn't Markswomen restrict themselves to hunting wyr-wolves and leave the rest to the clan councils?

Then along came the Taus and slaughtered every man, woman, and child in the peaceful little village of Veer. As the terrible news filtered through to the far-flung settlements of Asiana, the clans reacted with horror and fear. In the rumors and retellings that spread, the twelve death-sticks became a hundred, and the number of those killed multiplied to several thousand. The towns tripled their guard; the villages built trenches for self-defense. After all, it could have been any one of them. And it could be their turn next.

The killings at Veer accomplished what decades of diplomacy had not. The clans once again turned to the Orders, begging for help and acknowledging their supremacy.

The Orders moved fast, isolating the remaining known death-sticks in Asiana, and trapping the Taus in the sandy wastes of the Thar Desert. The outlaws would be disarmed and punished eventually, once a proper defense could be mustered. Meanwhile, the clan leaders would not question the continued reign of the Orders of Asiana.

"Fourteen years is long enough for the outlaws to have walked free," said Navroz. "Don't forget, there is another Order that can help us."

Derla threw up her hands. "The Order of Khur?" A note of disbelief crept into her voice. "Don't tell me you wish to involve those—*men*—in what is happening in the Thar. Kai is one of theirs. The elders of Khur were his compatriots."

"You know about that?" said Navroz. "It is something known only to elders. What else has Faran told you?" When Derla made no response, Navroz continued, "The elders of Khur do not like to talk about Kai, but this is precisely why they must be involved. They feel responsible for him and what he has done. Besides, Shirin Mam always believed that the Order of Khur should be treated as equal to the other Orders. She had cordial relations with Barkav."

"And your new Mahimata?" said Derla slyly. "What does *she* think?"

Navroz hesitated. Tamsyn's views on men and their place were rather well known. "The new Mahimata will do what she must, as will we," she said finally. "Tell Faran we will meet in Sikandra."

Derla rose to leave, declining their offers of more tea or a hot meal. The day was getting on, she said, and she had a village meeting to attend before sunset. Sandi Meersil was summoned to escort the visitor back to the Ferghana Hub.

When she was out of earshot, Felda said, "We have two problems, Eldest. First, how are we going to deal with the murderous outlaws in the Thar? Second, how are we going to deal with Tamsyn?"

"Pit them against each other," suggested Navroz, "and hope that Kai Tau wins."

The two giggled like novices. "She is too strong for us, Felda," said Navroz at last. "We cannot confront her. We will have to be indirect if we are to find out the truth of what happened the day Shirin Mam died." She recounted her unsettling encounter with Tamsyn in the Mahimata's cell.

"You did well not to try to open that package, Eldest," said

Felda. "If it is sealed by a word of power, then only the person it is intended for can safely access the contents. I wonder what's in it. Perhaps I will make some discreet inquiries."

A hint of steel entered Navroz's voice. "You'll do no such thing. Be careful, Felda. You are sometimes almost as obvious as Kyra was."

Felda bristled. "I most certainly am not!" she snapped. Her face clouded. "Where *is* that dratted girl? Those wyr-wolves . . ."

"Led us a merry dance through the woods, didn't they?" said Navroz. "Yet Akhtar was found coming from the opposite direction, from the hills of Gonur."

"You think she found a Hub?" said Felda. "It's the only logical explanation. I hope she hasn't taken it into her head to go off to the Thar and attempt vengeance on the Taus all by herself."

"I wouldn't put it past her," said Navroz. "All the more reason for us to act fast. Yes, child, what is it?"

It was Tonar Kalam, hovering at the edge of the red-brown carpet of leaves. She bowed and said, "To remind you, Eldest, that the petitioners are waiting. There are eleven today, six of them from quite far away. At least four require healing."

Navroz sighed, and both elders rose. Shirin Mam's death had done nothing to decrease the flow of petitioners. If anything, there seemed even more of them than usual these days, perhaps because Tamsyn did not deign to meet them. That work fell to Navroz.

She groaned inwardly as she surveyed the group of village folk squatting on the grass beneath the trees in the apple grove. There they were, waiting for their miracles, when all she had to offer was a combination of sensible advice, herbs, and a bit of thought-shaping.

Felda was already mumbling some excuse about a set of derivations and backing away. Happily, Navroz caught sight of Elena going toward the kitchen with her friend Nineth, and hailed the apprentice.

"I need your help, Elena," she called, and the girl came willingly enough, though Nineth fled into the kitchen as if wyr-wolves were after her—no doubt trying to wheedle food out of Tarshana, the wretch.

Thank the Goddess for Elena with her nimble hands and eager mind. If not for her, Navroz would have been hard put finding anyone to train as her eventual replacement. Not that she planned on dying just yet. Still, she was seventy-seven years old, and of late she had been feeling every one of them.

If only Shirin hadn't died . . .

But there was no use thinking that. Shirin was gone, but Kyra was still alive, somewhere out there. And one day she would return to the caves of Kali. Navroz held on to that thought like a talisman as she approached the petitioners, Elena in tow.

PART III

From *The Weapons of the Great War*, recounted by a historian of the clan of Arikken to Navroz Lan of the Order of Kali

The Great War was fought many ages ago. The kings and queens who battled for supremacy are long since dust. Not even their graves exist; so many died that they were burned or buried in vast, shallow pits. Some drowned, throwing themselves in the water to escape the burning metal poison that flowed over the earth and hung in the air, dark and suffocating to those who breathed its noxious fumes.

No structures remain of the golden time before the war, save the Fort of Sikandra—and no written tablets survive to tell us what the world looked like then. Everything burned, and what didn't burn was looted by survivors, and what wasn't looted succumbed to the wind and rain of the centuries that followed. We have no monument to these men and women of long ago.

Except their guns. Kalashiks do not erode with time. They glow darkly, as if new. Dust will not settle on their smooth flanks. They

sit in our underground chamber in a gleaming row, waiting to be picked up and used again.

But we will never commit that sin. This is the injunction that our forefathers laid upon us: guard them well, but do not touch them. Do not even look upon them, or you will be in their thrall.

This is what we know: a kalashik can fire fifty rounds per second. It does not need to be reloaded. There is a replicating mechanism within the chambers of the weapon that constantly replenishes the ammunition, drawing energy for this task from its surroundings, or perhaps from its handler. A drawing made a hundred and twenty years ago by one of the more gifted elders of our clan partially reveals its inner structure.

This is what we guess: the metal of the kalashik is telepathic, like kalishium, but in a deformed way. The metal was made with evil intent and that evil lives on in the machines, twisting the minds of all but the strongest who attempt to wield their power. It is said that the machines are haunted, that they carry the memory of all the men and women they have killed.

Perhaps the truth is even stranger than that. Perhaps the machines are living beings, immortals that will outlast the human race. Or maybe they are just artifacts, and their power exists only in our imagination.

The fact of their perpetual existence remains, a bane to our peaceful way of life, a threat to the balance we have established in the long years after the war. It is said that a time will come when these weapons will leave the world forever, at the hands of one who commands the destiny of the human race. But even the wisest cannot see how or when that will happen.

CHAPTER 18

NIGHT IN KHUR

The wind screamed and battered the tent. Kyra's teeth chattered as she tried to dig herself deeper into the layers of rugs that made up her bed. The stove was burning and she wore every scrap of clothing that she had, but she was still cold.

How did the Marksmen sleep every night with the wind wailing in their ears and the cold seeping into their bones? For that matter, how did they live in what must surely be the most desolate place in Asiana? There was nothing but sand and rock, sun and wind, for miles around. The little grove and the shrubs planted on the dune only emphasized the barrenness of the desert, and the absurdity of trying to grow anything in it. The vast emptiness hurt the eyes and you wanted to look anywhere but *there*, at that distant horizon, the towering dunes and pale sky. You wanted to consider anything but *this*, that you were stuck in a freezing desert and your only hope of returning home was to defeat the most feared Markswoman of Asiana in single combat.

Kyra closed her eyes and moaned. Ten days of lessons with

Rustan and all she had to show for it was a scattering of bruises in all sorts of interesting hues. She had yet to last more than a few minutes on her feet sparring with her reluctant teacher. Toward the end of the first week, Rustan had thrown up his hands in exasperation and said that he hoped she was better at wielding a katari than her hands as a weapon, otherwise he didn't see her surviving long enough against Tamsyn for it to even be called a duel.

It was galling. Kyra was not among the best at Hatha-kala in the Order of Kali, not by a long shot, but she had thought she knew how to fight. That was before she saw how Rustan moved, the way his limbs seemed to blur with speed as he attacked, evaded, or parried her blows. Of course, she knew that he was Ishtul's assistant and was exceptionally talented in combat, but she still didn't understand how it was possible for him to be so young and yet so skilled. It normally took several years of dedication to reach a level of proficiency in dueling. But not even the elders of Khur—save Ishtul and Barkav—could have stood against Rustan.

Ten days in this hellish place, and Kyra longed for the wooded slopes and tumbling streams of Ferghana with an ache that was almost physical. She missed Elena's gentle voice and Nineth's cheerful grin. She missed the vast, womb-like silence of the caves at night. She missed the ancient mulberry tree outside the caves of Kali, and the small pool surrounded by cherry trees not far off, where she used to bathe. Washing in half a bucket of freezing well water was *not* the same thing.

Most of all, Kyra missed riding Rinna, letting the mare gallop across the valley, fast as the wind, light as a leaf.

Was Rinna being looked after? Did she miss Kyra? What about Akhtar, had he made it back to the caves safely? Of course, thinking of Akhtar reminded her of Shirin Mam, and what she had seen in the secret Hub—how she had lost time. A familiar nausea welled up in her. She longed to confide in someone, to tell them what she had experienced.

Still more did she long to unburden herself of what Astinsai had revealed about her mother and Kai Tau. Now that some days had passed since that first, terrible night, she had begun to disbelieve the story, even though she knew the katari mistress would not tell an outright lie. Perhaps Astinsai was mistaken in some crucial way that would change the whole story. She wished Shirin Mam were still alive so she could demand the details from her.

There were times when she had almost confided in Rustan. Exacting and stern he might be, but there was something about him that made her feel she could trust him with her innermost fears and secrets. Perhaps because it appeared that he was troubled by secrets of his own. He rarely joined the others during mealtimes, and she'd noticed the way his mouth hardened and his dark gaze turned inward, in those quiet moments when he had given her a set of moves to practice, and settled down to meditate. These were the moments when she found herself on the verge of opening up to him. And might he not have knowledge of his own to share, especially about Kai Tau?

That Kai had once been a Marksman of Khur was almost as unbelievable as the claim that he had been her mother's lover, but it would explain what Astinsai had said about something being "owed" to her. Was this why the elders had allowed her to stay with them, and assigned one of their best to help her train for the duel with Tamsyn? Did they think they had some sort of debt to her, and it would be so easily repaid?

The tent flap seemed to untie itself. Kyra leaped up, heart pounding, as a cold rush of wind gusted through the small space, sending the stove flame dancing.

A tousled head ducked inside and a familiar voice said, "Good evening, gorgeous one."

Kyra lay back and groaned. "Shurik, you gave me such a fright! What are you doing here?"

Shurik crawled in and tied the flailing tent flap closed with practiced ease. He sat down and cocked his head, grinning at her.

"Seeing if you're all right. This is the first night since you arrived that we have a bit of wind, and I thought you might be awake."

"A bit of wind," repeated Kyra in disbelief. "I'm thankful it hasn't blown the tent away and me with it."

"That happens sometimes in spring and early summer," said Shurik. "Eight years ago we had such a storm that we had to take shelter in Akal-shin. We hid in a crevice while the wind screamed around us. It took everything we had: tents, wind-breaks, shrubs, even some of the camels. But this hardly ever happens later in the year. There's no need to worry."

"Well, thank you for the words of comfort," said Kyra drily. "Now if you have satisfied yourself that I am alive and well, perhaps you will leave? I don't know what the elders would do if they found you in my tent at night, but I wouldn't want to be around to watch it happen."

Shurik put a hand on his heart. "For you I will risk the wrath of all the elders of Khur, dead and alive."

He tried to say this in a dramatic whisper, but the effect was somewhat spoiled by his having to shout to be heard above a particularly loud screech of wind.

Kyra looked at him with a mixture of exasperation and amusement. It had taken Shurik all of three days to convince himself that he was in love with her, the Kanun be damned. She liked him, of course, and he was a good-looking boy with his curly brown hair and merry smile. But she had been as discouraging as it was possible to be without hurting his feelings. The rules about chastity and obedience might be in place only to lend weight to the text of the Kanun, but she had not made her vows to Shirin Mam lightly. Besides, he was young—the youngest Marksman in the Order of Khur. He had taken down his first mark with Rustan while rescuing a caravan bound for Kashgar from a band of nomadic outlaws, but he'd confessed Barkav hadn't assigned him any marks since then—a fact that clearly rankled.

"Tell me what's troubling you." Shurik stretched out next to her and leaned his head on his arms, gazing at her out of warm brown eyes.

Kyra moved a few inches away from him. His nearness made her feel a bit awkward. Not that she was the least bit attracted to him, she told herself, but she didn't want him getting any ideas.

"What makes you think I'm troubled?" she said. "I mean, apart from the fact that I'm probably going to get sliced in half by Tamsyn's blade."

It was the wrong thing to say.

Shurik frowned, the change in his face from sunny to dark so abrupt that she involuntarily moved another inch away from him.

"I won't let you do this," he said. "Throwing your life away will do no good to your Order. And you *will* be throwing your life away, if what I hear from Rustan is correct."

"What have you heard from Rustan?" demanded Kyra, ignoring his peremptory tone.

Shurik waved a hand. "Oh, that you are not ready. Perhaps if you trained for ten years, you would be a match for such a one as Tamsyn Turani. But now, he says, you are like a child playing with fire, who won't know until it's much too late that fire can burn."

Kyra sat up, the cold forgotten in her anger. Rustan thought she was like a child?

"I know about fire," she said. "I know about death. Far more than you and your precious friend can possibly imagine. Dying doesn't frighten me."

"Hey, don't talk like that," protested Shurik, looking wounded. "If you die, what will happen to me? I'll have to run away and become a hermit or something."

Kyra smiled unwillingly. "You're already a hermit," she reminded him. "You live in the middle of a desert. There's nowhere to run."

Shurik gave a deep sigh. "And to think I was content with my lot until I laid eyes on you."

"You do talk nonsense." Kyra gathered her rug more closely around herself.

"It's the truth," insisted Shurik. "All I ever wanted was to be a good Marksman. Now all I want to do is scoop you up in my arms and take you far, far away from here, to a place where no one can follow us."

"Shurik," warned Kyra, "behave yourself. What would Barkav say if he could hear you talking like that?"

"He'd have him doing penances from sunup to sundown, and push-ups in between," said a dry voice, and for the second time that night Kyra nearly jumped out of her skin.

It was Rustan. He had come in so quietly that neither of them had heard him. Now that Kyra thought about it, the wind's roar had slowly muted to a distant moan. Their voices must have carried beyond the tent. The realization heated her cheeks. How much had Rustan heard?

"And what are *you* doing here?" she demanded.

Rustan held out a small glass bottle filled with golden-green liquid. "I was walking and heard voices, and thought I'd give you this. Astinsai's spineleaf oil works well for muscular aches and bruises." He glanced at Shurik and his tone became cooler. "I trust I was not interrupting anything."

Shurik, who had sat up when Rustan entered, lay down again with his arms crossed behind his head. "Maybe you were and maybe you weren't," he said. "But I hope you're leaving soon."

"He most certainly is," snapped Kyra, "and so are you. I need to sleep and this is my tent, not a guesthouse. In future you will ask permission before you enter—*both* of you."

She stood up and pointed a finger at the entrance of the tent, ignoring Shurik's injured expression. They left, Rustan not even glancing at her as he flicked the tent flap away and stepped out.

Kyra bent down and tied the flap with a double binding knot. *Let's see them untie that one.* She shook her head in exasperation. *Men.* Thought they could walk in on her whenever they wanted, say whatever came into their arrogant heads, and stroll out without even an apology. Give her spineleaf oil for her bruises, would he? She picked up the little bottle Rustan had left behind and glared at it before tossing it into a corner. Serve them right if they were caught leaving her tent by one of the elders, preferably by Ghasil. He didn't like her at all, and he would pounce on any Marksman he thought was getting too familiar with her.

Kyra damped down the stove—the tent seemed warmer somehow—and lay back, still seething. She closed her eyes, trying to empty her mind. What had Shirin Mam said? A well-trained Markswoman should not need more than four hours of sleep a day. Well, she didn't have more than four hours before dawnlight anyway, so she didn't have much of a choice. A few hours and Rustan would once again be standing in front of her, flaunting his infinitely advanced dueling skills.

This thought was so irritating that her eyes flew open. She stared at the roof, at the round patch of night sky visible through the smoke hole, and wished with all her heart that she could for once knock Rustan down and wipe that superior smile off his face. Not that he smiled much, she had to admit. Most of the time he seemed to be gritting his teeth in an effort not to yell at her. Which was just as bad. Thought she was like a child playing with fire, did he? She'd show him. She'd win that duel and make him eat his words, and drink that bottle of spineleaf oil too.

❧

Rustan walked out into the cold night, trying to calm his mind. The wind had died down and the tents were dark. There was no light except the light of the stars. Marksmen conserved their fuel for when it was really needed: the heart of winter, when the cold could freeze the breath in your lungs, the words on your lips.

It was quiet and still and everyone was asleep except for that idiot scrambling after him, making enough noise to wake the dead.

"I don't know why you had to come in and ruin everything," Shurik muttered. "Another minute and she might have let me kiss her."

Rustan snorted. "Another minute and she might have punched you, more likely. Have you taken leave of all good sense, or just most of it?"

"Maybe I have. But she's so pretty. Don't you think she's pretty?"

"Not half as pretty as you will be after a switching," said Rustan. "I don't understand what's gotten into you and the apprentices, mooning after her like a bunch of camel-boys. Don't think the elders don't see what's happening. You're digging a pit to bury yourself."

"Don't lump me with the apprentices!" snapped Shurik. As the youngest Marksman in the Order, who had achieved his first mark more by accident than design, he did sometimes get lumped with the apprentices, and this was a sore point with him.

"Then don't act like them," Rustan retorted. "Don't forget who you are."

"I know who I am," said Shurik. "But who are *you*? My friend went to Tezbasti to take down a mark, and a stranger came back in his skin."

Rustan wheeled around to face him, anger and sadness building up until they wanted to burst out of him in a corrosive flood. But he managed to tamp them down. *Not Shurik's fault*, he reminded himself. Shurik was hurt and puzzled by the loss of his best friend. And didn't Rustan too miss those easy days of companionship and laughter? Wasn't his anger directed more at himself than at his friend, who had only pointed out the facts, and given voice to his pain?

Rustan forced himself to relax. "I'm sorry," he said quietly. "Perhaps you're right. I am different from who I was when I left that morning. Everything we do changes us, for good or ill. But I still remember the vows I made to my Order. Do you?"

He turned before Shurik could respond, and walked away without a backward glance. He could feel Shurik's eyes following him, and he almost paused. But what could he have said? The truth would only hurt, him to speak of it, and Shurik to hear it. And so he continued walking—past the tents and the grove, out into the dune field beyond.

When Rustan had walked far enough away that the grove of shrubs had melded with the dark shadows behind him, he sat down on a boulder and looked up at the star-studded sky.

He raked a hand through his hair and pressed it against the tense muscles of his neck. He had known fatigue before, but nothing like this soul-deadening sense of hopelessness, this surety that no matter what he did, he could change nothing. His very existence was meaningless. Everything he had worked and trained for, all the hours spent meditating in the grove or dueling in the sun—none of it mattered. The dead stayed dead, no matter how much he regretted the past.

The face of the innocent man he had killed floated in front of him once more—but now it was superimposed by another face, older than he remembered, but with the same serenity, the same smile.

He jerked to his feet, startled, but the vision changed and now it was Kyra's face in front of him, empty-eyed and blood-stained.

"No!" he choked out, holding his hand up to ward it away. The apparition vanished, leaving him alone in the dark.

Rustan collapsed on the boulder. The end was already written, with or without him. Kyra would die, Shurik would be heartbroken, and the Order of Khur would be even more isolated than before. And he—he would get no answers from the woman who had once promised him that she would acknowledge him to the world.

CHAPTER 19

WORDS OF POWER

She sensed the brilliance before her eyes were fully open. Even so, Kyra was almost blinded by the white light. She didn't know where she was—no longer in her tent at the camp of Khur, for sure.

Gradually the light resolved itself into the shape of a narrow bridge curving over a dark canyon. At the other end of the bridge stood the tall towers and white domes that she had seen once—it seemed so long ago—with Shirin Mam. A huge silver disc hung unsupported in the blue sky. The sun shone fierce and bright.

Anant-kal. How did she get here? Fear rose within her chest and she backed away from the bridge. How to get back to her own world? Perhaps she was only dreaming.

"*Only* dreaming?" A beloved voice echoed across the canyon. "Never ignore dreams, child. They may be what save your life."

At the other end of the gossamer-thin bridge was a gray-haired figure clad in black. *Shirin Mam.*

Kyra picked up her robes and ran. She forgot her fear of

the unsupported bridge and the bottomless chasm below. She forgot her unease at the strangeness of this world. She had eyes only for her teacher, clad in those familiar black robes, looking exactly as she had the day she'd died. Kyra's feet flew over the delicate metal tracery of the bridge. "Mother, wait for me," she called.

But Shirin Mam turned and walked away from the bridge. By the time Kyra reached the other side, she had vanished around the corner of a broad, smooth road lined with purple bougainvillea. Kyra raced down the road, determined not to let her get away.

Now that she was *in* the city, she couldn't help noticing that the towers seemed even taller than they had from across the bridge. Some of the structures were linked halfway up with transparent tubes. A wide metal rail curved across the sky like a giant question mark. Interspersed with the towers were massive, dome-shaped buildings resting on fluted columns and decorated with ornate marble sculptures.

But the city wasn't all glass and metal and stone. Woven through the buildings were lush gardens and fountains, as if the builders had known the importance of greenery to the human soul. Even some of the towers were draped with verdant foliage.

Around the bend, Kyra saw the Mahimata disappear into one of the huge towers, and quickened her pace. She caught a flash of gray on her left, and her skin prickled the way it had when wyr-wolves had appeared as she fled the caves of Kali. She and Shirin Mam were not alone here.

But Kyra did not pause to investigate. She sprinted to the metal door at the base of the tower. It slid open and she stepped into a small, blue-walled room, illuminated by a harsh light.

The door closed and the floor beneath her vibrated. It was like being inside a Transport Chamber, only smaller and more claustrophobic. But before her fears had time to coalesce, the wall in front of her melted away and a ray of light pierced her eyes.

Kyra stepped into the light and drew a sharp breath. She was in a white, marble-floored hall, so vast that she could barely see the other end. Carved stone pillars reached up to a distant ceiling. Diamond-shaped windows glittered in the sunlight.

And there, in the middle of that vast space, stood Shirin Mam. The symbol of Kali gleamed on her breast. Her hair was gathered behind in a neat bun. She looked for all the world as if she was about to give a class in Mental Arts.

Kyra moved forward eagerly, almost tripping over her robes in her hurry to reach Shirin Mam before she could disappear again.

Shirin Mam held up a warning hand. "Not too close. You will see me better from a distance."

Kyra came to a halt a few feet away from the Mahimata. Sure enough, Shirin Mam seemed less solid somehow, almost translucent, her edges wavering.

"Are you a ghost?" she whispered.

Shirin Mam gave a short laugh. "Look at yourself."

Kyra looked down and swallowed. She could see through her body to the floor below.

"So I'm not really here?" she said.

"Of course you are. But your physical self is elsewhere, and your katari knows it."

"What is this place?" Kyra looked around the hall. "Is it always daylight here?"

Shirin Mam shrugged. "This is simply a place I have been

drawn to, an aspect of *Anant-kal* that I think is safer than most. I imagine that this hall we are standing in existed a long time ago, and its form is embedded in the memory of my blade. As the mistress of my blade, I have some degree of control here. That is why I have brought you here, for one last lesson."

"But . . ." began Kyra.

"But I am dead?" said Shirin Mam. "What of it?"

Kyra looked at her in mute appeal.

Finally Shirin Mam relented. "We are in the mind and memory of my blade, which you have so tenderly placed under your pillow. It does not matter whether I am alive or dead in the physical world. My soul is imprinted on my katari, and it has drawn you here."

"Then I can see you again, whenever I need to?" said Kyra, a bubble of happiness rising within her.

"It is not that simple," said Shirin Mam. "This is something I planned on doing when I was still alive." Seeing Kyra's defeated expression, she said robustly, "Come, there is no time for idle chatter. Walk with me."

Kyra fell into step beside her and they walked down the hall. Was Shirin Mam going to take her through some advanced form of katari duel that would help her defeat Tamsyn? But to practice they would need their kataris. Kyra's hands were empty and so were Shirin Mam's.

"Observe the pillars," commanded Shirin Mam. "There are thirty-six, eighteen on each side. Look closely; there are carvings on each of them."

Kyra obediently looked at the pillars. The carvings were strange; one showed a woman—vaguely familiar—wrestling an enormous fanged serpent. Another showed the same woman holding a long, slim blade over the bent heads of a row of kneeling men and women. Kyra frowned. It was clearly a Markswoman, but who did she remind her of, with her rippling dark hair, triumphant smile, and that elongated katari that could almost be a sword?

The answer came to her in a burst of understanding. "These are carvings of the Goddess Kali."

"Perhaps," said Shirin Mam. "Do you admire my artistry?"

Kyra stopped short. "You made these? But *how*? Our physical selves are elsewhere, you said."

"*Nothing* is here in the physical sense," said Shirin Mam. "That does not make it any less real. I told you that I have some degree of control in this place. I have been here many times and shaped it to the best of my abilities. Remember every aspect of this hall, for you may wish to return here one day without my aid."

Kyra tried to do as she was told, but she was quite sure she wouldn't want to return to this eerie world without Shirin Mam. They had reached the other end of the hall and she dragged her eyes away from the last carving, a particularly horrible one of a three-headed monster with drooling fangs. The heads resembled those of wyr-wolves—*hungry* wyr-wolves, contemplating a meal.

"Each of these thirty-six carvings represents a word of power in the ancient tongue," said Shirin Mam. "It is your task to remember each word, the pronunciation as well as the tone. The price of error is high. The wrong word can bring death."

"*Thirty-six* words?" Kyra swallowed. The most that any young Markswoman usually knew was three or four, and even then, only the safest ones. Navroz Lan herself would not know more than ten or eleven. Words of power were a secret, passed on from one Mahimata to the next. Shirin Mam was showing great trust in her. "I am honored, Mother."

"Look, child." Shirin Mam stood next to the image of the three-headed monster. "The carvings will help you remember. Fix all the little details of the images in your mind. The word you need will spring forth when you summon the right image."

Kyra stared hard at the image of the three-headed monster, wishing that Shirin Mam could have picked something a little less terrifying. Kali sat astride the monster, her bare legs gripping its scaly hide. The Goddess looked into the distance with remote eyes.

Shirin Mam leaned toward her. "Now listen well to what I say, but concentrate on staying where we are. *Trishindaar.*"

The word reverberated inside Kyra's skull. The hall swam out of focus and she had the strangest sensation that she was surrounded by water. She opened her mouth to speak, but only bubbles escaped her lips. Suddenly, she couldn't breathe. She tried to move, but her limbs were too heavy and an oppressive weight pressed down on her chest, trapping her. Kyra flailed and fought her rising panic. Where was her teacher?

Shirin Mam had said to concentrate on staying where they were. And they were in a hall, weren't they? A hall with thirty-six pillars and a smooth marble floor.

Kyra shut her eyes and remembered the hall, forcing her mind to think of it and nothing else, forcing down her panic. The floor slowly solidified beneath her feet. She opened her eyes and exhaled, shaky with relief. She was back in the hall. Shirin Mam stood next to her, watching her.

"What—what does that word mean?" asked Kyra, hoping that Shirin Mam would not repeat it aloud.

"Look at the carving," said the Mahimata, instead of answering her. "What do you think the creature represents?"

"Kali is the demon-slayer. Perhaps this is a demon she has conquered?" Kyra hazarded.

"You are too literal," said Shirin Mam, "but that is one way of looking at it. Actually, the creature represents time. The three heads stand for the past, the present, and the future. Kali is beyond the reach of time and so too is the Markswoman who uses this word of power."

"I don't understand," whispered Kyra.

"You will," said Shirin Mam. Kyra wanted to ask for an explanation, but her teacher had already walked to the next pillar.

The next carving was even more ghastly than the previous one. A fire raged through a field, ravaging people and animals alike. Their faces and bodies were distorted, melting into one another. In the middle of the field Kali—untouched by the flames—stood in a familiar pose. Her right hand was raised in benediction. Her left hand clutched the severed, blackened head of a demon.

Shirin Mam pressed her lips together, disapproving. Then she gave a fierce grin and said, *"Agnisthil."*

And now Kyra was *in* the carving, screaming and twisting as the flames burned her flesh.

"Focus," came Shirin Mam's sharp voice. "Fix the hall in your mind and you will return to it."

Once more Kyra shut her eyes. But it was difficult to ignore the searing of her flesh and the thin, screaming sounds from her own throat. *It's not real*, she told herself. *It's the hall that's real.*

By the time she made it back, she was panting with the effort it had taken to wrench herself away from the flames.

"If you'd rather not go on . . ." said Shirin Mam softly.

"Do I have a choice?" demanded Kyra.

"You always have a choice," said the Mahimata. "The only binds are those that you lay on yourself, or those that you allow to be laid on you."

"What about you?" said Kyra before she could stop herself. "Did you *allow* yourself to be killed? If so, it was a poor choice."

Kyra expected Shirin Mam to deny this, or scold her for her impertinence. But Shirin Mam only looked at her, a little sadly, and Kyra grew warm with shame. "I'm sorry, Mother. Please go on with your lesson. What does the word—the word you said—what does it do?"

"It is the cleansing fire which destroys falsehoods and shows you the truth. Not to be used lightly, for the truth can hurt you worse than those flames did."

Shirin Mam walked to the next pillar. Kyra followed, apprehensive, but knowing that she did have a choice and she had chosen to continue with this lesson.

They went from pillar to pillar, image to image, and every word of power that Shirin Mam spoke snatched Kyra from the hall and threw her into a world of horror. She fell into the depths of an abyss, was trampled in the middle of a battlefield, and tossed by the giant waves of a dark, turbulent sea. She even struggled to emerge from a grave, choking as her mouth and nose filled with dirt. Gradually she got better at fixing the hall in her mind and was able to return to it more quickly. But by the time they came to the last pillar, she was trembling with fatigue and dizziness.

The last carving was innocuous, almost pleasant in comparison to the others. It was simply the carving of a door, plain and unadorned. Kyra stopped, and terror wrapped its fingers around her throat.

"No more," she said. "Please."

"One more," said the Mahimata, her voice implacable. "The word is *Tamam-shul*."

The hall vanished and nothing came to replace it. Kyra floated, a tiny speck in the vast emptiness of the universe. From somewhere came the distant, emotionless thought: *I have been here before*—and—*I am dead*.

Time passed, or perhaps it didn't. There was no way to tell.

A grating voice disturbed the darkness: "Come back."

No, thought Kyra. She floated farther, trying to get away from the voice. It was peaceful here.

"The hall, Kyra. Remember the hall." The voice was full of urgency.

What hall? Kyra tried to remember. It was hard to care, in the womb-like nothingness of this place, about the world that existed beyond it.

"Kyra, remember your blade."

Blade? Yes, she did have a blade. She had killed a man with it. She had plunged it into his heart, sending him to this same emptiness in which she now floated.

But wait, *she* wasn't dead yet. What was she doing here?

With sickening clarity, Kyra remembered the door in the secret Hub. She fought against the darkness, limbs flailing as she tried to claw her way out of it. The darkness didn't want to let her go. It held on, tendrils reaching into her nose, mouth, and eyes, choking and blinding her. Finally she wrested herself out of its grasp and fell to the floor, sweating and weeping.

The Mahimata knelt in front of her. "I almost lost you there. You didn't want to return."

Kyra took a deep breath, trying to calm herself. "It is that door," she rasped. "The third door of the secret Hub."

Shirin Mam bowed her head. "For each of us it is different. For you, a door. For me, it was a blade. This word of power tells us how we will leave the world."

Kyra sat up, brushing away her tears. "So you did die by a blade. I think I know whose hand held it, Mother, but I have no proof. Tell me, who killed you?"

Shirin Mam hesitated. "The Mahimata of Kali."

"Tamsyn. Just as I thought," said Kyra, and although Shirin Mam had affirmed her belief, despair flooded her. Had a small part of her hoped that she was wrong? That Tamsyn was not a monster, and that, perhaps, Shirin Mam had died a natural death?

Yes, of course. And then Kyra could have absolved herself of her own guilt in the matter—maybe even gone back to her Order.

But there would be no absolution now, not until she had defeated her teacher's murderess in a public duel. Kyra clenched her hands and despair was driven out by cold fury. "I am going to kill her, Mother. I will avenge you, I swear it. But why couldn't you see through her? Why can't the *others* see through her?"

"We all see what we choose to," said Shirin Mam. "Do not imagine that you know everything. Although I must say that you have done well today."

Despite the fact that she had been drowned, buried, trampled, burned, and finally killed off by this lesson—never mind that she wasn't even physically present—Kyra felt a glow of accomplishment. Shirin Mam rarely complimented a student, and to be told that she had "done well" was praise indeed.

"Of course," continued Shirin Mam, "you won't actually be able to use the words of power you have learned, not yet."

"But, Mother," protested Kyra, "you said that if I remembered the images I should be able to summon the right word. If I cannot use them, what was the purpose of this lesson?"

"Remembering them is only half the battle," said Shirin Mam. "You actually have to *need* the use of the word as well. And now," she added, rising from the floor, "it is time I left you."

"Wait." Kyra scrambled up. "There are many things I must tell you."

As briefly as possible, Kyra recounted the events that had taken place after Shirin Mam's death, and the strange things she had seen behind the doors of the secret Hub.

Shirin Mam listened with every outward show of patience and attentiveness, but Kyra sensed that she was not interested in much of what she had to say.

"I am with the Order of Khur now," she finished, "and Rustan is teaching—oh, not exactly teaching, more *practicing* with me—anyway, he's helping me get ready for the duel with Tamsyn. She was so angry that I got away with your blade, Mother, I'm sure she'll be happy for a chance to kill me in full view of the Sikandra Fort assembly."

"Rustan? Is that the name of the Marksman who is teaching you?" said Shirin Mam idly, seemingly unconcerned about the possibility of her pupil dying at the hands of her bloodthirsty rival.

"Yes," said Kyra impatiently. "And he's quite annoying. But what about the duel, do you have any advice for me? I don't want to die."

"There are worse things than dying," said Shirin Mam. "Death is just another door to walk through."

Kyra swallowed. For a while, she'd almost forgotten that Shirin Mam was dead. She cleared her throat. "Still, I'd rather live, at least until I have fulfilled my vow. Is there any way I can defeat Tamsyn?"

"If you can conquer yourself, you can conquer anyone," said Shirin Mam. "That's the best advice I can give you. Also, beware of *Anant-kal*. We are not the only ones who walk here."

Kyra remembered the flash of gray she had seen. "Who . . . ?" she began, but Shirin Mam interrupted her:

"One last thing."

Kyra leaned forward. "Yes?"

"Give my katari to this Rustan before you go to Sikandra."

"What?" Kyra stared at Shirin Mam in consternation. "Why should I give it to *him*?"

"It is no longer your burden," said Shirin Mam. "And he will have need of it."

"But if I give him your katari, I won't be able to talk to you anymore," said Kyra, striving to stay calm. The Mahimata's blade was the only link she had with her teacher. She had no right to it, but the thought of giving it up filled her with dismay.

Shirin Mam smiled. "You'll be able to talk to me as long as you remember what I have taught you," she said. She turned and the hall became dimmer, as if daylight was slipping away outside the windows.

"Wait," cried Kyra, desperate. "What about what I saw in

the Hub? Was that you behind the second door? What did it mean?"

Shirin Mam walked away, fading with the light. "Ask Felda," she said, her voice distant, as if it came from another world. "She knows far more about Transport than I ever did."

"Shirin Mam!" shouted Kyra. "What do you know about my mother and Kai Tau?"

But the hall was empty and Kyra was alone. She could have screamed with frustration. The walls around her began to dissolve, and the light went out of the world.

CHAPTER 20

THE HAND OF KALI

It was a golden late-summer day, the kind that made Nineth wish the warm season would last all year long. If Kyra were here, they would have gone riding every spare moment that they had.

No, don't think of Kyra. Not with Tamsyn standing right in front of you. Nineth emptied her mind and tried to focus on the lesson. Tried not to think about the disastrous events of yesterday, and what punishment Tamsyn might have in store for her.

Nineth hadn't planned on running away. Some half-formed idea of following Kyra's footsteps had taken hold of her; she'd gone to the horse enclosure and saddled Rinna. The worst of it was that she hadn't even left the enclosure before Baliya arrived and made her dismount. Nineth had felt like a complete fool.

Baliya would have reported her to Tamsyn right away. The longer Tamsyn made her wait for the penance, the worse Nineth felt.

They stood in a meadow not far from the caves. Chintil was testing them, and Tamsyn had stopped by to observe the class.

She seemed to think they were lagging behind in Hatha-kala somehow, especially the apprentices.

"Noor Sialbi," barked Chintil. "Name the twelve hands of Hatha-kala."

"Single Katari, Double Katari, Spear, Sword, Short Stick, Long Stick, Empty Hands, Tiger Prowl, Monkkat Dance, Breaking Bones, Vital Points, and Inner Strength," recited the small, round Markswoman.

Nineth, standing just behind her, groaned inwardly. Why couldn't she have gotten such a simple question that even a novice could have answered? But no, Chintil would see to it that Nineth got the most difficult question of all. After all, Tamsyn was watching.

Sure enough, the tall, strapping elder turned to her and said, "Nineth Dan, what are the five different kinds of vital points?"

That wasn't fair! Only Markswomen learned about the pressure points of the human body. Nineth racked her brain for what she could remember about the subject. "Skin, bones, nerves, joints, and . . . blood vessels."

"Correct," said Chintil, sounding both surprised and pleased.

Nineth sagged with relief as the elder turned her attention to another Markswoman. Thank the Goddess for Elena and her erudite discussions on the human body. But Tamsyn fixed an icy glare on her, and Nineth's feeling of relief evaporated. *Soon*, that glare seemed to say. *Soon you will learn the penalty for defying your Mahimata*.

Chintil's stentorian voice broke into her thoughts:

"Sheathe your blades and fall into pairs for Empty Hands practice. You may choose whatever stance and technique you wish. Your goal will be to throw your opponent, nothing more."

There was a general stirring and to Nineth's dismay, she found herself paired off with the loathsome Akassa.

Akassa dropped into the Elephant pose, a basic defense posture. Nineth eyed her warily before moving into Charging Boar, a simple yet effective hand-and-foot combination that could destabilize any opponent.

But Nineth stumbled in mid-kick and cried out with pain. Something had slashed her left shin. She saw the telltale glimpse of a bright blade before it disappeared up Akassa's sleeve. She hadn't sheathed her blade. The cheat! Nineth felt a surge of anger and, ignoring the pain in her left leg, stepped forward with her right foot, pivoted, and grabbed Akassa's back under the arms.

The smug look disappeared from Akassa's face as she tried and failed to counter the unexpected rear throw. Nineth flung her flat on the ground and rose, dusting her hands.

"Well done, Nineth," commented Chintil as she passed the pair.

Tamsyn pursed her lips in a thin line. "But not to be tried except as a last resort. Such a move is easily countered. Akassa, next time step to the side and answer with a reverse hip throw. Perhaps we elders can demonstrate, Chintil?"

"What?" said Chintil, clearly thrown off-balance. She stared at Tamysn for a moment, pursing her lips. "Well, all right."

Tamsyn stepped forward. "Please make the move that Nineth did."

A look passed over Chintil's face, there and gone in an instant. But it twisted something inside Nineth. She hoped Chintil wouldn't get hurt; what she really wanted was for the Hatha-kala Mistress to teach Tamsyn a lesson. But that, she knew, was too much to expect.

Chintil stepped forward, pivoted, and grabbed Tamsyn under the arms. Tamsyn slid sideways with a single step, smooth as a snake. She dropped her hips, grabbed Chintil by the waist, and fell backward, throwing Chintil sideways. Chintil landed with a thud that made Nineth wince. Everyone was perfectly still.

Tamsyn rose, graceful as ever. "See, children? I hope you have all learned something." She turned to Chintil and said in a concerned tone of voice, "I hope you are not hurt, Elder?"

"Not at all," said Chintil calmly, getting up. "Thank you for the demonstration. Now, if you will excuse us, I should get on with the class."

Tamsyn's teeth flashed. "Certainly. Please meet me in my chamber afterward."

She left, and Chintil continued with the class, but Nineth could tell that her heart wasn't quite in it.

"I don't see why we have to lift a finger to help the Order of Valavan." Tamsyn sounded bored as she gazed at the four elders standing in front of her. She had not invited them to sit—indeed, there *was* no place for them to sit in the Mahimata's cell except the floor. Tamsyn herself was behind her desk, playing with a linen-wrapped package—the same package she had dangled in front of Navroz, claiming that it was from Shirin Mam. Three scented candles burned at the desk, casting their yellow, uncertain light on the Mahimata's masklike face.

"It's not about helping the Order of Valavan," said Navroz. "It's a matter of responsibility. Shirin Mam gave the order to execute Kai's eldest son. Now he is amassing an army and using the dark weapons to kill innocent people. Perhaps the death of his son unhinged him, or perhaps he is taking revenge. He must be stopped before more people die. The Orders—*all* of them—must put away their differences to deal with this menace."

"I hope you are not referring to the Order of Khur," drawled Tamsyn. "They're nothing but a band of outlaws. Mere men, aspiring to our position."

Mumuksu frowned. "They exist, whether we wish it or not. It would be better to work with them in this case, as Kai was one of theirs."

Tamsyn leaned back and gave a humorless smile. "My point exactly," she said. "The Marksmen are unstable and dangerous and cannot be trusted. A man bonded to a blade is a perversion against the natural order of things. Besides, we don't need them. And we don't need the Order of Valavan. We can destroy the outlaws by ourselves on the condition that the Thar is recognized as ours."

The four elders stared at her, dumbfounded.

"That would be madness. Suicidal!" said Chintil. Navroz tried to catch her gaze. It was better not to display overt opposition to the new Mahimata; they would have to be more subtle if they were to have any say in the direction their Order took now. But Chintil would not look at her; her face had gone red, as if she suppressed great emotion.

"We cannot face the dark weapons on our own," said Mumuksu. "They would destroy us before we even came close to them."

"Who wants the Thar? Backward little desert full of bandits and outlaws." That last was from Felda.

Navroz groaned inwardly. She had spent hours talking with

the others before they could agree on how to present a calm and united front to the Mahimata, but Tamsyn was not making it easy for them.

Aloud she said, "There is no question of taking over any part of Valavian territory, Tamsyn. Faran Lashail would never stand for it, not if we cleaned the Deccan of every single outlaw that infests it. And what makes you think we can do this on our own? Kai is known to possess at least twelve kalashiks, and he must have amassed hundreds of more primitive weapons as well."

"It is simple, Navroz," said Tamsyn. "I am surprised that no one else has thought of it. I will present my plan at the meeting in Sikandra, and I am sure that it will be accepted. Please don't let me keep you any longer; I am sure your pupils await you." She waved her arm, signifying that the meeting was over.

"You aren't going to tell us what your plan is?" asked Felda through gritted teeth.

"Don't worry about it, my dear Felda," said Tamsyn sweetly. "Concentrate on those equations of yours—so critical to the well-being of our Order."

"You can hardly expect our cooperation if you do not tell us what you intend," said Chintil tightly.

Tamsyn laughed. "On the contrary, Chintil, I know you will cooperate fully with your Mahimata. As will the rest of you." Her voice was laced with the Inner Speech. Her dark eyes were filled with amusement. They rested on each of the four elders, one by one. When they came to Navroz they lingered a bit longer than on the others. Navroz stiffened, refusing to let slip the slightest emotion under that intrusive gaze.

Finally Tamsyn nodded, as if satisfied with what she had seen. "You may go," she said.

No one spoke until they were outside the caves. A cool breeze had sprung up, and Navroz inhaled the fresh air gratefully. An encounter with Tamsyn always left her breathless and with a pounding headache. She rubbed her temples, hoping the others wouldn't notice.

"Well, she certainly put us in our place," said Chintil.

Chintil Maya was younger than most of them, though not as young as Tamsyn, of course—and the best Hatha-kala teacher the Order had seen in generations. At one time, some fifteen years ago, Tamsyn had been her favorite pupil. That had been before Tamsyn overtook them all in both Hatha-kala and the Mental Arts, becoming second to none but Shirin Mam herself.

It was not only Tamsyn's talent, of course, that had prompted Navroz to announce her as the new Mahimata. In the shock and confusion surrounding Shirin Mam's death, it had seemed the right thing to do. Tamsyn was the Hand of Kali, the natural successor to Shirin Mam.

Now, however, Navroz was not sure that she had acted wisely. During the ceremony to initiate Tamsyn as the Mahimata, all the torches had flickered out, plunging them into darkness and dismay. It was an ill omen, a harbinger of the bleak times to come.

It was not only the debacle with Kyra, unfortunate as that was. It was the fact that Navroz was no closer to the truth of Shirin Mam's death than she had been that first night, when she saw the twisted shape of Shirin's body lying on the floor of her cell. In that moment she had the insight that nothing was as it seemed, that Shirin herself had arranged to be found like this by Kyra. But as time passed she was no closer to understanding why, or even how.

Navroz studied the faces of the other three. Gentle Mumuksu with her motherly ways, gruff Felda, who would be chagrined to know that even a novice could see past her rough exterior to the soft heart within, and capable Chintil, strong and unwavering in her convictions. How much did they know? How much did they guess?

"I have a bad feeling about the clan meeting," said Mumuksu, sitting down on the dry grass and fanning herself with a leaf despite the cool breeze. "She can undo in one day what it has taken Shirin Mam a lifetime to build. What are we going to do, Eldest?"

They all looked at Navroz expectantly.

"We do the only thing we can," said Navroz. "We wait."

The other three nodded as if she had said something of surpassing wisdom.

⁂

Nineth had been expecting the summons since yesterday evening. Still, when it came, her stomach seized. Tamsyn wanted her in her cell.

"Right away, apprentice," said Baliya. "Don't try to run away again, or I expect she *will* kill you."

"I wasn't trying to run away," said Nineth, scanning the cavern and the passages leading off from it. But there was no sign of Elena; perhaps she was helping Navroz with her healing work.

"Trying to find your friend?" said Baliya, catching her glance. "I wouldn't bother. She's in solitary meditation—a small penance for her terrible performance in Mental Arts today."

Nineth's heart sank. She followed Baliya down the corridor to the Mahimata's cell. What penance would *she* get?

They entered the Mahimata's cell and Baliya bowed. "Here she is, Mother."

"Thank you, Baliya," said Tamsyn. "You may leave. I will take care of our little runaway."

Baliya simpered and left, throwing a malignant glance in Nineth's direction.

Nineth stood in front of Tamsyn's desk, trying to slow her racing pulse. She didn't want to betray her fear. Tamsyn fed on fear, lapped it up like a cat slurping milk.

The Mahimata tapped an elongated nail on her desk. "Why were you at the paddocks yesterday evening, saddling Kyra's mare?"

Nineth licked her lips. "I wanted to exercise Rinna, Mother. No one rides her anymore."

"Indeed," said Tamsyn. "How thoughtful of you. And yet, that doesn't explain why you were carrying a sack of provisions."

Oh no. She'd forgotten about the food. "Provisions?" Nineth pretended confusion. "Oh, I asked Tarshana for some food because I had missed the midday meal. I thought I'd have a little picnic."

"You must have been *very* hungry, Nineth," said Tamsyn, "and planning a very large picnic, to need six pies and a whole loaf of walnut bread. You look surprised. Did you think anything would escape my notice? I have eyes and ears everywhere."

Of course you do, thought Nineth. *Baliya and Akassa and Selene, your spying toadies*. But she did not reply; it was better not to say anything. Tamsyn was going to punish her—the only question was how.

Tamsyn leaned back and laced her hands behind her head. She said, with a hint of the Inner Speech, "Give me your blade, Nineth."

It was the one thing Nineth had not expected. She struggled to resist the command, her mind crying in protest. But the katari slid out of her sheath and dropped onto the Mahimata's desk. She stared at it, bereft, a sob welling up in her throat.

Tamsyn smiled and picked up the blade. Nineth began to shake. Hot tears coursed down her cheeks. In that moment she hated herself. She wished she were strong, strong enough to snatch the blade and stab Tamsyn with it.

"My dear Nineth, do not be distressed," said Tamsyn. "I have only your best interests at heart. Your katari will be restored to you in due course. First, there is the small matter of penance. Running away, you see, is simply not allowed. The penalty is death. Perhaps you did not know that, having been here only five or six years? No matter. You are fortunate that Baliya prevented you from actually riding away."

"I'm sorry," whispered Nineth, her eyes on the deep blue blade in Tamsyn's hand. So close, and yet so immeasurably far from her.

"Of course you are," said Tamsyn gently. "You have been disrespectful to your Mahimata and disobeyed the most fundamental rules of the Order. Don't look anxious. There is a way to remedy your situation. An apprentice can be forgiven anything. You need not share the fate that awaits your friend Kyra. This is what I want you to do as a penance . . ."

Nineth leaned forward and tried to listen, but it was hard, with Tamsyn dangling her blade like that, just out of reach. She did the only thing she could, which was to agree with everything Tamsyn was saying. The full import of it did not hit her until she had left the caves of Kali.

CHAPTER 21

IN THE GROVE

The two kataris slashed and whirled in a lethal dance of colors. There was no need for guards, not with kalishium blades, and Kyra gave it all she had, trying to close in for the decisive thrust that would end this particular bout. But Rustan evaded her with his usual speed and grace, blocking every stab with a counter of his own. Despite the cold, sweat poured down her face and neck. They had been sparring since dawn and it was now midmorning. Kyra was hungry and thirsty and covered in cuts and bruises—all minor, of course, but they did nothing to help her mood.

Finally she lost her temper and rushed at him with her katari raised for an obvious overhead strike. Rustan blocked her with his own katari, pushed her weapon hand sharply to the right, pivoted, and secured her elbow in an armpit lock, forcing her to bend double and loosen her grip on her weapon. She hung there, gasping for breath, until he released her.

"You lost control there for a minute, but overall you're

improving," said Rustan, examining his own blade before sheathing it.

Kyra glared at him and mopped the sweat from her eyes with a torn and dusty sleeve. "You're joking," she muttered, wiping her palms on robes that were much the worse for wear after almost a month in the desert. "I have only been able to disarm you a few times."

"Yes," said Rustan. "But you make it more difficult for me all the time. If only you would anticipate me instead of reacting to me." He grinned, his teeth flashing white against his tan face.

Kyra threw up her hands in frustration. What did he think she was—a mind reader? "You keep saying that! But I cannot anticipate you. I don't know you. I don't know what you think or feel or dream. There is some small chance I could predict Tamsyn, but you—you are a stranger to me, even after all this time we have spent together."

A curious lump came in her throat. She swallowed hard and bent down as if to dust her robes so that he would not see her expression. When she straightened up, she was composed once more. But Rustan was frowning.

"I wish I could say the same about you," he said, his voice cool and hard. "After all, one does not care overmuch if a stranger lives or dies. But I do care about you. I care very much."

"That's not what I meant," said Kyra, her face heating up.

"What did you mean, Kyra Veer? What is it you wish to know about me?" He folded his arms across his chest and stared at her out of his deep blue eyes. Eyes you could fall into, if you weren't careful.

"I don't even know your clan," said Kyra after a moment, wishing fervently she had just kept her silence to begin with.

"Neither do I," said Rustan. "But I was adopted by the clan of Pusht. Barkav brought me here fourteen years ago, when I had seen but seven summers."

"Was it . . ." Kyra hesitated, then plunged ahead. "Was it hard for you? Leaving your adopted family and coming here?"

"Not as hard as it must have been for you," said Rustan, and his face softened in sympathy. "Barkav told me a little of what happened to the clan of Veer."

Here it was, the perfect moment to probe Rustan about Kai Tau. Kyra doubted he would be able to answer her questions; he would have been an infant when Kai turned renegade. But she had to try. "Do you know anything of Kai Tau?" she asked. "He's the one who killed my family. Astinsai told me he was once a Marksman." *And there is a small chance he might be my father*, she did not say—did not even want to think.

Rustan shook his head. "I don't know much. He left long before I joined the Order. I've heard that Maheshva, who was the Maji-khan of Khur at the time, recruited him from a street gang in Peking. Kai Tau was a skilled Marksman—probably still is. His blade, though . . ." He paused and considered. "Kataris are not meant for hands that have held a death-stick. It may have turned against him."

Kyra had not given a thought to the fact that a katari may have been present in the Tau camp when she took down her first mark. Because, of course, she hadn't known that Kai Tau had been a Marksman. Shirin Mam had not seen fit to share this information with her. "Maybe that's why it didn't alert Kai Tau to my presence," she said. She found herself telling Rustan about her first mark, and how close she had come to being killed herself, opening up completely for the first time in months.

"You'd think, wouldn't you, that it would make me *happy* to kill the eldest son of the man who murdered my family?" she concluded. "Instead, I could not even strike him until his hands were wrapped around my neck, squeezing the breath from my body. I wish I wasn't so weak!" Her voice was full of the frustration she'd been carrying for months, but she felt lighter after she had said that, as if confessing the doubt would make it go away.

"It's not weakness to care about a human life," said Rustan quietly. The intensity in his voice surprised her. "We are the protectors of the people, the upholders of the law. But far better to let a dozen murderers walk free than take a single innocent life." An expression of agony crossed his face as he spoke.

What are you not telling me, she thought, studying him. Aloud she said, "That doesn't make sense. Those dozen murderers could go on to kill hundreds more. You have to weigh that very real possibility against the small chance of error."

"Can you place a value on an innocent life?" he demanded, his eyes flashing.

"No," she said. The question made her uncomfortable, but she answered honestly. "But I would rather take that chance than let a murderer escape."

Rustan frowned. "That is immoral," he said.

"That is my vow," she shot back. "Both to my Order and to the memory of my clan. Perhaps if you had lived through what I did, you would feel differently."

"Perhaps if you had done what I did, *you* would feel differently," he countered.

Kyra longed to ask what he had done, but kept her mouth shut, knowing she was on the brink of an insight, or a confession from him—something that would expand her understanding of the man who stood before her, if only he would speak. She could not push him, not now.

But the moment passed and Rustan's face closed. "We can argue till we're out of words, and it makes not one whit of difference," he said. "First you need to win that duel with Tamsyn."

"You really think I've improved enough to defeat her?" The words were out before Kyra could stop them. She hadn't meant to ask him that; she didn't want him to guess the depth of her own doubts and fears.

"I have never seen the Hand of Kali fight, so I cannot answer that," said Rustan. "But you've improved enough to take on any Marksman in our Order, except Ishtul, our blademaster, and the Maji-khan himself. I think you stand a good chance, as long as you stay calm and controlled."

Kyra felt a stab of irritation. That was easy for *him* to say. She'd never seen him lose control, not once.

"What's the matter?" he asked, noticing her expression.

"Nothing," said Kyra. "Just wishing calmness and control came to me as easily as they do to you."

Rustan laughed outright at that, a genuine laugh that made her smile despite herself. "Of course they don't come easy. It's hard work. I've just had a bit more practice than you. And you're doing better than you were a month ago, both in temper and in technique."

"When I—*if* I manage to return to my Order, I'll have some new techniques to share with the others," said Kyra.

"You'll go back to your Order after the duel," said Rustan.

"If I win," said Kyra. "If I can anticipate my own teacher better than *she* anticipates me." She shook her head. "When I say it out loud, it seems impossible."

Rustan took a step toward her and grasped her shoulders, his touch warm even through her robe. "You have changed in the last month," he said, his eyes fierce. "You have learned new ways to fight, and she has not. You have the advantage, and don't forget it. Better you hide the remaining days of your life than walk into that hall thinking you're going to lose. Do you hear me, Kyra?"

His face was so close to hers, his expression so intense. Kyra had a sudden, inexplicable desire to reach out and touch his stubbled cheek with her fingertips.

Stupid, stupid. What was she thinking?

She said, fighting to keep her voice level, "I hear you, Rustan."

"Good." He released her after a moment. Was it her imagination, or was his breath slightly uneven? "Let's continue practicing after the midday meal."

She nodded, not trusting herself to speak. She lingered in the grove, waiting until he had gone before she settled down to practice Sheetali, the Cooling Breath.

CHAPTER 22

A GIRL WITH MANY QUESTIONS

A delicious aroma of vegetable stew and fresh baked bread rose from the cook tent, but Kyra hurried past it. She went straight to her own tent; mercifully, no one called out to her or asked her to join them for the midday meal. Perhaps Shurik had already started eating. She hoped so, anyway. He usually waited for her, but today her appetite was gone, for food or for company.

She ducked into the shade of her tent and drank some of the ice-cold water that she always kept in a covered pitcher beside the stove. The rest she splashed over her face and arms. She was dirty and tired and tense. There was sand in everything: hair, robes, boots, rugs. She began to comb her hair, yanking it with her fingers to get the tangles out. If by some miracle she got back to the Ferghana alive, she'd kiss the sweet grass and never leave again. Certainly she wouldn't be fool enough to end up in the company of men. What was wrong with her? Sheetali had done little to quell the tumult in her heart.

Just as she finished tying her hair, a voice called from outside, "Kyra, are you there? Astinsai wants you."

It was Jeev, one of the novices. Kyra almost growled in reply. She had avoided Astinsai since that first night—not a difficult task, since the Old One kept largely to her own tent. What did the crone want with her now?

"Jeev, please give Astinsai my deepest apologies," she said. "But I am . . ." She paused to swallow the awful taste of lying to the last living katari mistress. "I am not feeling well."

There was silence, and she could picture Jeev scratching his head. No one refused a summons from Astinsai, not even Barkav.

Finally a hesitant voice said, "Please, Kyra, I don't understand. Astinsai said to hurry up and fetch you, or she'd make me drink her bitter spineroot brew. Do come."

"In my opinion, you *all* need regular doses of bitter spineroot brew," muttered Kyra.

"What? Did you say something?"

Kyra sighed. "I'm coming."

She pushed aside the tent flap and stretched in the sun, trying to relax her limbs.

Jeev looked at her in relief. "Thanks, Kyra. I'd better get back to serving the food." He added, almost as an afterthought, "Shurik is looking for you too."

He grinned and scampered away in the direction of the communal tent.

Kyra grimaced with annoyance. All the novices and apprentices, and most of the Marksmen as well, knew about Shurik's silly infatuation with her by now. She had put a stop to his visiting her tent, and she tried to include others in their conversation at mealtimes, but it was too late. The damage had been done. And the truth was, he reminded her of Nineth, with his sunny smile and perpetual cheer. So she did like him—but not in the way he seemed to like her. Why couldn't he understand that and stop before he got into serious trouble with the elders?

Shaking her head, she made her way to Astinsai's tent at the southern edge of the settlement, keeping a wary eye out for Shurik. When she arrived at the Old One's abode, she paused. Should she ask permission to enter?

But she had no need to. "Come in," commanded a voice from within, and Kyra obeyed.

The interior was dark and smoky. The Old One was brewing something on her stove: something lethal, judging by the smell. Kyra knelt opposite her and schooled herself to stay expressionless.

"I grow blind," said Astinsai, not looking up. "But not so blind that I cannot see what is happening. What will happen."

Kyra said nothing, having resolved to stay silent unless asked a direct question.

Astinsai damped down the stove and lifted the large black iron pot with surprising ease. She poured a measure of steaming liquid into a cup, and looked up at Kyra, her eyes speculative.

"Rasaynam," she said, and proffered the cup. Kyra gaped at her in astonishment. Did the Old One mean for her to drink that awful-smelling potion? She had heard enough from the Marksmen to know what Rasaynam was, or at least what it was rumored to be: a potion to show you reality, but not a happy version of it, and never the whole of it.

"Why do you offer this to me?" she asked.

Astinsai placed the cup between them. "You are a girl with many questions, big and small. Rasaynam can show you the answers to some of them."

Kyra regarded the cup with a mixture of longing and revulsion. Yes, she had many questions. How had Tamsyn managed to kill Shirin Mam? What was the meaning of what she had seen in the secret Hub? What would be the outcome of the duel? Would she live to take revenge on the Taus for the slaughter of her clan? And—above all—what had happened between her mother and Kai Tau?

But was she ready for the answers that she might get?

Kyra wanted to reach out and quaff the contents of the cup in a single gulp. She wanted to run away from this tent and never set eyes on Astinsai again.

A long minute passed, with both impulses warring inside her. Finally she drew a deep breath and said, "I thank you for the honor you have shown me. But I am not ready for this potion of yours. Not yet."

"I thought as much," said Astinsai. She took the cup and poured its contents back into the pot. "Come to me when you are ready," she said. "When you think you have seen every-thing, when you think you have no more tears left inside. Come to me then. I'll still be around."

Kyra suppressed a shiver. She got up and bowed before leaving the tent, but Astinsai's attention had already returned to her herbs and potions.

⟨⟫

"There you are. I've been looking everywhere for you. Why did you miss the midday meal?"

Kyra gave a start as Shurik materialized by her side. She had been preoccupied after leaving Astinsai's tent and hadn't noticed where she was going. Her steps had taken her back toward the shaded grove. Shurik must have followed her in.

"I've been with Astinsai." Kyra told him what had happened, omitting the part about her being "a girl with many questions."

Shurik's face twisted in comic horror as he listened. "Don't ever drink that stuff," he warned. "Look what it did to Rustan."

Kyra stopped walking and sat down cross-legged in the shade of a jessora bush. "Rustan has drunk Rasaynam?" she said, surprised. "I thought none of the Marksmen had touched that potion in years." But even as she said it, she remembered the haunted look on his face. *Perhaps if you had done what I did, you would feel differently.*

"None but my good friend Rustan," said Shurik, sitting down next to her. "Astinsai made an exception for him, like she seems to have made for you. She must dislike you both very much."

Kyra laughed. "Don't be silly, Shurik." The katari mistress was surely above liking or disliking anyone.

"Don't drink it, okay?" said Shurik, suddenly anxious. "I couldn't bear for you to change, the way he changed."

"How did he change?" asked Kyra, glancing around to make sure no one was listening. It wasn't necessary; no one was around. The Marksmen rested in their tents after the midday meal, resuming classes and chores in the evening.

"He used to talk more and laugh more," said Shurik. "We sparred together every day. He would tell me if he had a new trick to disarm me, or if he was fed up with the food, or if he thought an elder was full of gas. Now he barely looks at me. And it's not just me. He hardly talks with anyone." He trailed his hand on the ground, clearly struggling not to betray his hurt.

"To be fair, he spends most of the daylight hours teaching me," said Kyra. "It doesn't leave much time for anything else."

"This happened before you came here," said Shurik. "Rustan was sent to take down a mark in Tezbasti. When he came back, Astinsai made him drink Rasaynam. I don't know what he saw, but it must have been bad, because he's not been the same ever since."

He gazed into the distance, his mouth compressed in a hard line.

"What do you think happened in Tezbasti?" asked Kyra, but she had begun to put two and two together. Something had gone wrong with the mark and he blamed himself for it. No wonder he was so grim all the time.

Shurik pulled at a stalk of grass and twined it around his finger. "I don't know what happened. He won't tell me. I tried to get him to talk once or twice, and had my head bitten off as a reward. But let's not talk about him anymore." He glanced at Kyra. "Let's talk about *us*. Do you think we can use the Akalshin door to get away from this place?"

Kyra stared at him in disbelief, too stunned by the turn of conversation to respond.

"We could go anywhere we wanted," he continued. "No one would be able to follow us. I wouldn't mind setting myself up on a farm somewhere, with nothing to worry about but the rain."

Despite herself, Kyra smiled. Shurik had grown up on a farm in the fertile Peral River delta, and a part of him still yearned for it, especially in this barren land where it was a struggle to grow anything.

Shurik caught her hand. "You smile. Surely you know by now how I feel for you. I love you."

Kyra withdrew her hand quickly, hot and uncomfortable. "Shurik, you do *not* love me. I happen to be the first girl you've met in ages, and so you believe yourself to be in love. What you're suggesting is crazy."

"You are not the first girl I've met," he said. "I've seen women in Yartan, Kashgar, and Tezbasti. Some were quite beautiful and I admired them from afar. I forgot their faces as soon as I left town. You are different. I see you when I close my eyes. I think of you even in my dreams." He caught her chin and drew her face to his. She gazed at him, mesmerized by the play of emotions on his face.

"Do not say I cannot love you," he whispered. "Say instead that you can learn to love me." He bent down to press his lips on hers. Kyra was so startled that a moment passed before she jerked her head away.

And looked right into Rustan's cold blue eyes. Kyra stared at him in consternation. He stood opposite them, leaning on the woody stem of an ephedra, looking as if he had swallowed some of Astinsai's bitter spineroot brew. How long had he been standing there, watching them?

I wasn't really kissing him! a part of her wanted to scream. But another part said—*What business is it of his? Let him think what he wants. It doesn't matter.*

But it did matter. It mattered when Rustan said, "I thought you wanted to continue your lessons this afternoon. It appears that I was mistaken."

He walked away, silent as he had come, as always. Kyra gazed at his retreating back in dismay, wondering if she should go after him and say that yes, she wanted to continue her lessons.

Suppose he refused? She became aware that Shurik was speaking:

". . . always interrupts us at the wrong time. It's almost as if he's spying on us. Thinks he's an elder already, I suppose. We'll be well rid of him when we're out of here."

Kyra glared at Shurik. This foolishness had gone further than she had thought possible. It was time to set the boy straight, before things got out of hand. She stood up and dusted her robe. Shurik rose and tried to embrace her again but this time she deflected his arms and stepped away with a warning look.

"You will not try to kiss me again," she said. "If you do, I'll hit you. Hard."

Shurik raised his hands, and a look of innocent protest entered his face. "I'm sorry, Kyra. I didn't mean to surprise you." His tone became warmer and he stepped toward her. "Have I told you how beautiful your eyes are? They are the color of—of the desert after rain. I could drown in them."

Kyra backed away, fighting a sudden impulse to laugh. "Stay away from me," she said severely, holding up her hand. "And listen well, because I'll only say this once. I am *not* running away with you anywhere. I have my duty, even though you seem to have forgotten yours. No more talk of love or pretty eyes. I do not love you, Shurik." Seeing his crushed expression, she added in a gentler tone, "I like you, though, and I hope we can continue being friends. But only if you give up this foolish love talk."

"If you like me, you can one day love me," said Shurik. "Don't frown. I'm not going to kiss you again. But I'm not going to stand aside and watch you die on Tamsyn's blade either. I want us to have a chance together. As long as you're safe and alive somewhere, I can bear us being apart, because I know we'll meet again. Give it up, Kyra. There must be another way for you to get back to your Order."

"There is no way other than a duel," said Kyra, exasperated. She had been over this many times, both with herself and with him. "Tamsyn *killed* Shirin Mam. She has the elders of Kali in her thrall. The only thing that protected me from her, letting me escape, was Shirin Mam's katari."

"Which you still have," Shurik pointed out, changing tack. "If you must duel Tamsyn, then use Shirin Mam's blade instead of your own. You will have a far better chance of winning."

Attractive though this idea was, Kyra had discarded it long ago. "It is not lawful to use any weapon but your own in a duel," she said. "I will leave Shirin Mam's katari in Rustan's safekeeping before going to Sikandra."

"That doesn't make sense," said Shurik. "Why would you give it to *him*? The one thing that kept you safe from the Hand of Kali!"

Kyra hesitated. How could she tell him that Shirin Mam herself had asked this of her? "I can't explain," she said. "But I know in my heart it's the right thing to do."

"The right thing is to protect yourself by any means possible," said Shurik. His face had gone red and he spoke with effort, as if trying hard to stay calm.

"I'm sorry," said Kyra. "I cannot use Shirin Mam's blade. I must face Tamsyn armed only with my own katari."

"If you will not listen to reason, there's no point in talking with you," said Shurik coldly. He walked away before she could say another word.

Was Shurik going to give up on her so easily? Kyra felt a pang at the prospect of him abandoning her. He was the only real friend she had in Khur and she would hate to lose him, especially when there were just a few days left before the journey to Kashgar. It was not a trip she was looking forward to: a week on camelback through the desolate landscape of the Empty Place, with only the dour and disapproving elders of Khur for company, and only the duel with Tamsyn to look forward to at the end of it.

With a sigh, Kyra slowly headed out of the grove, back to her tent. Perhaps she could get an hour of rest before the evening classes, when she usually joined the Marksmen in katari-play or Mental Arts practice.

But as usual, sleep evaded her. She twisted and turned on the rugs in her tent, unable to still the fluttering in her stomach. She touched her lips with her fingers, and recalled how it had felt to be kissed by Shurik. His lips had been soft against hers, his eyes passionate. But her primary emotion had been one of surprise, followed by embarrassment when she noticed Rustan watching them.

Rustan. What would he think of her now? And why, *why* did she care so much what he thought of her? And then the most traitorous notion of all: What would it be like to be kissed by him? This thought made her feel hot and cold at once, like shivering in a furnace. She got up and splashed her face with water, but it still felt as if she was on fire.

CHAPTER 23

ESCAPING THE SELF

Rustan strode out of the grove. Someone called out to him—was it an elder?—but he did not respond. Distantly, he sensed the fierce glow of the katari against his side.

Shurik, that pie-faced fool. He could have strangled him with his bare hands. As for Kyra, he had thought she had more sense than this. Shurik was hardly more than an apprentice. Perhaps she liked to be told that she had pretty eyes. Perhaps she liked boys mooning after her like brainless calves.

Rustan forced himself to appear expressionless. No one must know what he had seen. But he had to get out of Khur. Now. He was done with the girl and the complications she had brought into his life. If not for her, he would have left weeks ago. But he had stayed; he had obeyed his Maji-khan and taught her what he could. It was out of his hands now.

When he reached Barkav's tent, he had to wait his turn to meet the Maji-khan. Saninda and Ghasil were inside; he could discern their voices. A full ten minutes passed before the elders left the tent. They greeted him in surprise. He gave them a quick bow before asking Barkav's permission to enter.

The Maji-khan was kneeling on the carpeted floor, a pile of letters in his hand. Barkav often spent the afternoons reading petitions that arrived with the camel caravans on their way to Kashgar. He looked up when Rustan entered and broke into a smile. "Come, Rustan. It has been a while since you sought me out."

Rustan bowed and sat down. "Yes, Father. I had a task to do, and there was no point in bothering you with my presence. It would have been impossible for me not to bring up what happened in Tezbasti."

"Ghasil has executed the real killers in front of the entire village," said the Maji-khan, stroking his beard. "It will not happen again. That is all you need to know."

"And it is not for me to seek vengeance," said Rustan. "I understand." And a part of him did. Vengeance would have assuaged his ego, nothing more. Hard as it was for him to accept it, Barkav had been right not to send him back to Tezbasti.

But Rustan could do nothing about the anger he still felt, the guilt that dogged his waking hours and haunted the edges of his dreams. At first he had thought the raw pain of it would finish him off, that his own blade would turn against him and reject him.

Then the Markswoman arrived by the Akal-shin door, and the news of Shirin Mam's death overshadowed everything else.

Rustan looked up to see Barkav watching him, his eyes calm as ever, and it hit him that Barkav had chosen him to teach the Markswoman for a reason—a reason that had nothing to do with his dueling skills. Bitterness rose in his mouth and he spoke more harshly than he had intended:

"I salute you, Father. You have succeeded."

Barkav's brow creased, but he did not say anything.

"I have begun to care for the Markswoman. That is what you wanted, is it not?"

"What I wanted was for her to have a capable teacher," said Barkav. "What is the matter, Rustan?"

Rustan stared at him. *Everything*, he wanted to shout.

"I have taught Kyra all I can. There is little more I can do in the week that is left, except torture myself with looking at her face, and imagining how she will die."

"I see," said Barkav. "You wish to give up your assignment because it is too hard?"

Rustan started to argue, but Barkav forestalled him. "When you are given a task, it is your duty to finish it," he said. "I am aware of how—*trying*—circumstances have been for you this past month, but that is no excuse for a Marksman."

"I have taught her all I can," Rustan repeated. Unable to sit still any longer with the Maji-khan's penetrating gaze on him, he stood up and began to pace the tent. "Give me another assignment, Father. There must be something you need doing away from here."

"You not only wish to give up your assignment, you also wish to leave Khur. You would flee, rather than stay with your pupil to the end?" There was no judgment in Barkav's voice, and yet the words cut deeply.

Rustan spun around to face the Maji-khan, anger heating his face. "What would you have me do?" he demanded, throwing up his hands in frustration. "Surely you would not have me accompany you to Sikandra?"

"It is not for me to decide whether you should go to Sikandra," said Barkav. "I can give you another assignment if you like. But don't delude yourself. You cannot run away, no matter how far you go. There is no escaping the self."

Rustan looked up, stricken. Had Barkav guessed the true depth of his feelings for Kyra? But Barkav's face was expressionless. "Help me, Father," he pleaded.

Barkav was silent. "I need a man in the Thar Desert," he said finally. "But first, I want to find out what happened to Samant."

Rustan frowned. Samant was the eldest of the elders of Khur and the Master of Meditation. He had left for the Kashgar Hub almost a month ago, shortly after Kyra's arrival. His destination was Herat, the home of the Ersanis, a clan of cultivators and carpet weavers. The trip was supposed to be a brief prelude to scoping their young boys as possible novitiates. Samant should have been back a week ago, but had yet to return.

"You can go to Kashgar ahead of us and Transport to Herat," said Barkav. "We will meet you in Kashgar, on our way to or back from Sikandra Fort, depending on how long it takes you to find Samant. In Kashgar, you can make your choice: come back to Khur or go to the Thar Desert. By then the Markswoman will have met her fate, and perhaps you will be able to think more clearly."

Rustan's heart constricted. The Maji-khan made it sound as if Kyra was sure to die. If he cared at all about the outcome of the duel, why didn't he teach her himself?

"Is there anything else, Marksman? I have much to do this afternoon." Barkav waved a hand at the letters scattered around him.

"Who will teach her when I am gone?" asked Rustan.

"She may join our classes, if she wants to. It is not your

concern anymore. Go to Herat and find Samant. I will see you in Kashgar, God willing."

Rustan bowed and left the Maji-khan's tent, unable to put words to his thoughts. He knew that Barkav was disappointed in him. He had been liberated from the task of teaching the Markswoman, but instead of the sense of relief he had expected, all he felt was doubt and the gnawing guilt that he was somehow betraying her.

At least he was getting away from Khur. He would be gone by nightfall. He would not have to see Shurik's face for weeks. Or Kyra's. But the thought that he might never see Kyra again created a painful twist inside him, and he walked faster, trying to ignore it. He would go to Herat, he would find Samant, and he would bring him to Kashgar. In Kashgar he would decide what to do next.

One step at a time was all he could take.

CHAPTER 24

BEND LIKE A REED

Behind the hill that housed the caves of Kali rose another, steeper hill. No caves punctured its slopes, but a rocky overhang halfway up provided some shelter from wind and rain. Here Nineth sat in the lotus position, numb with pain. Tamsyn had instructed her to spend four days and four nights meditating, alone and without food. This was her penance for trying to run away.

Water was not a problem; a little stream tumbled down the rocks not far from where she sat, and she had a clay pot that she kept filled at her side. But Nineth was sick of eating the sour red berries and dry walnuts that were all the sustenance she could find this late in the season.

She was not supposed to eat anything at all, and she had fought her hunger pangs the first and second day. But by the third day her self-control was gone. She crammed berries into her mouth, letting the juice dribble down her chin. She hunted for walnuts under the silvery gray tree that stood like a sentinel below the rocky overhang. She smashed the nuts open against the rocks and pried them out with her fingernails.

Now she had cramps, but whether from the food she had foraged on the hillside or from sitting in the lotus position, she did not know.

Concentrate, she told herself. But it was no good. She couldn't. Her thoughts kept wandering in the most wayward fashion. What had Tarshana cooked for the midday meal? Was Kyra alive and well? How far could she herself have gotten if that sly Baliya hadn't followed her to the paddocks? Did any of the elders know and approve of her penance?

Tamsyn had commanded her not to talk to anyone about the penance, saying that it would be "prideful" on her part. Nineth had agreed, of course. Anything to make Tamsyn stop speaking to her in that voice that drilled into the back of her skull like so many nails. She still had a headache from that, even four days later.

Would today be the day that Tamsyn sent for her, to welcome her back to the Order? And if she did not, couldn't Nineth simply walk back home herself, penance over, all forgiven, to be reunited with her katari?

No. Of course she couldn't. Nineth almost cried when she thought of this. The caves of Kali were but a half-hour walk from here. But they might as well have been at the other end of Asiana. Tamsyn had been most explicit in her commands. Here she was to stay until sent for.

But Tamsyn had also said four days. Surely she had said four days. Another night here would kill Nineth. She had her cloak, but it did little to keep out the cold and damp. Sleep, when it came, was filled with terrifying dreams of being chased by an unseen evil through a dark and dripping forest. She was always relieved to wake up in the morning and find that there was no monster.

But even the bright sunlight was no longer a comfort. It mocked her with its cheery disregard. Look, it said, the world turns without you. The birds sing, the squirrels store nuts for winter, the Markswomen of Kali carry on with their daily work. You are not needed. You are not missed.

A tear trickled down Nineth's cheek and she wiped it away. *Don't weep, you ninny. What would Shirin Mam think?*

But the thought of Shirin Mam brought a fresh wave of sadness. She would have broken down and wept right then, but was startled by the sound of twigs crackling in the undergrowth. Were those footsteps? Hope flared in her chest; she wiped her face with a sleeve and stood up, swaying. The roof of the shelter was not high enough for her to stand erect, and she had to bend down as she hobbled out.

Tamsyn stood before her, arms crossed, a little smile on her lips. Her black robe flapped in the wind, but she looked as elegant as ever. "My dear Nineth," she said, wrinkling her nose. "You have begun to smell."

"I'm sorry, Mother," said Nineth, and she hung her head.

Tamsyn waved her hand. "No matter. After all, there is no one here to smell you. Have you done as I instructed?"

"Yes, Mother," said Nineth. "I have been meditating, like you told me to."

Tamsyn uncrossed her arms and examined her long fingernails. "I despair of these young ones," she said to herself. "One of them has run away like a thief, and another lies to me, her Mahimata."

"I did not lie," Nineth protested, although a small voice warned her to stay quiet. "I have been meditating."

Tamsyn did not stop smiling. If anything, her smile became wider. Her arm shot out in a backfist punch that caught Nineth on the chin, throwing her against the rock wall.

Nineth got back to her feet slowly, her head spinning, tasting blood. The hope that had flared in her chest flickered out. Had she thought it would be so easy to return to the safety of the Order?

"I did not like to do that, Nineth," said Tamsyn. "And I do not like to leave you here for another four days. But you give me no choice. This was supposed to be a penance, not a picnic. You have been gorging on nuts and berries, haven't you? You should not even have moved from your place inside the shelter. And I did tell you quite specifically not to eat."

Nineth knew there was no point in arguing.

"YOU WILL STAY HERE," Tamsyn commanded, and Nineth shook as the Inner Speech rolled into her head. "YOU WILL NOT MOVE FROM THE LOTUS POSITION. YOU WILL NOT EAT." She paused and said in a normal voice, "You can drink, if you wish, so keep some water with you. You see, I am not unreasonable. I will come again in four days. I hope that this time you will take your penance seriously and I can return this to you."

She made a flourish, like a magician, and Nineth stared at the katari that lay revealed in her hand. If only she could get hold of it again.

But a vast and growing gulf separated Nineth from her beloved katari. She could no more have reached for it than she could have touched the sky and the stars.

Tamsyn flicked the katari back inside her robe and said, with a hint of the Inner Speech, "Take your position now. Do not let anyone know that you are here." She paused and cocked her head. "Not that anyone has asked after you, of course."

She left, but Nineth did not see her go. A darkness came before her eyes. No one had asked after her. No one missed her.

She crawled inside the shelter and settled slowly, painfully, into the lotus position once more. It was said of the Boddhisattva Vajrakanta that he had stayed in the lotus position for more than a year before attaining salvation, but Nineth doubted that she could emulate his feat.

Shirin Mam had said that strength lies not in the body but in the mind. If the enemy is stronger than you, bend like a reed. Yield your blood but not your heart. If you are overpowered and hurt, understand that all states are temporary and this too will pass. The only true weakness is to accept defeat and succumb to despair.

Nineth strove against the despair that threatened to overwhelm her. She pushed away the thought of the slow, lingering death that awaited her in this little hole, and thought instead of the life she had lived.

The scenes flashed one after the other, gathering momentum like a story-play. A pleasant and uneventful childhood among the herders who dwelled in the eastern end of the valley. The surprise and fear at being chosen as a novice by the Mahimata of Kali. Her success at the coming-of-age trial, and the joyful reverence with which she beheld her new blade. *Katari-mu-dai*, the moment of bonding. Meditating on a grassy, moonlit patch under the guidance of Navroz or Shirin Mam. Collecting blackberries with Kyra for one of Tarshana's pies, their hands scratched from the thorny bushes, their mouths stained with berry juice. Rubbing down the horses in the enclosure, the smell of sweet grass and sweat commingling in the spring air.

It had not been a particularly noteworthy existence, but it had been a happy one. Certainly it could not have continued so forever. Sooner or later, she would have had to take down her first mark. She had been filled with doubts about this. Could she bring herself to kill another human being, no matter how evil? Too late now to find out.

"Are you all right? Here, drink this."

A worried whisper of a voice, faintly familiar, intruded on Nineth's drifting thoughts. She tried to open her eyes, but her eyelids were too heavy.

The owner of the voice touched her arm, and the pain she had succeeded in banishing from her consciousness flooded through her. She would have screamed if she could, but all that escaped her throat was a small moan.

Something sweet and fiery trickled into her mouth. She gulped it down. It burned as it slid down her throat, but it lessened her pain.

"Easy does it," said the voice. "You don't want to take too much. Let's get out of here first. We're too close to that witch for comfort."

Nineth felt herself being lifted up from the ground and swung around by a pair of broad, muscular shoulders. Her eyes fluttered open.

Darkness. She had a moment of panic. Had she gone blind?

No, it was simply the dark of a cloudy night. She could see a small patch of starry sky. Somewhere, a horse whickered.

Who are you? Where are you taking me? she wanted to say. But all that came out was a hoarse groan.

"Don't worry," said the voice. "You're safe."

The moon sailed out from behind a cloud and its light fell on the face of the man carrying her. *Hattur Nisalki.*

Nineth stared at him in shock. She was dreaming. She had to be.

He grinned at her. "Aren't you glad I followed you to your caves that night?" he said. "Kept an eye on you. The caravan's going south to the Tajik Plains for the winter, and you're coming with us. Neri's the fastest horse we have. I'm rescuing you."

Rescuing? *Let me go, idiot.* Nineth tried to shout, tried to move, but she was too weak.

"Hush, don't try to talk," he said. "You can thank me later." He lifted her onto the saddle and leaped up behind.

After a while Nineth gave up trying to speak and drifted off into a state of semiconsciousness that was strangely like the first-level meditative trance. Dimly, she wondered if she would ever see Elena or Kyra again.

Chapter 25

THE SPIRIT OF VARKA

At first sight, Samant looked dead. His body was thin beneath the ragged blanket, shrunken like a starving child's. His cheeks were hollow with a dark, unhealthy flush. A smell of decay emanated from the bed. But his chest rose and fell; life clung on, despite the odds.

Rustan knelt next to the wooden bed and felt a wave of fury at the superstitious fools who had left the elder to waste away in their "death hut" instead of giving him medicine or sending for a healer when he fell ill. There were herbs to treat fever and deliruim, but the Ersanis professed not to know of them. A mere mile away from the walled town of Herat with its libraries and schools, they might as well have been in the middle of a jungle with their thatched huts, ragged children, and the twitchy shaman who had tried to prevent Rustan from entering the village in the first place.

Rustan laid Samant's blade on his chest and reached for the elder's hand. It was dry and burning hot. Samant shuddered and opened his eyes.

"It's all right, Elder," said Rustan softly, "I'm here now, and so is your katari. As soon as you're well enough to ride, I'm taking you to Herat to be treated by a medicine woman."

Samant looked through him, unseeing. Rustan forced a few spoonfuls of sugar water into his mouth and, after a few minutes, the elder slipped back into sleep. Rustan leaned back on the mud-daubed wall, numb with weariness. He had ridden hard and fast across the Empty Place to reach the Hub of Kashgar, stopping only for a few hours every afternoon to rest his camel.

But no matter how hard he'd ridden, he hadn't been able to get away from Kyra. Her face, words, and gestures were seared into his mind. Every step that he took farther away from her only sharpened his pain.

His anger toward her and Shurik had begun to cool as soon as he mounted his camel and left the camp of Khur. He regretted leaving abruptly without a word of explanation or farewell. But what could he have said that didn't sound forced or melodramatic?

On the way to Kashgar, with only his camel for company under the silent stars, Rustan had allowed himself the luxury of emotion—grief for the one who had gone, fear for the one who stood poised on the edge.

He would find Samant and return to Kashgar, he'd decided. If he hurried, he could make it back before they all left for Sikandra Fort. He could at least say goodbye to Kyra, and wish her well.

Then he'd arrived in the village of the Ersanis, and Samant's plight had taken precedence over everything else.

Now he longed to sleep, but he didn't dare let down his guard, not with Samant in this perilous state and the Ersanis gathered outside the death hut, muttering darkly to each other. No telling what they might do if they thought a stranger was interfering with the directives of their ancestral spirits. Burn the hut down with the two Marksmen inside it, maybe.

But the death hut was too precious for the Ersanis to burn. It was where they laid their dying kin to feed the spirits of their ancestors. That was the only reason Rustan hadn't moved Samant yet. It was currently the safest place for them in the entire village.

Samant's breathing came shallow and uneven. Rustan closed his eyes and prayed that his breath would not stop. Samant was the Master of Meditation; at one time, many years ago, he had even taught Barkav. It was his skill, perhaps, that had kept him alive in the last ten days of utter isolation, without food or water, fever devouring his flesh and his katari buried in the soil beneath the entrance of the hut. An offering to the spirits, the Ersanis had told Rustan. Had been *forced* to tell him. He'd been surprised at their resistance, at the intensity of the Inner Speech he'd been compelled to use to get their compliance.

He could hear their thoughts: it wasn't fair, depriving the spirits of what was rightfully theirs. The old Marksman was sick, he was meant to die. Another day or two and he *would* have died. Not their fault. Not anybody's fault. And then that young one had to come along, digging up the blade offering, *entering the death hut.* No one was supposed to enter the death hut and live.

Right when Rustan captured that thought, and sensed the approach of the six terrified men who had been ordered to attack him, an alien smell hit his nostrils—a strong, musky odor, like that of a wolf. Rustan's eyes flew open and he leaped to his feet, heart thudding.

It *was* a wolf. No, not an ordinary wolf. A wyr-wolf. It sat on its haunches just inside the door of the hut, a massive, gray-furred beast exuding an aura of power, regarding him out of pale yellow eyes. Though he should have been frightened, it was awe and wonder that swept through Rustan. It was the first time he had ever seen a wyr-wolf, although, like every Marksman, he had heard many stories about them.

And then the men burst inside the hut, moving *through* the wyr-wolf as if it did not exist.

Stunned as he was, Rustan had ample time to withdraw his katari. He could have killed the first with a quick thrust, spun around to stab the second, used the Inner Speech to immobilize the rest, and dispatched them one by one. It would have taken a lot out of him, but he could have done it.

Yet he didn't. He had read the men's intentions as soon as they entered. *Stay your hand*, a quiet voice told him, even though it went against his training, against his own instinct for self-preservation.

He was never sure, later on, whose voice it was. The wyr-wolf, who had by now vanished from the hut, if indeed it had ever been there? Or the blade that smoldered against his side? Or was it a voice from within, born of his own guilt?

It took every ounce of self-control he possessed, but Rustan stayed his hand. He let the men grapple him to the ground and tie his hands and feet. The katari they could not touch—it burned the hands of those who tried to take it, right through the scabbard.

The men dragged Rustan out of the hut into the afternoon sun and rolled him to the feet of the waiting shaman. Men and women cheered and gathered more closely around them. Rustan spat dirt and squashed his misgivings. He had done right, and if he was going to be lynched by a mob gone out of control, then so be it.

"We have no quarrel with you, Marksman," said the shaman, a thin, bony man in a sheepskin robe. "But if you interfere with our rites, it will bring ruin on us all. The elder must die peacefully and be absorbed into our spirit world. If you object, then you must join him."

"I saw a wyr-wolf," Rustan blurted out. "In your death hut. Your men walked right through it."

It had only been a hunch, but the effect on the shaman was remarkable. His face went pale and the staff dropped from his hand. He turned to talk with some of the older men and women behind him—elders of the village council, Rustan guessed. One ancient woman stepped up to him.

"Tell us exactly what you saw, Marksman," she rasped.

Rustan described the huge beast, its thick gray fur, the intelligent eyes, the steady gaze. He told them how his six attackers had walked through it, and how it had then vanished from sight.

When he had finished, the woman exhaled. "He has seen the spirit of Varka, the wyr-wolf," she announced.

There were murmurs and cries from the listening crowd. The shaman spoke a word of command, and one of the young men who had dragged Rustan out bent to untie him.

Rustan got to his feet and rubbed his wrists with relief. He wasn't about to be lynched after all. "Who is Varka?" he asked the shaman.

"Our oldest ancestor," said the shaman. "Varka the wyr-wolf fled the poisonous aftermath of the Great War and found refuge in Herat. He married Ersani, the youngest daughter of the Herati headwoman, and founded our clan."

"How do you know of him?" asked Rustan. "The war ended over eight centuries ago."

"We have dozens of ancient manuscripts, locked in trunks and buried in cellars, that tell this story," said the shaman. "Most are in a script we do not understand, but some of them have been translated by our predecessors. Very few of us now have the gift of learning."

"If your manuscripts are that old, you possess a treasure trove indeed," said Rustan. "I could request the Maji-khan to send an elder to help you copy and catalog them."

An expression of horror crossed the old man's face. "Never! Strangers are forbidden to touch those sacred pages. They will crumble to dust and our heritage will be destroyed."

Rustan sighed. Another superstition. "You can send some of your children to schools in Herat," he said. "Perhaps, as they grow in years and learning, this task could be entrusted to them."

"Perhaps," said the shaman, noncommittal.

Rustan knew it was unlikely that the Ersanis would ever send their children to the town of Herat, but at least he had planted the idea in the shaman's head.

"What happened to Varka and Ersani?" he asked. "Why did they leave Herat?"

"Jealousy," replied the shaman. "Varka was too powerful, too strong. Ersani's siblings grew afraid of him, and poisoned their mother's ears against him. She banished Varka and Ersani from Herat. They made their way here, to till the land and start a family. To start a new clan." A glow of pride lit his wrinkled face. "We have wyr-wolf blood in our veins."

A likely story, Rustan thought. But he remembered the wyr-wolf he had seen in the death hut, and kept quiet.

The Ersanis gave him little trouble after that. Apparently,

the spirit of Varka had not been glimpsed in almost a century, and he was very fortunate to have seen it. Everyone wanted to touch him and speak to him. In all the excitement, Samant was almost forgotten. But Rustan asked for, and received, permission to bring Samant out of the death hut and into the shaded porch of the village council hut.

He showed a woman how to boil water to make it safe for drinking, and gave an impromptu class on herbs and healing as he made a tincture for Samant. Not that he knew much about it, and he was hampered by a lack of all but the most basic materials he had carried with him: dried peppermint and garlic, a bunch of sacred basil, a bottle of spineleaf oil. But he hoped that some of what he told them would filter into their own practices, and prevent needless deaths in the future.

That night, Samant recovered sufficiently to ask for a glass of water. He held his katari gripped in one skeletal hand, as if afraid someone might snatch it away again. After he had drunk the peppermint-infused tea Rustan brewed for him, he drifted back to sleep, his breathing quiet and regular.

The rest of the village also slept, quiescent under the moonlit sky. From somewhere a bulbul called, piercing the night with its sweet cry. The wind wafted through the porch of the council house, filled with the scent of jasmine. Rustan blew out the lamp and stretched out on a woven grass mat next to Samant, allowing himself to relax for the first time in days.

He watched Samant's sleeping form for several minutes, then turned his face to the darkness above, his thoughts drifting, as always, to Kyra. Her fierce expression when she fought, the way she pushed the hair away from her eyes when she was angry, the depth of her gaze, and how it seemed to plumb the very depths of his soul.

"Do you know, Elder, why I came here?" he whispered. "It was not to save you. It was to escape myself."

Samant gave a tiny snore. Emboldened, Rustan talked on in a low voice, unburdening himself to the sleeping elder. He told him about the tragic mistake in Tezbasti, the arrival of the Markswoman through the Akal-shin door, and the news she had brought. "Barkav made me teach her dueling," he said. "I was so busy doing that, I mostly forgot everything else. And then I discovered I cared for her. Cared too much. And so I left Khur. Is it so wrong, Elder, to love a woman?"

Samant cleared his throat and said, "No."

Rustan sat up, horrified. Samant was *awake*.

The elder regarded him out of calm, lucid eyes. "You should return to Kashgar," he said, his voice hoarse but steady. "Return before it is too late."

PART IV

From the copy of *The Kanun of Ture-asa* possessed by the Order of Kali

There are those who believe, and those who do not. There are those who remember, and those who forget. There are those who worship, and in their worship is the stink of fear.

To them all I say, the Ones who wait and watch in the sky know everything that has happened, and everything that can happen. You have broken covenant with them, and still they do not abandon you. See, they leave you their most precious metal kalishium, which can look into your inmost heart. They leave you their doors. Why else, if not to return?

There is darkness now all around us. There are none left to listen to me. My son is dead, and soon I will die too.

But a time will come when my words will be known to all that live in Asiana. Twenty, fifty, a hundred years from now, the smallest child will gaze into the dark bowl of the sky and know that we are not alone.

The fractured clans will unite to form the Orders of Peace and return harmony to Asiana. The Markswomen, as they will come to be called, will use blades fashioned from kalishium to mete out justice. Thus will they keep faith with the Ones, for only kalishium can look inside the soul and be true to its keeper. All must obey the Orders, for in them lies the hope of Asiana and the future of our race.

It is I, Ture-asa, the last king of Asiana, who says this to you.

To all who would repudiate me, I say that you are deaf and dumb and blind. You turn your face away from the light, and so you cannot see. You clap your hands on your ears, and so you cannot hear. But look up at the star-filled sky one night. Look for the blue disc of Amaderan, the home star of the Araini. See if you dare deny the Ones.

CHAPTER 26

ACROSS THE EMPTY PLACE

It was the hour before dawn in the Empty Place—almost time to move. Time to leave this frozen, desolate landscape that had begun to feel, despite everything, like an unforgiving kind of home.

Kyra rested her hands on the two kataris, sensing their power. One blade so much a part of her, the other ancient and alien. It was beginning to weigh on her now. Well, she wouldn't have to bear it much longer. Shirin Mam had made that clear. Kyra would give it into the Maji-khan's safekeeping before the duel, to pass on to Rustan when he rejoined the Order. She wished with all her heart she could have given it to him herself, but that was no longer possible. Rustan was gone. Barkav had summoned her one morning and told her that he had left Khur.

"Left for where? Left why?" she had asked in dismay, but he was vague about that. *Business of the Order,* he said, and waved his hand in dismissal. She walked back to her tent, oddly bereft.

Had he gone because he'd seen Shurik kissing her? No, that was too ridiculous. More likely he was simply fed up with teaching her, day in and day out. She had swallowed the painful lump in her throat and focused on her training.

Kyra went to all the classes that she could in her last week at Khur, joining the Marksmen in Mental Arts, katari-play, and unarmed combat. She even volunteered to cook the midday meal once, and was quite pleased when it was not an unmitigated disaster. She asked the fabled Gajin for help, and he gave it willingly enough, telling her how much salt and water to add to the millet and how long to cook the potatoes. The elders thanked her for the meal and Barkav joked that she was good enough to be an honorary Marksman of Khur. She had to smile at that, even though the elders' expressions ranged from mildly disapproving (Saninda) to terribly shocked (Ghasil).

Still, she had been lonelier than ever before in her time at Khur. She missed Rustan's lessons, his patient voice as he told her the fine difference between churi-katka and katari-kaat, or why she was holding the katari the wrong way. *It is not a weapon apart from you, but an extension of your being,* he had said, pushing the dark hair away from his forehead and gazing at her with burning eyes. *Feel it.*

She couldn't understand why it hurt that he was gone. He had only been teaching her on the Maji-khan's command. All their time together had been spent in katari-play; they'd never talked of anything else, except on that last day. Yet somehow being with him had kept the darkness within her at bay. She hadn't thought about it earlier, but she'd had fewer nightmares; the ghosts had been less insistent. When he left they returned in full force, knocking on her dreams once again, demanding to be let in.

Well, it was time to lay down her ghosts, one way or another. Kyra sheathed the blades, her own in the wooden scabbard by her waist, and Shirin Mam's in the black metal scabbard on her back.

"We move at dawnlight," Barkav had said. "Pack your things."

Kyra donned her camel-wool cloak and knee-length boots. As if she had any "things" to pack. One brown robe with the symbol of Kali, two kataris, and three prayers were all she had. First, that she could somehow win the duel with Tamsyn. Second, that her friends were all safe in Ferghana. And third, that she could once again find her path to avenging the slaughter of her clan.

Kyra stepped out of the tent, clutching the tiny bundle of her belongings. The cold took her breath away, even though there was no wind yet. A hint of orange lit the eastern sky, but elsewhere the dark of night still held; the stars still shone. She was halfway to the camel enclosure when a figure materialized out of the darkness.

Kyra's heart sank when she saw who it was. Was Shurik going to make a scene now, when she was about to leave?

Shurik had grown more and more withdrawn as the time for them to part drew near, until he barely acknowledged her at all. It was better this way. But she still missed his easy companionship and cheery grins, especially after Rustan left. She had been paired with Shurik for a mock duel in one of Ishtul's classes and he had done a poor job of it, wildly thrusting his sparking katari into the air until the elder told him to go join the apprentice class. He went off red-faced and scowling, and ignored Kyra after that.

Now here he was, looming in front of her with a determined expression on his face, dressed in thick robes and boots, a bulky bundle tied on his back.

"I'm going with you to Kashgar," he said without preamble. "Don't bother saying no, because I already asked the Maji-khan's permission."

Kyra bit down her impulse to whoop for joy and said, "Whatever for?"

"It will be boring here with practically half the Order away," said Shurik. "Barkav can use me to stock up on provisions in Kashgar while you all go to Sikandra."

Kyra breathed a sigh of relief. At least he wasn't attempting to dissuade her from going to Sikandra, or talking of his supposed love for her. Perhaps he had finally seen reason.

"I'm glad to hear it," she said. "I wasn't looking forward to having just the elders for company."

The way Shurik's eyes lit up when she said that made her think she shouldn't have spoken.

⚜

There were six of them besides Kyra: Barkav, Saninda, Ghasil, and Ishtul, all bound for Sikandra, and Shurik and Aram, who would remain in Kashgar to take care of the camels and buy provisions for winter. The remaining elders, along with Astinsai, were to stay behind at Khur. Kyra learned that this was the way the elders had done it for years, rotating duties among themselves so that they each got a turn to represent Khur at the clan assembly.

They set off at dawnlight, as Barkav had promised. Everyone showed up to bid them goodbye. Astinsai sprinkled a few drops of a strong-smelling potion on each of their heads, muttering a blessing for their safe return, her ancient face darkly planed in the half-light.

Kyra mounted her camel and settled as best as she could on the saddle between its humps. The men who remained stared at them half in envy, half in gloom. It would be several weeks before everyone returned and the Order dug in for winter. Kyra waved to them, smiling. It was strange, how she'd longed to get away from this place when she first arrived, and how, in a little over a month, she'd come to regard it as a refuge. She'd sparred with the Marksmen, been taught by their elders, and grown to love the stark beauty of the desert sky. She wished she could say or do something memorable to thank the Marksmen for taking her in.

Then the camel she was sitting on lurched to its feet and she almost toppled over, saving herself by grabbing a hump. She scrambled back upright, flushing as she sensed the grins behind her back. So much for a graceful exit. Well, at least she had given those glum faces something to smile about.

They rode in single file, the camels casting long shadows across the golden sand. Barkav led the way, picking out the route they would travel, skirting the edges of the vast dunes and jagged cliffs. Saninda brought up the rear, behind Kyra. In the middle were two camels loaded with their provisions.

The sun slipped higher in the sky, its white light bleaching the sands and hurting the eyes. Kyra lowered the hood of her robe. The swaying motion of the camel together with the fierce light of the sun made her dizzy, but she hung on, determined not to show any weakness in front of the Marksmen. The men sat with the ease of long years of practice traveling in the desert, squares of white cloth tied around their heads.

By the time Barkav called for a halt in the shelter of a cliff, Kyra was so sore from riding the camel that she almost wept with relief at being able to get off. Why couldn't they have made that wooden saddle more comfortable to sit on? A bit of padding wouldn't have hurt. She winced as she got off and stretched her body. Aram was already unloading waterskins and bundles of food from one of the camels, and she hobbled toward him.

Aram was a few years older than Shurik, a taciturn youth whom Kyra did not know well. He had been given the task of loading the camels and making sure that they had enough food and water to last the week's journey to Kashgar.

Aram looked up as she approached and handed her a waterskin. Kyra drank little, despite her thirst. A few mouthfuls now and then, Barkav had said, would take you further than long, greedy gulps.

The camels sat down and rested in the shade while Aram and Shurik served the food. It was a simple meal of millet bread, dried dates, and camel cheese; there would be no actual cooking except at dinner. After they had eaten, the men stretched themselves out on the sand to rest.

Kyra walked to the edge of the cliff's shadow and gazed at the vast dune field that surrounded them. One full week of this might well kill her before she ever reached Sikandra.

The softest of footfalls behind alerted her to Shurik's presence. He hadn't spoken to her since morning, had behaved in the most exemplary fashion, in fact. Without turning around, she said, "Are you not tired, Shurik?"

Shurik sat down beside her. "No more than you," he said. "And I can hardly rest with Ghasil wheezing on one side of me and Ishtul snoring on the other. Those two have given me more grief than all the rest of the council combined."

Kyra chuckled. She had observed the elders glare at Shurik for no particular reason, had seen him duck his head and shuffle away from their beady eyes. "Why you have volunteered for this trip, I cannot fathom," she said. "It is like a fish jumping into the pan, begging to be fried."

Shurik sighed. "I can remember the taste of freshly caught Peral River fish," he said, his expression turned to some distant memory. "Juicy, succulent, and flaky, cooked on a slow fire with lemon juice, pepper, and turmeric. We used to eat it with steamed rice and fried onions."

"Could be the last taste you remember," teased Kyra. "I can feel the elders' eyes on us right now."

Shurik scrambled up and hurried back to the camp without a word. Kyra suppressed a grin. He would find it difficult to misbehave on this journey.

Three hours later they were on their way again, Kyra wincing as she eased herself into the saddle once more.

Dusk lengthened the shadows of the camels on the sand. The sky burned a fiery orange as the sun sank and the wind rose. There was nothing all around but a sea of sand. Kyra prayed that the wind would not keep up all night. It had been cold enough inside a tent with a stove; what would it be like to sleep out in the open, exposed to the bitter night? They had not brought any real shelter with them; Aram had been surprised when she asked. They had a couple of stoves, but the fuel was too precious to waste on anything but cooking and brewing tea.

Hours later, when a yellow sliver of moon hung low in the sky and Kyra was just about ready to topple off her camel, dignity be damned, Barkav called for a halt behind a vast, curving dune.

"Dinnertime," he said, dismounting and smiling as if they were at a feast. The men gave a cheer. Kyra slid off her camel, numb with fatigue.

Aram lit the stove. Kyra knelt in front of it and held her hands out to the flickering flames. How strange they must look—a small circle of life in the vast, empty darkness of the desert.

"Tell me," she said, "what do we do if the wind *really* gets going tonight? Like in the spring when it can blow the tents away?"

Aram glanced at her, his face unreadable. "We die," he said, and put a pan of water on the stove.

So much for trying to make conversation. Kyra ignored Aram after that, merely thanking him for the cup of tea he gave her. She drank quickly; they all did. At that temperature, the tea would have become cold and useless in half a minute.

Shurik lit the second stove and Barkav himself made the stew. He tossed in potatoes and onions with the millet, joking and laughing as if they were not in the middle of the most godforsaken place in Asiana. Kyra told him about the Ferghana Valley, the beauty of its tumbling streams, the wooded slopes and wild horses. Even Ghasil and Ishtul unbent sufficiently to ask her about the system of teaching at the Order of Kali, murmuring to each other at the similarities, and exclaiming at the contrasts. The biggest difference, of course, was the wyr-wolf hunts of Kali. The vicious beasts, ubiquitous in the fertile valley and uplands of Ferghana, were absent in the desert. It was the biggest plus point of living there that Kyra could think of.

As Kyra described the hunt in which she had ridden and the massive wyr-wolf she had killed, the men grew quiet. Finally, sensing that something was amiss, her words petered out and she looked at Barkav, questioning. Had it sounded like she was boasting?

"Tell me, Kyra," said Barkav. "Why does your Order hunt wyr-wolves? Is it for sport?"

"Certainly not!" Kyra was shocked. "Wyr-wolves are dangerous. They aren't a bit like ordinary wolves. They can kill and carry off a grown man, never mind a small child. They plague the villages of the Ferghana, especially during winter when game is scarce."

"Why don't you tell her?" said Barkav to Aram. "Tell her the story about Zibalik's wolves."

Aram scowled at the stove. A few moments passed before he started to speak, his voice hesitant at first, and gathering confidence as his story progressed:

"Did you never wonder why they are called wyr-wolves? It was Zibalik who named them so: Zibalik, the founder of Khur and the first Marksman of Asiana. He wanted to learn whatever he could from all the Orders of Asiana before establishing his own, and he first heard the lore of dangerous wolf-beasts from the Markswomen of Kali. But it is said that he understood what they were only when he left the Ferghana Valley and set off to seek the Order of Zorya in the far north.

"The Zoryan Markswomen played a cruel game with Zibalik; perhaps it was a test. They evaded him for months, leaving tantalizing trails across the bogs and through the forests. As winter darkened the days and stripped the trees, Zibalik began to despair. Snow covered the ground and the lakes froze. If he did not find the Zoryans soon, Zibalik knew he would die. He was almost at the end of hope when the wolves first appeared."

Aram paused and glanced at Barkav, his face uncertain, as if asking permission to go on. Kyra held her breath. Barkav inclined his head, and Aram resumed speaking:

"Zibalik said later that the wolves spoke to him in his dreams and told him where to find the Zoryans. Then he woke one bitter morning to find the wolves sitting in a circle around him. They gave him the warmth of their bodies and shared a buck that they had killed. They saved his life."

"That's impossible," Kyra burst out, unable to contain herself. "The fangs of a wyr-wolf inject venom that causes paralysis. He'd have *died* if he'd eaten that buck. If you believe this story, it must be because you have never come face-to-face with a wyr-wolf yourself."

Aram glowered and the elders bristled. Even Shurik frowned at her. Kyra squirmed and wished that she had held her tongue.

But Barkav only said, "Not everything that is passed on is to be taken literally. We believe the essence of it, as do the Zoryans, which is why we follow the injunction Zibalik laid on us to never raise our blades against wyr-wolves."

Kyra frowned. Easy for them to say, living as they did in the Empty Place. Try telling a herder in the Ferghana who had lost his finest calves that wyr-wolves were not to be harmed.

But there was something else Aram had said that she didn't understand. "That doesn't explain why Zibalik named them wyr-wolves, though," she said.

Shurik spoke fast, before anyone else could: "'Wyr' means 'man' in the ancient tongue. By giving the wolves this name, Zibalik recognized them as equal parts wolf and human."

Barkav gave a slight smile of approval. Ghasil snorted and muttered, "Show-off."

Kyra hid a grin at Shurik's expression and didn't ask further questions when the topic changed to the Zoryan style of fighting. Although she was curious to know more about Zibalik, she suspected that she would hear more malarkey about how wonderful the wyr-wolves were. The men of Khur were a cred-ulous lot, to believe such a tall tale.

The dune provided some shelter from the wind, and the camels surrounded them in what Kyra found was a comforting circle, almost as if they were protecting the humans. With the two stoves lit in the middle, one could almost ignore the cold, dark night. After they had eaten, talk petered out. They sat in silence until Barkav announced that they had six hours before dawn and they had better use them to get some sleep. Aram damped down the stoves; the loss of the little light and warmth was almost painful.

Kyra wrapped herself in all her blankets and, after a moment's hesitation, rested against her camel as the others were doing. She looked up at the twinkling stars and the crescent moon; it was higher in the sky now, and paler. The night sky was crystal clear; she could see the milky river of light arcing across it that Felda had once explained was the light from stars that could not be individually distinguished.

What had Astinsai said? *There is always a price to pay for beauty. Or for love.* Kyra shivered and closed her eyes.

Of course, sleep was no easier to come by here than it had been in her tent. She wriggled, trying to find a more comfort-able spot against the camel's hard, furry flank. Her thoughts turned to Rustan, as they did every night. Where was he now? Was he safe? Did he think of her at all? Why had he left with-out even saying goodbye?

She knew he had merely done what he had been ordered to do, and gone on to another mission. He was a Marksman, after all. And *she* was a Markswoman. Feelings played no part in that truth.

It was a long time before Kyra could sleep, and she could not keep Rustan's face out of her mind. After a while she stopped trying, and let her thoughts wander where they would. What did it matter? She would not see him again. But she could think of him. She could remember what he had taught her. She could remember the way his eyes pierced her when he was trying to make her understand something. Or the rare smiles when she managed to surprise him: a move he did not expect, a punch that he didn't see coming.

And she could imagine. She imagined what it would be like to see him again. She would be cool and polite with him, of course. He would ask her if she wanted some practice sparring, and she would agree. She would send him sprawling facedown in the sand, as he had done many times to her. There would be sand in his mouth and hair and he would look at her in surprise and respect. *That duel is as good as won*, he would tell her. She would laugh lightly, and he would smile that smile of his that made him look not much older than one of the apprentices. He would grasp her hand in his and say that he had missed her. He would bend toward her, and press his lips to hers . . .

One of the elders coughed and Kyra jerked out of her little dream with a start. Hurriedly she began to count her breaths: breathe in, hold it, hold it, breathe out. It would never do to allow the elders the slightest glimpse into her mind. She breathed and counted until she had calmed enough to try to sleep.

It was on the afternoon of the fifth day that the sandstorm hit. It had been deathly still since morning. Barkav kept scanning the horizon every few minutes, his brow furrowed.

They had been on the move since dawn and Kyra's limbs were stiff, her throat parched. Sand and wind, sun and sky—she felt as if she had never known anything else. When Barkav called for a halt in the shelter of a cliff, she almost fell off in her eagerness to dismount. Two more days and she could get off this camel, guzzle as much water as she wanted, and have a bath.

Kyra was doing a stretching exercise to loosen her limbs when she heard the cry go up behind her:

"Calima! Calima comes."

She straightened up, and her heart sank. Over to the south, perhaps thirty or forty miles away, sky and sand had merged into a solid, terrifying wall of red-brown dust. Even as she watched, it grew larger, billowing toward them with uncanny speed.

"We have fifteen or twenty minutes at most," said Saninda. "Do we run or do we hunker down?"

Barkav moved his lips; he seemed to be calculating the odds. "We hunker down. We can't outrun that and this is the only shelter we've seen for miles."

Even Shurik's face was grim. He worked with Aram, tethering the camels to the large rocks jutting out of the sand on the leeward side of the cliff. Kyra helped Saninda and Ghasil secure their food and waterskins rapidly, wrapping them in layers of canvas and tying the bulky bundles with ropes to the rocks at the base of the cliff.

The sky overhead darkened to a dull orange as the wall of dust closed in on them. Kyra kept glancing up at it nervously. It was huge; it looked almost a mile high. How could they possibly outlast it? Despite her dehydration, sweat trickled down her face and back, and she threw up a fervent prayer to the

Goddess. *Please, let me live, so I can confront Tamsyn in the Hall of Sikandra.*

"Cover yourselves," Barkav shouted over the wind. "Get as close to the cliff as you can. Lie facedown and hold your blanket over your head. Hold on to each other as well."

Kyra obeyed at once, knowing the advice was for her. The others were already moving into position, holding their blankets tightly over their heads. She lay facedown and immediately got sand in her mouth.

"Keep your eyes and mouth closed," came Barkav's muffled voice. "Don't look up or the sand will blind you."

Kyra closed her eyes and pressed her lips together, trying to ignore the sharp bits of rock digging into her skin through her cloak.

The sandblast hit the cliff in a howl of fury. They were almost swept away with the sheer force of it. Kyra hung on to Shurik and Saninda, who were on either side of her, but her blanket was snatched away. The sand scoured her exposed neck and pelted her on all sides. The wind tore at the cloth tied around her face. She kept her eyes closed, but the sand got into her nose and mouth. Just when she thought she wouldn't be able to take another breath, Shurik dragged her under his blanket and breathing became a tiny bit easier. She lay quite still, glad of his arm around her.

It felt like hours before the storm passed. Kyra didn't dare move until she heard a husky voice saying, "Well, that wasn't so bad, was it? Nothing like the storm last summer."

Nothing like the storm last summer? These men were crazy.

Kyra coughed out sand and pushed Shurik's arm away. A mountain of sand had accumulated on them; they staggered to their feet and dusted themselves off. Kyra's muscles ached from the effort of holding still for so long while being buffeted by the gale. There was sand everywhere: in her hair, mouth, nose, and ears. It had gotten inside her clothes and cut her skin. Her neck and hands, which had been exposed for only a few minutes, were bleeding.

Aram bent down to examine their provisions. After a moment, he said, "About half our supplies are still here."

A ragged cheer went up and Barkav announced that it was time for tea. Five minutes later, after using a bit of the precious water to rinse their mouths and eyes, they were all sitting around the stove, cracking jokes about how Calima, the wicked wind, was getting old and toothless. Kyra sipped her tea and listened in disbelief. Aram had a cut lip and Ishtul had a nasty gash on his cheek where a flying piece of rock had hit him. Shurik had cut his hands in protecting her, but he grinned at her foolishly as if they were at a courting party.

Finally Kyra could not bear it any longer. She got up, tore her face cloth into strips, and wet them. She didn't have any ointment and there wasn't much water to spare, but it was essential to keep wounds clean or they would fester. Even the Marksmen ought to know that, for all that they didn't consider healing important enough to merit a full class.

The elders looked up suspiciously as she approached. Ishtul protested that he didn't need her help, but she ignored him. She wiped his cheek until the grit and sand were gone, and tied a clean strip around his face.

"There," she said, stepping back. "That should do until you can see a medicine woman in Kashgar."

"I thank you," said Ishtul, patting his cheek and looking more hook-nosed than ever.

Aram took a couple of strips from her for Barkav and Saninda.

Kyra glanced at Shurik, and he held his hands out to her with a pathetic look. She bit back a smile and bent over them, examining the cuts and cleaning them as gently as possible. Shurik winced several times but didn't complain, even though it must have hurt.

The moon had risen when they finally resumed their journey. They had lost half a day and half their provisions, but this was little compared to what might have been.

Swaying on her camel under the moonlight, feeling the stillness of the night like a blessing, Kyra thought how close she had come to death. All of them could have died that day, their bodies preserved by the desiccation for some unsuspecting nomad to find years later. And there would have been no one left to avenge the death of Shirin Mam.

But the Goddess had decided their fates otherwise. Kyra was still alive, and her story wasn't quite finished yet.

CHAPTER 27

IN KASHGAR

They arrived in Kashgar the next day, late in the afternoon. The change from the silent emptiness of the desert was abrupt, almost shocking. One minute they were riding between dunes and towering black rocks with the sun beating down on their bowed heads. The next minute they crested a dune and Kashgar lay before them, a vast jumble of adobe buildings dotted with blue-green domes, surrounded by ten-meter-high mud walls. Kyra gawked while Shurik explained that Kashgar was the biggest and oldest town under Khur jurisdiction. It had been settled soon after the Great War ended, eight hundred fifty years ago.

They passed through the walls by the main gate, a massive arched doorway with iron spikes on top. Burly Kushan guards dressed in ceremonial red and gold robes stood on either side of them, bowing deeply, clearly recognizing the group of Marksmen. Barkav and the elders called out greetings, but Kyra kept her face and katari hidden, though she longed to stare at everything. She didn't want to draw attention to herself. Several clans and tribes had gathered in Kashgar ahead of the annual clan meeting, and it wouldn't do to start rumors of a strange Markswoman in the company of the Marksmen of Khur.

They dismounted outside a large, rectangular two-story building near the main gate with the grand name "Jewel of Kashi" painted on the arch of its entrance. This, Kyra guessed, was the guesthouse where the men of Khur stayed when they were in Kashgar. Certainly they were expected. The proprietress, a middle-aged woman dressed in sober gray, hurried forward to greet them with cups of fragrant mint tea. Two young boys led their camels through the entrance to the open courtyard inside the walls.

Kyra followed the Marksmen into the vast courtyard, stunned by the size and beauty of the blue and white building. The courtyard was surrounded by dozens of stables, housed between elegant arches. The arches were decorated with a mosaic of glazed blue tiles that gave the effect of intricate floral patterns. The courtyard itself was paved with stone, but in the center was a square garden with a well, overhung with olive trees. Sandstone benches lined the garden on all four sides.

Most of the stables were already occupied by horses, mules, or camels. The guest rooms, Kyra deduced, must be on the floor above, arranged along a gallery facing the courtyard. The spicy, fruity smell of the olive trees mixed with the earthy smell of the animals, and Kyra inhaled deep, feeling herself relax.

The courtyard was crowded with people—merchants and traders for the most part, but clan elders were present as well. All talk and laughter faded as the Marksmen walked past, Barkav in the lead. Everyone fell back and gave space for their little party to pass, bowing and murmuring respectful greetings.

Kyra could feel their curious eyes on her, and hear some loud thoughts:

Who is this strange girl with the untidy hair?

What is a woman doing with the Marksmen of Khur?

And, worst of all:

What are the Marksmen coming to, dragging their floozy to a respectable guesthouse like this?

Kyra's cheeks burned with anger but she kept her eyes down. She wished she could disabuse the idiot who had thought that, but now was not the time to reveal herself.

They climbed a marble staircase to the gallery on the first floor, the proprietress bobbing up and down as she showed them their rooms, urging them to call her if they needed anything. Kyra could make out elaborate gold letters painted on each door. Although she couldn't read the script, Shurik told her that each room was named after a fruit or a flower. Kyra's room was called *Shisqa*, a type of date.

It was a relief to enter the snug little room she had to herself, and warm her cracked hands in front of the small fire that had already been lit for the evening. Kyra sat on the wooden chair by the fireplace and regarded her room with pleasure. The arched ceiling was of brown sandstone, and the floor was covered with crimson patterned rugs. A narrow bed was pushed against the wall; it had a thick red and yellow patchwork quilt that looked very welcoming. Here the cold and discomfort of the journey could be put aside, the sandstorm forgotten like a bad dream. Kyra wished she could stay longer than the three days that were left before the clan assembly in Sikandra.

Dinner was a delicious bowl of steaming hot noodle soup, loaves of freshly baked bread, ripe cheese, olives, and roasted nuts. They ate in the dining hall downstairs, attended by a dour and capable old man, who refilled empty plates and bowls without being asked. Everyone ate without speaking, so intent were they on their food, although Shurik managed to wink at Kyra across the table when none of the elders was looking. Kyra ignored him. After a week of millet stew and potatoes, this tasty food deserved all of her attention.

But what washed off the fatigue of the journey was a trip to the bathhouse after dinner. Kyra had heard of these wondrous buildings but never entered one herself. She learned that there was only one bathhouse in the Jewel of Kashi, with separate hours for men and women; the men could bathe in the mornings and the women in the evenings.

At the entrance, Kyra put on the wooden clogs that had been thoughtfully provided so that bathers would not slip on the wet floor. She stripped off her grimy robes and handed them to a female attendant to wash. The attendant bowed and gave her a colorful checked bathrobe to tie around her waist, a thick white towel, a scrub, and a square of jasmine-scented soap.

The bathhouse consisted of three interconnected chambers: a domed "hot" room with a heated marble platform in the middle for sweating, a rectangular "warm" room with alcoves and stone basins for washing with soap and water, and an airy "cool" room with comfortable divans for relaxing, dressing, and maybe having a cup of tea.

Kyra didn't stay long on the marble platform of the hot room; the steamy air made her feel claustrophobic, although it also loosened her tense muscles. She made her way to the warm room, where a bored-looking masseuse sat on a stool, waiting to offer up her services to the next guest. She perked up on seeing Kyra, who did not have the heart to deny her, although she had never had a massage before and was reluctant to have a stranger's hands on her body.

But the masseuse was as skilled as she was garrulous, and Kyra soon found herself lying facedown on a stone slab, trying not to drift off to sleep while the woman massaged her aching limbs with fragrant sandalwood oil, and kept up a constant flow of inane chatter. Finally, Kyra escaped into an alcove to soap herself, and the masseuse went to the cool room to prepare mint tea for her customer.

By the time Kyra emerged from the bathhouse, rejuvenated and refreshed, night had fallen on Kashgar. The courtyard was lit with several small fires. Men and women who couldn't afford rooms clustered around them, cooking food and warming themselves. Kyra paused on the stairs to drink in the scene. So many people. There were even some children, presumably traveling with their families. What spurred them to make the arduous journey across deserts and mountains without the help of doors? Was it only the chance of profit? The livelihoods of many depended upon the markets of Kashgar. But it was a hard way to make a living, being on the move for several months a year, with the ever-present risk of losing your wares and your life.

Kyra turned to resume climbing, and stopped short. Someone was cat-footing along the first-floor gallery ahead of her. Even without her blade, she sensed it was Shurik. Sure enough, he appeared a few moments later, his boyish face framed by the light of the oil lamp hanging at the top of the stairs.

"What are you doing still up?" asked Kyra, wary.

He shrugged. "Couldn't sleep. Thought I'd wait for you." He

came down the stairs and sniffed. "You smell nice. I'm dying to have a bath myself."

"You'll get your turn tomorrow morning," said Kyra.

"Yes, I can just picture myself, sweating in the hot room between Ghasil and Ishtul," said Shurik with a wink.

But Kyra sensed that his heart was not in it. "What's the matter?" she couldn't help asking, although she could guess, and she didn't really want to hear it spoken aloud.

Shurik ran a hand through his hair and sighed. "I don't know," he said. "I thought I could do this, come here and run whatever errands the elders wanted me to, and wish you godspeed with a smile. But it's too hard. I can't bear the thought of losing you." He added hastily, "As a friend, of course."

"It's hard for me too," said Kyra, choosing her words carefully. "But the right thing is rarely easy to do. In fact, that's probably an excellent way to choose your course: What's the most difficult and thorny path of all? And then take that one."

"What?" he stared at her, surprised. "Kyra, that might be the dumbest thing I've ever heard. Or the wisest. I'm not sure."

"Thank you," said Kyra drily, shaking her head, moving past him up the stairs. "Now, if you will excuse me, I need to sleep."

"Stay awhile and talk?" said Shurik, trailing after her. "In three days you'll be gone and God knows if I'll ever see you again, and all you want to do is sleep?"

"Hush," she hissed. "You'll wake them up." They were walking past the rooms that had been given to the elders.

"I don't care," said Shurik. "Let them wake up. I'm not scared of those old bats."

"Bats?" drawled a familiar voice. "That's a new one, Shurik."

Kyra stopped, astonished. It was the Maji-khan, leaning against the railing of the gallery ahead of them. How had they missed seeing him in the lamplight? Perhaps he had the gift of camouflage, like Ria Farad.

Behind her, Shurik cleared his throat. "Gnats. I was complaining about the gnats. They're always flying about at this time of the night. I think I'd better go to bed."

"Yes," said Barkav. "You had better go before those gnats decide to come after you."

Shurik left so quickly that Kyra could have sworn she felt a breeze. She quenched the mirth rising up inside her and met Barkav's gaze.

"Has the boy been troubling you?" he demanded. He raised a hand. "No, don't answer. I know that you will not admit it. I have let this go on for far too long. Perhaps I should not have let him come with us to Kashgar. Saninda did speak against it."

Kyra stifled her indignation with difficulty. What did he mean, he had let *this* go on for far too long? What was *this*? "I don't know what you mean, Father," she said. "Shurik is my friend and I have been glad of his company. There is no trouble of any sort."

"You know what I mean, Kyra," said Barkav. "I'll not see a promising young Marksman—one who is exceptionally gifted in the Mental Arts—lose his wits because of a childish infatuation. I will send him back to Khur tomorrow morning."

Kyra bit her lip. He would send Shurik back through the desert alone? Suppose he was attacked by a gang of outlaws or caught in another storm on his own? How would he survive?

"Father, there is no trouble," she said at last. "I will come to you if there is. You have my word. There is no need to send him away. It's only a matter of three days."

Barkav frowned. "Yes. Three days before the meeting in Sikandra. I will be busy with the Kushan and Turguz clan elders, but perhaps I can spare Ishtul to work with you on the different forms of katari duel."

Kyra quailed at the thought of individual lessons with the dour Ishtul. "Thank you for the offer, but please don't trouble the elder," she said. "Rustan has taken me through all the forms in great detail. I can practice them on my own."

"Fine, see that you do," said Barkav. "You may take a couple of hours to explore Kashgar tomorrow morning, but after that I expect you to practice for the rest of the day. I will send for you in the evening, and then you will duel with me."

Kyra gasped, but Barkav slipped away before she could say another word, silent and graceful as a cat despite his bulk.

She went to her room, bolted the door from within, and collapsed on the bed. Duel the *Maji-khan*? She doubted even Rustan had done that.

❧

After an early breakfast of fruit and milk brought up on a tray by a serving girl, Kyra set off to explore the town. She took her own katari, leaving Shirin Mam's blade underneath the bed, buried in her little bundle of clothes. Ever since Shirin Mam had told her to leave her katari with Rustan, the ancient blade had begun to feel more and more like a burden. Was that why she had also not heard her teacher's voice in so long? Despondent, Kyra slipped out of the guesthouse, careful not to draw attention to herself.

The narrow, dirt-packed streets outside were filled with more people and palanquins, shops and vendors than Kyra had thought existed this side of the Tien Shan Range. How did they all survive in such cramped quarters? She squeezed past people and pack animals, narrowly avoiding being run over by a horse cart. Vendors thrust their wares under her nose, wheedling her to part with her precious coin. She ignored them and continued walking, deeper into the bustling heart of the town, half-dazed by the noise, color, and commotion.

She stopped short at the edge of a vast, dirt-packed square. Row upon row of stalls jostled for space with prospective customers of every hue and garb. Goats and people milled about. At one end of the square was an enclosure for camels; at the other end a strip of sand had been cleared for testing the horses that were on sale. This must be the fabled weekly market of Kashgar. Kyra stood on tiptoe, trying to spot an opening in the press of people so she could join the throngs fingering fabrics and poking melons.

"I wouldn't go into the crowd, if I were you," said someone behind her. "Not unless you wish to have your purse cut."

Kyra's heart leaped at the sound of that voice. *Rustan*.

He stood there smiling, holding a covered basket in one hand and the reins of a loaded mule in the other. All the anger and loneliness she had felt at his abrupt departure from Khur evaporated, and she grinned back at him, the first real surge of joy she'd felt in days rushing through her. She was relieved that she had had a bath the evening before and washed her hair. Thank goodness he hadn't seen her when she arrived in Kashgar, filthy and exhausted.

He was trim and striking as ever, with his black hair cropped short and his blue eyes regarding her with amusement. Even holding a basket of potatoes, he was every inch the Marksman, the symbol of the winged horse on his robe and the unadorned heartwood scabbard hanging from his waist belt. She noticed a circle of space had opened up around him. People backed away after a single glance at his face. How come they didn't do that around her? True, she hid her scabbard in a fold of her robe, but still.

"Barkav told me I'd probably find you at the market," said Rustan. "He gave me a list of things to buy, and here I am, at your service once more."

He gave a mock bow, but the effect was rather spoiled by a half-bray, half-whinny from the mule. Kyra burst out laughing and Rustan straightened, shaking his head in disgust.

"Where have you been?" she demanded, hoping she didn't sound breathless. "I thought you were away on a mission for the Order."

Why didn't you tell me you were leaving? I thought I'd never see you again.

Better if you hadn't.

Kyra blinked, startled. Had they spoken aloud?

But Rustan said, "I *was* on a mission. I went to Herat to look for Samant, the elder who was visiting the Ersani clan. I found him delirious with fever, lying alone in a hut while the Ersanis waited for him to pass into the spirit world."

"What?" said Kyra. "Why didn't they give him medicine?"

"Superstition," said Rustan. "They think sickness is a possession by the spirits. Fortunately, I've managed to bring Samant here for treatment. He should be fine in a few days." He looked at the square. "What were you planning to buy today? Perhaps I can help." A teasing note entered his voice. "Thieves will steal the robe off your back if you're not careful."

"I only wanted to look," said Kyra. "I don't have much coin, and not much time either. The Maji-khan wants me to spend the rest of the day practicing. He said he would duel me this evening."

She hoped Rustan would offer to practice with her, but he simply nodded. "We shall have to be quick then. Follow me."

He plunged ahead into the crowd, which seemed to part magically for him and his mule. Kyra hurried after him, a little disappointed. What had she been expecting? Rustan had taught her what he could; Barkav had said as much. His being in Kashgar at the same time as her was happenstance, and she had best not act like a fool around him.

Rustan watched as Kyra touched a roll of fabric on the counter of a tiny stall manned by a sharp-eyed Kushan woman. It was Jili silk of the finest quality, spun by silk farmers of the Zhejiang province. It was emereld green in color, much like her blade.

When Samant told him he should return to Kashgar before it was "too late," he had been mortified, and also terrified he would somehow miss her, that the contingent would have left for Sikandra Fort already, and he would never see her again. But there was no way he could endanger the life of the elder in his care. It was Samant, finally, who had insisted on leaving the Ersani village as soon as he could stand.

Stay alive, Kyra.

She looked at him, frowning, and Rustan blanked his thoughts. She turned her attention back to the fabrics on display, but he could sense her confusion, the disarray of her emotions. She had not expected to see him again and it was difficult for her to hide her feelings. Although, he supposed, he wasn't doing such a good job of it either. He had known he would be happy to see her again; he had thought of her every day since leaving Khur, and it had seemed like months rather than weeks since he'd last laid eyes on her. But what he hadn't expected was this fierce desire to take her in his arms.

Rustan winced inwardly, remembering the kiss he had witnessed in Khur. And the inescapable fact of Shurik's presence in Kashgar.

In three days it wouldn't matter how he felt. She would be gone from their lives, one way or another. If she won the duel, as he hoped and prayed she would, she would return in triumph to her Order, and they would not meet again, except in the most formal of circumstances. If she lost . . . but here his mind refused to go.

There was nothing he could do about it, nothing. Except—he could be a witness to the last. He owed her that much. Samant thought so. Barkav did too, not that he had said anything outright. But Rustan could still remember the disappointed look the Maji-khan had given him when he'd asked for another assignment. What had he said? *Don't delude yourself. You cannot run away, no matter how far you go.*

In Herat, after inadvertantly confessing his feelings to Samant, Rustan had known he had to come back. There was no way he could influence the course of the duel. But he would be there for Kyra till the end. He would give her—give *himself*—that.

CHAPTER 28

COMPULSION

Kyra walked along the gallery to her room, humming, cradling the lovely roll of Jili silk Rustan had insisted on purchasing for her, despite her protests. But it wasn't the silk that made her happy; it was the fact that Rustan had been unable to hide his pleasure at seeing her again.

"Never mind," he had said about the silk, with a smile that made her heart flutter in the most alarming way. "Perhaps you will find an occasion to wear it one day."

It was foolish, of course. She would never wear that silk. She would never wear anything but the robes of her Order as long as she lived. But she couldn't help running her hands over the delicate material, imagining how it would feel against her skin. Imagining how Rustan might feel, seeing her in it, how it might make him want to touch her the same way she was now stroking the fabric.

They had returned to the Jewel of Kashi together, the mule following them through the narrow streets. At the guesthouse they shared a brief midday meal, which Kyra was not able to taste or remember. She was too aware of Rustan's eyes lingering on her face. Finally he left to run some errands for Barkav, reminding Kyra that she needed to practice before the duel with the Maji-khan.

The rest of the day dragged by. Kyra tried to concentrate on the forms of internal strength, but her thoughts kept returning to Rustan, and the way he had looked at her when he bought the green silk.

When Aram knocked at her door that evening and told her Barkav was waiting for her, Kyra woke from her daydreams with a guilty start. She hastily tied her hair and tightened the belt across her robe, trying to overcome her nervousness. She followed Aram down the stairs and into one of the empty stalls facing the courtyard. To her dismay, Shurik, Rustan, Ishtul, Saninda, and Ghasil were also present, standing just outside the stall, blocking it from the view of curious onlookers.

The elders gave her a brief nod, but otherwise remained expressionless. Rustan gave her an encouraging smile. As her teacher, this was as much his test as hers, but he did not look unduly worried about it. Shurik, on the other hand, could barely disguise his anxiety. *Good luck*, he mouthed at her. Kyra bowed to the elders, and gave a reassuring look to her friend. *It's all right. I know what I'm doing.*

And then she entered the stall and faced the Maji-khan. Her heart quailed. He stood in a pool of light cast by two oil lamps hanging at the entrance, immovable and solid as a mountain, his face like granite. He was at least twice her size. But Chintil had taught her that size had nothing to do with the outcome of a duel. You could use someone's strength against them, if you had the skill.

Kyra bowed to the Maji-khan, and he inclined his head.

"I could break you in two like a twig," he said, his deep voice booming in the empy stall. "Are you worthy of my katari?" He made a tiny movement, and a soft golden-yellow light appeared in his hand.

Kyra swallowed. He was testing her will and courage. "I am as unbreakable as my blade," she said, keeping her voice steady. She unsheathed her own katari, and felt its warmth travel up her arm.

He moved forward, so fast that she almost stumbled back in fear, and thrust his katari toward her throat in a sudden, upward strike. Behind her, she heard Shurik gasp. But Kyra had no time to spare a thought for him. She blocked the Maji-khan's katari with her forearm, wincing as she hit the flat of his blade. If this wasn't a mock duel, the katari would have sliced her arm in half. She brought her own katari slashing down on Barkav's shoulder. At the last moment, she twisted it so it glanced off harmlessly, and at the same time hooked her right leg around his left leg to try to sweep him off his feet.

It was like trying to fell a gigantic pile of rock.

Barkav grabbed hold of her right leg and twisted it so she fell on her face. She steadied herself with both hands before she hit the ground, losing her katari in the process, and jabbed her left foot up in the direction of his face. The foot connected, and she was rewarded by a surprised grunt. But then Barkav grabbed hold of her other leg as well and hauled her up so she hung upside down, the blood rushing to her face as she tried in vain to scrabble for her katari.

"Not bad," said Barkav, chuckling. "Can't remember the last time someone managed to hit my nose. But let us see if you can handle a surprise attack better than that."

He released her gently and allowed her to get to her feet.

As she bent to retrieve her katari, she caught Rustan's gaze. He gave her the same encouraging smile as before, as if determined not to betray any other emotion. The elders looked grim, as if they were witnessing a funeral. But Shurik turned and strode away before she could see his expression. *Probably can't stomach seeing me beaten*, she thought wryly.

After another mock fight—which, predictably, she lost—the Maji-khan began to teach her in earnest. He took her through eight lesser-known styles of katari duel. One by one, the elders left for various meetings after wishing her well. Rustan too was summoned by Ishtul and had to leave, and finally it was just Kyra and Barkav who remained.

The Maji-khan taught with patience and lucidity, even though she knew he had returned from a daylong meeting with the Kushan clan elders and had many more petitions to hear before he could sleep that night. When she finally managed to disarm him—after several tries—he applauded her with delight. She left the stall aglow with a sense of achievement, feeling more confident about facing Tamsyn than she had before, and full of gratitude for the Maji-khan.

They gathered together for the evening meal a little later—all except Shurik. Kyra wondered where he was and what had made him miss dinner. That wasn't like him at all.

When the meal was over, she lingered at the table, hoping to speak to Rustan alone again. She wanted to know what he thought of her duel with Barkav. But the elders wouldn't budge from his side. They plied him with questions about what had happened in Herat and how Samant had fared with the Ersanis. Finally she gave up and decided to go up to her room.

Shisqa was as cozy and welcoming as ever. Firelight flickered on the walls, reflecting the glow inside Kyra. She threw herself on the bed and sighed. Today had been wonderful. She wished every day could be like this. If only she could stop time so that nothing moved and nothing lived except her and Rustan. She would wear that green silk for him and they would walk hand in hand through the empty streets of Kashgar, with no one to look at them, no one to point and whisper.

She drifted off to sleep thinking about this, smiling.

It was a sound that woke her up—a rustling, as of someone in the room. Her eyes flew open and she was instantly awake. Had she forgotten to bolt the door? The fire had gone out but she sensed movement near the end of her bed. Her hand slipped under the pillow for her blade, but before she could withdraw it from the scabbard, a voice spoke in the dark:

"Leave your katari and come. Do not make a sound."

The mental bonds fell on her like a heavy net. She opened her mouth to scream but no sound emerged. She tried to will her hands toward her katari, but they refused to obey.

Tamsyn, she thought, her insides congealing in fear. Tamsyn had found her. Kyra would never have a chance to challenge her to a duel now. She would be dead long before then.

"Follow me."

Kyra's legs made her stand and move with the dark figure out of the room. She tried to claw her way out of the panic fogging her mind. She had to warn the Marksmen that the Hand of Kali was here. She tried desperately to remember what she knew about Compulsion. *Misuse of the Inner Speech. Breaking of the rules. Breaking of the mind.*

Tamsyn was the Mistress of Mental Arts, the most powerful

Markswoman the Order of Kali had seen in decades. How would Kyra break free from her long enough to call for help, let alone make a run for her katari?

But in the light of the lamps hanging in the gallery outside, Kyra received her second shock. The figure striding in front of her wasn't Tamsyn.

It was Shurik.

What are you doing, you fool! she wanted to scream. *Let me go.*

But no words emerged from her mouth. Barkav had mentioned that Shurik was exceptionally gifted in the Mental Arts, but Kyra hadn't thought anything of it at the time.

Heart pounding, Kyra followed Shurik down the wooden staircase to the courtyard below. It had to be the middle of the night, for no one was awake. The courtyard was dotted with groups of people huddled under blankets. Somewhere a horse stamped and neighed.

At the bottom of the stairs, Shurik veered left, heading for the gate. Kyra tried to stop, and once she stumbled and fell, but he hauled her up again. His face was a stranger's face. Why was he doing this to her?

He led her into a stable near the gate. The light of an oil lamp fell on a young boy holding the reins of a saddled horse. Shurik tossed the boy a coin; he caught it deftly and scampered off into the night. The hope that had flared in Kyra at the sight of another person flickered out.

Shurik pointed at the horse.

"GET ON THE HORSE," he said. "We're leaving Kashgar."

Kyra's mouth worked with the effort of trying to speak against a direct order. "Why?" she whispered, leaning against the wall for support, her body trembling as she fought the command to mount the horse.

Shurik gazed at her out of calm brown eyes. "Because I love you," he said. "I'll not stand by and let you go to your death. Did you not tell me yourself to choose the most difficult path of all? This is the hardest thing I've ever done. LEAVE WITH ME."

Kyra shuddered as his voice rolled into her skull, obliterating everything else. Oh, how it hurt. She reached for the reins with shaking hands. Her eyes stung as she thought of her katari, buried under the pillow in her room. Would she ever see it again? She would rather die than be parted from it forever.

"What do you think you're doing?"

Shurik whirled around and swore.

A tall, lean figure was silhouetted against the entrance to the stall. Rustan? Kyra tried to turn toward him, but Shurik had gripped her upper arm. His blade was out.

"We're leaving," said Shurik. "Don't try to stop us. Kyra has changed her mind about the duel and I'm helping her escape."

"Is that so?"

Rustan closed the gap between them. Shurik's grip on her arm tightened. The horse whinnied nervously.

"I thought I heard you use the Inner Speech," said Rustan.

"Oh?" Shurik paused before answering. "I had to make sure that groom didn't go about telling tales of us come daybreak."

"Strange," said Rustan. "The boy who came running out of here was so eager to describe your long and tender embrace that I could almost believe the opposite."

Some of the fog lifted from Kyra's brain. Shurik must be losing his concentration. She struggled to free herself, holding on to the image of her blade.

"You're jealous," said Shurik, his voice scornful. "I know how you feel about her, even if no one else does. I'm honest enough to admit my feelings, but you—you're a coward and a hypocrite. Now get out of our way."

It was too much to be borne. Kyra's anger finally broke the last of the bonds Shurik had laid on her, and she twisted her arm free of his grip. "How dare you!" She was barely able to get the words out. Her throat felt parched, like it had after the sandstorm. "How dare you compel me like this!"

Shurik stepped away from her and raised his hands. "Compel? My sweet, you came to me of your own free will, remember? Begging for a way out of here. Don't lose your courage now because of Rustan. He cannot stop you. He will not even tell the elders if we ask him not to."

Kyra's head swam. Shurik's voice was subtly laced with the Inner Speech. Could Rustan not sense it? She looked across the stable to where Rustan stood, his eyes troubled as they rested on her.

"Help me," she begged.

"That's exactly what I'm trying to do," said Shurik. "Get on the horse. We must leave before daybreak."

"Wait," said Rustan. "Where is your katari, Kyra?"

"In my room," she said, and it was hard to admit, even though it should have been a relief to have someone else know she had been forcibly separated from her katari.

Rustan looked at Shurik, anger darkening his face. "As if she would leave without her blade. What the sands were you thinking, you idiot? You've broken one of our most fundamental rules. You must have known you wouldn't be able to keep her under Compulsion for long."

"Long enough," said Shurik, his voice brittle. "A couple of days was all I needed. A couple of days and she would have been mine—if not for *your* interference."

Without warning he raised his hand and a silver blue streak flew straight at Rustan. Kyra cried out in horror and threw herself toward him. But Rustan moved faster than she did, almost out of reach of the blade. *Almost.* It grazed his shoulder and he slid down the wall, breathing hard.

Kyra was in front of him in a second, a cold pit opening up in her stomach. Reaching out, she gently touched his arm. "You're bleeding. Let me fetch the Maji-khan."

She straightened up but Rustan said, "No. It's only a minor wound. Please don't call Barkav. You can bind it up for me."

With what? Kyra looked around for some cloth. Her eyes fell on Shurik, who was staring at Rustan with an expression of shock, his hand still raised.

"Give me your headcloth," she snapped at him. She had to repeat herself before Shurik seemed to hear her. He unwrapped the red and brown square of cotton from his head with hands that shook slightly, and gave it to her without a word. She deftly tore it into strips and knelt before Rustan.

Rustan looked up at Shurik. "You would have killed me?" He swallowed hard.

Shurik hung his head. He looked young and scared and lost—no longer the stranger who had compelled Kyra. As if, in that one terrible act of throwing his blade, he had remembered who he was—or at least who he was supposed to be.

"Talk to me," said Rustan, a note of command entering his voice. "Tell me you understand what you just tried to do."

"I . . . I'm sorry," said Shurik, raising his head, anguished. "I . . . I do understand and it's unforgivable. I don't know what came over me. But she's going to die now. I thought I could save her."

"We all die," said Rustan. "The most we can hope for is that the time and manner of our death are of our choosing. Kyra has chosen to challenge the mightiest Markswoman in Asiana, and it might be that she will die for it. How long could you have kept her safe? How long before you broke her mind, or she escaped, full of hatred for you?"

They were talking about her as if she wasn't even there. Kyra glared at Rustan, but he had eyes only for Shurik. "I know you're thinking of running away right now," he said. "But don't do that. Please. Go to the Maji-khan and plead for clemency."

Kyra finished binding the gash in Rustan's shoulder, jerking his arm a bit harder than necessary as she tied it off. Thankfully, it was not too deep. Then she stood up, wrapping her arms around herself in an attempt to still the cold fury racing through her.

"How will the elders punish me?" asked Shurik. "Will they exile me? Take away my katari?"

"I don't know," said Rustan. "The katari belongs to you. But you need to make sure that your emotions don't rule your blade. You must take it to the Maji-khan and let him decide." He picked up the katari from the floor and held it out to Shurik, who eyed it as he might a spitting cobra.

"We all got lucky today," Rustan went on. "I arrived before you could take Kyra away, and the blade missed my vital organs—but you can't rely on luck in the Order. I think, at the very least, Barkav will make you retrain with the apprentices. You'll have to earn your blade back."

A spasm of pain rippled across Shurik's face. "As long as they don't send me away," he said. "As long as *you* can still bear to have me around."

"Of course I can," said Rustan. "I wouldn't be able to bear *not* having you around. You're my friend; you always will be."

He held his arms out. Shurik reached down and hugged him, carefully avoiding his injury.

Kyra was stunned. Shurik had almost killed Rustan a few moments ago, and now they were embracing like long-lost brothers. She would never understand them. At that moment, she didn't even want to. She had a splitting headache and she was thoroughly shaken from the ordeal Shurik had put her through. "If you will excuse me, I want my katari," she said. "I'm going to my room now." Her voice was hard and flat, alien to her own ears.

Shurik drew away from Rustan and said, in a pleading voice, "Kyra, I'm so sorry, I . . ."

Something in her snapped. "Don't you ever say my name again!" she shouted. "If you're not gone by morning, I'll speak to the Maji-khan myself. I thought you were my friend. But you betrayed my trust. You broke the law. You entered my *mind*, Shurik." She shuddered anew at the violation she had suffered.

Shurik looked down, his face crimson. "I'm sorry," he repeated, his voice a husky whisper. "I will confess to the Maji-khan, and be gone by morning."

"Kyra," began Rustan, but she didn't wait to hear what he had to say. She couldn't bear to be in Shurik's presence one second longer. Or Rustan's, for that matter. Not right now.

She marched out and made her way across the courtyard, giving a wide margin to the groups of people still sleeping out in the open. Her face burned as she thought of the story Shurik had paid the little groom to circulate about her. Why, oh why hadn't she warned the Maji-khan not to let Shurik travel with them? She had known the kind of feelings he had for her, after all. But she'd never dreamed he would be capable of . . . of *this*!

She burst into her room and snatched her katari from under

the pillow. She withdrew the blade from its sheath and touched it to her forehead, whispering, "I'm sorry, I'm sorry."

She huddled in the quilt, clutching the katari to her chest. Her headache dissipated as the warmth and power of the blade flowed into her. Never again would she be parted from it. She would wear it in a scabbard around her neck while sleeping. It was shameful, the way she had been caught. Shirin Mam would have been most cutting. She could hear her now, in her most caustic voice:

A Markswoman without her weapon is like a horse without legs.

Kyra sat up, startled. It was a long time since she had heard her teacher's voice. She bent down to retrieve Shirin Mam's blade from the bundle of clothes underneath her bed, but at that moment there was a rap on the door.

Kyra tensed. She knew it was Rustan. She didn't want to see him or talk to him. It wasn't his fault, what had happened, but he had witnessed her awful humiliation, her almost-abduction by his so-called best friend and fellow Marksman.

He probably saved you from a great deal of pain, my child.

Kyra winced. Shirin Mam again. *Get out of my head, please,* she thought.

She put on her blandest face and opened the door.

Rustan stood outside, looking as edgy as she felt. He had donned a fresh shirt and there was no evidence of the wound beneath. Beyond him Kyra could hear the clatter of a wagon across the courtyard and the stamping of hooves. Dawn, and people were already on the move.

"Who were you talking to?" said Rustan, walking in and shutting the door without so much as a by-your-leave.

"I don't know what you mean," said Kyra coolly. "As you can see, there is no one here besides us."

Rustan crossed his arms and leaned against the wall, study-ing her. It made her uncomfortable, as if there was not enough space in the room for both of them.

When she could no longer bear his silent scrutiny, she burst out, "Have you come seeking my gratitude?"

Rustan's eyes widened. "Three things," he said, holding up his fingers. "One: the worst thing that can happen to a Marks-man or Markswoman is the loss of his or her blade. You have been careless."

Kyra closed her eyes. First Shirin Mam and now Rustan. She *was* ashamed. Did he have to rub it in?

"Two: even though you have been careless, you cannot blame yourself for what happened."

Kyra's eyes flew open, and she swallowed the lump in her throat. "I knew how he felt about me," she whispered. "I should have told the elders, made sure he didn't come to Kashgar with us."

"Shurik is a Marksman," said Rustan harshly. "We all choose how we act. He chose to break the law, and he will be punished for it." He paused and said in a different tone, "I knew some-thing was wrong with him last night, but I couldn't figure out what. I woke at some point and sensed you both out in the corridor. I followed as quickly as I could. I . . . I don't want you to think I was testing you in any way, Kyra, when I asked you where your katari was. There were a number of ways the scene could have played out, and I wanted to do it with the least possible damage."

Despite herself, Kyra gave a tentative smile. "Least damage?" She pointed to his shoulder. "He almost killed you."

Rustan's face relaxed and he almost smiled himself. "I was never in danger. Shurik has terrible aim. Besides, he didn't really want to kill me." He shook his head. "No, the real danger once I arrived was to Shurik. I needed to free you without harming either of you. Ultimately, you freed yourself, and I did not have to use my blade. I have learned, the hard way, to stay my hand."

"Well, I have not," said Kyra fiercely. "If I'd had my katari, I would have stabbed him."

"You are right to be angry," said Rustan. "I don't expect you to forgive him."

"What will happen to him?" asked Kyra.

"He has gone to Barkav to confess," said Rustan. "I imagine he will be sent back to Khur, and the elders will pass his sentence after the meeting in Sikandra."

Kyra shivered as she thought of how the Maji-khan could crush a person with a single dark look. She wouldn't want to be in Shurik's boots for anything. On the other hand, she would never be stupid or cruel enough to try to do what he had done.

"I should go now," said Rustan. "The elders will want my version of what happened."

But he lingered in the room, his eyes resting on her face, as if reluctant to leave.

Then don't leave.

"What's the third thing?" said Kyra hastily, wanting to hide that thought.

"What?" said Rustan, as if his mind was elsewhere. The way he was looking at her made her feel hot and cold all at once.

"You said 'three things' when you entered my room," said Kyra. "You've only told me two of them."

"Ah yes, the third thing," said Rustan. "When Shurik called me a hypocrite and a coward, he was right."

They stared at each other across the room and something ignited between them. He took a step toward her, and the blaze of desire in his eyes almost made her stumble back over the bed. He caught her with one hand and pulled her to him, tracing her face with his fingertips, down to the hollow of her neck and up to her lips. Kyra stood still, heart thudding inside her chest, his fingers leaving trails of goose bumps on her skin.

Slowly, never taking his eyes from hers, Rustan leaned down and pressed his lips against hers.

Kyra closed her eyes and swayed. The world turned, the moment stretched. Rustan smelled of the desert, the hot sun, the cold wind. She could not breathe, she could not think. Unable to stop herself, she parted her lips and reached for him, twining her fingers in his hair. She heard him gasp, and his arms encircled her.

But the next moment he released her and stepped away, breathing hard.

She felt bereft. *Don't stop*, she wanted to shout. *Don't leave.* He must have known what she was thinking, what she wanted, and yet he made no move toward her. She could have wept with disappointment.

"Kyra . . ." he said, a plea entering his voice.

"Don't," she whispered. "Don't say anything." She couldn't have borne it if he had apologized.

Rustan looked at her, his face tight with suppressed emotion. He turned and left, as abruptly as he had come.

Kyra sat down on the bed and exhaled the breath that had been trapped in her chest while Rustan was in the room. She had never been so utterly in someone's power before, not even when Shurik laid the bonds of Inner Speech on her.

A tight band of pain encircled her heart. Was this what it was like to love someone? She was glad, *glad* that the meeting in Sikandra was only two days away.

The dam broke and she cried, sobbing into the pillow to muffle the sounds.

CHAPTER 29

LIVE LONG AND
DIE WELL

Kyra splashed cold water on her face and got dressed. It was time to leave the Jewel of Kashi. She dragged out the little bundle of clothes from underneath the bed and withdrew Shirin Mam's katari from its scabbard. She touched it to her lips. Time to say goodbye.

She had given up hope of meeting Shirin Mam in *Anantkal* again, but at least while she carried the blade, she could imagine that her teacher was somehow still with her. It was a wrench to give it up, but Shirin Mam had been quite clear in her instructions. Rustan was to have the katari before Kyra left for Sikandra, and now she had the chance to give it directly to him. She had known from the beginning that she would not be able to keep it for long.

She donned her brown Markswoman robe with the symbol of Kali. She didn't want to hide who she was anymore, but Barkav had insisted she wear a hooded cloak over the

robe until she declared herself in the Hall of Sikandra. Kyra
had agreed, knowing that the longer she could keep her
identity a secret, the stronger the element of surprise for
her enemy.

She glanced at the window and was startled to see how light
it had become. She would have to hurry if she wanted to catch
Rustan before he went down for the morning meal.

She slipped out the door and went down the corridor to the
last room but one, hoping none of the elders would notice her,
and trying to quell the nervous flutter of anticipation that rose
in her chest. She hadn't seen Rustan alone even once after that
kiss. This would be the first time—and probably the last, she
reminded herself.

Again and again she had been drawn into a wretched argu-
ment with herself. What had happened in the room between
them that day? Why had he kissed her? Why had it hurt so
much when he stepped away from her and left the room?

She hardly knew him. He should mean less to her than
Nineth or Elena did, less than the memory of those she had
loved and lost. Why did thoughts of him consume her waking
moments? She longed to be alone with him again; at the same
time the force of her feelings frightened her. Such feelings
were surely a sign of weakness in a Markswoman. Would they
be what broke her during the duel with Tamsyn?

A Markswoman belonged to no one but her Order. She
could not allow personal desires to get in her way. This was
what Shirin Mam had said, and certainly what the Maji-khan
believed too.

Kyra quaked inwardly at the thought of what Barkav would
say if he knew of the kiss. First Shurik and now Rustan. He
would forbid the Order of Khur from having anything to do

with her, ever again. As it was, Kyra had gleaned from talk among the elders that Barkav had been furious with Shurik. He had questioned both Shurik and Rustan closely, and sent Shurik back to the camp of Khur. Shurik had gone at once. Apparently, he would have to relinquish his blade to Astinsai until the Maji-khan returned and decided what to do with him. Kyra had waited on tenterhooks to be summoned to the Maji-khan herself, but he had not asked for her. She didn't know whether to feel relieved or anxious about that.

Kyra reached the door of the last room but one and drew a deep breath. *Watch yourself now*, she thought. She raised a hand, but the door flew open before she could knock on it.

Rustan looked disheveled, as if he had woken up a short while ago. Behind him, she could see robes and underclothes strewn about his chamber. A knapsack lay open on his bed. She had caught him in the middle of packing. It was too intimate somehow, and she could feel her face flush as she began to say that she would come back later, but Rustan gently pulled her inside and told her to sit down.

"To what do I owe the pleasure of this early morning visit?" He spoke lightly, but she could tell that he was not quite at ease.

She smiled, trying to appear as cool and polite as him. "It's not that early, you know," she said. "It will soon be time for the morning meal. In an hour we leave for Sikandra."

"Oh, really? I'd better hurry up." He began to throw his things higgledy-piggledy into the knapsack.

That puzzled her. "Are you leaving too?" she said. "I thought you were going to stay here until the elders returned from Sikandra."

"I'm going with you." Rustan closed the straps of his knapsack and straightened up.

"But . . . but why?"

"Surely you can guess?" said Rustan. "I taught you what I know of dueling. I don't know if it was enough, but it is my duty to see you through this. The Maji-khan agreed."

"Oh." Kyra wasn't sure what she had wanted him to say, but his answer was a bit deflating in its practicality. He was accompanying her out of a sense of duty. What had she hoped for, declarations of undying love? Neither of them had any use for those. Just as the silence between them turned awkward, she remembered why she was there and held Shirin Mam's scabbard out to him. "I give this to you for safekeeping."

Rustan accepted it without a word, tying it to the belt around his waist.

Kyra felt a sense of anticlimax. "Aren't you going to ask me why I gave that to you?" she said, a touch acerbically.

Rustan looked surprised. "Who else is there? I suppose you could have given it to the Maji-khan, but he would probably have passed it along to me anyway. I'll take excellent care of it, don't worry."

Kyra frowned. "I gave that to you because Shirin Mam *told* me to," she said, and was gratified to see the look of shock on Rustan's face.

"What do you mean? When did she tell you?" he demanded.

"Some weeks ago. In a—I guess it was a dream." To Kyra's dismay, tears sprang to her eyes. She got up and turned away before he could see them. "I'd better go finish my packing," she choked out.

She slipped out, relieved that he did not stop her. She went back to the room that wasn't hers anymore, and gave in to a fit of silent weeping. Giving up the katari was like losing Shirin

Mam all over again. But when she had cried herself out, it was as if an unseen weight had lifted from her shoulders. She took out her own silvery green blade and kissed it.

"It's just you and me now," she said.

Her katari sparkled in response.

Rustan held himself rigid until he was sure that Kyra was out of earshot. Then he pounded his fist against the wall, growling in frustration, until his knuckles were bruised and the pain brought him back to his senses. He pushed away from the wall and swore under his breath. By all the gods of Asiana, that had been close. Standing so near Kyra, in this confined space—it had taken iron self-control to not reach for her, to not kiss her the way he had in her room, to talk to her as a friend . . . as more than a friend. He knew she was upset. But if she had known how close he had come to touching her . . .

He slumped on the bed and held his head in his hands, focusing on his breath. It was all right. The danger was past. He had restrained himself.

When his breath had evened out, he withdrew Shirin Mam's katari from its sheath. He gently touched the translucent blade, wondering if anything would happen.

As he had expected, nothing did.

Rustan frowned, twirling the blade in his hands. Why had Shirin Mam wanted him to have her katari?

You will have need of me before you are done.

Rustan dropped the blade in shock. Shirin Mam's quiet voice, heard after so many years, sounded exactly the same.

Except that it wasn't a voice, not exactly. More like hearing someone's thought, clear and low.

Rustan picked up the blade again, but although he concentrated for several minutes, he heard nothing more.

Saninda's voice, sharp and demanding outside his door, snapped him back to the present. Rustan sheathed Shirin Mam's katari, slung the knapsack on his shoulders, and hurried to join the others downstairs.

⟡

The Hub of Kashgar was below a ruined temple in the heart of the old town. It was hard to say whether the temple had been built because of the gleaming corridors of Transport underneath, or in spite of them. Those who had laid the foundations of the temple were long dead, their skeletal remains hidden in stone chests in the burial chamber beneath the main hall. People stayed away from the temple now; it was rumored to be haunted.

Kyra, following Barkav and Saninda down the uneven, rock-hewn steps to the burial chamber, could believe that it was so. The air was dank and musty; there was no light, save the glow of their kataris.

"Why didn't we bring a torch?" she muttered to herself.

"A local superstition," said Rustan from behind her. "They do not wish to wake the dead."

Kyra almost stumbled, but Rustan steadied her with his arm, his touch warm against her skin. Her breath caught. She hadn't realized how close behind he was.

"Watch your feet now," said Barkav. "The last step is broken."

Kyra shook off Rustan's arm and felt her way to the bottom. They reached the end of the stairs and stood, as far as she could make out, in an unadorned chamber lined with stone chests that were covered with inscriptions. Knowing what they contained, she avoided looking at them. Her gaze went instead to the door on the far side of the room.

"The Hub of Kashgar," said Saninda. "Shall I?" The elder strode to the door and inserted his katari in the slot. A moment later the slot glowed blue and the door swung open.

Kyra's heart accelerated. She wouldn't survive another Transport experience like the last one. It would break her mind if she saw things and lost time again. She began to hyperventilate, her breath coming in short gasps, the dark abyss yawning before her.

"It's all right, Kyra," said Rustan softly in her ear. "This is the Hub of Kashgar. We use it all the time. No reports of anyone getting lost. And we're all with you."

Kyra forced her breathing to slow, but it didn't help that Rustan was standing so close to her they were practically touching. "I'm perfectly all right," she said, her voice uneven, and marched toward the open door. Behind her, Rustan followed.

Barkav and Saninda had disappeared into the darkness of the corridor ahead. Ghasil and Ishtul must already be at Sikandra Fort, having Transported an hour ago with the Kushan and Turguz clan elders.

The door swung shut behind them, and Kyra was once more in the strange yet familiar landscape of Transport: a dark, winding corridor, lit only by the slots on the doors and the glowing kataris of the Marksmen.

"It's the fifth door on the right," came the Maji-khan's voice. "Go on, Saninda, you know the code."

This corridor had doors on both sides. It was a vast, complex Hub that possibly connected Kashgar with every corner of Asiana. Except, of course, that many of the doors were unusable, having shifted over time.

But Felda had discovered that special sets of primes could unlock any door in any Hub. Kyra's stomach clenched as she thought of the vast possibilities of this, as if she teetered at the edge of some great insight. It was too much to grasp, too much power for anyone to have. Was this why the old war had been fought? She fingered the fraying parchment with the secret codes in her pocket. She would have to keep it safely hidden.

The Transport Chamber opened and its light—brilliant after the dimness of the corridor—beckoned them in.

Kyra followed the others into the circular room, taking one of the seats melded to the floor. It moved beneath her, as she had known it would, adjusting to her weight and shape. She shuddered.

Barkav and Saninda talked about the meeting, but Rustan was quiet, watching her. The room began to spin and Kyra schooled herself to stay calm.

Barkav stopped talking and glanced at her. "Once we arrive at Sikandra, you're on your own."

"Yes, Father." It made sense. The Order of Khur could not afford to take sides until the duel had been fought and the outcome decided.

"The use of Mental Arts is not permitted in the Hall of Sikandra, where clans and Orders meet as equals," said Barkav. "This is to your advantage. Stay hidden until you declare yourself to the assembly. We will pray for your success."

The chamber stopped spinning, the door swung open, and the Marksmen stood up. To Kyra's surprise, Barkav leaned forward and gently kissed her forehead. "May you live long and die well," he murmured. He left the chamber without a backward glance.

Saninda put his bony hand on her head, his touch featherlight. "Live long and die well," he repeated gruffly, before following Barkav out of the chamber.

And then she was alone with Rustan and he was holding her so close she could hear the beating of his heart and feel his breath on her cheeks, and she wanted the moment to go on forever, because it felt so right, so safe, so *good*.

Rustan released her, his eyes burning into hers. "You can defeat her. I know you can."

Kyra smiled reassuringly, not trusting herself to speak.

Then Rustan was gone too and for the first time in months, Kyra was quite, quite alone.

CHAPTER 30

THE HALL OF SIKANDRA

K yra stepped out of the Sikandra Hub, which stood half-way up a rocky hill, surrounded by the arid brown of the Uzbek Plains. But it was what brooded on top of the hill that held her gaze and caught her breath: a massive fortress surrounded by an unbroken stone wall.

She had heard about the fabled Sikandra Fort from the elders of Kali but had never paid much attention, or imagined that anything man-made could be so huge. The gray stone of the crenelated walls glinted in the sun, doing little to hide the two magnificent towers rising within the complex, one on each side. Two huge bronze statues—one of a man, and the other of a woman—crowned the flat roof of each tower. Notches and rectangular gaps punctured the walls that surrounded the fort—to allow for the discharge of weapons, Kyra guessed. Were those battlements older than the war itself? She could remember a history lesson in which Navroz had mentioned that Sikandra Fort was one of the few monuments remaining of the Age of Kings.

The Age of Kings . . . that was before the war, perhaps even before the Ones arrived in Asiana.

There it stood in the middle of nowhere, defying time and space. The nearest village was by Lake Azkal, almost a hundred miles away. Yet the fort must have been of great importance in the olden days. The Sikandra Hub, after all, had been built at its feet.

A stream of people filed out of the Hub ahead of Kyra, men and women talking and laughing as they recognized one another and exchanged news. No one gave her a second glance, cloaked and hooded as she was.

She climbed up the hill behind the crowd heading for the fort, on a steep and twisty road that snaked between boulders and sheer drops. It was much warmer here than it was in Kashgar, and Kyra was soon sweating under her cloak, wishing she could discard it. Almost everyone else was dressed as if for summer in the Ferghana Valley, in pastel cotton shirts and loose trousers. There was even one group of wild-haired folk who wore nothing but strings of beads and animal skins around their waists.

The entrance to the fort was through an arched stone gateway, guarded by a watchtower on each side and topped by notched parapets. The air was cool here; the walls were several meters thick. Kyra followed the crowd through the gateway, craning her neck to see the carvings on the distant roof above—warriors on horseback, sword-wielding women, a row of archers. She tried to imagine a time when sentries manned the gate and archers prowled the parapets above, while kings and queens plotted conquests within the secure heart of the fort.

And then she was through the gateway and Sikandra Fort

rose before her in all its splendor. The floor beneath was paved with cool gray stone. A massive, rectangular edifice lay directly ahead, surrounded by a covered portico. Smaller buildings and intricate sculptures dotted the paved courtyard in which Kyra found herself. And to each side of the main building were the tall towers she had seen from the hill.

Kyra longed to linger and read the inscriptions on the sculptures, and explore the small buildings, which looked like temples or memorials. But there was no time. She made her way to the main building, like everyone else. Serving girls and boys were stationed at the top of the steps leading to the entrance hall. Kyra accepted a welcome drink of strained yogurt and stood aside, wincing at its sour taste.

There were so *many* people, of every hue and garb imaginable. Kyra knew that there were hundreds of clans and tribes in Asiana under the Kanun of Ture-asa. But knowing was one thing, and seeing quite another. The representatives flowed up the stairs, chattering to one another in myriad tongues. This was Asiana, and Sikandra Fort was the heart of it all—at least for one day in the year. How Nineth would envy her this particular adventure.

As she thought of Nineth, her excitement drained away, replaced by numbness. No, Nineth would not envy her. Nineth would tell her that she was mad for challenging Tamsyn, and attempt to drag her to safety, much the way Shurik had.

Thinking of Shurik turned out to be better. Some of her anger returned and Kyra squared her shoulders, straightened her back, and strode in behind the last of the stragglers with such a firm step that she almost bumped into three elderly women in front of her. Embarrassed, she apologized and slunk into a corner, keeping her face hidden beneath her hood. She scanned the people around her, trying to spot the elders of Kali.

But the crowd was too thick, and the hall itself simply enormous, a vast, circular space lined with arched doorways and elongated windows of brilliant colored glass that let in a muted light. A domed ceiling soared overhead, painted in rich detail with animals, people, and what looked to be strange hybrids—half-human, half-machine. The floor was smooth marble, patterned with concentric rings of an intricate geometric design that made you dizzy if you looked at them too long. Yes, it was easy to imagine that kings had once held court in this graceful space.

The Hall of Sikandra reminded Kyra of the place Shirin Mam had taken her to in *Anant-kal*, the night she gave her a "last lesson" in words of power. There were differences in the shape and size of the halls, and in the quality of light that streamed into them. But the *feel* was the same. They both belonged to a different world, a world that was now gone. They were all gone—the kings and queens, the men and women of learning and talent, and, above all, the mythic Ones who had graced Asiana with their presence all those hundreds of years ago.

But Kyra could almost believe that their ghosts still lingered in the hall. Almost see, with her inner eye, the red velvet robe of a queen dragging on the marble floor as she walked, arm in arm, with her consort.

"Hear me. Hear me now." The stern voice echoed across the hall, and all laughter and talking died away. Kyra craned her neck to see who had spoken.

In the center of the hall stood a bent old woman with a wrinkled face and silver hair, leaning on a staff that appeared to be almost twice her height. When she was satisfied that she had everyone's attention, she spoke again:

"I, Unduni Arallin, headwoman of the clan of Arallin, keeper of the Black River Forest, do welcome you to Sikandra for the two hundred fifty-third clan assembly of Asiana. May the light of the Kanun shine on you."

"May the light of the Kanun shine on you," they murmured in response.

"As the mediator," continued Unduni, "I stand between Order and clan. Heads, sit down, please. We had best not waste time, for I see that we have many items to discuss, or shall I say, *argue* about, today."

There were a few dutiful titters and a great rustling as people began to sort themselves out. Everyone obviously knew where to go and how to arrange themselves. Clan elders and heads sat down on chairs, surrounded by the younger members of their families. The Orders walked past Unduni and settled down behind her in five tight little groups.

Kyra stood petrified in the middle of the purposeful rush, not knowing where to stand or with whom.

And then she spotted Tamsyn strolling to one of the chairs behind Unduni, looking as elegant and lethal as ever. Kyra held her breath and released it slowly, trying to still the panic that rose within her at the sight of her deadly enemy. All the time she had spent with the Order of Khur, learning new ways to fight, seemed to blow away like dust. Kyra felt like a novice again, weak and unprepared for the challenge she had set herself.

Navroz, Mumuksu, Chintil, and Felda sat down behind Tamsyn. Kyra's heart gave a little swoop of fear and longing as she regarded the elders of Kali. Navroz looked old and tired in a way she never had before. Mumuksu wore an expression caught between fear and anticipation. Chintil's face was mask-like and she held herself rigid, as if she wished to hide every emotion she had ever felt. Only Felda looked her usual gruff self. Kyra longed to reach out to them, get their news, and share her own. She wished she could somehow communicate with them without alerting Tamsyn.

Or did she? How far could she trust even them? Perhaps Tamsyn had subverted them to her way of thinking by now. Perhaps Shirin Mam and her teachings were but a distant memory, and Kyra a mere irritant to be removed.

Kyra stopped herself. She had to focus on the duel; the elders could be dealt with later. She was lucky that the use of Mental Arts was forbidden in the hall, or Tamsyn would certainly have sensed her presence by now.

She edged near a group of men and women standing close to the center of the hall. It would appear as if she belonged to their clan, and she would be able to see everything that was happening. Her eyes went past the mediator to the lone group of men, and her heart did another somersault. There was Rustan, looking as if he had swallowed a stone that was slowly poisoning him. There was the Maji-khan, grave and impassive, his hand resting on Rustan's shoulder.

Kyra could hear the thoughts of the Markswomen surrounding the Order of Khur:

Mere men, sitting here as if they are our equals.

Men wielding kataris, it's a disgrace.

Why don't they stay away in that godforsaken desert of theirs so we aren't reminded of their existence every year?

And, oddly:

That young dark-haired one is rather good-looking. I wonder who he reminds me of?

Kyra gave a start. Who had been thinking that perilous thought? Her gaze swept over the Markswomen, but their impassive faces gave no clue to what was going on in their individual minds. No way to find out without using the Mental Arts.

The Marksmen, for their part, seemed impervious to the cold glances and occasional mutters aimed at them. Perhaps they were used to it, but Kyra felt a stab of indignation on their behalf.

If anyone had the right to bear the Order of Khur a grudge, it was her. But living with the Marksmen, she had never once thought that they were the enemy, or even that different from her. Of course, she didn't understand the way they processed emotions. And there had been that debacle with Shurik, which still hurt and angered her to think of.

But on the whole, she had got along with the Marksmen just fine. She even liked most of them—okay, no one could *like* Ishtul, but he was an elder and elders didn't count. The only person she had disliked at Khur was Astinsai, and Astinsai was a woman.

Why were the other Orders ill at ease with Khur? Could it be that the Markswomen were afraid of the Marksmen, and they hid their fear under a layer of disdain?

Unduni rapped on the floor three times with her staff. A chair had appeared behind her and a girl stood next to it with a tray, presumably for when the mediator got tired or thirsty. But for now Unduni stood, her eyes somber, her face grave.

"First, I must inform you that Shirin Mam, Mahimata of the Order of Kali, is dead."

Murmurs and sounds of distress broke out among the people gathered in the hall. It appeared that not everyone present had heard of the passing of the old Mahimata of Kali, although they must have marked her absence at the assembly today.

"She will be missed," continued Unduni. "A great leader, who brought several clans of Asiana under the aegis of the Kanun. May she find peace in the world beyond."

"May she find peace," echoed the hall.

Unduni's voice assumed a brisk tone. "Tamsyn Turani has succeeded Shirin Mam as the Mahimata of Kali. I am sure you will join me in extending our good wishes to her for a long and peaceful reign."

The hall was utterly silent as people took in this news. The Hand of Kali was famous in Asiana, but Kyra doubted the word *peaceful* had ever been used in conjunction with her name. Even Unduni looked skeptical as she said it.

Tamsyn got up and said in sweet, sorrowful tones, "I thank you, Unduni Arallin. Shirin Mam was my teacher and friend. It is a great honor to be appointed in her place, but I am not worthy. *No one* is worthy."

Kyra dug her nails into her palms at the sound of Tamsyn's voice. Time had done nothing to dilute her hatred of it. The lying hypocrite. Could no one else see through her?

It appeared Unduni could, for she said, a shade coolly, "Indeed. Moving on to my second announcement, I have great pleasure in welcoming the tribe of Vedarsa from the island of Cochy to this assembly." She gestured with her hands, and the group of scantily clad folk Kyra had seen earlier rose from where they were squatting on the floor and gave deep bows. Everyone cheered and clapped.

Tamsyn sat down, her face betraying nothing, but Kyra could imagine how angry she was. She would already be planning some distant, long-range revenge against Unduni for not giving her the proper respect that was her due as the new Mahimata.

Unduni continued speaking, moving from one item to the next with rapid ease, pausing only to take a few sips of tea. More deaths and appointments were announced, as well as reports on the rainfall and crops produced in different regions and the volume of trade between major towns.

Finally Unduni put away the scrolls she had been consulting from time to time, and sat down with a sigh of relief. "Well, that's all the routine items dealt with. We move on to a far more serious issue, that of outlaw activity in the Thar Desert. I ask Faran Lashail, the head of the Order of Valavan, to make her report to the assembly."

Kyra craned her neck as Faran Lashail strode to the center of the hall and stood next to Unduni's chair. The head of the Order of Valavan was tall and graceful, with oak-dark skin and flashing black eyes. Her hair was coiled like a serpent on her head. A katari hung around her neck, glittering aquamarine against her pristine white clothes—a sleeveless blouse cropped at the midriff, and a rectangular length of cloth wrapped around her waist like a skirt, with one end draped over her shoulder.

"Thank you, Unduni," she said, her voice deep and musical. "I do have rather disturbing news from the Thar. It appears that the Taus, the only outlaws in Asiana armed with death-sticks, are amassing an army in the desert. We do not yet have the exact numbers, but our spies report that they are training over a thousand men to fight."

There were gasps in the hall. Kyra crossed her arms, cold

and light-headed. Was this because of her? Had her first mark set this chain of events into motion? She should have killed Kai Tau that night in the Thar when she had the chance.

No. Her mark had been Maidul, and no one else. And surely Shirin Mam would not have assigned her such a mark if she knew what they risked.

A voice called out, "To fight whom? And why?"

"Precisely what I asked myself," said Faran. "The Taus have kept to themselves for years and I wondered why they would escalate their activities in this blatant way. Then I found out that a Markswoman of Kali had entered *our* territory," and here she threw a cold look at the elders of Kali, "and executed Maidul, the eldest son of the outlaw leader Kai Tau."

Voices rose in excited discussion and Unduni rapped the floor with her staff again. "Silence!" she said. "I ask Tamsyn Turani to speak to the hall, and explain what happened."

Tamsyn stood up and spread her hands. "What can I say? Shirin Mam did not consult any of us in this matter, or I at least would have spoken against it. Suffice it to say that the Markswoman in question was a girl named Kyra Veer. You will remember that the clan of Veer was slaughtered by the outlaw Kai Tau and his men. It was a matter of revenge, I understand, and the girl would not rest until the Mahimata agreed to send her to the Thar. She had an inexplicable fondness for the girl, and could not refuse her."

Kyra's cheeks burned in anger. That was not how it had happened, and Tamsyn knew it. She was making it sound as if Kyra was some sort of a spoiled favorite of the old Mahimata.

Faran gazed at Tamsyn in an assessing way. "What's done is done," she said. "We must find a way to meet this threat. Kai Tau is obviously planning to attack the Orders; we are all that stand between him and absolute control of Asiana. He can wreak havoc with those kalashiks. Dozens of innocent people have already been killed—and that's just the start."

Kyra's stomach clenched. People were dying and it was all *her* fault. She would have to find a way to defeat Kai Tau. It was no longer just a matter of vengeance for the slaughter of her clan.

"Surely we can deal with the outlaws?" came a throaty, contemptuous voice. A large, fair-haired woman rose from one of the chairs, adding, "May I speak, Unduni?"

"You may, Ikina Furshil." Unduni inclined her head.

Ikina Furshil. That was the name of the head of the Order of Zorya. Kyra remembered the story of Zibalik's wolves. Barkav had implied that the Zoryans did not hunt wyr-wolves, believing, as the Order of Khur did, that the wolves were part human.

Ikina glided forward with catlike grace, the white falcon embroidered on her midnight blue robes rippling as she walked. She stared at those gathered around, her stormy gray eyes so compelling that many flinched away from them. "What are a few outlaws against the might of the Orders?" she demanded. "We can break a man's mind before he thinks to reach for a weapon. Fourteen years ago we promised to protect the clans from these murderers. It is time we fulfilled our promise and destroyed the Taus, once and for all."

Murmurs rose at this, subsiding as Unduni waved an imperious hand.

"How many will you kill?" said Faran. "A thousand? Two thousand?"

"It will be enough to kill the Taus," said Ikina. "Leaderless, the rest will lay down their weapons quickly enough."

"And how do you propose to get close enough to the Taus to overpower them?" inquired Faran. "They are armed with a dozen death-sticks—or have you forgotten?"

Ikina's eyes flashed. "There are ways of approaching unseen—or have *you* forgotten? We steal in upon them, we take them by surprise."

"Too risky," said Faran. "They will be expecting us. Perhaps they are even inviting us. All it would take is one guard armed with a single death-stick to take down dozens of Markswomen before one of us gets close enough to use the Inner Speech."

"And even that would not work against Kai Tau himself."

All heads jerked toward the Order of Khur. Barkav's thoughtful voice, deeply male, seemed to send a current through the Markswomen around him. Some glared at him openly, while others crossed their arms and turned their faces away. Kyra was torn between amusement and anger at their reactions. Did they not understand that he was on *their* side?

Tamsyn rose from her chair. "I wonder how many present here are aware that Kai Tau is skilled in the Mental Arts?" she said. "That he developed his skills at the Order of Khur, under the tutelage of Maheshva?"

An uneasy hush fell on the hall. Kyra held her breath, wondering how many were learning this for the first time. Tamsyn had timed her interjection well.

Unduni cleared her throat. "Well, that's all in the past, and we are here to discuss what to do about . . ." Her voice trailed away as Barkav stood, his bulk menacing compared to Tamsyn's slender form.

"Yes, Kai trained at the Order of Khur," said Barkav. "He

became a renegade over twenty years ago, as you must be aware."

Tamsyn's eyes widened. "Oh, I didn't in the least mean to cast any blame on the Order of Khur. But I thought—since he was one of yours—that you may wish to be at the forefront of any assault on the Tau camp. It is fitting, is it not? Unless"—and her tone became amused, a little condescending—"unless you think you and your men are not quite up to the task."

Faran and Ikina both turned to stare at Barkav. There was pin-drop silence in the hall.

Kyra's fists clenched. Tamsyn had trapped Barkav by implying that Kai Tau was *their* responsibility, and if there was dying to be done, the Marksmen should be the ones doing it. She hoped that the Maji-khan would not rise to the bait.

Barkav's eyes had become flints. Beside him, the Khur elders looked furious. But Rustan's face was blank, as if his mind was elsewhere.

When Barkav spoke again, his voice was as calm as ever. "Yes, it would be fitting. We would have gone after Kai years ago, were it not for the words of our seer and katari mistress, Astinsai. According to Astinsai, there is another who must be consulted on the fate of the Taus."

Kyra realized to her horror that Barkav was looking straight at her. He meant *her*.

Tamsyn gave a silvery little laugh. "As I expected, the Order of Khur wriggles out of its responsibility with words that mean nothing." Before Barkav could respond, she addressed Faran. "I have the perfect plan to eliminate the Taus without risking a single drop of our blood. You may leave it to the Order of Kali. I need from you only two things."

Faran raised her eyebrows. "Indeed. And what may those be?"

Despite herself, Kyra leaned forward, spellbound.

Tamsyn held up one finger. "First, you grant jurisdiction over the Thar to the Order of Kali."

Chaos broke across the hall. The elders of Valavan stood up and began to shout. For a while it was difficult to make out what anyone was saying. Unduni frantically rapped the floor with her staff until the noise died down.

When everyone at last fell silent, Unduni glared around the hall at the entire assembly, including the Markswomen of Valavan.

"I remind you," she said, "that I am the mediator of this clan assembly. Does anyone wish to speak? Please raise your hand if you do. No?" She raked them with her eyes. "Good. You may continue, Tamsyn."

"Thank you, Unduni," said Tamsyn. "As I was saying, the Order of Kali will take care of this whole outlaw business. All we need is jurisdiction over the Thar—for how else may we enter it?—and second, we need access to the cache of dark weapons that the Order of Valavan has kept hidden."

This time Unduni did not even try to control the pandemonium that broke out. She stared at Tamsyn, disbelief etched in every line of her ancient face.

"You're *mad*," said Faran. "You would use the dark weapons? The *death-sticks*? Shirin Mam would have flayed you alive for even thinking it."

Barkav was waving his arms, his face red with anger, having finally lost control of his temper. Even the elders of Kali were shouting. Kyra guessed that they hadn't been informed of Tamsyn's brilliant plan beforehand. But Ikina looked thoughtful, as if she was actually considering what Tamsyn had said.

In fact, Kyra realized with a sinking heart, quite a lot of people in the hall looked thoughtful. Tamsyn smiled a self-satisfied smile; her words had divided the assembly and set them thinking the unthinkable: Markswomen armed with death-sticks.

It made sense, in a horrible sort of way: use the dark weapons against the outlaws. It was the one thing they would not expect, the one thing they would not escape. In her mind Kyra saw rivers of blood, hundreds of bodies cut down by bullets, limbs scattered and guts spilled on the crimson earth. She felt sick, as if she was remembering a terrible event from the future, that had happened in her past, and would happen again and again, unless she did something to stop it.

Tamsyn held up a hand. It was a mark of how her power had increased that everyone fell silent at once.

"I know that what I say is blasphemy to some," she said. "I am not unaware of the power of the dark weapons. But consider this; Markswomen are protected by kalishium blades from the madness that leaks from death-sticks. We would not use them indiscriminately. Think of it as an execution like any other. Only quicker, safer, and much more efficient. Once the Taus are eliminated, the dark weapons—*all* of them, including the Taus'—can go right back into the safekeeping of the Order of Valavan. The whole of Asiana will be a safer place, and we would not be putting our lives at needless risk."

"But we would be risking our souls."

Kyra's voice, high and wavering, caught even herself by surprise. The group of men and women in front of her parted and she walked to the center of the hall, willing her steps to be steady. There was a gasp of recognition from someone, Navroz perhaps.

And then she was standing before Tamsyn. The Hand of

Kali stared at Kyra, shock and rage twisting her beautiful face. Her voice rang out, heavy with the Inner Speech. "RENEGADE! BOW BEFORE YOUR MAHIMATA AND BEG THE MERCY OF HER BLADE."

Kyra's knees buckled. *No.* She was not a renegade. Tamsyn was not her Mahimata. She. Would. Not. Bow.

Her forehead beaded with sweat and she trembled with the strain, but she straightened up. Shurik's betrayal had been good for something, after all. Compulsion had hardened her. She had broken Shurik's bonds, and she wouldn't let Tamsyn take over her mind. Not now, and not ever again. Tamsyn's expression changed from rage to disbelief.

Unduni rapped her staff on the floor. Her voice was stern. "I will have no use of the Inner Speech during this meeting, Tamsyn. Is that understood?"

Tamsyn bowed to the mediator. When she looked up to speak, her face was composed. Only Kyra could know the effort this cost her.

"I apologize, Unduni. May I be allowed to speak?"

"Of course," said the headwoman of Arallin, the relief on her face palpable.

"This is none other than Kyra Veer," said Tamsyn, "the Markswoman I spoke of earlier, the one who executed Maidul Tau. What I did not tell you is that she is a thief and a renegade. On the night of Shirin Mam's death, Kyra stole the blade of the old Mahimata and used it to make her escape. I have been trying to find her for months, both to retrieve Shirin Mam's katari and to persuade her to return to the Order."

Unduni frowned. "This is an internal matter of the Order of Kali and does not belong in the assembly. You will talk to her later, yes?"

"No," said Kyra, her voice a croaky whisper. Unduni gave her a questioning look.

"No!" she said, her voice stronger. She stepped forward and faced Tamsyn, her heart pounding. There was no going back now. It had to be done. From the corner of her eye she could see Rustan, his face devoid of color.

He thinks he is about to witness my death. She felt a surge of pity for him.

"Do I have permission to speak?" she asked Unduni.

"You do," said the headwoman, leaning forward on her staff, her face attentive.

Kyra took a deep breath. "I speak not only for myself, but for those who have no voice in this assembly: the novices and apprentices of Kali. We did not know how blessed we were to have a teacher like Shirin Mam. When she died, we lost not only our leader, but also our spiritual guide. Tamsyn will lead the Order of Kali to ruin. Witness her suggestion that we use the dark weapons. Who knows better than I how evil they are? Only someone morally corrupt would even think of using the death-sticks. And only someone utterly heartless would kill her own teacher to become the Mahimata herself. I do not recognize Tamsyn's right to rule the Order of Kali. I hereby challenge her to a katari duel."

Shock waves rippled through the gathering. Tamsyn actually gasped. For once, Kyra had managed to catch her off guard. She felt a small stab of satisfaction at that.

"You have made a serious accusation, Markswoman," said Unduni grimly. "Do you have any evidence to support this claim?"

As Kyra hesitated, she saw Tamsyn's lips curl in a sneer. None of those present would understand about *Anant-kal,* or believe that she had met Shirin Mam after her death. Finally she said, "I have no evidence. But it is what I know to be true, nevertheless. Tamsyn has gained the title of Mahimata through murder and deceit."

"It is within your right to challenge the head of your Order to a duel," said Unduni. "But you are young, and you are the last of the clan of Veer. I ask you to reconsider."

Kyra bowed her head. "Yes, I am the last of my clan," she said, "and I have sworn to avenge the killing of my family. But my first duty is to my Order, and while Tamsyn casts her shadow on the caves of Kali, none of us are safe."

"My dear Kyra," said Tamsyn, looking like a snake about to strike, "you are mistaken. I had nothing to do with the untimely death of our dear teacher. I loved her, as you did. Return to the Order, and please give me a chance to prove you wrong."

There were murmurs of agreement in the hall and Kyra could imagine what people were thinking: such a wise, patient Mahimata, to not lose her temper with this insolent child.

Kyra kept her voice as calm as Tamsyn's. "Give you a chance to murder me, you mean? No thanks. Here there are only you and I, and the sharpness of our blades."

Tamsyn gave a tinkling laugh that made Kyra feel as if a spider was walking up her spine. "Indeed. And what is it that makes you so bold, little deer? The blade of Shirin Mam, I warrant."

"I no longer carry the blade of Shirin Mam," said Kyra. "I will fight you with my katari alone."

Tamsyn's eyes narrowed. "Oh really? Then pray tell, where is Shirin Mam's katari?"

"It has found another guardian," said Kyra. "Someone who can protect it until its true destiny is revealed."

"The blade of Shirin Mam protects itself." Rustan stood and every gaze turned toward him. "But I carry it until it is needed elsewhere."

He reached into his robes, withdrew the ancient blade from its scabbard, and held it aloft. It caught the afternoon light filtering through the stained glass windows of the hall, and sparkled joyously. There were gasps of wonder from the assembled people.

Tamsyn caught her breath and hissed, "The blade of Shirin Mam belongs to the Order of Kali. By what right do you hold it captive, Marksman?"

"A right greater than yours," Rustan countered.

Kyra frowned at that. What did Rustan mean? Why had he even spoken? She hadn't meant to reveal that the katari was with him.

"Explain yourself, Marksman," said Unduni.

"That's right, Marksman. *Explain* yourself," taunted Tamsyn. "Who are you to lay a claim on Shirin Mam's katari?"

Rustan looked at the blade and it glowed in response, throwing myriad colors of light on his face, which seemed different, exalted somehow. Kyra's heart pounded an unsteady rhythm in her chest. She was almost afraid of what he would say next, though she didn't know why.

"It is strange, how we interpret things," said Rustan softly. "My mother once told me that she would acknowledge me to the world. I did not believe her, not until today. I lay no claim on her katari but that of kinship. I am Shirin's son."

CHAPTER 31

DEER AND SNAKE

It was a while before Unduni could bring any order to the assembly in Sikandra Hall. When Rustan announced that he was Shirin Mam's son, the elders of Kali leaped up as one and started shouting at him. Tamsyn advanced on the young Marksman, eyeing Shirin Mam's blade. She stopped short when Barkav blocked her way, his face ominous. Tiny Unduni rushed between them before they could draw their kataris, and implored them to sit. She swooped down on the elders of Kali, scolding and pleading alternately until they too subsided.

At last she returned to her place at the center of the hall. She mopped her brow with a sleeve and said hoarsely, "If I have to shout one more time, I will lose my voice. You will have to continue without me." She reached for one of the cups on the tray, and quaffed its contents in a single gulp.

The hall went silent. Rustan sat down and sheathed the transparent blade, his face calm.

Kyra stared at him in shock, unable to believe what she had heard. Rustan couldn't . . . he just *couldn't* be Shirin Mam's son.

Could he? Now that she thought about it, his eyes, his chin, his brow, even his manner of speaking—they were all rather like Shirin Mam's. No wonder she had felt she could trust him, almost from the start. Why had she not seen the resemblance before?

Because it was impossible. Markswomen did not take mates. They did not have children. It was against the Kanun. Why hadn't Rustan told her?

Never once in all their time together had he given her a hint of the connection. She had spoken to him of Shirin Mam, given him the terrible news of his mother's death, and yet he had kept the secret close to his heart. It hurt that he had not confided in her. Although she understood that it was not entirely his secret to share.

Rustan met her gaze and frowned. *Focus*, that frown said. *Now is not the time.* She tore her gaze away from him and back to Unduni.

The mediator spoke, her voice uneven: "What—what the young Marksman has declared is unbelievable, but it is not a topic of discussion for the clan assembly. The day passes. There is a matter still to be dealt with. Do you, Kyra Veer, still wish to challenge your Mahimata?"

"I do," said Kyra, and the two words fell like the funeral tolling of a bell in the deep silence of the hall.

"So be it," said Unduni heavily. "It has been many decades since a duel was fought in the clan assembly, and I will repeat the rules for the benefit of those present. There will be no use of the Mental Arts. No weapons may be employed except the kataris of the duelists. No one may interfere or influence the course of the duel in any way, on pain of exile. The duel is not deemed finished until one of the combatants is dead or mortally wounded. The katari of the vanquished will pass into the custody of the victor." She took a deep breath and raised her hands in benediction. "May your blades be true this day."

She backed away, waving her staff at the men and women gathered around. They withdrew to the edges of the huge hall, clearing a space in the middle for Kyra and Tamsyn. The scene took on a dreamlike quality in the light of the late afternoon sun.

Tamsyn dropped into the hidden snake stance. "Are you ready, little deer?" she asked almost tenderly, stretching an arm out. Her blade flashed bloodred in the hollow of her out-stretched palm, and for a moment Kyra felt the fluttery wings of fear beat against her face. The hall went dark and she thought she would faint.

The words of her teacher (which one?) came back to her: "Be aware of who you are. Know yourself and your surroundings. Anticipate her when you can."

I know you, Tamsyn. You have taught me and hated me for years. I know every move that you can make.

Kyra stood motionless in the middle of the space that had been cleared for the duel, retreating inward until it seemed as if she was the only person in the hall. There was no Tamsyn, no Unduni, and no audience of excited people, shoving against one another in order to get a better view of the duel. There was only herself, and the warmth of the katari in her hand. It was in this moment that she finally understood what Rustan had been trying to teach her: that stillness which was at the center of all things, life flowing around it like an endless stream. Kyra sought the calm at the core of the tumultuous universe, and welcomed it into her being.

Tamsyn cocked her head. "Come come, little deer. It is time

to take your stance. Or do you regret your rashness and wish to surrender? I will be merciful if you make a public apology. I will let you live. I may even welcome you back to the caves of Kali."

But Kyra stayed where she was, still as a rock.

Tamsyn clicked her tongue impatiently and began to circle Kyra. The blade in her hand glowed brighter. Still Kyra did not move.

Tamsyn darted forward, quick as a cobra to strike down her prey. But her katari slashed through empty air. She spun around, her face a mixture of rage and astonishment. Kyra was standing a few feet away. She had slipped out of range at the last moment.

Tamsyn's teeth flashed. "You have learned a few things, little deer. Good. This will be more interesting than I imagined."

Kyra did not allow Tamsyn's voice to penetrate the shield of silence around her. She concentrated on seeing, with her inner eye, the flow of movements that made Tamsyn such a feared Markswoman. When Tamsyn turned her back on her, as if to walk away in boredom, she knew it was a diversion. She held herself still, listening for the minute breath of air that would tell her when Tamsyn threw her blade. When it came, she danced aside so quickly that those watching would have sworn she appeared to be in two places at once.

Tamsyn's katari clattered across the floor and Kyra launched herself at her foe, knowing that this was the moment to attack.

Tamsyn gave a snarl of fury and blocked Kyra's katari with one hand, suffering a deep slash on her elbow, while with the other she delivered a stunning blow to the side of Kyra's head. Kyra stumbled back, dizzy with pain, almost losing her grip on her katari. Tamsyn lashed out at her head again with a powerful side kick, but Kyra saw it coming and rolled away so that she got but a glancing blow on her shoulders. As Tamsyn bore down on her, her face contorted into a mask of hatred, Kyra thrust her katari up toward her enemy's heart.

But Tamsyn grabbed her hand and twisted it aside. Kyra's katari dropped to the floor. Her fingers scrabbled for the blade, but Tamsyn held her wrist in a lock with one hand. The other hand she wrapped around Kyra's throat. Kyra choked and clutched her hand, trying to loosen the fingers that were squeezing the breath out of her. Tamsyn bent over her, smiling and panting. The next moment the smile was wiped off her face as Kyra kneed her in the stomach. Tamsyn's grip loosened and Kyra broke free.

She dropped into a defensive stance, her head throbbing, her breath coming in painful gasps.

Tamsyn stood before her laughing in triumph, blade glowing in her hand. She had called her katari back, and it had obeyed. Too late, Kyra realized that she should have done the same.

The next moment seemed to stretch out forever. Kyra saw, as if in slow motion, the moving red slash that was Tamsyn's blade, traveling toward her heart. She moved—oh so sluggishly!—to avoid the death-strike. She knew, even before the blade tore into her right side, that she had not been fast enough.

She fell to the floor and a deathly silence filled the hall. Kyra felt the wetness of blood seep into her robes, heard the rasp of her own breath. Then came the pain, a piercing, screaming pain that drove everything else from her mind. She opened her mouth and a single moan escaped her lips.

I have failed, Mother. I wasn't good enough.

Her sight blurred. Was she dying already? Die then, get it

over with. Anything was better than this terrible pain, this crushing weight on her chest, the bitter knowledge that it had all been for nothing. The last of her clan, and no one left to avenge them. Tears slid down her cheeks. She was crying. The final humiliation.

Footsteps. Tamsyn was walking toward her.

Kyra pressed her lips together, willing herself not to make a sound. She would not give Tamsyn the pleasure of her distress. *A few minutes more*, she thought. Hang in a few minutes more. The door of death would open; already, she could see it. A door like any other, except that there was no coming back. She closed her eyes and the pain dimmed.

Stay alive, Kyra.

Her eyes flew open. Who was that? Certainly not Tamsyn, whose smiling face now filled her vision.

Kyra turned her head sideways and locked eyes with Rustan, standing at the front of the circle around them.

Stay alive, Kyra, he pleaded, and his voice was a hook that snagged her, pulled her back from the door that had begun to open. The pain came back in a red rush and she bit back a scream. No, no, no! Why couldn't Rustan let her go?

"It is a pity," said Tamsyn. "So young and rebellious. I would have spared her life, but a duel demands death." She gazed with concern into Kyra's eyes. "Does it hurt, little deer? Do not worry; I will put you out of your misery now." She reached for the blade that was still buried in Kyra's flesh.

Afterward, Kyra would not know what impelled her to it. But as Tamsyn's fingers closed over the hilt of her katari, the image of a scaly three-headed wolf-monster with an empty-eyed Kali sitting astride it filled Kyra's mind.

"*Trishindaar*," she whispered, and everything went dark.

CHAPTER 32

TRISHINDAAR

They stood at the edge of a narrow, bustling street. Kyra blinked and felt a shock of recognition as she took in the grubby shop fronts, sloping roofs, and smoking chimneys. She had been here before. It was the same street she had seen through the first door of the secret Hub. The only difference was that it was late evening now; lamps were lit on the shop fronts, casting their uneven glow on the faces of those hurrying by. Shadows pooled in the corners of the buildings. A dark feline shape slinking along the open drain took one look at them and fled, yowling.

Tamsyn looked even more stunned than Kyra felt.

"*This* is your talent?" she said. "Where have you brought us?"

Kyra had no idea, but she wasn't about to tell Tamsyn that. She glanced at the elder. Strange, she had never seen Tamsyn afraid before. She, on the other hand, felt an odd sort of peace, as if she wasn't bleeding right this minute on the floor of Sikandra Hall.

Her wound—where was it? Kyra looked down the front of

her robe, but it was clean and dry. The place on her belt where her katari usually hung was empty. Tamsyn, she was glad to see, did not seem to have her katari either. Of course she didn't; it was still buried in Kyra's flesh—wasn't it? Yet it must have been Tamsyn's katari that had brought them here.

No, it was Kyra who had brought them here, using the word of power Shirin Mam had taught her. Tamsyn's katari had merely been the conduit for that power.

Shirin Mam had said that the Markswoman who used this word of power went beyond the reach of time. That meant— what exactly? If only Shirin Mam had been more explicit.

Kyra stepped away from the wall and began to make her way down the street. Could the people in this place, this time, see her? The cat had certainly seen them, or at least had sensed something amiss. Perhaps people could sense them as well, for they flowed around her, without seeming to notice what they were doing. Kyra was glad of that. She wouldn't have wanted anyone to walk *through* her.

Tamsyn followed her. "Where do you think you're going?" she hissed. "You take us back to Sikandra Fort right now."

Kyra did not respond. She kept walking. There was something here, something that held the key to Tamsyn. Why else would her katari have channeled them here?

A note of panic entered Tamsyn's voice. "Take us back now, you fool. You don't know what you're playing with. Listen to me!"

"Why, Tamsyn, are you in a hurry to leave?" said Kyra. "I am not. There is much to learn from words of power. Did you not once offer to teach me some yourself? Luckily, I had a far better teacher than you."

But Tamsyn was no longer listening to her. She was looking

at something beyond Kyra, her breath coming in little gasps, her face stricken in the smoky lamplight.

Kyra glanced over her shoulder, but there was nothing much to see except another street, emptier and darker than the one they had left behind. She sighed. A part of her had thought Shirin Mam would turn up and take care of Tamsyn, but that was probably too much to hope for.

A man with an ill-kempt beard and long, straggly hair wove drunkenly down the narrow street. It was this man that Tamsyn was watching, Kyra realized. Two children followed close behind him. Kyra felt a jolt of recognition as they came closer. They were the same two children she had met before, the ones she had wanted to help. What had the boy said his name was? Arvil. They were dressed as outlandishly as ever, in overlarge hand-me-downs.

The man shouted at the children. They shrank from him and clung together, yet they followed his unsteady footsteps.

Kyra flattened herself against the wall as the pitiful trio passed. Would the children be able to see her this time as well?

But they had eyes only for the man they followed. As he passed the two Markswomen, Kyra heard Tamsyn take a deep, sobbing breath.

She scrutinized the elder. Tamsyn's eyes were closed and she leaned against the wall for support. And all at once Kyra *knew*. This man, and these children, were the key to Tamsyn.

Without a word she detached herself from the wall and began to follow the trio down the street. What would she do if Tamsyn did not follow her? Would she be able to find her again in this place?

But Tamsyn fell into step next to her. Perhaps, having been

brought here by Kyra's word of power, she was tied to her in some way. They walked in silence for a few minutes. Kyra kept her eyes on the two children ahead.

"This changes nothing, you know," whispered Tamsyn. "You will still die."

The boy tripped over something, the man roared at him, and his sister helped him up.

"Perhaps," said Kyra, frowning. She didn't like this man. She wished there was something she could do for the children.

Tamsyn glanced at her sideways. "You will die without having fulfilled your vow," she said. "The last Veer, and none left to avenge your clan. What a pity."

A fist of pain closed inside Kyra's chest. Yes, she was the last Veer. Yes, she was dying in Sikandra Hall without having avenged the brutal killings that had destroyed her world.

But did it matter? Kai Tau would die one day, if not by her katari, then by another's.

Or maybe he would live to a ripe, happy old age and die peacefully in his sleep.

Still, one day the door of death would open for him, and he would have to face the numberless innocents he had killed. Was that not punishment enough? Against eternity, what were a few years more or less?

Kyra took a deep breath and the fist of pain dissolved, leaving her lighter. She had wasted so much time in the last fourteen years, hating, remembering, planning her revenge. Now, finally, she could let it go.

They passed beyond the last few huts, the last flickering lanterns on the street. The ground was unpaved now, the darkness unrelieved but for the sliver of a young moon. From somewhere ahead of them came the gurgle of a river, and the creak of a wooden bridge.

Tamsyn stopped short, her face working.

"It can't be," she said. "This is not how it was."

Kyra heard a short scream and a splash, and she ran ahead, her heart thudding.

The man knelt at the edge of the dark, swirling water. Moonlight fell on his back and his arms, which seemed to be holding something down under the river's surface. The two children were nowhere to be seen.

"You liar, this is not what happened!" Tamsyn's voice rose in a scream. "He fell in. We tried to save him, but we couldn't."

"That's *you*?" said Kyra, stunned. "The little girl he's drowning is you?"

Tamsyn did not reply. In the moonlight her face looked half-demented. "We went to an inn," she said feverishly. "We ate stew and dumplings and rice pudding. We came here to cross the bridge; he'd left the horses tied on the other side. But Arvil bent down to look at something in the river, and fell in. We both jumped in to save him, but only I survived."

That was definitely not what was happening. Kyra ran to the bank where the man still crouched, breathing hard.

"Stop it!" she shouted, but the man didn't hear her. In desperation she struck at the man's neck with a double fist punch.

It went through him and Kyra almost fell into the river herself. At the last moment she managed to right herself and draw back.

The man must have felt something, because he grunted and stood up, pressing his hand on his neck and casting his eyes about suspiciously.

Kyra pushed past him and bent down, scanning the river. It was shallow near the banks. Perhaps she could save the children.

But there was no sign of them. The river ran dark and fast, utterly uncaring. Behind her, the man muttered under his breath and stumbled away.

Kyra's shoulders slumped and she rose. Her eyes caught a movement near the opposite bank, a flash of pale skin. A body perhaps, caught in the tangle of rushes.

Kyra didn't stop to think. She ran across the creaky wooden bridge, intent only on reaching the place where she had seen the movement.

The opposite bank was wild, dense with grass and wet underfoot. Kyra scrambled through it, panting. If she was not physically present here, she should be able to simply float through the undergrowth. Maybe it was a question of mental practice.

Finally she reached the edge of the water, and caught sight of the body she had seen from the opposite bank. It was the little girl. Kyra crouched down next to her. The girl's eyes were closed and she lay awkwardly half in and half out of the water.

But she was alive. Kyra could see the rise and fall of her chest as she breathed in and out.

She heaved a sigh of relief and straightened up. "Poor girl," she said, gazing down at the pale, damp face, the sticklike arms, and the thin body.

Tamsyn's voice came cold and ragged from behind her. "You pity me? Don't. Would you like to know how your precious Nineth died?"

Nineth dead? Kyra felt the breath leave her body.

Tamsyn smiled, a shadow of her old, cruel self playing on her face. "I thought that would get your attention, little deer. Your beloved friend is no more. I wish I could tell you that she died easily. But she didn't. Poor Nineth, she looked quite emaciated when last I saw her. She starved to death, you see. It took many days, and gave me much entertainment."

Kyra closed her eyes in pain. Her poor, darling Nineth.

"Who do you think you are, playing with my memories like this?" Tamsyn's voice took on a note of command. "We will go back to Sikandra Fort now. It is time to die, time to join the rest of your pathetic clan."

The river and the night swam out of focus and Kyra had a moment of panic. She was drowning, unable to breathe.

Stay alive, Kyra.

She could do this. She could stay where she was, maintain the link with this time, this place. Kyra concentrated hard, shutting out Tamsyn's taunting voice, seeking once again the stillness at the core of her being.

The world solidified once more and she breathed, exulting at Tamsyn's surprised face.

Tamsyn recovered quickly. "We will have to go back sooner or later. You can't stay here forever."

Kyra gave one last look at the little girl lying on the bank. There was nothing more she could do for her. Time to deal with the adult Tamsyn.

"No," she said. "I can't stay here forever. But I can leave *you* here." She began walking back to the bridge.

Tamsyn thrashed through the undergrowth after her. "Of course you can't leave me. My katari brought us here, and it will take us both back."

"I should leave you here," said Kyra. "It would be a fitting punishment, to be banished forever into the worst moments of your past. To be forced to see yourself and your brother drown, time and time again."

"That is *not* what happened," Tamsyn spat. "Our father loved us. He would never have hurt us."

They had reached the bridge. Kyra stopped and whirled around. The bridge swayed, groaning in the wind. "Your father tried to kill you both," she said. "Words of power cannot lie, and you know it."

Tamsyn was still as a statue. "You've tricked me somehow," she said finally, her voice wavering. "This is not what happened."

Kyra shrugged. She was cold and weary. "You've spent your whole life lying to yourself. Stay here and see if you can get the past to reflect your lie."

"You can't go without me," cried Tamsyn.

But Kyra, walking on the desolate bridge, suspected that she could. The only question was, *should* she? Tamsyn was a monster. If Kyra had had any doubts about that, they were quashed when she gloated about starving Nineth to death.

Nineth. Dead. A sob racked her chest, but she controlled it. Now was not the time to weep. That would come later, if there was a later.

She heard Tamsyn's light, running footsteps behind her, swinging the bridge.

"You're not going without me." This time there was a thread of panic in Tamsyn's voice.

Kyra smiled. Good. Let her wonder, let her suffer. Had Nineth too been torn between hope and despair, granted a reprieve one minute, and condemned the next?

"*My* katari brought us here," said Tamsyn. "Mine, not yours."

"You are in my debt and your katari knows it, even if you don't," said Kyra, more sure of herself with every passing minute. "If I wish to return without you, your katari will obey me."

Tamsyn's brow wrinkled. "In your debt?"

"I saved your life," said Kyra. "If I hadn't distracted your father, he would have held you down long enough to kill you. There would have been no Tamsyn Turani, famed Markswoman of Asiana, killer of innocent apprentices."

"You saved nothing," said Tamsyn. "We are in a distorted memory of the past, that is all."

"It is no mere memory," said Kyra. "We are here, Tamsyn. Your father actually sensed me."

Tamsyn glared at her, breathing hard, her eyes slits of hatred. Moments passed before she spoke in a flat voice, "Fine, little deer. What do you want in return for taking me back to Sikandra?"

"Your katari," said Kyra. "It is mine now. You will leave it buried in my flesh and walk away. You will announce to the hall that you yield the duel, and relinquish your post as the Mahimata of Kali, as well as your right to bear a weapon. You will leave Sikandra Fort and never show your face in Ferghana again."

"You're mad," hissed Tamsyn.

"It's up to you," said Kyra. "I can leave you here, and you can spend eternity figuring out a way to come back on your own. I will win the duel in any case."

"If you live."

"There are worse things than dying," said Kyra. "To be trapped in your past—that is one of them."

"To give up your katari—that is another."

"Stay if you will," Kyra told her, calm now. "I don't care one way or another. If you wish to come back with me, you must do as I have said."

"Wait," said Tamsyn. "If I do as you say, how do I know that you will not kill me?"

"I'm bleeding to death myself," Kyra reminded her. "I don't think I'm in a state to jump up and strike you dead. We'll have to keep that for later."

"Later, yes." Tamsyn cocked her head, eyes gleaming with malice. "We're not done yet, little deer." She bared her teeth and held out one long-fingered hand. "I give you my word. I will yield the duel if you take us back to the Hall of Sikandra."

Kyra leaned against the railing of the bridge, feeling exhaustion creep up on her. The wind had died down and the night was still, the stillness before dawn that brings the strangest dreams. It was time to leave. She eyed Tamsyn's outstretched hand.

Tamsyn's face gave away nothing. She could not be trusted, but she had given her word. It was probably the best Kyra could wring from her. In any case, Kyra could not maintain the link to this place indefinitely. She clasped Tamsyn's hand in her own. It was like trying to hold on to air, but she supposed it was the principle of the thing that counted.

She bent her mind to the hall they had left behind, to that moment when Tamsyn had grasped the hilt of her katari. The river and the night blurred like a damaged painting; superimposed on it now was an image of the Hall of Sikandra. Tamsyn's hand solidified in her own.

It was then that Tamsyn chose to strike, in that in-between place where two realities clashed and converged.

She twisted Kyra around, grabbing her midriff with one arm, and choking her with the other. "Foolish little deer," she panted. "Did you truly think I would yield to you?"

Kyra bucked and tried not to panic. *No.* Not now, not after everything. She could not let Tamsyn defeat her. She gripped the arm around her neck, trying to loosen its deadly hold, and concentrated on recovering her link to Tamsyn's past. But the night stayed out of focus, and Tamsyn's hold on her did not weaken. Black spots danced in front of Kyra's eyes and she gasped for air.

Do it for Nineth, then, if you can't do it for yourself. Shirin Mam's voice, calm, compassionate, and full of love.

"Nineth," choked Kyra, and with a last burst of strength pried the arm from her neck. She swung her assailant around and Divided the Wind, breaking both of Tamsyn's wrists with the sides of her palms. Tamsyn cried out in pain and stumbled back at the precise moment that the bridge solidified around them once more.

Kyra took an involuntary step toward her, but it was too late. The barrier broke and Tamsyn tumbled into the rushing black water beneath.

Kyra knelt at the edge of the broken railing and gazed down at the river, panting. But there was no one and nothing to see. Tamsyn was gone. The river had claimed its victim, once and for all.

She pushed herself away from the edge and collapsed on the wooden slats of the bridge, trying to recover her breath. "Goodbye, Tamsyn," she whispered. "You will not be mourned."

She hurt everywhere. Her throat and palms burned, and from somewhere deep inside, the ghost of a wound inflicted in another world began to pulse.

Time to go back and face that world, that wound.

"*Trishindaar,*" she said, and Tamsyn's past dissolved. For a moment Kyra fought against the drowning sensation. With an enormous effort of will she closed her eyes and yielded herself to the currents of time.

CHAPTER 33

LAST TWIST

Pain, red pain that held her in its bloody embrace. Why wasn't she dead yet? Kyra closed her eyes, shivering. Cold. She was so cold. If life were to end now, she would welcome the release. The duel was over, although she could not remember now why it had been so important.

She heard the sound of running footsteps. People bent over her, talking.

"She's lost a lot of blood."

"She will live! She's young and strong, and the blade missed her lung."

"Out of my way, young man. I think I know a little bit more about healing than you do."

"Stay alive, Kyra!"

"We must take the katari out now, before it puts her beyond our reach. Mumuksu, you will staunch the flow of blood when I remove it."

And on the borders of the group gathered around, the uneasy whispers, the fear-filled thoughts:

What did she do to Tamsyn Turani?
Where has the Mahimata vanished?
What black magic is this?

Someone applied pressure to her side. Someone else grasped the hilt of the blade. Kyra's eyes flew open and Navroz's face crystallized before her.

"Yes, it will hurt," said the elder. "But it must be done now if we are to save you."

She pulled the blade out: carefully, slowly.

The pain rose to an unbearable crescendo, obliterating everything else. Kyra could hear an agonized screaming echoing in the hall, and feel the gushing wetness of blood pouring from her wound.

Darkness, and in the darkness a vision: a blue-skinned, four-armed figure with a vermilion-streaked forehead. In three of her hands she held a lotus, scissors, and a sword. The fourth was held out in benediction.

Kali. The Goddess . . .

And Kyra knew no more.

ACKNOWLEDGMENTS

This book would not exist without the help of several wonderful people. First and foremost, my editor at Harper Voyager, Priyanka Krishnan, who made me reach deeper within myself for the truths of my characters and the world they live in. Thanks also to the team at Harper Voyager for all their hard work in making this book possible.

My deep gratitude to my agent, Mary C. Moore of Kimberley Cameron & Associates, for believing in my story, and to Pooja Menon for passing it on to her.

Thanks to my sister, Prinks, for being my first reader, to my mom for proofreading, to writer Karl Schroeder for his gentle encouragement, to Amy Goh for the lovely map, and to the friends who shared this journey with me: Charlotte, Ariella, Erika, Valerie, Debbie, Lesleyanne, Victoria, Kristin, Vanessa, and Marie-Lynn.

For all you math geeks, Kyra's pyramid of palindromic primes is taken from "Palindromic Prime Pyramids," by G. L. Honaker and C. Caldwell, in the *Journal of Recreational Mathematics*, 30:3 (1999–2000).

Lastly, thanks to you, dear reader, for picking up this book and taking a chance on it. Until we meet again, the Goddess be with you.

ABOUT THE AUTHOR

Born and raised in India, Rati Mehrotra makes her home in Toronto, Canada, where she writes novels and short fiction and blogs at ratiwrites.com. Her short stories have appeared in Apex Magazine; AE: The Canadian Science Fiction Review; Abyss & Apex; Urban Fantasy Magazine; *PodCastle; Cast of Wonders;* and many other publications. Find her on Twitter @rati_mehrotra.